I0762853

INVASIVE SPECIES

INVASIVE SPECIES

ELLERY ADAMS

HANOVER
SQUARE
PRESS

ISBN-13: 978-1-335-00153-5

Invasive Species

Hanover Square Press
22 Adelaide St. West, 41st Floor
Toronto, Ontario M5H 4E3, Canada
HanoverSqPress.com

HarperCollins Publishers
Macken House, 39/40
Mayor Street Upper,
Dublin 1, D01 C9W8, Ireland
www.HarperCollins.com

Printed in U.S.A.

Í minningu Lilly.

"I should have been a pair of ragged claws
Scuttling across the floors of silent seas."

—T. S. Eliot

INVASIVE SPECIES

1

Mrs. Smith

Cold Harbor, Long Island, New York
June 1982

Mrs. Smith read the final sentence of the *Cosmo* article titled "How to Eat Like a Thin Person" and flung the magazine aside in disgust. It struck the water hard, creating several tiny tsunamis that rose over the lip of the hot tub and splashed down onto the bathroom floor.

The cover model, a brunette with feathered hair and a hesitant smile, began to sink. The water added shadows to her pearl-smooth skin and twisted her smile. As she sank, she seemed to be staring up at Mrs. Smith, silently begging to be rescued.

Mrs. Smith stared back. She didn't think the brunette looked like a supermodel. She looked like a frightened child wearing an ill-fitting dress and too much makeup.

Mrs. Smith had seen plenty of frightened children over the course of her very long life and hadn't felt an ounce of pity for any of them. She'd never shown them mercy or sympathized with their plights.

She expected them to be scared when she was close by. After all, even simple creatures knew when they were about to die.

For a brief moment, Mrs. Smith wondered what it was like to be afraid. But she was unable to comprehend the emotion. She had never cowered in terror. Never scrabbled backward, searching for a place to hide. Fear was for the weak. For prey.

Mrs. Smith was a predator.

The heavy magazine slowly dragged the cover model deeper under the water's surface, but Mrs. Smith grew tired of the girl's insipid face, so she pushed it to the bottom of the hot tub with a curved nail, thick and black as an old fishhook.

The magazine's pages fanned outward like the wings of a manta ray. The sight stirred a familiar longing in Mrs. Smith's bones, so she sank lower into the tub, submerging as much of her body as she could. There, in the saltwater tank that kept her scaly skin hydrated through the interminable hours of daylight, allowing her to rest in safety and seclusion, she closed her eyes and thought of her children.

She would be with them again when darkness fell.

Tonight, after her neighbors were asleep, she would leave her cage of a house, where she was confined to tanks and tubs like a minnow in a bucket. Without the sun shining its spotlight on her, arousing the curiosity of the neighbors and the boats in the harbor, she could walk down to the beach. She would cast off her robe and leave it crumpled on the boathouse floor, her naked body electrified by the salt-kissed air. Her feet, too large to fit in women's shoes, would ache to sever contact with the dry land. Her long arms would stretch forward to meet the embrace of the incoming tide.

Soon, she would swim.

Soon, she would hunt.

Until then, she would wait in her hot tub. She would wait and consider the message of the magazine article. She would hear the words of the woman who wrote to the editor echo inside her mind like whale song.

"Help!" the woman had written. "I can't lose any weight because I'm always hungry!"

Mrs. Smith suffered from the same affliction. She, too, was always hungry.

She ran her tongue along her teeth, which hung like icicles from the roof of her mouth, and considered the words of the woman who'd written the editor, searching for answers. The woman wanted to shed twenty pounds before her wedding but couldn't seem to control her appetite.

Mrs. Smith couldn't control hers, either. For her own protection, she ate many things she didn't want to eat. She ate food that sustained her. Food that kept her alive but failed to satisfy her cravings. No matter how much she bit and chewed and swallowed, the hunger remained. It burned in her belly, refusing to let her sleep for more than a few hours. It called to her, even from her fragmented dreams.

The hunger would not be satisfied until she'd consumed the sweetest of all flesh.

Soon, she would have her fill of it.

Soon, she would feast.

2
Natalie

Natalie Scott checked her lipstick in the rearview mirror one last time before climbing out of her station wagon. As she moved through the employee parking area behind the Gold Coast Realty offices, she wished she had a more stylish car. Like Beth Pulaski's Jag.

But a sporty little two-seater wouldn't work for Natalie. Not with three kids and two dogs. And where would she put groceries for a family of five? Or plants? Or suitcases?

Sure, Beth could put her Jag's top down and race around the curves of Little Neck Road on her way to the butcher shop or the deli, but she had to borrow Natalie's car to go to the garden center.

Maybe I'll buy myself a convertible. I'll sell so many houses that Jimmy can't complain about me spending money. An image of her husband's face flashed in Natalie's mind, and she set her jaw in defiance. *He doesn't think I can handle a job, the kids, and the house, but I'll show him. I'll show everyone.*

She entered a sunflower-yellow, shingle-style building through the rear entrance and walked straight to the kitchen. She put her lunch bag in the fridge, which was in desperate need of a good cleaning. As she scanned the countertops of the room that had once been the heart of a family home until the house was gutted and turned into an office space, she saw dirty coffee cups and a spray of spilled sugar. Someone had left the milk out next to the coffee maker. A banana peel hung like a used condom from the trash can's rim.

Not my job, Natalie thought, suppressing the urge to scrub everything until it gleamed. But, because she couldn't help herself, she put the milk back in the fridge. Then she stepped out into the hall, where her boss was leaning on the water cooler, wearing his oily car salesman grin.

"Here you are! Our baby agent!" he boomed. "Come into my lair, my dear."

Natalie followed him into the only private office in the building.

Sid Bosworth dropped into the leather swivel chair behind his massive desk. Smoothing his yellow tie with one hand, he gestured at a steel-and-leather guest chair with the other.

When Natalie sat down, the leather cushion groaned. It groaned again when she crossed her legs.

Sid studied her shiny patent leather heels. Then his gaze slithered slowly up her body. Finally, he looked her in the eye. "How ya feeling this morning, Nat? Ready to take on the world?"

The corners of Natalie's mouth dipped. She'd already told Sid that she never went by Nat.

He's your boss. You need this job.

"Yes, I'm—" she started, but he talked right over her.

"I see you're wearing your 'Gold Standard' scarf. Good, good, good. You and Gina are really gonna liven up the place. Two lovely ladies. *Very* lovely." He waited for her to smile in appreciation before laying a hand, pale and square as a slice of Wonder Bread, on top of a file folder. "I've got your first listing right here."

Natalie felt a stirring of excitement. This was what she'd been waiting for.

That folder represented her future. She'd worked hard for this chance, and she was going to work even harder now that she had it. She was going to shine.

She couldn't wait to study the listing, meet the current owners, and plan what she'd say to potential buyers and their agents. She pictured the For Sale sign at the curb, and she saw herself tying yellow balloons to the sign before welcoming eager buyers to the open house. She'd pick up cookies from Hubie's Bakery and arrange them in a spiral on that pretty china platter her mother brought back from England. She'd put yellow roses in a white vase and position the cookies and vase just so in every kitchen.

The yellow roses will be my trademark.

She'd lead prospective buyers through a clean and shining house. Every surface would gleam. Every pillow would be plumped. The buyers would picture themselves eating dinner in the spotless kitchen and hosting parties in the spacious living room. They'd imagine the sewing machine in the den. New cars and a workbench in the garage. They'd envision their future children in the cozy bedrooms. On the swing set in the backyard.

For once, Jimmy would be in charge of the kids while Natalie worked. He might even have to take them to church or make their lunch while Natalie prepped the sale property or showed it to clients. He wouldn't like it, she knew, but how many times had she taken them to birthday parties, movies, Sunday school, scout meetings, soccer practice, dance class, and swim team events? How many times had she been both mother and father while Jimmy was away on business? How many times had she been alone with the kids while he drank beer in Frankfurt or ate beef Wellington in London?

Natalie wanted to start this new phase of her life right now. This very second. She was dying to study her first listing, but the folder was still trapped under Sid's meaty hand.

"I'm not gonna yank your chain, Nat. This one will be a challenge for a baby agent. But don't worry your pretty little head about it, because we're a team. A win for you is a win for all of us. If you need help, don't be afraid to ask. My door is always open. Okay?"

"Absolutely."

Sid placed a rectangular box on top of the folder. "And here's a little gift from me to you. You're a Golden Girl now, Nat, and you've got the cards to prove it."

His desk phone lit up. Glancing at the number, he said, "Sorry, sweetheart, I've gotta take this. It's about the Deerfield property." He reached for the phone with one hand and pushed the folder toward her with the other. "Shut the door on your way out. That's a good girl."

Natalie backed out of the office and gently closed the door.

Clenching the box and folder in her hands, she walked down the hall into the main room, where ten desks were arranged in a cluster, each separated by a chest-high partition.

Natalie shared a cubicle wall with Gina, a short, dark-haired woman with olive skin and a body as curvy as a mountain road. She looked like the pinup girls painted on the noses of World War II bombers.

"The scarf looks good on you," Gina said with a smile. She wore bright red lipstick, which made her teeth look fish-belly white. Natalie wanted to ask if she brushed with baking soda, but they'd only been colleagues for two weeks, and after reading a dozen articles on workplace behavior, Natalie had learned it was best to keep personal questions to a minimum until her job was secure.

There would be no job security if Natalie failed to sell a

house. She was on a ninety-day trial, and though she hadn't worked in an office for fifteen years, she was a quick study. And she was determined. Nothing was going to stop her from having a career. Nothing.

Gina was Gold Coast's top-selling female agent because she'd been the only female agent. Now there were two women in the office, and Natalie had no intention of sharing the spotlight. Gina might be younger and fresher than Natalie, but she hadn't given birth to three children. She hadn't managed a household of five people, trained two dogs, run a garden club, served as PTA president, or organized the carpool schedule, yacht club fundraisers, and scout troop field trips. When it came to juggling tasks, she couldn't possibly hold a candle to Natalie.

Natalie eyed Gina's glossy black hair with envy. Throwing a smile her way, she said, "The scarf looks even better on you. I wish I could get my hair to curl like that."

"I just got it permed. I'm going to a new place in Huntington. It costs an arm and a leg, but like L'Oréal says, I'm worth it." Gina jerked her chin, indicating the folder. "Have you peeked yet?"

Natalie wanted to examine her first listing without an audience, but the way Gina leaned forward made it clear she wasn't going to focus on her own work until her curiosity was satisfied.

Sighing inwardly, Natalie opened the folder.

Inside was a grainy black-and-white photo of a ranch house she instantly recognized. Idle Day Drive was the next street over from where Natalie lived on Tidewater Terrace. Everyone in the neighborhood knew the couple on Idle Day because they owned three ancient cocker spaniels that barked around the clock. The McCreedys had no kids. They didn't play bridge, attend block parties, or buy a single box of Girl Scout cookies. They turned out their porch light every Halloween and never put up Christmas decorations. They spent most of their time walking their dogs and watching TV in the front room. They never planted flowers or trimmed their bushes. The lantern at the end of their walk was filled with the corpses of dead bugs. Their lawn was riddled with fungus.

Gina whistled. "It needs work, but at least it's in the good part of town. If it's totally nasty inside, you can still sell the school district."

"Sure," Natalie murmured absently.

"I see you got your business cards. What name did Sid put on them?"

Natalie blinked in confusion. "What do you mean?"

"Sid gives everyone nicknames. Except for me. He couldn't think of a way to shorten Gina, so my cards have the name my parents gave me." She tapped the name tag pinned to her blouse, making her left breast jiggle like jam with too little pectin.

Natalie opened the box Sid had given her and pulled out a business card. It was the crisp white of a new undershirt. The right corner featured a graphic of a yellow house. In the center, under *Gold Coast Realty* and *We Have the Golden Touch*, was Natalie's name, business phone number, and office address.

Only it wasn't Natalie's name.

"Guess you're Nat now. Good luck with that listing, *Agent Nat*," said Gina, quirking a pencil-line brow.

Natalie was seized by an urge to slap Gina. She could almost hear the satisfying smack and watch her handprint surface like a bright pink starfish on the younger woman's cheek. She'd love to wipe away that smug expression, to see shock and a smidgen of fear appear there instead.

Glancing down at the business card, Natalie muttered, "I'm not going to get used to it. My brother used to call me Nat the Brat when we were kids, and I swore I'd never let anyone use that name again." She shoved the box lid back on. "I'll just have my own cards made."

Gina shook her head. "Better not rock the boat. Not until you're on the board."

Natalie looked at the sales board affixed to the rear wall. All the spaces next to her name, Nat Scott, were blank. No open houses, no closings, no exclusive listings, and no sales.

She was perfectly aware that she was here on a trial basis and didn't need Gina to remind her of that fact.

If Natalie didn't make a sale in ninety days, she'd be gone.

And it'll be another summer of laundry, vacuuming, cooking, grocery shopping, and swim meets.

Natalie pictured the blue rubber gloves she used for washing dishes, the Electrolux in the hall closet, the mop in the laundry room, and the trash can under the kitchen sink. If she were at home right now, she would've spent the past hour cleaning up after the kids' breakfasts, feeding the dogs, and loading the dishwasher. After that, she would've refilled her coffee cup and sat down at the kitchen table to make her grocery list and sort through her coupons.

But she wasn't sitting at her kitchen table right now. She was sitting at her desk. At work. In her office. She could get coffee from the staff room whenever she wanted. And the only lunch she'd made that day was her own.

She wasn't wearing shorts and a T-shirt. She'd traded those for a pencil skirt and a silk blouse. The grubby sneakers she wore for yard work were sitting in the garage, and her narrow feet were encased in a sexy pair of heels.

I can leave my other self at home. I can be a different person.

Natalie could forget about her kids, her pets, and her house without feeling an ounce of guilt because she had Una.

Una would be waiting for the kids when they got off

the bus. She'd fix them a snack and tell them to play outside before starting their homework. When they came back in, she'd have a pitcher of homemade lemonade waiting. She'd listen to them talk about their day before sending them to their rooms to study or read. The dogs loved Una, too. They'd snooze at her feet while she ironed Jimmy's shirts or flop on the kitchen floor to watch her chop vegetables or boil potatoes.

Without Una, Natalie could never have gone back to work. Una cooked, cleaned, and took care of the kids and the dogs. She was soft-spoken and thorough. Everyone on Tidewater Terrace wanted to hire Una, but her time was already taken by the Scotts and Natalie's two best friends, Beth and Elaine.

Natalie never stopped to consider that Una might also want to be a different person—that she hadn't immigrated from Iceland thirty years ago with dreams of becoming a housekeeper for an upper-middle-class family on Long Island. Natalie had no idea what Una dreamed about. She'd never thought to ask because she needed Una to stay exactly as she was. She needed Una to step into her place while she auditioned for a new part. Because Natalie Scott was ready to play the lead.

On the other side of the cubicle wall, Gina pushed her chair away from her desk. The wheel squeaked, snapping Natalie back to reality.

"I'm grabbing a coffee. Want one?"

Natalie nodded. "Sure."

"Don't tell me how you take it," Gina commanded. "I'm *really* good at guessing." Folding her arms across her chest, she openly appraised Natalie. "You've had three kids, but you still have a great bod. Your clothes are classy. Your nails are polished, but they're short, so you work with them. Dishes, gardening, that kind of thing. And you're a neat freak. I bet you like strong coffee with just a splash of milk."

"That's incredible!" Natalie laughed despite herself. "Are you a palm reader, too?"

Gina tapped her temple. "I don't need to read your palm to know that you're going to have a hell of a time selling that property."

Natalie's smile vanished as she gazed down at the photo. "It just needs a little work."

"Yeah, you could find a buyer even if the roof needs replacing, and there's zero curb appeal, but those aren't your real problems. The *location* is your real problem. *Her* woods are right behind that backyard. And on the other side of the woods is *her* house."

Natalie didn't need Gina to spell out who she meant by "her."

Mrs. Smith.

Gina pointed at the McCreedy listing. "Everyone who goes out to the back patio will see those creepy woods. They're like something out of *Wicker Man.*"

"What's that?"

"A horror flick." Gina put her hands on her hips. "Ever heard of Michael Myers? The guy who wears a white face mask and goes around stabbing people to death? He'd be right at home in those woods. My boyfriend and I watch horror movies all the time, and that house is just like the one in *Salem's Lot.*"

Natalie had seen that movie, but she thought the Marsten House was larger and more sinister than Mrs. Smith's.

"Wait! You live super close to her, don't you?"

The gleam in Gina's eyes raised Natalie's hackles. "We're two lots away. There's a big empty lot between us."

Gina shuddered. "That would be *way* too close for me. I'm glad I'm on the other side of the harbor."

"On the waterfront?" Natalie asked, knowing it was very

unlikely. Gina probably lived in a tiny cape near the train station or the high school, whereas Natalie and her family lived right on the water. They had their own private beach. Their own floating dock. Their own boat.

"No. I'm off Church Street." Gina leaned over and spoke in a stage whisper. "Have you ever seen her?"

Only once. In the middle of the night. She was walking over the grass toward her boathouse. Her gait was awkward. One leg dragged behind the other. Her hands were spearheads, hanging limply at her sides. Her body was reed thin, all shadows and sharp angles, like the bones were trying to break through her skin. Her head was capped by a mass of dark hair. It shifted in the wind, like worms in a bait bucket.

She was completely naked.

In the middle of March.

"No."

The lie came easily because Natalie had told it many times before. At swim practice and teacher conferences. While waiting for Jill's Girl Scout or J.J.'s Youth Group meetings to finish. She'd been asked at the library, the beauty salon, and the deli. Even at the Macy's makeup counter.

Mrs. Smith was the most talked about woman in Cold Harbor.

Natalie didn't believe her neighbor was a witch. Or a psychopath. She didn't think she'd escaped from prison or the loony bin. She wasn't a convict or a lunatic, but she wasn't normal, either.

Normal people went outside.

And they don't swim naked. At midnight. When the ground still crackles with frost.

Gina scooped her coffee cup off her desk and said she'd be back in a minute, but Natalie didn't hear her.

She stared down at the McCreedy listing like she was trying to memorize every detail, but she wasn't thinking about their house at all. She was thinking of the woods that formed a protective horseshoe around Mrs. Smith's house.

Mrs. Smith's woods were made up of sharp, spindly trees crowded together like needles in a pincushion. Some were lightning-scorched. Others were storm-lashed and bowed close to the ground like penitents. Curtains of poison ivy hung down from their branches and oriental bittersweet vines girdled their trunks.

The vines curled skyward in thick ropes, squeezing the trunks and branches in their vise-like embrace. Masses of green leaves with serrated edges exploded from every vine. Half of the woods were shrouded in oriental bittersweet.

Eventually, the trees would suffocate under its weight.

Eventually, they would die.

When that happened, the vines would seek new hosts. They'd slither over fences and walls in search of healthy trees. The roots would burrow under a forest floor pockmarked with holes.

The soil in the woods was treacle brown and always smelled of decay. Rocks jutted out of the ground, colorless and jagged as broken teeth. In the few places the sunlight penetrated, there were weeds with knife-sharp leaves and fetid flowers. Giant tangles of pricker bushes formed a perimeter around the woods. The thorns were as big as arrowheads and the berries were the color of dried blood.

Mrs. Smith's woods were always chilly, even in the middle of summer. Frost whitened the ground well before winter's first freeze and clung to the ice and snow long after the spring thaw.

Natalie had never seen a squirrel or songbird in Mrs. Smith's woods. Occasionally, a murder of crows would haunt the trees, and at night, moon-pale moths would flutter out from dark cavities, only to be devoured by swooping bats.

Natalie and her friends had spent countless garden club

meetings complaining about Mrs. Smith's property, but short of dousing it in gasoline and tossing a lit match into the heart of the eerie forest, there was little they could do about the neighborhood eyesore.

Gina's laughter tripped down the hall, followed by Sid's hyena chuckle.

Natalie rolled her eyes. She'd never flirt with their boss. She planned to earn her way to the top of the sales board without tossing her hair or giggling at his stupid jokes. But seeing as Gina was busy sucking up to Sid, Natalie decided to peek inside the folder on her coworker's desk.

When she saw the property, a charming three-bedroom cape within walking distance of the elementary school, she felt a hot surge of jealousy. Natalie knew the house well. It was daffodil yellow with a covered porch and a spacious backyard. A family with young children would grab that house in a New York minute.

This should be my *listing. What does Gina know about kids? About all the food they eat. Or all the laundry they create. Or how their stuff takes over every room. Their clothes, their toys, their bikes, their video games. Does she have any idea how their noise travels through a house? How much energy it takes to make sure they're safe, healthy, and happy?*

"She doesn't have to know," Natalie grumbled. "That house will sell itself."

Closing the folder, she returned to her desk to focus on her own listing. Pulling a legal pad out of her briefcase—an old one of Jimmy's—she sat straight as a ruler and prepared to make a list.

Natalie loved lists. She loved tidiness and order. She loved organizing things and was happiest when she was given the chance to beat chaos into submission with colored pens, file folders, and a pocket planner. With organization came control. And that was what she wanted. Control. Power.

It would take a lot of creative thinking to sell the McCreedy place. And the first thing Natalie had to do was to start seeing 9 Idle Day Drive as the first house she was going to sell.

This meant finding a way to make Mrs. Smith's property less threatening when potential buyers gazed at it from the McCreedys' backyard. She had to find positive phrases to use when describing Mrs. Smith's gloomy gray house and oppressive woods.

Natalie wrote:

Single occupant who keeps to herself
Quiet
Wooded buffer / Nature preserve
Historic mansion

Studying her list, she wondered what she'd do if a potential buyer asked if Mrs. Smith's house was haunted. And they *would* ask. They might laugh nervously as the question left their mouth. They might blush in embarrassment, but they'd ask all the same.

Is the house haunted?

Are the woods cursed?

Gina returned carrying two cups of coffee, and Natalie put her pen down to accept the steaming mug from her new coworker. She took a sip and stared forlornly at her list. Next to her, Gina made a slurping noise that set Natalie's teeth on edge.

She glanced at the other woman, taking in the lipstick stains on her mug. The gap in her blouse that revealed a red satin bra. The beauty mark on her round, smooth cheek.

When Gina slurped her coffee a second time, Natalie saw herself pushing the tip of her pen right through her coworker's beauty mark.

Fed by this fantasy, something dark uncoiled from deep inside Natalie. It moved through her, seizing control of her muscles and nerves, causing her to add a note to her list in spidery block letters that bore no resemblance to her precise and elegant cursive.

LIE THROUGH YOUR TEETH

3

Una

Una Einarsson pulled her VW Bug into the driveway of a split-level brick ranch and turned off the engine. She was early. Too early to knock on the door and expect Beth Pulaski to answer.

Beth always took long, luxurious showers. And when she finally got out of the shower, she'd put the radio on and sit at her vanity, applying her makeup and drying her hair into a long, straight waterfall of gold. She'd sing along to whatever was playing on WPLJ while picking out an outfit from one of her four closets. Finally, she'd admire herself in the Cheval mirror Una cleaned once a week.

By the time Beth emerged from her bedroom—dressed in curve-hugging jeans, or a low-cut jumpsuit, or a dress with such a high side slit that she couldn't get out of her Jag without flashing her panties—she knew exactly how good she looked.

Beth Pulaski, age twenty-eight, was the Marilyn Monroe of Cold Harbor. She knew how to move her body to attract attention. When she walked, her hips rocked like a boat caught by a river current. Her breasts rose and fell like waves rolling into the shore. Her hair shimmered like sunlight on sand.

In high school, she'd been the cheerleader who could do the deepest splits and the most roundoffs. She was the flyer of every pyramid.

Ten years later, she still used her petite frame to her advantage. At the grocery store, she'd stand on tiptoe to reach for items on the highest shelf. She liked the whisper of her skirt sliding up her thighs. She liked feeling tendrils of cool air creep under her dress. She liked knowing people's eyes were moving up her toned legs to her tight ass.

"I work hard for this body, and I want people to see it," Beth told Una back when she first started cleaning for the Pulaskis.

Una had plugged in the vacuum and met Beth's Delft-blue gaze. "They see it."

"Don likes it when other guys stare at me. It turns him on. But men are easy. When a woman stares? That's what *I* like. Because women understand beauty. Women's bodies are works of art, don't you think?"

Una's gaze slid from Beth's lovely face to the toast crumbs on the counter. "I suppose so."

"I know what they say about me, the women in the neighborhood. They call me a slut. They think I want to seduce their husbands. They won't let their sons walk past my house because I might lure them over and say something naughty. But they've got me all wrong. I just want people to *look*. I only want to be touched by Don."

To Una, it seemed like Beth's main occupation was seducing her husband. She had drawers full of lingerie. Silk nighties and robes hung from padded hangers in her closet. The trunk at the end of her bed held costumes that Una would find on the bedroom floor from time to time. The French maid was clearly a favorite. As was the nurse.

Beth owned a lot of clothes. Fuzzy sweaters, leather pants,

pleated miniskirts, whisper-thin blouses. Wrap dresses, ribbed dresses, strapless dresses. Dresses made of mesh, of soft cotton, of shimmering silver sequins or metallic gold. Beth had racks of shoes, too. Thigh-high boots, stilettos, strappy sandals, and wedge heels.

"Don likes me to model whatever I buy," Beth once explained. "It's a game we play. After dinner, he makes a drink and goes to the den. I put on my new outfit to show him, and he tells me to walk around or spin—to act like a model. If he likes what he sees, he'll take it off, nice and slow. That means I'm keeping the outfit. If he's not in the mood, or he's more interested in the game than in me, I return what I'm wearing. If I can't make Don horny enough to look away from a bunch of sweaty guys in uniforms, I blame the clothes."

When Una first started cleaning for the Pulaskis, she was shocked by the things Beth told her. She'd never met a woman who revealed such intimate details about her sex life.

Una had grown up in a small village north of Reykjavik where women prided themselves on modesty and humility. It made her uncomfortable to listen to Beth talk about things that should be kept between herself and her husband.

Una had wanted to quit after her first time cleaning the Pulaskis' house. She couldn't imagine picking Beth's thongs off the carpet or seeing her parade around in a state of undress ever again.

But she didn't quit.

She kept cleaning for Beth Pulaski because Gunnar's scholarship didn't cover room and board at Cornell. Nor did it cover the cost of his textbooks. No one from Una's family had gone to college. The same went for Kristofer, her husband. Their son, Gunnar, would be the first—and as an engineering major no less—so Una went back to the Pulaskis the next week.

Una never encouraged Beth to confide in her. She gave no indication that she was interested in the details of Beth's marriage. In fact, she tried to send her thoughts elsewhere during their one-sided conversations, concentrating on what to clean next or mulling over what to make for dinner.

She managed to remain emotionally unattached until the day she found Beth huddled in the corner of her bathroom, crying like a lost child.

Una dropped to her knees and took Beth's hand in hers. "What is it, sweetheart?"

Beth let out a sob. "I just got my period. I was four days late, and I'm *never* late, so I thought . . . I hoped . . . I've been praying so hard!"

Una stroked Beth's soft, smooth hand. "You want a baby?"

"More than anything!"

"Have you been trying for a long time?"

"Years." Beth's face crumpled in pain. "I got pregnant once, but I lost the baby. There was blood in the toilet and when I went to the doctor, he couldn't find a heartbeat. It was just gone. I think about that all the time. How I flushed it down the toilet. How I didn't even know it was there. My baby. The doctor said I didn't do anything wrong, but there *must* be something wrong with me. With my body."

Una wrapped an arm around Beth's shoulder. As the younger woman sobbed into her chest, smearing Una's blouse with tears and snot, Una smoothed her golden hair and hummed a lullaby from her homeland.

Það er margt sem myrkrið veit,
minn er hugur þungur.
Oft ég svarta sandinn leit
svíða grænan engireit.
Í jöklinum hljóða dauðadjúpar sprungur.

There is much that darkness knows,
My mind is heavy.
Often I've seen the black sand
Scorching green meadows.
In the glacier rumbles deadly deep cracks.

Eventually, Beth had stopped crying. She'd gotten to her feet and moved to the sink to wash the sorrow off her face.

Una had returned to her cleaning, but not before noticing the stack of *American Baby* magazines in the cabinet under the sink. They were all worn and water-wrinkled, as if Beth sat in the tub, paging through them over and over again, seeing her future child in every fair-haired, dimple-cheeked cherub. She read about diaper rash and milestones until the water turned cold. Then she'd pull the plug, letting gravity take her dreams and the dirty water down into the dark.

Unlike her other clients, Beth had never given Una a key.

"Who knows what you'd walk in on?" Beth had teased. "If I don't come to the door, and you see Don's car in the driveway, you might have to wait outside for a few minutes if you know what I mean."

Today, Don's car—a boxy look-at-me red sports car—was in the driveway. This meant Una had to wait.

The sun slanted through the old dogwood tree in the Pulaskis' front yard, dappling Una's face with light and shadow. The chiaroscuro effect softened the lines around her eyes and mouth, transforming her from a sixty-two-year-old housecleaner to the young bride who'd immigrated to the US from an Icelandic fishing village three decades ago.

Even now, after all this time, she still rejoiced in the feel of sunlight on her skin. She was eternally the cat, seeking a square of sunshine. She spent her childhood yearning for this bone-warming light. She'd read about it in books. Her uncle spoke of it when he shared tales of his travels. He'd been to many places. He'd met Mickey Mouse in Florida and climbed the Statue of Liberty all the way up to her crown. He'd ridden in taxis and visited museums. He'd eaten at a Burger King and slept at a Howard Johnson's. He made it sound like everything about America glowed. Everything was bigger and brighter. Even the sun.

Una pictured her uncle on a stool close to the fire, packing his pipe with work-worn fingers. She could see the wisps of smoke rise toward the rafters and smell the peaty scent of his tobacco. As she sank into an ocean of memories, her eyelids grew heavy.

She hadn't been sleeping well lately. Every morning, she woke sticky with sweat. Her tongue was dry as sandpaper and her head felt like it was stuffed with cotton.

She couldn't remember her dreams, but she knew they were troubled. Something was calling to her from that other place—that close but faraway place where the mind wanders in the small hours of the night. She felt the echoes of this other world even after she woke up—disturbances in her psyche where things from the dream place had latched onto her like a sucker fish.

It had been a long time since she'd taken a nap, but she allowed her stiff neck and knotted shoulders to relax deeper into her seat. Her breathing slowed. She concentrated on the vision of smoke curling out of her uncle's pipe and her father's laughter, which sounded like an avalanche of snow. She could see his eyes, the blue of a frozen fjord, sparkling with merriment. His beard wagged like a sheep's tail as he chortled and slapped his thigh.

In the memory, he was wearing his favorite sweater—the one Mamma made for him last winter. There was a hole in the elbow and another where his collarbones met. A fishhook had landed there, biting into the weave, stretching and pulling until the wool finally gave way.

Pappi.

Una's dream self yearned for her father to see her, to turn away from his brother and cast a smile in her direction.

The image shifted, and the little room in her amma's turf house disappeared. Una and her father were on the deck of his fishing boat. The sea was a wild stallion, bucking and kicking. Waves rose like mountains, blotting the horizon as they tried to soak the clouds. White foam bubbled from the curling crests, making Una think of rabid animals. The only thing between her and the hungry waves was the thick wood of Pappi's boat.

Without warning, the bow dipped.

Una would've been thrown forward onto her face had she not grabbed a rope and wound it around and around her forearm.

Pappi shouted something, but Una couldn't hear him over the banshee shriek of the wind. She turned his way, slitting her eyes against the rain, and saw him gesture at the port side of the boat.

She followed his gaze but saw nothing but churning water. The sky had darkened to the same shade as the sea. The clouds were thick as porridge.

When she looked back at her father, his mouth was stretched into an oval of fear.

He gesticulated at the port side again, his free hand clamped around the wheel. His leather gloves were gone, leaving his bread-pale hands bare. The skin had peeled away from his knuckle bones, and they stuck out of his ruined hands like the spine of a prehistoric lizard.

Una tried to scream, but the wind stole her voice before she could make a sound.

Pappi's eyes rolled in their sockets. He stabbed his pointer finger into the air, wordlessly commanding Una to move, to release her rope and cross the heaving deck to the other side of the boat.

But Una's body was like petrified wood. She just stood there, clinging to her rope, as the boat groaned and plunged into another trough. Suddenly, the planks beneath her feet fell away until there was only air under her boots. She was weightless—an insect frozen in ice—and then the deck came racing upward again, slamming into her feet, buckling her knees.

She heard a cry over the howl of the gale. Her father's voice, sharp and urgent. *"Svana!"*

Una stared at him in horror. Her sister! Where was her sister?

She must be tangled in the netting!

Without a second thought, Una let go of the rope.

She immediately lost her footing. Sliding and scrambling, she practically rolled to the other side of the boat. Her stomach lurched with the waves, and she lowered her head against the smack of sea spray. The jerking movement allowed her braid to escape from beneath her oilskin coat. It writhed in the air like an agitated snake.

Svana.

Una pulled herself up to the rail and peered over the side of the boat.

Salt spray smacked her face, torturing her eyes with the needlelike sting of jellyfish, but she squeezed the water away until she could see directly below her.

The nets were gone.

Svana was gone.

But something was there, just below the surface.

A mass of darkness, even blacker than the sea.

The mass was as big as a whale.

No. It was bigger.

Its teeth were not a whale's teeth. This creature had rows and rows of long, pointed fangs. They looked like stalactites and stalagmites jutting out of its cave of a mouth. Its eyes were two black marbles, glinting with predatory hunger.

It held something in its octopus arms.

A girl.

Svana.

The monster stared up at Una, and she felt a biting cold course through her body. Frost crept into her blood. Her skin froze. The air in her lungs turned to ice. Her heart stopped beating.

From a very great distance, a car door slammed, and Una jerked awake.

The dream was already out of reach as she blinked against the daylight. She unclicked her seat belt and waited for Don to back his car out of the driveway before gathering her cleaning supplies and knocking on the Pulaskis' front door.

"Halló!" she called out, cracking the door. "It's Una!"

Beth poked her head out of the kitchen, phone pressed to her ear. She waved Una in and then leaned against the wall.

Una always started her work in the kitchen. This room was the beating heart of every house, and every house was happier when it was clean.

As usual, the stove needed her attention. Beth was a messy cook, and the cooktop was speckled with oil droplets and a crusty brown sauce.

"I'm telling you, Paula, Don hasn't been himself since he went to see Mrs. Smith." Beth spoke in a clipped tone. "She's that creepy lady who lives in the ugly mansion at the end of the street. She bought a car from his dealership, a Porsche 911 Turbo, though I have no idea why. I mean, the woman doesn't leave the house. Why does she need a fucking Porsche? Anyway, *Don* went to see her."

Una pulled on her rubber gloves and began scrubbing the cooktop, trying not to listen. Don Pulaski swore all the time, but Beth only swore when she was really upset.

"He's been weird ever since he went there. It's been over a week, and he hasn't touched me. Not *once*. No sex. No grabbing my ass. Not even a kiss. He barely looks at me!" Her voice was high and shrill. "Last night, I cooked dinner, opened a nice bottle of Chianti, and told him dessert was a surprise. I gave him a little time to digest his steak, then I called him for dessert. I was in the kitchen with a lacy negligee and a bottle of Hershey's syrup. I waited and waited for him to come in, and guess what? He never did! He just shouted that he didn't want dessert."

Underlying Beth's indignation was a note of fear.

"I want a baby more than anything, but I can't get pregnant by myself. He's acting this way because of *her*. Don practically bit my head off when I asked why Mrs. Smith needed a car when she doesn't even drive. He said the commission's gonna pay for our trip to Jamaica, so I should shut up and be happy. Don has a temper—everybody knows that—but he's never talked to me that way before. Not *once*."

Una had heard Don fly off the handle many times. He was a loud and brash man. He yelled at sports teams and news anchors on TV. He shouted at the mailman, the garbage collectors, and kids who walked on his grass. He was a bulldog of a man with a barrel chest, slicked-back brown hair, and dark, hooded eyes. He barked and bellowed unless he was talking to Beth. With her, his voice was spun sugar, all airy sweetness.

"I have no idea what she looks like," Beth said, twining the phone cord around and around her palm. "Don didn't see her. She put a check in an envelope and taped it to her front door. I know it sounds crazy, but just being that close to her *did* something to him. Just being on her property, it cursed him somehow. Like in a fairy tale." Beth shot Una a plaintive look. "You believe in curses, don't you, Una?"

Una nodded. She'd seen old women in her village carve runes into sheep bones and bury them outside an enemy's house. She'd seen painted stones left on windowsills and heard dark mutterings fly up the chimney with the smoke. She'd seen animals grow sick from curses and recover when curses were lifted.

Yes. She believed in curses.

She watched Beth clutch the gold cross nestled in the hollow of her throat. "I've *been* to church, Paula. Four times since Don went to her house. I lit candles. I prayed to Saint Anne and the Blessed Mother. My mom thinks I'm being punished for dressing like a hooker, which is ridiculous. I could wear a potato sack, and men would still look at me like I'm a lollipop they want to lick. Except for Don. *He's* not looking at me in that way anymore. He's looking right *through* me." Beth walked over to the window. "It's Mrs. Smith. She's coming between us. The woman's a spider, and I'm going to flush her out into the light and squash her. Yeah, I *do* have an idea. If I can get my garden club to help, we can make Mrs. Smith wish she lived on a different street."

Beth ended the call but didn't return the phone to the cradle. She just stood in front of the window, staring at the treetops in the distance. She couldn't see Mrs. Smith's house, but Una knew she was thinking about it. About *her.*

When the jarring off-the-hook alert blared from the phone speaker, Beth thudded it into the cradle. She left the room, a hornet's buzz of angry muttering trailing after her.

Una had no idea what Beth was planning, but she was scared for her.

You're here to work. Don't get involved, Una reminded herself.

She turned the knob at the kitchen sink and waited for the hot water to flow onto her sponge. While she waited, she also glanced out the window, her eyes locking on the cluster of jagged treetops in the distance. She couldn't see Mrs. Smith's house from here, but she could feel it. She could feel its presence and the presence of the woman within.

Danger waits there, she thought.

Suddenly, the water from the tap turned viciously cold. So cold that it burned. Una felt like her fingers were freezing inside her glove. She'd had frostbite before, but this sensation was a thousand times worse. It was like touching the red eye of the cooktop for several agonizing seconds.

Jerking her hand away from the water, Una peeled off her glove to find scarlet blisters on every finger. They looked like tiny toothless mouths. Like the open sores left by a cluster of leeches.

Wrapping her hand in a clean rag, Una pressed it against her belly and waited for the pain to subside. Then she reached for the Comet and, using her uninjured hand, began to scrub the sink.

She did not look out the window again.

4

Jill

Jill Scott stood at her bedroom window, watching her mother drive away. When the station wagon reached the top of the driveway and turned right, something loosened in her chest. With her mother gone, she could relax.

She finished making her bed, folding the top sheet over the powder-blue comforter and smoothing away all the wrinkles. Then she put her nightgown away, placing it neatly in the drawer next to her socks and underwear. When she shut the drawer, a tiny shudder ran through the piece of furniture, causing one of the carousel horse music boxes on the hutch to play the opening notes of "You Light Up My Life."

Locating the source of the sound, Jill ran her fingers over the yellow roses on the porcelain mane. The horse had been a Christmas gift from her parents, an addition to her collection, and though she'd pretended to love it, she hid it behind the other horses to avoid looking at it.

She didn't like its open mouth or the way its lips peeled back in a snarl. It looked like it wanted to take a bite out of something with its little Chiclet teeth. Its black eyes seemed accusatory, as if it was Jill's fault that its body was impaled by a silver pole.

There were eight carousel music boxes on the shelf. Jill's favorites played "The Way We Were" and "Greensleeves." She was about to turn the winding key on the horse with the blue flowers woven into its mane when she heard the rattle of Una's car.

Dimples popped on Jill's cheeks, and her braces flashed as she smiled.

She waited until she heard Una's key scratch the front door lock. She gave her time to put her things down and to call out a greeting before emerging from her room.

Justin, her baby brother, was less reserved than Jill. He came racing out of his room at the end of the hall and hurled himself into Una's arms.

"Good morning, my darling." Una giggled. "Soon, you'll be so big and strong that you'll knock me over like a bowling pin."

Justin raised his little arm and flexed his bicep, mimicking J.J., the oldest of the Scott children. Justin was a surprise baby, which explained the seven-year age gap between himself and Jill, who was twelve, and J.J., who was thirteen.

"Oh!" Una admired Justin's arm. "I could use muscles like that in the garden today. What do you say?"

Justin nodded and ran back into his room. Within seconds, Jill and Una heard him talking to himself and making car engine noises.

"He loves his Hot Wheels," Una said, her eyes shining with affection.

Jill's face clouded. Everyone loved Justin. Her mother most of all. She was always hugging and kissing her youngest child. She stroked his hair, rubbed his back, and let him climb onto her lap when they all watched TV. Jill couldn't remember the last time her mom had spontaneously reached out to hug or kiss her.

"Mom got him a new pack of cars for being good while she was at work."

"He's always good," Una said. "And so are you. Do you want me to braid your hair?"

Jill didn't have much time before she had to catch the bus. Their stop was at the top of the road, and their house was at the very bottom, perched on a narrow stretch of lawn overlooking the harbor. It was an uphill walk to the bus stop, which Jill hated, but a downhill ride whenever she rode her bike home from her best friend's house, which she loved.

Grabbing her hairbrush and two hair ties, Jill followed Una into the kitchen and sat at the table while Una filled the kettle with water.

Una started every shift with a mug of tea, and Jill loved the scent of it. Una carried the tea leaves in her purse and would scoop them into a little silver ball. When she lowered the ball into her mug of hot water, the aroma of herbs and flowers would fill the air.

Once, when Jill had asked about the tiny purple flowers in the tea, Una had gotten a faraway look in her eyes. "That's Arctic thyme. It grows in Iceland. My amma loved to use it for tea. Now I do, too. But mine also has mint. Keeps my breath nice and fresh."

Jill loved Una's scent, which was a blend of mint, lemon furniture polish, and Pond's Cold Cream. It was nicer than the perfumes her mom wore, or the body spray the older girls at school used after gym class.

"Alright, let's get your braids in," Una said, running the brush gently through Jill's dirty-blond hair. Using the edge of her fingernail, she parted Jill's hair down the middle. In the background, the water in the kettle gurgled softly.

Jill said, "I need to tell you something."

Una started braiding. "Okay."

Jill thought she heard a sound coming from down the hall. A few notes of music, tremulous and strange. She pictured the carousel horse with the bared teeth slowing turning.

She wanted to hide the thing away—to shove it in the back of a drawer. But if she did that, her mom would notice. And what could Jill tell her? That the horse creeped her out? If she told her the truth, her mother would frown or let out a sigh, her face etched with disappointment.

It would've been easier if Jill collected trophies instead of music boxes. J.J.'s shelves were stuffed with dozens of shiny gold swim trophies. He had so many that he barely had room for his comics or D&D handbooks, and after this summer, he'd have to find another place for his other possessions. Summer was right around the corner, and for J.J., summer meant more trophies.

Jill had a few trophies. None were gold. Hers were the color of old pennies.

Just once, she wanted to see her name on one of the big two-tier, first-place trophies J.J. casually collected, but she had to make the team first.

Every day this week, she and J.J. had come home from school, changed into their swimsuits, grabbed goggles and towels, and headed to the yacht club for tryouts.

To get to the yacht club, they'd cross the back lawn and jump off the seawall onto the strip of beach behind their house. Heading west, they'd pass a vacant lot, then Mrs. Smith's boathouse and beach, then another vacant lot. A seawall topped with a thick layer of concrete marked the beginning of the yacht club's property. From there, it was a short walk past the snack bar to the outdoor pool.

J.J. always increased his pace when they reached the parking lot. He didn't want to be seen with his sister. At school, she was the more popular of the two, but he was the king of the pool.

A year ago, Jill and J.J. were the same height. Now J.J. towered over Jill. He was tall with wide, powerful shoulders and strong legs. He could outswim the rest of the boys in his age group with ease.

Jill wasn't fast or strong. She kept hoping she'd shoot up in height—for the equation of her body to balance out. Instead of getting taller, she just got thicker in the waist and thighs.

"You need to watch what you're eating. You don't want to look like the Pillsbury Doughboy. Boys like a girl with a slim figure," her mother had said a few weeks ago when Jill was trying on last year's swimsuit to see if it still fit. "I'm not going to spend good money on a new suit until we see which team you'll be on, but if you want to move up, you should exercise more and snack less."

Jill had desperately wanted to be a Flying Fish. All week, she'd been worried about spending another year as a Bluefish, losing any chance of winning one of the coveted gold trophies at the end-of-season banquet and finishing another season with a small participation trophy.

But at the end of yesterday's tryouts, Coach Patrick had read out the names of the newest members of the Flying Fish, and Jill had made the team. Fueled by joy, she couldn't wait to share the news with her parents.

Though J.J. had made the team without even trying, he'd been in a foul mood on their walk home.

Jill had seen his sullen look when Coach called her name, and she knew he didn't want to share his place in the spotlight. The idea made him angry, and when J.J. was angry, he was cruel.

"Hey, Jill!" he'd yelled when they reached Mrs. Smith's beach. "Wait up!"

The false note of brightness in his voice didn't fool Jill. She pulled her towel tighter around her shoulders and kept walking.

"Don't you want to hear what Aaron said about you?"

This gave Jill pause. She'd had a crush on Aaron from the moment he'd boarded the school bus last September. With his chiseled cheekbones and head full of soft coffee-brown curls, he looked like one of the Greek statues she'd seen on a field trip to the Met. And when he'd smiled at her, his eyes shining in the morning sunlight, her heart had somersaulted inside her chest.

Every time she saw him, she felt breathless. She could never think of anything to say to him, so she just stared at him when he wasn't looking. At home, she wrote stories about him. In every story, he fell in love with a girl just like her.

She didn't think Aaron had said a word about her to J.J., but there was a small chance her brother was telling the truth. Swinging around to face him, she said, "What'd he say?"

"That it was cool you made the team."

Jill glowed with pleasure. She wanted to run to her room and shut the door so she could picture Aaron's face from every angle as he talked to J.J. about her. She wanted to hear Aaron's deep voice repeating the line over and over again, even if it was only in her head.

J.J. gave her a few seconds of happiness before sliding the dagger in. "Mike said something, too. *He* said you should get a new suit because everyone can see your mosquito bite boobs through this one."

Jill's skin grew hot with embarrassment. She wrapped her towel around her torso, mortified by the thought that her suit was actually see-through.

Why didn't you tell Mike to shut up? she wanted to shout at

J.J., but he wasn't that kind of brother. He never defended her. He always joined in when other kids teased her, eager to see her taken down a peg or two.

"Mike's an asshole, and so are you!" she spat.

J.J. feigned innocence. "Don't get mad at me. I didn't say it! But *I* know how you can get Aaron to like you back. All you have to do is pick a dandelion from Mrs. Smith's lawn. I dared him to do it, but he was too scared. If *you* did it, he'd think you were totally awesome."

Jill glanced from where her feet were safely planted on the sand to the scraggly grass shooting up behind Mrs. Smith's boathouse and felt a frisson of fear.

Mrs. Smith's property was off-limits. No Trespassing signs were nailed to dozens of trees bordering her property. Others hung from the high iron fence surrounding her house or were taped to the inside of the boathouse windows.

Kids were always daring their friends to invade her property. They tried to shame, cajole, or bribe one another into ignoring Mrs. Smith's signs, but no one was dumb enough to try. A powerful sense of self-preservation held them back. The same kids who'd break into the yacht club's snack bar or sneak into the planetarium without paying refused to see if the boathouse door was locked or pick blackberries from the thickets huddled against Mrs. Smith's fence.

But last night, Jill had felt strangely invincible.

If I can make the team, I can make Aaron like me, too.

Now, as Una wound a hair tie around her second braid, Jill murmured, "I said I'd do it. I'd pick a dandelion."

The kettle began to shriek, and Una moved it off the burner. She poured her tea and sat down across the table from Jill. A small crease appeared between her brows. "What happened?"

This was why Jill loved Una. She didn't scold her for ignoring Mrs. Smith's signs. She didn't call her foolish or stupid. She didn't get angry. She just waited for Jill's story to unfold.

"I saw a dandelion. A big one. Right behind the boathouse. I figured I'd only be on the grass for, like, thirty seconds, but when I ran over to pick it, it was gone. There weren't *any* flowers in the grass, even though I saw tons of them when I was on the beach."

Seeing Jill's confusion, Una made an encouraging noise.

"I was about to give up when I saw a bud. I knew it was a dandelion because of the leaves, so I ripped it off the stem and ran back to the beach."

Jill's eyes were glassy. She was no longer sitting at the kitchen table. She was standing in the sand, her hand fisted around a flower bud.

"When I showed it to J.J., he said it didn't count because it wasn't a dandelion. It was yellow, but it wasn't a flower. He *knew* it was a dandelion. He was just being an idiot." The anger she'd felt yesterday came bubbling back to the surface. "I hate him!"

Una shook her head. "No, you don't. You're mad at him, and you'll be mad at him lots of times before you're both grown. Now, finish your story."

Jill's eyes flashed. "I wanted to throw that stupid flower at his stupid face, but he walked away."

"Look *gullible* up in the dictionary, Jill the Pill!" J.J. had shouted over his shoulder. "Your picture's there!"

Under the table, Jill's fingernails carved half-moons into her palms. She held on to her fury because it was hot and energizing and far better than the weird sensation the flower had given her. The moment she'd touched it, she'd felt fear slip under her skin like a needle, injecting something oily and cold into her veins.

Jill lowered her voice. "The bud wasn't normal. It had a

bump. Like a wart, but it felt hard—like there was a pebble inside. When I peeled it open, this yellowy thing fell out into my hand." Jill squeezed her eyes closed and spoke so softly that her words were nothing more than a fragile whisper. "It was a tooth."

Una went very still. "A tooth?"

Jill nodded.

"From an animal?"

Jill shook her head and pointed at the metal braces glued to her front teeth. "It had one of these on it."

When Una gave her a searching look, Jill knew what she was thinking. Everyone knew how much Jill liked telling stories. She had notebooks full of them. She whispered them to her friends at school assemblies and during sleepovers. She added details to real-life events to make them more interesting. She was always getting in trouble for bending the truth, but she wasn't lying now. She prayed Una could see that.

The second hand on the kitchen wall clock ticked and ticked. If Jill didn't leave soon, she'd miss her bus. But she couldn't go until she told Una everything.

Finally, Una said, "What did you do with it? The tooth?"

Jill let out a sigh. That was where things really got weird.

"It freaked me out, so I dropped it. I yelled at J.J. to come back because I wanted him to see it, but he wouldn't stop. When I looked back at the sand, I saw the tooth . . . sink. It happened so fast—like it got sucked up by a vacuum." A tear slid down Jill's freckled cheek. Her story sounded so ridiculous that she couldn't blame Una for not believing her. "I'm not lying. I swear."

Una came around to Jill's side of the table and gave her shoulders a squeeze. "My amma would've said the tooth was a piece of elf treasure. Did I ever tell you the story of the men who tried to build a road through a hill belonging to the elves?"

Jill didn't care if she missed her bus. If Una could explain what she'd seen, Jill could forget all about the gross tooth. She could stop feeling scared every time she remembered how it had looked sitting in her palm. "No."

Una returned to her seat and cradled her teacup in her hands. "Elves are invisible, but just because you can't see a thing doesn't mean it isn't there. The men who wanted to build a road learned this the hard way. They used every machine they could get their hands on, but the machines failed. The engines jammed. Rocks cracked the shovel blades. The men tried dynamite next, but every time they lit the fuses, a strange burst of wind or sudden rainstorm would snuff them out. Finally, the men brought in the strongest horses in the country to pull down the trees. The horses refused to budge. The men threatened them with whips, but the horses wouldn't move. One night, they ran away and were never seen again. In the end, the road was built somewhere else, and the elves were left in peace."

"So, your grandma would've said the tooth belonged to the elves?"

Una nodded. "All they want is to stay hidden—to be left alone. If you don't disturb them, they won't harm you. If you make them angry, they'll seek revenge. But since you gave the tooth back, they won't be angry."

Relieved, Jill got to her feet and pulled her book bag onto one shoulder.

"What would your amma say about Mrs. Smith?"

Turning in her chair, Una glanced out the window facing Mrs. Smith's yard. "Amma believed in witches, trolls, ghosts, demons, wind spirits, and all kinds of monsters. She wore charms around her neck and wrists. She carved runes over the door and into the leather of her saddle. She believed people needed protection from the wild things. She would've told you to stay away from Mrs. Smith's yard." Una made a shooing motion at Jill. "Now, hurry, or you'll miss your bus. J.J. left ten minutes ago!"

Jill did as she was told.

She hadn't heard J.J. leave, but because his room was in the basement, he used a different door.

Will he hold the bus for me?

He probably wouldn't, but Jill's friends would. It was the last week of school, and her entire grade would be watching a movie after lunch. Jill didn't want to miss it, so she ran as fast as she could up the driveway, her book bag bouncing on her back like a loose turtle shell.

As she left her house behind, she felt a feathery tingle on the nape of her neck, like someone was watching her.

And even though Jill had never seen the woman, she knew it was Mrs. Smith.

Everything about Mrs. Smith's property was wrong.

The thorns on her pricker bushes were too big. The berries on her winter creeper oozed a bloodred sap. No matter the season, poison ivy and poison sumac clung to every inch of the fence. Deep purple mushrooms with gills that moved as if they were drawing breath sprouted all over her yard.

Then there was her soot-gray house.

It sat on the hill like a howling wolf. Its top half was narrow and pointed, while the bottom half looked like the haunches of a large beast. No windows faced the street on the ground floor, and the windows that gazed out over the harbor were tall and skinny. Sunlight never winked off the glass or the metal railing of the widow's walk. Shadows spilled out from under the eaves and the front porch and pooled around the bushes and trees.

Jill and J.J. didn't agree on much, but they both believed the house was meant to be some kind of fortress. The iron fence surrounding the property had spear-tip finials, and the electric gate across the driveway sent a clear message that visitors were not welcome. There were no potted ferns or rocking chairs on the porch. No dining table with an umbrella and chairs on the patio. No wind chimes or gazing balls in the overgrown garden.

The only splash of color came from the pair of round windows in the attic turret. Made of stained glass, their central figure was a purple octopus suspended in blue water. Because the purple was so dark that it was nearly black, and the blue was a deep indigo, it was difficult to see the octopus. It hid on sunny days but came alive during lightning storms.

These windows were the eyes of the house. One watched the cars on the road. The other watched the boats in the harbor. They watched people walk on the beach or fish off the dock. They watched Jill and her family as they went about their lives. They saw everything. Jill was sure of it.

The windows, the spiky fence, the creepy plants—they were all an extension of Mrs. Smith. Jill was sure of that, too.

The sensation on the back of her neck spread. It felt like a thousand earwigs were crawling over her body.

She ran faster.

As she put distance between herself and Mrs. Smith, Jill tried to focus on Una's gentle face and soft voice. She wanted to reclaim that feeling of relief. Of safety. But she couldn't.

She was almost thirteen—too old to be soothed by tales of wise grandmothers or trickster elves.

She knew there must be more teeth like the one she'd found. Braces were glued to the teeth and connected by wires. The wires on the tooth Jill found had been snapped.

Where are the rest of the teeth?

As soon as the thought formed, she wished she could retract it. She never wanted to know the answer to that question.

5

Natalie

Natalie attended the weekly sales meeting at the office, and after listening to Gina brag about the number of potential buyers expressing interest in her new listing—the adorable cape across the street from the elementary school—she had to get out of the office.

Did Gina get a listing like the McCreedy house when she first started? Natalie wondered as she watched Gina give Sid a flirty slap on the arm.

She knew the answer was no. Sid liked Gina. He wanted her around. She laughed at his jokes and nodded enthusiastically when he talked. She stroked his ego.

It's probably not the only thing she's stroking.

It had taken a Herculean feat of willpower for Natalie to ignore the platter of jelly donuts and sesame bagels on the conference table. She'd been too busy cleaning up dog puke that morning to eat breakfast, but donuts and bagels were fattening, so she kept her mouth occupied by drinking coffee.

By the time the meeting was over and she was free to leave the office, she had a bellyful of acid and a bitter taste in her mouth. She sat in her car for a few minutes, chewing a stick of spearmint gum. It tasted like envy.

Natalie was a confident person. She knew she could do things better than most people, but now her thoughts spiraled into an unfamiliar realm of self-doubt.

Does Sid want me to fail so he can hire a younger woman? Another Gina? Or is one female agent enough? Maybe someone higher up on the Gold Coast ladder told Sid to bring more women on board, but he doesn't actually want us to stay.

"I'm not going anywhere," she muttered, tossing a glare at the Gold Coast building.

As she backed out of her parking spot, she started a mental list.

First, she needed food. After stopping at the deli for a sandwich, she'd head to the garden center.

Natalie knew she had to improve the curb appeal of the McCreedys' bedraggled split-level before she drove a Gold Coast sign into the ground.

When she'd asked Sid if the company provided a budget for cleaning supplies, balloons, or flowers, he'd laughed so hard that he'd nearly fallen out of his chair. When he recovered, he said, "You'll have to look under the sofa cushions for your balloon money, Nat. Gold Coast pays your commission, but you have to earn it first."

Natalie had wanted to stick her Gold Coast pen into Sid's balloon of a gut. Instead, she'd thanked him and backed out of his office.

I'll show you, she thought as she pulled into her favorite corner deli, where she ordered salami and cheese on a kaiser roll. She ate the sandwich in the car on the way to Greenlawn Garden Center.

She made a beeline for the annuals, hoping to find colorful blooms to brighten up the McCreedys' mailbox bed. Begonias were on sale, but Natalie wasn't a fan of the orange-red flowers. Petunias were also discounted, and even though she didn't want to spend time deadheading the spent blooms, they'd give her a good bang for her buck.

She loaded two flats of purple petunias into a Radio Flyer wagon and was mulling over whether to mix the purple with two flats of bright pink when she heard the velvety voice of her friend Elaine Bernstein.

"Fancy meeting you here."

"Hi!" Natalie smiled a genuine smile for the first time all day. "I'm glad I ran into you. I'm buying plants for the McCreedy house, and I could use your opinion."

Elaine glanced at the petunias. "Where are these going?"

While Natalie shared her vision, Elaine's gaze swept over the annuals. "So, the goal is to distract people from the house?"

"And the woods in back," Natalie added. "If I plant pretty flowers, trim the bushes, and mow the lawn, buyers can see the place as a family home. The neighborhood is lovely. We've got good schools. Beach access is two streets away. If a buyer is new to the area, they won't know about the creepy house on the other side of the woods or have heard rumors about its mysterious owner."

"Mysterious? I'd use other words to describe Mrs. Smith." Elaine practically spat the woman's name.

Natalie stared at Elaine in surprise. Her friend always spoke in soft, dulcet tones and rarely said a mean word about anyone. She was the epitome of a lady. Well-mannered, elegant, and inscrutable. She moved her body with the calculated grace of a dancer. Her clothes were stylish and expensive. She favored neutral colors that complemented her strawberry-blond hair. Natalie had never seen her sweat or lose her temper.

If the Scotts were Mrs. Smith's closest neighbors on the bottom of the hill, the Bernsteins were her closest on the top of the hill. There were three houses on the cul-de-sac, but only two regulation mailboxes on wooden posts. Mrs. Smith's mailbox had been built into the stone pillar next to her electric gate. She had a mail slot in her front door as well, but it was a relic from a bygone era and hadn't been used since the gate was erected.

"Did something happen? Something involving Mrs. Smith?"

Elaine nodded. "It's about Charles."

Of course it is, thought Natalie.

Elaine's whole life revolved around Charles. He was Elaine and Benjamin's only child, and he was a loser.

Natalie and Elaine had been pregnant at the same time. Natalie with Jill, and Elaine with Charles. Natalie had watched Charles grow from a fussy baby to a spoiled toddler. Eventually, he'd stopped being a clingy child and had morphed into an unattractive, awkward preteen.

Charles didn't make eye contact with anyone outside his family. His gaze was always fixed on the ground, and he had a funny way of walking. His was a short, hurried gait, and he swung his arms without bending them at the elbow, which made him look like a toy soldier on the march.

He didn't carry himself like the other boys, who slung backpacks or beach towels over one shoulder, loping along in an easy, casual manner. The neighborhood boys were rarely alone, preferring to travel in packs of three or four. They exchanged playful punches and laughed often.

Charles wasn't one of those boys. He'd been walking alone since he took his first steps.

Natalie knew most of the kids called him Chuck instead of Charles. When they were feeling uncharitable, they called him Upchuck. They made fun of his red hair, his chalky skin, and the riot of splotchy freckles covering every inch of his face. They made fun of the strange and halting way he moved his body, his unusually deep voice, and how he turned tomato red whenever a girl spoke to him.

Elaine and Benjamin rarely argued in public, but when Natalie and Jimmy were at their house for a Memorial Day cookout, Benjamin had come right out and said that his son's only friend was a much younger boy from Hebrew school.

Elaine had rushed to her son's defense. "That's not true! He has friends. Jill's one. Right, Natalie?"

"Absolutely," Natalie had agreed to spare Elaine's feelings. In reality, her daughter didn't like Charles at all.

"And not just Jill. There are other kids in the neighborhood, too," Elaine had insisted.

Everyone knew this was untrue, but no one said as much.

Instead, Benjamin had pressed Elaine's hand to his lips and said, "He needs to toughen up, *motek*. The boys in his class pick on him. I know this because he told me. And they'll keep doing it until he makes them stop."

Elaine had stared at her husband in horror. "Why should *he* have to do anything? He's a wonderful boy. If they can't see that, it's their loss."

"Help me out here, Jimmy," Benjamin pleaded.

Jimmy had taken a swig of beer and leaned back in his chair. "In junior high, I was a skinny kid. I didn't play sports, so I wasn't friends with the jocks, and those guys ran the school. The captain of the football team decided he didn't like me. He and all his buddies loved to mess with me. They pushed me against the lockers, smacked the lunch tray out of my hands—shit like that. My dad told me to go after the leader or they'd never leave me alone. He said I'd probably get my ass kicked, but if I wanted to hold my head up high and be a man, I had to do something."

"What'd you do?" asked Benjamin.

"I went after the captain in the middle of the hall, between classes, so everyone could see. I didn't wait for him to pick a fight, either. I just ran at the guy. I landed one good punch—

bam!—right in his nose. And then, just like my old man said, I got my ass kicked." Jimmy laughed. "But the jocks left me alone after that. You know why? Because I wasn't an easy target anymore."

"You see?" Benjamin turned to Elaine. "That's what Charles needs to do. Even if he gets knocked on his tushy, one black eye is better than being pushed around for the rest of his life."

Elaine had dismissed the idea with a languid wave of her hand. "School's almost over. Charles's bar mitzvah is in July. He won't need to punch anyone after that. Trust me. Kids will crawl over each other to get an invitation. It's a better solution than telling him to punch people in the nose. Now, who wants another drink?"

When she'd gone inside to make another pitcher of margaritas, Jimmy made a snipping motion with his fingers. "Charles will be thirteen this summer, Benjamin. Time to cut the apron strings."

Several margaritas later, Natalie had gone down to the Bernsteins' basement to tell her kids the party was over.

J.J. was on the sofa, his attention fixed on the TV, while Justin played with a LEGO set in the corner. Jill was on the floor with her back pressed against the sofa. Charles was on his knees, facing Jill. He wore a striped shirt that made him look like Ronald McDonald.

"Hold on, Mom," Jill had said without turning around. "I want to see if he can pick my card."

Charles had fanned the cards in his hand and made a big show of selecting one. He flipped it over, his face shining with hope. "Behold! I give you the jack of hearts."

Jill shook her head. "I had the jack of diamonds."

Natalie had looked at her pretty, golden-haired children and felt a stab of sympathy for Charles. Having produced the wrong card, his cheeks were aflame. He ran a hand through his wavy red hair, and it stuck up in peaks like a torch.

She might have said something kind to Charles, this ugly boy with no friends, but the nearly empty popcorn bowl next to Jill's leg had caught her eye.

That girl eats every second I'm not watching her!

"Let's go, Jill," she'd barked. "Clean up your mess, all of you, and then come upstairs and say good night to Mr. and Mrs. Bernstein."

"I can show you another trick," she'd heard Charles whisper to Jill. "It'll take two seconds! I was saving my best for last."

Natalie knew Charles had a crush on her daughter. She also knew that Jill couldn't wait to escape the Bernsteins' basement. Jill felt sorry for Charles and was never mean to him, but his obsequiousness made her squirm. Natalie had barely made it out to the patio when Jill appeared, holding Justin's hand, and politely thanked Elaine before heading down the hill toward home.

"I'm glad they're doing swim team together again this year," Elaine had said after Jill left. "Charles is doing sailing camp, too. He doesn't want to, but Benjamin insisted. Are J.J. and Jill sailing, too?"

"They are. I need to fill their days because I'll be at work and Una will have enough on her hands taking care of Justin, the house, and the dogs."

The Bernsteins didn't have any pets. Elaine claimed that Charles was allergic to pet dander, but Natalie didn't believe her. Elaine just didn't want a cat or dog scratching the white leather sofas or shedding on the cream-colored shag rugs. Elaine's house was photoshoot ready at all times, as if she were constantly anticipating a magazine spread.

To be fair, the Bernsteins' home had been featured in magazines. Six of them, to be precise, a fact which Elaine seemed to mention at every yacht club dinner and neighborhood party.

Elaine was enormously proud of their big, blocky, modern house. She loved to talk about its architectural details, the art hanging from its walls, or how the light passed through the banks of floor-to-ceiling windows to warm the spacious rooms.

Working with a team of decorators from Manhattan, Elaine had filled the house with Lucite, chrome, and glass. She'd rejected the trendy Laura Ashley prints, pastel walls, and bold geometric rugs in favor of an elevated art deco look. Everything had been painstakingly chosen, from the living room lamps to the salad bowls.

The Bernsteins were the wealthiest family in the neighborhood. If Elaine wanted something, she got it.

Benjamin was nothing like Jimmy. Natalie was always explaining why she'd spent money on new swimsuits, shoes, and school supplies for the kids. At the end of every month, when Jimmy went through the bills, he'd grumble about various doctor, dentist, or orthodontist visits. Natalie would keep her temper until he asked her to justify the price of women's haircuts or asked why she needed more perfume when he'd gotten her a bottle from the duty-free shop last year.

"This is why I want to go back to work!" she'd snap every time. "I'm sick of sitting here, like I'm being called into the principal's office, and explaining every item on the Visa bill. I want my own money so we don't have to do this ever again!"

Elaine shopped at Lord & Taylor. Natalie shopped at Macy's. For once, she'd like to spend money the way Elaine did. She'd like to hand her Visa card to the clerk with the disinterested ease of someone who could do whatever she wanted. Who could buy things without guilt. Who could take pleasure in shopping for herself.

Looking at the petunias in her wagon, Natalie decided to

invest a few hundred dollars making the McCreedys' house look good. She was impatient to get started, but first, she needed to find out what was bothering Elaine.

"What's wrong with Charles?"

"Nothing's wrong with *him*. It's his bar mitzvah."

Inwardly, Natalie rolled her eyes. She'd been hearing about this bar mitzvah for six months. It was all Elaine talked about, which was why Natalie already knew that there'd be a ceremony at Temple Beth-El followed by the biggest, most memorable soiree in Cold Harbor history.

"For one night, we want to be the Jewish version of Jay Gatsby and Daisy Buchanan," Benjamin had said one night over dinner.

Jimmy assumed his friend was joking, but Natalie knew he wasn't. Elaine had converted her entire dining room into her bar mitzvah "war room." The table was covered in articles, magazine clippings, a desk calendar, and a chalkboard listing possible themes. One by one, the themes had been crossed off. Safari, outer space, arcade, candy factory, pioneers, underwater, punk rock, rock climbing, travel around the world—they'd all been rejected.

"I thought you found a great party planner and everything was going well," Natalie said, noting the shadows under Elaine's eyes.

"It was. We *finally* came up with a theme, and I'm ready to have the invitations printed. However, there's a hitch, and it's Mrs. Smith. If we weren't in public, I'd call her something that rhymes with *hitch*."

Natalie was intrigued. Elaine expected Charles's social status to do a total one-eighty because of this bar mitzvah, and she was so used to getting what she wanted that Natalie couldn't wait to hear how the neighborhood recluse was standing in her way.

"What's the theme?"

Elaine wagged a manicured finger. "I'm not telling. You'll find out when your invitation comes, but I *will* need Jill and J.J.'s help with something."

"Sure," said Natalie, lifting her voice at the end of the word as if not quite willing to commit.

"The temple kids will come to the party with their parents, but for this to be a true success, I need kids from outside the temple to show up. And I have a plan. It came to me when Charles went to Ian Fielder's bar mitzvah and got a Walkman as a party favor."

Natalie whistled.

"That's nothing." Elaine pulled a shriveled petunia flower off its stalk and tossed it to the ground. "At Robbie Weitz's, the boys got baseball gloves signed by Dave Righetti, and the girls got sterling silver bracelets. A few months ago, I would've sold the house if I thought I could get cassette tapes signed by Michael Jackson or lightsabers signed by a *Star Wars* actor, but I can't. And that's okay because our party favor is better than any of that stuff."

"What is it?"

"An Atari 2600 system with two all-new games. *Empire Strikes Back* and something called *Donkey Kong.* That game isn't supposed to be out until August, but Benjamin knows someone at Atari, so Charles's friends will have it before anyone else."

Natalie was impressed. J.J. and Jill would be over the moon to be gifted a new gaming system. "Wow."

Looking pleased, Elaine went on. "If *your* kids are excited about going to the party, they'll get their friends to go, and we'll have a full house. Will they do that? For Charles?"

Seeing the naked need in Elaine's eyes, Natalie said, "Leave it to me. Every kid in Cold Harbor will be running to their mailbox, hoping to find an invitation. But what does any of this have to do with Mrs. Smith?"

After casting a furtive glance at the other women in the annuals section, Elaine said, "Let's move over to ground covers. I need a few flats of pachysandra."

Natalie pulled her wagon past tables of shade-loving plants until she and Elaine reached the section devoted to ground covers. Elaine walked all the way to the back, where rows of sedum, trailing periwinkle, and creeping juniper were packed tightly on a long table.

"I don't want to spoil the surprise by telling you what I have planned for the party, but I can tell you it'll be at the yacht club," Elaine began. "Linda, the woman I'm working with at Premium Parties, called yesterday to let me know that Peter couldn't sign off on the fireworks."

Peter, the yacht club president, was one of the most congenial people Natalie had ever met. "What's the problem?"

"Peter told Linda about a special clause in the bylaws. The club doesn't own the land it sits on. They lease it from Mrs. Smith, and part of the lease agreement stipulates that she has to approve all club-related events that take place outdoors after ten at night. I guess she said no to the fireworks, because Peter denied my request."

Natalie was taken aback by this news because Benjamin and Elaine were Commodores, the highest level of membership. Not only did they pay a king's ransom in dues, but Benjamin's company donated very generously to club fundraisers and sponsored several regattas each year. After all the Bernsteins had done for the club, how could Peter turn down Elaine's request?

"He says his hands are tied," Elaine said. "So, I contacted Mrs. Smith myself."

"Really?"

"You know I'd do anything for Charles. *Anything.* This woman isn't going to ruin my son's big day." Elaine smoothed her hair. "It's not like I haven't tried to be nice to her, either. Remember when we first moved in and I went over to introduce myself, but she never came to the door? Then I went back the next day with that potted hydrangea. It was a gorgeous plant."

"I remember it turning brown on her front porch."

Elaine scowled. "She came out to collect her newspapers—probably in the middle of the night, because I've never seen her do it—but left that plant out there to die."

"It stayed there until one of her yard guys took it away." Natalie's gaze went glassy. "All these years we've lived next door to her, we've only seen the yard guys and the hot tub repairman pass through her gates."

"And Don."

Natalie's mouth fell open. "What? *Beth's* Don?"

"Yes. He strolled through the gates, casual as you please, and took an envelope taped to the front door."

"When was this?"

Elaine shrugged a delicate shoulder. "A week ago. Maybe more. Benjamin saw the whole thing and didn't think to mention it to me until today. Anyway, I called Beth to ask her about it, but she said she'd tell us tomorrow night at garden club."

"Why would Mrs. Smith be writing *Don*?" Natalie was practically panting. This was the juiciest gossip she'd heard in ages.

"I don't know, but if she can tape an envelope to the door for him, she can reply to my letter the same way."

When Natalie had pulled into the garden center, she'd been in a huge hurry to buy plants and get to work at the McCreedys', but her desire to sell a house was completely overshadowed by what Elaine was telling her. "Wait. You already wrote her?"

"Yes. I politely asked for permission to shoot off fireworks the night of the party and told her why it was such an important event for our family. She might've brushed off Peter's request, but I won't take no for an answer."

"What if she doesn't reply?"

Elaine tossed her head. "Then I'll stand on her porch and ring her doorbell until she opens the damn door and speaks to me. The woman lives in a neighborhood, which means she's part of a community. She can't just hide in her house and make decisions that affect her neighbors without looking us in the eye."

Elaine's intensity discomfited Natalie. On one hand, she thought her friend's obsession with a party for a thirteen-year-old was ridiculous. She couldn't imagine spending such a crazy amount of money on a kid. Then again, Natalie had three kids. Three times the expense of Elaine's one child. But even if she and Jimmy could afford such an extravagant party, they wouldn't throw their money away to impress a bunch of teenagers.

Elaine thinks she can buy friends for Charles, but it won't work.

The kids would be nice to him for a while, but when the afterglow of the party and the satisfaction of having received a new Atari faded, so would his newfound popularity.

"They should ship him off to boarding school," Jimmy had said more than once. "He'll be a sissy for the rest of his life if he doesn't get away from his mother."

Deep down, Natalie was envious of Elaine. The Bernsteins flew first-class to Europe twice a year and spent every spring break in the Caribbean. Elaine had the most exquisite clothes, jewelry, and purses. She owned several fur coats. She had her hair and nails done every Friday. Every three years, Benjamin bought her a new Mercedes.

Benjamin's company, Rose's Frozen Foods, was the main

supplier of frozen kosher meals for all Long Island. He had several hundred employees and an army of delivery trucks bearing the company logo and a big blue rose. These trucks zoomed from the distribution center in Queens to grocery stores all over Nassau and Suffolk Counties.

"Benjamin might expand into New Jersey next year," Jimmy had whispered to Natalie a few nights ago. "If that happens, he *will* be the Jewish Gatsby."

"It'll take more than money to fix Charles," had been Natalie's petty response.

Jimmy had kissed her neck, his hand sliding under her nightgown to stroke the silky skin of her inner thigh. "You could fix him. You always know what to do."

Turned on by the hint of pride in his voice, Natalie had shrugged out of her nightgown and pulled her husband on top of her.

Now, standing in a quiet corner of the plant store, Natalie didn't feel jealous of Elaine. She felt admiration.

Elaine Bernstein was going to tangle with Mrs. Smith.

"What can I do to help?"

Elaine smiled. "You can make me a double G&T tomorrow night. Either I'll be celebrating a victory, or I'll need some liquid courage before I make my next move. Because if she doesn't give me what I want, I'll be declaring war on Mrs. Smith."

6

Mrs. Smith

Mrs. Smith lurched over the dewy grass in her bare feet, her yellow toenails spearing the soft soil. Dark purple spider veins covered her bony limbs like tattoos. As she moved, flakes of salt-white skin drifted to the ground, leaving a feast for the mites and pill bugs. Her black hair was matted. The moonlight probed the bald patches on her skull.

She moved as fast as she could in her decaying human form.

Ahead, the water waited like a lover lying prostrate on black satin sheets.

It was just past midnight, and all was quiet.

To Mrs. Smith, however, it was never quiet. Even now, in the dead of night, her ears vibrated with a cacophony of human noise. She heard steel lines clanging against aluminum boat masts. The persistent hum of air-conditioning. The rush of water through pipes. The roar of a motorcycle. Somewhere, far above her, a plane whined as it cut through the clouds.

The quiet had been spoiled long ago. So had the darkness.

As she made her way to the boathouse, Mrs. Smith's sensitive eyes were assaulted by a thousand pricks of light. Lights glared from buildings and docks on the opposite shoreline. Lights on the sailboats swayed as the vessels rocked in their sleep. Lights from the windows, decks, and porches of her neighbors' houses trespassed onto the fringes of her property.

If she could, she'd squeeze every bulb until it shattered. She'd slice through every power cable, restoring the true blackness of night. The night did not belong to the humans sleeping in these air-conditioned houses. It belonged to creatures like her.

Predators.

Killers.

Light was the refuge of the weak.

Mrs. Smith always waited until the light and noise was at a minimum before venturing outside. Eager to escape terra firma, Mrs. Smith entered her boathouse through the back door.

This close to the water, her skin began to itch. The muscles in her legs tensed. Her teeth and nails tingled.

She shed her robe and approached the channel cut through the middle of the floor. A sleek powerboat hung suspended above the water. Draped in ash-gray canvas, it looked like an orca's carcass.

The boat could be lowered into the channel, which maintained a depth of six to nine feet, and eased out into the harbor through the main door. However, it was nothing more than a prop. The boathouse served another purpose. It allowed Mrs. Smith to enter the water without being seen.

She was very, very careful to avoid being seen in her human form and even more so after she transformed. Her survival depended on concealment.

As her ragged toenails scraped over the wood floor, she sensed her children waiting for her. They'd be just past the sandbar, wriggling with anticipation.

I'm coming, children.

The itching intensified, but a smile touched Mrs. Smith's

thin lips as she padded over the rough floorboards and jumped into the channel. The water embraced her, its liquid fingers cooling her skin.

The saltwater hot tubs in her house kept Mrs. Smith's scaly limbs hydrated during the day, but she hated them. She hated their fiberglass basins and chrome dials. She hated their ridiculous jets and bubbles, their inane cupholders.

She spent most of the day languishing in one of several large tubs, reading books or flipping through magazines. She had piles of magazines because she owned a company that printed hundreds of them every month. She had piles of books, too. She belonged to the Literary Guild, the Dollar Book Club, the Book of the Month Club, and the Doubleday Book Club. She also had a library of antique books and would revisit old favorites when she couldn't stand to face yet another vapid novel by the likes of Jackie Collins or Danielle Steel.

When Mrs. Smith grew tired of reading, she'd fall into a restless sleep and dream of a younger world.

She dreamed of oceans without boats, of jagged icebergs thrusting deep down into glacial waters, of colossal sharks and finned serpents. She dreamed of submarine-sized eels. Of creatures moving soundlessly through the depths. Creatures like her. Creatures with teeth. Powerful, magnificent, hungry hunters.

They were all dead now. All but her. And here she was, soaking in hot tubs and sneaking into the water under the cover of night. It was too dangerous to hunt during the day. Human eyes were everywhere. The time when she could doze in underwater caves, knowing she would never be discovered, had passed. She had to live a half-life among the creatures she despised most or cease to exist at all.

Mrs. Smith retained her human form as she slithered under the gap in the boathouse door.

She swam like a frog for several strokes—taking care to remain below the surface—before finally shedding her fragile human husk.

Her legs divided into thin, elongated limbs. At the end of each rubbery, eel-like appendage was a needle-sharp barb. Her skin darkened. Diamond-shaped scales erupted all over her body.

The bones in Mrs. Smith's arms shattered and rearranged into spines. Her arms grew longer and longer, like pieces of pulled taffy, and her fingers morphed into hooked claws. As her torso stretched and narrowed, her breasts flattened into calloused disks. Her head swelled like an oval balloon, row after row of serrated teeth cutting through her gums. When she opened her flexible lower jaw, her ink-black tongue wriggled out of her mouth like an adder slithering out of a cave.

Gills sliced through the flesh of her neck, and for the first time in many hours, Mrs. Smith could breathe.

The transformation had been painful. It always was. But the pain was already fading as she swam away from the shore, as her eyes became bigger, rounder, and beetle black.

She had the cold, calculating stare of a great white, but the intelligence in her gaze made her far more terrifying. The most formidable sharks in the ocean ate without discernment. They'd bite anything once. Mrs. Smith was far more selective.

Tonight, she would spurn her diet of whales and fish. It was the summer solstice, which meant her season of renewal had finally begun. For nine months, she'd been fasting, eating only to survive. Now she would eat for pleasure.

These were the old laws—blood oaths put into place when humans first became a threat to ancient creatures. The laws between the species were binding. And eternal.

The oath had been sworn so long ago that the humans no longer remembered it. Their numbers had grown too quickly.

Their lives were too short. They were born, reproduced, and died in the blink of an eye. Their blood became diluted. The oaths and old ways were forgotten.

But Mrs. Smith remembered. The laws were etched into her DNA. They'd been transferred from mother to daughter for millennia. Back when the humans were little more than apes dragging their knuckles on the ground, they had vowed not to hunt her kind.

In return, the Mother of Eels promised not to hunt humans unless they failed to give her what she needed at the end of her hundred-year life cycle. If they failed to sacrifice their own to her when she asked, she could take what she needed.

There were no sacrifices now, but all Mrs. Smith had to do was devour the flesh of nine man-children between the summer solstice and the fall equinox and she would be reborn.

Nine Pure Ones.

Nine unsullied pieces of flesh.

Nine was the number of power. The number of mastery. Of all timeless things. The creature in Mrs. Smith's stained-glass window had nine tentacles. Seven sprouted from her hips and two from her torso. These muscular appendages propelled her through the water like a spear.

Mrs. Smith opened her mouth and emitted a sound beyond the range of human hearing. She swam under the moored boats, moving faster and faster as she headed for the mouth of the harbor.

Diving deeper, she felt the caress of an eel's body. And then another. And another.

Soon, there was a swirling, writhing cloud of eels. They swam in a mass above her, shielding her, camouflaging her. The eels turned her into a shadow. A meaningless smudge on a ship's sonar screen. An anomaly.

An anomaly is precisely what she was. She moved with

such speed that it was difficult to distinguish her body from the water. She was a harpoon in animal form, swimming with her viper-shaped head jutting forward, her arms pinned to her sides. The thrusts of her lower tentacles were explosive.

With her children swimming above her, Mrs. Smith entered the deep waters of the Sound. The eels couldn't keep pace with their mother. They were not the giant eels of old but their smaller, slower descendants.

Still, they were legion, and as one swarm tired, a fresh swarm would suddenly appear to take over. Together, the dark, undulating mass continued moving east until the land forked.

Here, at the northern tip of Long Island, in a place the humans called Plum Gut, Mrs. Smith would wait for her prey.

The waters in the channel between Orient Point and Plum Island were turbulent. The rip currents were strong even when the surface of the water was smooth as ice. Squalls manifested out of nowhere, whipping the sea into a frenzy and effortlessly capsizing small boats.

This is exactly what Mrs. Smith was hoping for.

At sunrise, the sea looked deceptively glassy. Mrs. Smith knew the commercial fishers and sports fishers would listen to the weather forecast one last time before loading their boats with supplies and motoring away from their safe harbors.

Their misplaced faith in science would drive them into the channel where she lurked. They'd lower their nets, hooks, and traps into the water, their engines excreting noxious gas and oil sheens. They'd launch aluminum cans and food wrappers over the sides of their boats. Flick cigarette butts. Dump piss and feces.

Mrs. Smith smelled every contamination, no matter how small. She tasted every corruption. As she drifted along the bottom, her children weaving back and forth above her like threads of yarn on a loom, the abuse of her domain enraged her.

Her fury seemed to summon the storm.

Birthed to the Bermuda Triangle, the system was inconsequential at first. But as it passed over the jet stream on its way to the shores of Long Island, it collided with a mass of cold water. And just like that, it had teeth.

Mrs. Smith felt the storm long before the fishermen knew of its existence. The bigger boats with their larger crews saw the future on their radar screens and fled, but many of the sports fishermen, ignorant of the incoming squall or too full of hubris to run, stayed put.

By the time they realized their mistake, it was too late.

The wind struck the boats from the side, making them rock back and forth like bathtub toys. The rain pelted the decks and men fought to keep their feet on the slippery surfaces. Some were pitched into the lifelines, which saved them from catapulting overboard. Others reached for the same lifelines and missed.

The instant their bodies were flung into the roiling sea, Mrs. Smith felt their terror. It aroused her appetite. She salivated as she imagined curling her tentacles around their legs and pulling them down, down into the dark.

Her first victim wore an orange life jacket and rubber boots. Mrs. Smith severed his left arm in one bite. Blood poured from the wound, feathering around her face and flooding her nostrils with its sweet scent.

After devouring the other arm, she shredded the life jacket with a single swipe of her claws. Embracing the lifeless body of her prey, she ate greedily.

It had been too long since she'd tasted tender flesh. Rich blood.

She felt a shark approaching from below, rocketing up at her with its jaw open in a lethal grin. She smashed it with a tentacle while sinking her teeth into the dead man's neck. The loose ligaments in her jaw stretched and her mouth opened wide enough to take in his whole head. Then she clamped her jaw shut, crushing the skull like a conch shell. As the brain matter slid down her throat, she waited for the flood of euphoria that came from feasting on a man-child.

It did not come. The human had been too old.

When her second victim arrowed into the water, Mrs. Smith left the legs of her first victim to the sharks and darted to the surface to collect a more valuable prize.

This human wore no life jacket. Unlike the man she'd just eaten, he was a strong swimmer. He'd barely stopped his downward trajectory before he began to scissor-kick toward the surface.

Mrs. Smith could practically feel the air burning in his fragile lungs. She watched his pale, ineffective limbs for several seconds, delighting in his weakness, but then her hunger surged, and she grabbed him by the feet, reeling him in like a yo-yo on a string.

The man-child couldn't see her in the darkness, but he was aware of her shape and the rubbery tentacle curling around his ankles. She sank her teeth into his torso, puncturing his heart and lungs, and his world went black.

The blood pumping into his chest was nectar to Mrs. Smith, pure and bright and strong. It electrified her body like a lightning strike, instantly healing and regenerating her tired cells.

As she crunched the man-child's bones, her spine arched in ecstasy.

Humans were perfectly ripe only once in their short lives. This occurred during the two or three years when they were caught between childhood and adulthood. During this time, their hormones surged, flavoring their blood with possibility and promise.

Long ago, when Mrs. Smith had been called by other names, humans had willingly sacrificed their Pure Ones to her. In those glorious days, the man-children walked into the water, naked as seals, and she had feasted on them. In return, she had allowed the rest of their tribe or band or village to live. This had been part of the oath between her and their kind.

As the centuries passed, the humans continued to feed her. They gave her their weak or deformed children. They gave her slaves and prisoners or those who'd broken their laws.

Back then, Mrs. Smith had her fill of man flesh. Back then, the Pure Ones were gifted to her—wrists and ankles bound like a present wrapped in ribbons.

The sacrifices made Mrs. Smith lazy. Complacent. She watched the humans evolve. She bore witness to their advancements, never imagining the day would come when she was no longer the most powerful of the two species. She couldn't foresee a future in which humans dominated the planet, forcing her to hide in the shadows.

When such a future arrived, she had to adapt.

She no longer received sacrifices. She had to skulk about, biding her time until she could strike. She had to avoid boat propellers, commercial fishing nets, submarines, and sonar. She had to pick off humans when they were alone or in the middle of a storm. Detection would lead to her death, so she became one with the shadows.

Truth be told, she relished the hunt. She was born to stalk. To tear. To devour. She would make the humans pay for diminishing her. For forgetting that she should be worshipped as a god.

By the time her third victim entered the water, the sharks were waiting. They circled around Mrs. Smith, frenzied with hunger.

Mrs. Smith recognized their need, but she was the apex predator of every ocean. The sharks would have to make do with her scraps.

This man-child was hers and hers alone.

She enfolded him in her serpentine arms and carried him all the way down to the bottom. She would make the pleasure of eating him last as long as possible.

Every bite was dizzying. Orgasmic. The effect on her body was a miracle. She felt the years slough away like old snakeskin. Her muscles were infused with strength. She'd be twice as fast now. With her renewed stamina, she could spend more time out of the water. Her human shell would look younger. Its skin smooth with no trace of scales. Her bony body would fill out. Her flesh would be as soft as a ripe pear. Her hair, fine as corn silk. Her teeth would gleam like pearls. Her uneven gait would be gone. Instead, she'd move with the lithe grace of a dancer.

The summer had just begun, and she'd already consumed two Pure Ones. Seven more and she would live for another century.

With her belly stretched tight as a drum, she fell into a doze, her body hovering above the ocean floor. She woke only once to vomit a pair of watches, a wedding ring, a belt buckle, three zippers, and a handful of undigested teeth. As she slipped into sleep again, the eels cloaked her body.

They would stay with her until the moon rose and the tides shifted. They would stay until she slipped back under the gap in the boathouse door. And when she was gone, walking on the hard, dry earth with her grotesque human legs, her children would glide away to their clumps of seagrass to wait.

They would wait for the Mother of Eels to call to them. They would wait until it was time for the next hunt.

7
Jill

Jill didn't realize her mom was in the laundry room until her fingers curled around the cool metal of the refrigerator handle. The laundry room was steps away from the fridge, and Jill snatched her hand back as if she'd been burned.

Her mother slammed the dryer door closed, straightened, and pinned Jill with a glare.

"Where's your brother?" It was just past nine in the morning and Natalie's voice was already edged with anger. "There isn't a drop of water in the dog dish. Why do we pay you kids an allowance when you never do your jobs?"

"He's downstairs," said Jill.

"Listening to music, with his door closed, I suppose?"

Jill nodded.

Her mother released one of her weighted sighs and picked up the water bowl. "I have to do everything around here. Absolutely *everything.* But not today. Today, you and J.J. are helping me with yard work. Go get dressed."

Jill let out a moan of complaint, but it was half-hearted. There was no use arguing when her mom got that Cruella de Vil look in her eye, so she trudged down the hall to her room and pulled on shorts and a striped T-shirt that used to be J.J.'s.

In the bathroom she shared with Justin, she gazed at herself in the mirror as she brushed her teeth. She saw a girl in a seriously ugly shirt. Not only were the colors hideous—brown, yellow, and orange—but it was too short for her. The bottom hem sat just above the waistline of her shorts, which meant her skin would be exposed every time she moved.

I'm going to ruin you, Jill thought, testing the thickness of the fabric with her fingernail.

Yard work meant sharp tools. Clippers, hand rakes, weeders. All she had to do was make a big enough hole, and her mom would finally let her throw it out.

Stepping out of the bathroom, she heard raised voices from downstairs. Her mom was yelling at J.J., and he was yelling right back.

Jill stood at the top of the spiral staircase, listening. She was relieved that her brother was in trouble instead of her. Jill felt like she was always in trouble. Always disappointing her mom.

The list of Jill's faults was long. Her hair was always tangled. She didn't chew with her mouth closed, use good posture, or wait her turn to talk. She didn't sit like a lady, speak like a lady, or eat like a lady. She had a terrible sweet tooth, which was why she was on the chubby side. She ate unhealthy snacks in her room in between meals. She pouted when she didn't get her way. She wasn't good at math. When cornered, she lied.

Downstairs, her brother shouted, "I'm not going!" and slammed his bedroom door.

"Wait until your father hears about this!" her mother threatened before screeching, "*Jill!* What's taking you so long?"

Jill hurried down the winding stairs and followed her mother into the garage.

"We need gloves, clippers, a rake, a shovel, and garbage bags."

Jill began gathering the tools, but stopped when her mom

lowered the tailgate of the station wagon. The rear cargo area was completely stuffed with flats of colorful flowers. "Where are we going?"

"To the house I'm selling."

Jill shot a sideways glance at her mom. There'd been something unfamiliar about her tone. There was a lightness to it. She sounded almost . . . happy.

"Mr. and Mrs. McCreedy's house?"

"That's right. Put the tools on the floor behind your seat," she said, slamming the tailgate. "There isn't any room back here."

As they drove up Tidewater Terrace and rounded the first of three bends in the road, Jill glanced at Heather Anderson's house, hoping to catch sight of her best friend, but guessing she wouldn't.

There was no reason for Heather to be outside this early on a Saturday morning. Heather was probably still in her pajamas, eating a bowl of Cap'n Crunch's Crunch Berries on the sofa while watching cartoons.

The last time Jill slept over, she'd filled her cereal bowl to the brim with the sugary cereal. She'd picked out all the red spherical Crunch Berries first, crushing each one between her molars, the sweet flavor flowing over her tongue and coating her gums. Next, she'd eaten the rectangular cereal pieces. They scratched the roof of her mouth like sandpaper, but she didn't care. The only cereal her mother bought was Raisin Bran or Grape-Nuts. Raisin Bran was okay because of the raisins, but the flakes got so soggy by the end that Jill didn't want to put them in her mouth. And Grape-Nuts was totally disgusting. It was like eating twigs and acorn caps.

"It's good for you," her mother always said when she caught Jill grimacing.

Heather wasn't forced to eat Grape-Nuts. Her pantry was

always stocked with tasty cereals like Cap'n Crunch, Lucky Charms, Frosted Flakes, or Apple Jacks. Heather's mom let her have soda with dinner and ice cream for dessert. She never told Heather she needed to watch what she ate or that boys didn't ask fat girls out for dates.

Jill's mother always asked what Heather's mom had given her to eat, and Jill always lied. If her mother knew she'd had a TV dinner followed by an ice cream sundae on Friday night and sugar cereal for breakfast the next morning, she'd never let Jill sleep over at Heather's again.

As if reading her mind, her mother frowned at the Andersons' crooked mailbox. "Why don't you ever ask Heather to stay over at our house? She owns a sleeping bag, doesn't she?"

Jill tightened her jaw. She couldn't let her mother see how important it was to have Heather's house as a refuge. Spending the night there was like going on vacation. She could eat whatever she wanted. She and Heather could watch whatever they wanted on TV. No one told them when to go to bed or when to get up in the morning. No one told them to brush their teeth or put their plates in the dishwasher.

Jill was a different person at Heather's house. She was more relaxed. She laughed all the time. She didn't have to worry about being loud. She could say she was hungry without feeling like a pig.

She couldn't let her mother take the Andersons away from her, which meant she had to pretend that she didn't cherish every minute she spent with them.

Shrugging one shoulder, she said, "It's easier for me to go to her house because she has two beds in her room."

Her mother arched her brows. "Is that the only reason?"

Jill knew she had to throw her mom a bone. She had to tell her something to make their family seem better than the Andersons.

"Heather and I get to pick the movie we want to watch," she admitted. "Erik doesn't have to agree because he has a TV in his room now."

"That explains why he barely passed the tenth grade," her mother muttered. "Kids shouldn't have TVs in their bedrooms. It's ridiculous."

Knowing she had to let her mom have the last word, Jill stayed silent for the rest of the short car ride.

Her mother pulled into the driveway of a lettuce-green ranch house Jill had ridden past on her bike a hundred times. All the kids took the dirt path connecting Tidewater Terrace to Idle Day Drive on their way to the hobby shop or pizza place. The McCreedys' dogs always barked at them, their lips curling back into nasty snarls as they pushed their snotty muzzles through the fence rails.

Sometimes, Mr. McCreedy would whip his door open to see what had set his dogs off. He'd stand on the stoop in a pair of velour sweatpants and a dingy white undershirt that never covered the full mound of his hairy stomach, and he'd glare at the kids.

Mrs. McCreedy hardly ever went outside. She was a droopy-faced woman who wore shapeless housedresses and a head full of pink rollers. She never said a word to the kids. She just flicked the ash from her cigarette in their direction, watching them through slitted eyes.

Jill had written a story in which Mrs. McCreedy was really Medusa in disguise. It had been a huge hit on the school bus.

"We're going to improve the curb appeal of this place," Jill's mom said as she turned off the engine. "I'll plant flowers in front, and you'll weed in the back."

"Where are the McCreedys?"

"In Florida for the summer, thank God. Their miserable dogs are gone, too, so there's nothing to stop us from getting some real work done today. Put all the petunias next to the mailbox. I'll get the other flowers."

While Jill lined up pots of pink and violet petunias on the grass near the mailbox post, her mom unloaded two terracotta planters. After carrying the planters to the front door, she went back to the car to collect the flat of red geraniums, white lobelias, and asparagus ferns. She was humming to herself as she pulled on her garden gloves. Jill paused to listen, wondering if she recognized the tune.

Her mom made a shooing motion. "Get a move on. We have a lot to do."

Jill walked around the side of the house to the scraggly backyard and looked around. There wasn't much of a lawn. The grass was green in a few places, but for the most part, large patches of brown bordered garden beds overrun by weeds.

Directly behind the house was a dirty brick patio surrounded by sickly looking bushes. A wooden fence marched along the entire length of the property. It bulged in places where the trees from Mrs. Smith's woods leaned heavily against its rails. Vines streamed down from the trees and poured over the fence. Jill could see dozens of thin tendrils stretching across the McCreedys' sparse grass.

She recognized the vines. Her parents had taught her everything they knew about plants. She knew how to sow, water, and feed vegetables and flowers. She also knew how to prune bushes and kill weeds.

There was a ton of killing to do in the McCreedys' yard.

Jill gazed at the trees behind the fence. The ropes of oriental bittersweet coiling around the trunks were python thick. Their foliage was so dense that she couldn't see any farther into the woods. There was nothing but green leaves and shadow.

She felt sorry for the trees, which were being smothered by the vines. Woven into a great, heavy net, they soaked up all the sunlight and drank up all the rain—stealing everything the trees needed to survive. They'd taken over the woods. Now they were coming for the McCreedys' house.

Turning her back on the woods, Jill began weeding the garden beds. She pulled out clump after clump of chickweed, filling a black trash bag in no time. Next, she used her trowel to dig up stubborn dandelion and crabgrass roots.

After an hour, her arms were coated with a sheen of sweat and dirt. Her hairline was damp. Her mouth was dry. She wanted a drink of water from her mom's thermos, but she didn't want to stop working until she'd cut a few vines with the hedge clippers.

For the next fifteen minutes, the scissor-like blades bit through the vines hanging over the fence. They tumbled to the ground like clumps of hair, and by the time she'd created a small channel of space between the trees and the fence, she was ready for a break.

Wiping her wet brow with the bottom of her T-shirt, she stared into the woods.

They were too quiet.

There was no birdsong or drone of insects.

There was nothing.

In the silence, Jill could sense the vines moving.

She could almost feel their tiny, maggot-white root hairs wriggling through the soil. Stretching and probing. It was only a matter of time before fresh, young shoots climbed over the fence. Without constant trimming, they'd spill down and blanket the brown-bellied juniper bushes. After that, they'd crawl over the patio and come for the house.

Jill imagined them growing and spreading until they couldn't be stopped.

These vines were the reason behind the concrete drainage gully running between their property and the empty lot next to Mrs. Smith's house. As soon as the vines reached the ditch, Jill's dad would cut them back and douse the lacerated stalks with weed killer.

Year after year, the vines tried to creep onto the vacant lot. They were a constant nuisance, and no matter what Jill's father did to them, they always came back. But if he didn't stop them, they'd invade the Scotts' property.

He told Jill that oriental bittersweet couldn't be burned. It had to be attacked at ground level. However, trying to rip the spiderweb of orange roots out of the dark earth was only a temporary solution. The roots tunneled deep into the soil, branching out like hundreds of tiny lightning bolts. A severed root could regenerate like a lizard's tail.

The vine was a survivor. It had found a home in Mrs. Smith's woods. And now, it wanted more. It wanted to spread, smothering and choking every living thing in its path.

I bet Mrs. Smith wants that, too, Jill thought with sudden clarity. *It's all over her property. She must love it.*

Jill swiped at her sweaty forehead and glared at the woods.

She was angry.

She hated the sight of the suffocating trees. She hated having to spend her Saturday cutting the insatiable vines. She was hot and thirsty. And hungry. The bowl of Raisin Bran she'd eaten for breakfast seemed like a distant memory. She wanted to tell her mom that she'd had enough—that she was going to the pool to hang out with her friends. She wanted to sit with them on the hot stone steps and eat a sun-softened ice cream sandwich while they talked about boys.

She knew she wasn't going anywhere until her mother was good and ready. Then they'd load the tools into the car and head home, and her mom wouldn't even thank her for helping. She'd just tell her to scrape the dirt out from under her nails before she sat down for lunch or not to wear her dirty shoes in the house.

And lunch would probably be a turkey and cheese sandwich on that dry-as-sand wheat bread. Jill would get apple slices or carrot sticks while Justin could have a mountain of potato chips. He could have whatever he wanted. Chips. Oreos. An orange Creamsicle. Grilled cheese on rye.

If Jill asked for any of those things, her mother would say, "Have a nice glass of milk."

J.J. should be here, Jill thought, her anger building. *It's not fair.*

A jagged rock poked out of a brown patch of grass close to Jill's sneaker. She pried it out of the ground and hurled it toward the woods. It sailed over the fence and was instantly swallowed by the dense vines.

She heard a faint rustle when her missile struck the foliage, but although she waited for the muffled thud of the rock hitting the ground, it never came.

The silence was as dense as the woods.

Jill felt eyes on her. There was something behind the trees, back where the shadows stitched together. Something was there, watching her.

Mrs. Smith.

Fear knotted Jill's stomach.

She took a step backward. She couldn't see a thing beyond the tangled mass of vines, but she knew she was no longer alone.

Jill grabbed the garden trowel, clippers, and the garbage bags stuffed with withering weeds. Then she ran to the front of the house and told her mother she'd finished her work.

Behind her, the vines she'd cut were already healing.

8

Una

Una closed her book with a sigh of satisfaction.

"It was good?" asked Kristofer.

Una smiled at her husband. "Very good. It's also the last one from my pile. I'll have to go to the library today."

"I'll come with you. I want to get that book by Kissinger." Kristofer folded his newspaper and drank the last of the coffee in his mug. "Are you ready for me to brush?"

Una nodded and pulled her chair away from the patio table and the protective shade of its umbrella. As the morning sun lit her face, she closed her eyes and raised her face to the sky.

"You look like a cat," said Kristofer, laughter in his voice. "A cat with long, silver fur."

Standing behind his wife of forty-two years, he began to brush her hair using gentle, rhythmic strokes. Una had washed it earlier that morning and left it to dry in the summer air. While Kristofer showered, she'd made breakfast and carried it out to the patio overlooking their garden. For the next hour, they ate, drank coffee, and read. A mystery novel for her and *The New York Post* for him.

Saturday mornings were Una's favorite time of the week, especially during the summer. She and Kristofer would sit outside in companionable silence broken only by birdsong. When he was done reading the paper, he'd pick up her brush and run it through her hair, which fell down her back like a curtain of silver water.

"Like Skógafoss," Kristofer always said. To him, Skógafoss was the most beautiful waterfall in the world. It was where he'd asked Una to marry him, where he'd taken her hands in his and declared that he'd found the lost treasure hidden in the cave behind the falls. "You're the treasure. I found you."

Una had thrown her arms around him, dizzy with happiness. There'd been no silver in her hair when she'd kissed him on the rocks below the falls. She'd been young and glowing with promise. Her cheeks had been wet from mist and tears, and when Kristofer told her to look up, she'd seen a rainbow dancing across the sky.

Even though she'd been young and inexperienced with the ways of the world, she'd looked into Kristofer's kind face and known that he would never take her for granted. He'd brushed out her hair on their wedding night, and he'd been doing it ever since. His touch was as tender as it had been all those years ago. He was still the kind, appreciative man she'd kissed by the waterfall.

She saw how time had marked the skin on his hands as he laid the brush on the patio table, but she loved him all the more for his brown spots and swollen knuckles. They'd earned their wrinkles together, the two of them. They were the lucky ones.

After dropping a kiss on Una's forehead, Kristofer collected their breakfast plates and went inside the house.

Una stayed where she was, surveying her garden while she braided her hair into a long rope. She then wrapped the braid around and around into a bun and pinned it in place.

A bee hovered over the table, demanding something from

her, so she poured a little water into a saucer for it and turned back to her garden.

The bulbs Una had planted in the autumn had survived the winter. Nestled in the soft soil, they'd received all the rain they needed in April and May. By June, every bulb had burst out of the ground, ripening in the sun until the buds fell open to reveal jewel-toned flowers.

The red lilies were especially vibrant. Una had read somewhere that red lilies were a symbol of fertility.

I should bring some to Beth Pulaski next week, Una thought.

She wished she could do more for Beth. If only she could remember which plant her amma would have used to make a fertility tea.

As a girl, she'd had no interest in fertility or childbirth. Her amma's tinctures and teas meant little to her. It was Amma's stories Una craved.

For Beth's sake, Una wanted to remember, so she moved through her garden, touching the plants and whispering their names in her native language, hoping to spark a memory.

She walked to the edge of their property, where the cucumber vines and pole beans covered the back fence in a curtain of green. Next, she checked the vegetables for signs of insect damage. The lettuce leaves had small spots around their ruffled edges, but nothing to be concerned about. The carrot tops looked like a small, lush forest—a place for the elves to hide.

Stepping over a row of onions and radishes, Una saw nectar-dusted honeybees tunneling in and out of the golden lily flowers. She followed the flight of a singular bee for a while before making her way to the herb bed below the kitchen window.

After scanning the tidy rows of dill, basil, and wild garlic surrounded by a border of marigolds, she pinched off a dead marigold head and thought about the tooth Jill had found.

There are no elves in this land. But there are monsters.

Despite being bathed in sunlight, Una shivered and turned toward the north, toward the harbor.

Mrs. Smith was on the other side of town, secreted inside her ash-gray house, but Una could still feel her. She could sense her power.

Her darkness.

Una worried about the two families living in her shadow. No, it was more than worry. She was frightened for Charles Bernstein and the Scott children. She didn't know Charles well because she usually cleaned for the Bernsteins when he was at school, but she'd seen his shy smile in photos and heard the love in Elaine's voice when she spoke about him. He seemed like a nice boy. A nice but vulnerable boy.

As for J.J., Jill, and Justin, Una loved them dearly. She'd watched them grow up. They were like a second family. She wanted to shield them from the presence inside Mrs. Smith's house.

Something was stirring behind the closed door and shuttered windows; she could feel it like the shift in the air before a storm.

Something was waking.

Something strange and terrible.

Una hadn't shared her fears with Kristofer. He was a man of facts and figures. Of newspapers and biographies. He liked freshly ironed clothes and a ham and cheese sandwich wrapped in wax paper in his lunch box. He listened to classical music on the radio and watched sports on TV. He went to church on Sundays and grabbed a beer with his coworkers on Fridays. His penmanship was neat, his papers were stored in a file cabinet, and his socks were lined up in his dresser drawer like a row of turnips in a garden bed. He kept the gutters cleared and the grass mowed.

Kristofer's amma never told him the old stories. He didn't

believe in hunches. He didn't think there were messages hidden in a person's dreams.

Then again, his dreams weren't haunted. Not like Una's.

Una believed in the impossible because she had reason to, which was why she'd spent a decade trying to block out Mrs. Smith's presence and the shadow cast by her sinister house.

But she couldn't ignore the feeling in her gut. Turning her back and averting her gaze wasn't going to work anymore. It was time to learn what kind of creature lived next door to the Scotts and the Bernsteins. What sort of monster had human teeth buried in the lawn.

"Kristofer!" she called, entering the kitchen and depositing her coffee cup in the sink. "Ready to go?"

"Ready!"

He met her at the door carrying a tote stuffed with their library books. Una took the tote, and he scooped up the keys from the wobbly clay bowl Gunnar had made. He'd been in the second grade then, a dark-haired, gap-toothed boy, as sweet as the raisin buns Una's mother used to bake. Like most American children, Gunnar loved hamburgers and hot dogs. He loved Shake 'n Bake pork chops and fried chicken. Kristofer joked that they were raising a giant, and by the end of junior high, his prediction proved to be true. Their bright, handsome college boy was now six-four with linebacker shoulders and lumberjack legs.

Last summer, Gunnar had lived at home. Una had cooked all his favorite meals and fussed over him whenever she got the chance. This year, however, he was working on campus and would spend only the month of August with his parents.

"Gunnar would like today," Kristofer said as if reading Una's mind.

"It's perfect beach weather."

"Maybe not enough wind. You know he likes big waves. We'll go to Fire Island when he comes home."

Una liked Fire Island. The sand was smooth and sunbaked. It wasn't riddled with the broken shells and horseshoe crab husks like the beach behind the Scotts' house. There were no sharp things to draw blood from the bottom of her foot. No eels hiding in the shallows.

Ever since her amma had told her of the *hrökkáll*, a giant eel that oozed venom from its skin and could slice a person open with its razor-edged fins, Una had been afraid of eels. She was afraid of things in the water she couldn't see, so she never swam too far past the sandbar. She stuck to the shallows, where she knew exactly what moved beneath her.

"Come on, slowpoke," Kristofer teased as Una climbed into the car.

The library was busy that Saturday morning. Patrons browsed the shelves and milled around the newspaper and magazine section. There was a line at the checkout desk, which wasn't unusual. Mrs. Stapleton liked to chat while she stamped the cards in the back of their books.

There were no copies of Kissinger's book, but Kristofer said there were other fish in the sea and meandered away to browse the biography section.

Una headed for the rows of books with a magnifying glass decal on their spines. She was so familiar with the mystery section that she easily found the latest releases in the Brother Cadfael and Amelia Peabody series, as well as number eleven in the Inspector Wexford series. Cradling these treasures in one arm, she also selected books by Martha Grimes and Anne Perry, authors she'd yet to try.

Knowing that Kristofer always took twice as long to choose his books, Una wandered over to the card catalog. Pulling out the drawer labeled COD–CON, she flicked through the cards until she reached a listing for a book called *Cold Harbor: A Timeline.*

She closed the drawer and returned to the stacks. As she scanned the 900s in search of 974, she realized how little she knew about the town she called home. She'd been too busy building a life to learn the story of Cold Harbor.

She knew it had started as a fishing village and that its most famous landmark was a mansion built by one of the Vanderbilts. The yacht club was the social and recreational focal point of the area, and while there were a few stores and churches, all the schools and major businesses were located in adjacent towns.

Una wanted to discover the history of Mrs. Smith's house. It had stood on its lonely hill for a century before the rest of the houses on Tidewater Terrace were built. As old as it was, Una hoped to find a record of its origin.

She plucked *Cold Harbor: A Timeline* from the shelf and, after placing her stack of mysteries on the floor, began to read.

The slim volume was mostly a pictorial history. Una flipped through pages of grainy photographs, mostly of grim-faced fishermen, occasionally pausing to read captions about saltbox houses that no longer existed.

These flat-faced, unadorned structures were nothing like Mrs. Smith's house.

"Not here," Una muttered.

The other local history books devoted only a few pages to Cold Harbor. Most focused their attention on larger neighboring towns like Northport or Huntington.

Una was on the verge of abandoning her search when she spied a book with a plain brown cover on the top shelf. The words on the spine were faded, and a current of unease ran through her body as she opened to the title page.

"*The Secret History of Cold Harbor* by Jonathan Stapleton," she murmured to herself.

She flipped to Chapter One and was quickly engrossed by what she read.

> First established as a fishing hamlet in 1705, the area now known as Cold Harbor was originally called Bone Harbor. According to local lore, the name stemmed from the vast number of whale skeletons found along the beaches. This was over a century before the whaling industry became prevalent in the waters around Long Island, and there is no documentation to explain the presence of hundreds of carcasses of varying species. The Matinecock Indians living in present-day Huntington warned the settlers away from Bone Harbor, claiming the waters were haunted. Their people refused to fish in the area, and though they retrieved bones to use as tools and ornamentation, they took care when collecting these treasures and would walk the beaches only during low tide on a clear day.

A rush of cold air swept over Una's skin, raising gooseflesh on her arms. She glanced up, expecting to see a vent in the ceiling, but the ceiling tiles over her head were solid.

Returning her attention to the book, Una kept reading.

> Bone Harbor was renamed Cold Harbor in 1836 following a particularly long and bitter winter. By the end of the nineteenth century, the whaling trade was in full swing, and docks popped up around the harbor's edge like rib bones. Fishermen built huts around the new mill, while wealthy merchants and captains erected spacious homes with large tracts of land sweeping down to the water.

As Una studied pen and ink drawings of these houses, another blast of icy air slammed into the back of her neck.

The cold sank deep into the vertebrae of her spine and spread across the wings of her pelvis. Pivoting this way and that, she searched for the source of the phantom gust. There were no vents near the stacks, in the ceiling, or on the wall under the window.

She heard the buzz of an agitated insect and saw a massive horsefly battering against the window glass. Scuttling toward the end of the bookshelf, Una looked in the direction of the checkout desk to see if Kristofer was ready to go. No one was waiting in line, so she continued to study the drawings of nineteenth-century houses.

None were familiar to her, which was no surprise as more than a dozen had been destroyed by fire in 1873. Those untouched by the flames had either been razed or renovated so many times that they bore little resemblance to their original structures.

Una turned the page and froze.

A photograph of Mrs. Smith's house filled the entire page. Una took in every detail, comparing it in her mind to its current state.

There was no electric gate, of course, but the fence with its spiked finials was there. In the photo, the fence gates were closed, and the house looked just as hostile and unwelcoming as it did now. The windows were shuttered. Vines clung to the walls. Ragged shrubs dotted with arrowhead-sized thorns grew in waves along the length of the fence. Banks of dark clouds drifted behind the steep roof.

There was a figure on the porch. A woman in a long black dress and oversized black hat. She must have been in motion when the camera shutter closed because she wasn't quite in focus. Her face was turned to the side, revealing a flash of pale cheek and a swoop of dark hair that covered her ear and rose upward until it vanished under her hat. Her hands, shrouded in a pair of dark gloves, were knotted into fists. The pointed toes of her black boots peered out from under the hem of her dress. Her brow was lowered. Her mouth was set in a hard line.

"Didn't want your picture taken, did you?" Una whispered.

Tearing her gaze away from the woman's blurry profile, Una read the caption on the opposite page.

> Eel's Nest, home of Captain Josiah Smith. Photo taken in 1881 by the author's grandfather, Edward Stapleton.

Una wondered if the Stapleton who'd written this book was related to Mrs. Stapleton, the librarian. She tried to remember Mrs. Stapleton's first name but couldn't concentrate because the fly's buzzing suddenly increased in volume. The small engine whir of its wings became the throaty roar of a sports car.

The fly hurled its body around the window frame, torpedoing into the glass over and over again. Between each impact, its translucent wings vibrated with anger or desperation; Una couldn't tell which.

She was about to close the book splayed open in her hands when her gaze was abruptly snagged by the woman in the photo.

She was no longer looking off to the side. She now stared directly out at Una, and her face was no longer blurry.

"No!" Una cried, dropping the book as if it had burned her.

It landed on its spine, its pages spread to the photo of Eel's Nest and the woman in black. Her mouth was a menacing slash. Her eyes were two pinpricks of hatred.

Those eyes catapulted Una into the past.

She had seen them before.

Their soulless blackness. Their otherness.

She'd seen them staring up at her from beneath the waves. She'd seen them in her nightmares.

They were the eyes of a monster.

A killer.

"No, no, no. That can't be," Una whispered, backing away from the book.

She put a hand out to steady herself on the shelf, but instead of feeling the cool metal of the bookshelf under her fingers, she felt a sting of pain.

The horsefly squatted on the back of her hand. It had stung her once and seemed poised to sting again. Its green eyes flashed. Its hairy legs stroked her skin.

She swatted at the fly with her other hand, but it flew back to the window and pressed its body to the glass. It hung there, unmoving, as if waiting for her to attack.

Una cradled her throbbing hand, surprised by how much it hurt.

As a gardener, she'd been stung by all kinds of insects. Ants. Mosquitoes. Wasps. Horseflies. No bite or sting had ever felt like this. It felt like a hot needle was embedded just under the surface of her skin.

She turned away from the window and saw Kristofer standing at the end of the row.

"Did you get lost? This isn't the mystery section," he teased. Catching sight of her face, he stopped smiling. "*Elskan mín.* My love. Are you okay?"

Blinking back tears, Una pointed at the book. "I was looking at that when a horsefly bit me. It was a big one. It's on the window."

Kristofer glanced from the raised bump on his wife's hand to the window. "Well, it's gone now." He scooped up the book, and his eyes went wide. "Look at this! The most famous house in Cold Harbor." He shook his head. "It was ugly then, too."

Una rubbed at her eyes. "The woman in the picture. Is she facing the camera?"

"No, she's looking to her right. Her face is a little out of focus, but it looks like someone caught her in a bad mood." He closed the book. "Are we taking this with us?"

Una wanted to say no. She wanted Kristofer to put the book back on the shelf. Or in an incinerator. She wanted to bring her mystery novels to the car and then walk up the street to the bakery. She wanted to order a cookie with rainbow sprinkles—Justin's favorite—and take it home to have with a cup of tea later that afternoon. She wanted to be in her garden, to feel the sun on her skin. She wanted to get out of this library—to run from the strange eddies of glacial air, the horsefly, and the woman on the porch of a house called Eel's Nest.

She thought of Justin eating a cookie with rainbow sprinkles, his little face crinkling with pleasure. Of Jill, scribbling a story in one of her notebooks. Of J.J., singing ABBA behind the closed door of his bedroom. She thought of Charles and all the other children who lived near the water, and she knew she couldn't leave without the book.

Una had to know if Mrs. Smith could turn her blood to ice with the flick of her gaze. She had to know if she had the same eyes as the woman in the photograph. The same eyes that had haunted Una for most of her life.

For the children's sake, she had to know.

"Yes," she said, rubbing the sore skin on the back of her hand. "We'll take it."

After piling all of Una's books on top of his, Kristofer walked Una to the checkout desk.

Mrs. Stapleton chatted as she stamped Kristofer's two biographies and Una's novels. When it came time to stamp the slim history book, she beamed with delight. "My father wrote this. He knew more about this town than anyone I've ever met. He always said no one would care about its history until it was too late."

The phrase echoed in Una's head.

Too late, too late, too late.

"What did he mean?" she asked.

"I have no idea. Maybe he just didn't know many people who collected bits of local history the way he did. Before he got sick, he was working on his second book. I have all of his research at home. Boxes of letters and postcards and photos. Newspapers, too. I keep meaning to sort everything, but whenever I have free time, I end up in a chair, reading. I can't resist the lure of a good novel. Hazard of the profession."

Una waited for Mrs. Stapleton to finish stamping the card before turning to the photo of Mrs. Smith's house. "Do you think there's more information about this house in your father's boxes?"

A shadow crossed Mrs. Stapleton's face. "Not that house, no."

She wasn't a very good liar, but before Una could question her further, Kristofer loaded the last book into their tote bag and wished Mrs. Stapleton a good day. The librarian smiled weakly at him before glancing away.

She's afraid, Una thought as she followed Kristofer to the exit.

As they approached the double doors, she heard laughter from the children's area and the whir of the Xerox machine. There was another noise, too. A faint, persistent sound coming from the stacks.

Una shouldn't have been able to hear it because she was too far away. But she knew what it was and where it was coming from.

It was the thump of the horsefly, beating its body against the window, again and again and again.

9

Natalie

Natalie took the tray of homemade desserts from Beth's hands. The pastries were beautiful. They looked like they belonged on the cover of *Good Housekeeping.*

"I made extra for the kids," Beth said. "I know how much they love chocolate."

"Jill needs to learn to love it a little less," Natalie murmured. She put the tray down on the coffee table and handed Beth a Tom Collins.

Elaine was perched on the sofa, her legs crossed at the ankles, a martini glass in her right hand. She used her free hand to pat the sofa cushion next to her. "Saved you a seat."

Beth sat down and took a sip of her drink. Smiling at Natalie, she said, "Oh, my God! Is this straight gin?"

"Lemme fix it for you." Natalie leaned over the coffee table and dropped a lemon wheel into Beth's glass.

Beth laughed. "All better." She sank into the sofa cushions with a sigh and turned to Elaine. "Where are your men tonight?"

Elaine pointed at the spiral staircase leading to the Scotts' basement. "Charles is downstairs, and Benjamin's having dinner with friends from the temple." She looked at Natalie. "What's Jimmy up to?"

Natalie tried to give a breezy reply, but a sour note snuck into her voice "He's still in the city. He's taking clients to dinner and a play. They're going to *Medea*, which burns me up because I've been dying to see that one."

"He's so lucky. What did he take his clients to last time?" asked Beth.

"*Joseph and the Technicolor Dreamcoat*," Natalie said.

"Starring Bill Hutton." Beth wriggled her brows. "He can invade my dreams anytime."

Natalie returned to the bar cart and filled a shot glass with vodka. "The man of my dreams would be wearing coveralls and painting every inch of the McCreedy place before the open house. Last night, I dreamed I made the kids paint. Even Justin. It was your run-of-the-mill child labor dream."

The women laughed.

"Once, I had a dream that Charles was in the kitchen, making me breakfast," said Elaine. "I knew it was supposed to be a surprise, so I stayed in bed. When I woke up, I expected to find a big mess in the kitchen. I was relieved when everything was neat and tidy, but also a bit sad. Charlie's too old to do something like that now. How did the time go by so fast?"

The conversation moved on to disastrous breakfast-in-bed experiences and Mother's Day mishaps.

Natalie made a fresh round of drinks while telling a story about the time J.J. overturned an entire tray of food onto her bed. Her comforter had been drenched in oatmeal, bacon, orange juice, and coffee. J.J. had burst into tears and fled, leaving Jimmy to clean up the mess.

"And you can imagine how useless *that* was," she said. "The man looks at the dials on the washing machine like they're the control panel of a Russian rocket."

She and Elaine chortled with mirth. Beth didn't join in.

Natalie knew how much Beth wanted a baby, which was why she tried not to mention her children too often in front of her. But it was hard to avoid. Most of her time and energy was devoted to her three kids. Even with her new job, the things she needed to do for them were always on her mind. The calendar in the kitchen was filled with their swim meets and sailing regattas. J.J. had a dentist appointment this month, and Justin had his annual checkup with the pediatrician. And she was always thinking about their meals and snacks, planning menus, and making shopping lists.

Just change the subject, she chided herself.

Turning her attention to the dessert platter, she said, "I've been starving myself all day because I knew you'd be bringing goodies tonight."

Elaine pointed at a row of cake triangles made of layered wafers drizzled with chocolate. Chocolate buttercream peeked out between the layers. "Remind me what these delicious morsels are called."

"*Andrut*," said Beth. "It's a traditional Polish dessert. Last time, I made them with plum butter. This time, I went with chocolate and almond. It's French buttercream. Very light and silky."

"Hmmm." Natalie leaned closer to the platter. "Keep talking, baby."

Grinning, Beth pointed at the next row of treats. "You've had the *karpatka* before, too. It's a sandwich cake with creamy filling. And these are *kolaczki* cookies with three different fillings. Apricot, raspberry, and poppy seed."

"They're so professional looking," Elaine said. "You really

should sell your desserts. Have you talked to Don about your home business idea? I think you'd make a killing."

"Me, too," said Natalie. "Birthday cakes, desserts for dinner parties—I've never met anyone who can bake like you do."

Seeing the defeated look in Beth's eyes, she reached over and squeezed her arm. "Hey. What's wrong?"

"Don and I aren't talking about my home business idea because we're not talking," Beth mumbled. "I feel like I'm living with a stranger."

Elaine cocked her head. "What do you mean?"

"He comes home late, gobbles down whatever gorgeous meal I've spent hours cooking for him, and then goes to the den to watch TV. When I ask about his day, he gives me one- or two-word answers. And he's not touching me at *all*." Beth lowered her voice. "In bed, he pretends to be asleep."

An affair, Natalie thought.

She wasn't surprised. Don flirted with every woman between the ages of sixteen and sixty. He saw himself as a Casanova, and while Natalie enjoyed his gregarious nature, she didn't find him attractive. He was too loud and way too hairy for her taste.

"Did you two have a fight?" she asked Beth.

"That's the crazy thing. Everything was hunky-dory between us one day and totally weird the next. He's not mean. We're not arguing. It feels like he's not really there." Beth tapped her temple. "When he's watching TV or brushing his teeth, he looks totally spaced out. When I say his name, it's like I'm waking him up. Like he didn't even realize I was in the room."

Elaine studied Beth over the rim of her glass. "How long has this been going on?"

"About a week. Ever since he sold a car to Mrs. Smith."

Natalie stared at Beth. Then she glanced at Elaine. Judging by the look of shock on her face, this was news to her, too.

"A *car*?" Natalie couldn't wrap her head around it. "Does she even drive?"

Elaine pointed toward Mrs. Smith's house. "I've never seen the woman. She could walk right past me and I wouldn't know who she was."

"She'd have to come outside to walk past you," Beth said snidely. "And if she doesn't come outside, why does she need a car?"

"What did Don say about it?" Natalie wanted to know.

"Just that she called the dealership and asked for him by name. Said she saw the Porsche in his newspaper ad and wanted it." Beth pushed one of the pastries on the platter back in line. "She told him she'd pay the sticker price. In *cash*. All Don had to do was collect the check from her house."

Elaine narrowed her eyes. "She's ignored all of us for years. Why reach out to Don now?"

"I don't know," murmured Beth.

Tapping her nail against the glass top of the coffee table, Elaine declared, "I wrote her a letter yesterday."

Now it was Beth's turn to be surprised. "Why?"

As Elaine launched into her story of woe about the fireworks for Charles's party, Natalie wanted to shout, *Why does every conversation end up being about your son's goddamn bar mitzvah?*

Clearly, Beth didn't feel the same way. She was hanging on Elaine's every word.

"Did she write you back?" Beth asked when Elaine was done.

"Not yet. I called her several times this afternoon, but the phone just rang and rang. She never answered and we all know she was there." She speared Beth with a sharp glance. "Or is she driving around town in her new Porsche?"

"It hasn't been delivered yet. It's paid for, but she hasn't told Don when she wants him to drive it to her house." Beth passed her hands over her face. "I wish she'd leave him alone. I don't want a trip to Jamaica if it means he has to go back there."

Natalie took Beth's empty glass out of her hands and carried it to the bar cart. "Mrs. Smith is a thorn in all of our sides. I'll never sell the McCreedy house if potential buyers are afraid to move in behind her. Jill just clipped the vines in their backyard, and they're coming from Mrs. Smith's property. Every year, her vines encroach into other people's yards." Natalie stabbed at the air with the ice tongs. "If this goes on much longer, she'll bring down all of our property values."

"Those vines have already breached the yacht club property," Elaine said. Her blue eyes were feverish with anxiety. "I want to put the party tent on the side lawn because it's nice and flat, so I asked President Peter if we could cut the vegetation back to the property line, and *he* said I'd have to get Mrs. Smith's permission because the yacht club leases the land from her. As if asking permission for the fireworks isn't bad enough. I mean, does the woman own the sky?"

Natalie grinned at her friend. She liked it when Elaine got tipsy. With every cocktail, she was less poised. Less perfect. She snorted when she laughed. She raised her voice. Occasionally, she'd even chew ice, grinding it between her molars like a cow masticating hay.

"If Mrs. Smith can buy a new Porsche, she can afford to do something with her yard," Natalie said. "I have the open house on Sunday, but I'm going to church first. I plan to sit with Les Holton, who's on the town board. I'm going to ask him what can be done about the oriental bittersweet vines. They're contained to our neighborhood right now, but if we don't get rid of them once and for all, they'll spread."

"Les can only do so much." Beth reached into her bag and

withdrew a clipboard. "I thought we could start a petition. Get the rest of the neighbors to agree that she needs to clean things up. That she's driving down property values and allowing the spread of invasive vines."

Elaine pointed at the clipboard. "Then what?"

"We show it to Cliff Hodges. Les is great, but he's only a board member. Cliff is the town supervisor."

Natalie scanned the petition. "You might be onto something. Remember when Cliff did that talk at the yacht club two years ago? He's a Master Gardener. If we could get him to come out and look at Mrs. Smith's place, he might—"

"Slap her with a fine," finished Elaine. "And nothing will change."

Beth's eyes went to her clipboard. "Maybe we should skip the petition and bring cuttings of her invasive plants right to Cliff. That would really get him fired up."

"It would," Elaine agreed. "She has more than one variety, too. There's the oriental bittersweet, the Japanese honeysuckle, and I'm pretty sure I've seen patches of garlic mustard from my bedroom window."

Natalie raised her glass in the air. "Beth, you're a genius."

Elaine shook her head in dismay. "But what if the power of the town supervisor's office is limited? Maybe all Cliff can do is give her a warning or a fine?"

"I remember his yacht club talk, too," said Beth. "He wants to make his mark on the town by increasing public gardens and green spaces. Today's newspaper mentioned a fundraising campaign to put in a garden around the Cold Harbor sign. If someone wrote a big check to the campaign, I bet he'd do more than give her a fine."

Now Elaine raised her glass. "Benjamin and I would be happy to contribute."

Natalie heard a shuffling sound coming from the hall and

turned to see Justin standing in the doorway. He was in his dinosaur pajamas and carried a tattered blanket in one hand and a toy car in the other. He looked out of sorts.

Beth opened her arms and he floated into them.

"Hello, angel," she whispered into his hair. "Would you like a cookie?"

When he nodded, she looked to Natalie to be sure she hadn't overstepped.

Natalie smiled at her son. He was such a darling boy. Sweet and cute and smart. She knew she wasn't supposed to have favorites, but she did, and everyone knew it. "Just one. But then you'll have to brush your teeth and go right to bed."

Beth picked out a cookie with raspberry jam. She put it on a plate and showed it to Justin. "This is the best one."

"Thank you," Justin murmured sleepily.

While he sat on the edge of Beth's chair and nibbled his cookie, Natalie's friends smiled at him. Women were always taken in by his round, flushed cheeks, the sweep of his dark eyelashes, and his thick, tousled hair. His small feet dangled above the floor, and he clicked his heels together as if he wanted to teleport home from Oz.

When the cookie was gone, Justin handed Beth the plate and snuggled against her. Beth's expression turned dreamy, and Natalie knew she was pretending that Justin belonged to her—just for a moment—so she let her son stay where he was.

She immediately regretted this decision. Justin's presence had altered the mood. The momentum the women had begun to build in their campaign against Mrs. Smith was fizzling, and she couldn't allow that to happen.

At some point, and Natalie couldn't say when, she'd decided that Mrs. Smith was the only thing standing between her and her first sale. Why should this woman whom she'd never seen or spoken to wield so much power by ignoring conventions?

It was high time Mrs. Smith took responsibility for the eyesore that was her house and property. Natalie refused to let one woman thwart her success. She wouldn't let anyone condemn her into spending the next ten years cooking, cleaning, and driving the kids all over town.

Beth gently swayed from side to side, and when Natalie saw Justin's lids growing heavy, she tenderly wiggled his big toe.

"Go brush your teeth like a big boy. I'll come kiss you good night in a minute."

When Justin slid off Beth's chair, he dropped his Hot Wheels car. It tumbled on the rug between Natalie and Beth, but Beth stretched out her arm to retrieve it before its wheels had stopped spinning. She handed it to Justin and, after whispering his thanks, he trundled down the hall to the bathroom.

Beth took a gulp of her cocktail and stared after Justin. "I want to bake things for little boys like him. Choux pastry cars. A cinnamon-swirl brontosaurus with raisins for eyes. Boat-shaped cakes floating on a pudding ocean. I want to make cupcakes with sprinkles in the middle and brownies with monster faces. I want to make things for my own kids."

Natalie took hold of Beth's hand and was about to offer words of encouragement when she noticed the marks on her friend's arm. "Did Don do that?"

Beth tried to pull down the sleeve of her blouse, but it was too late. Natalie had already seen the purple, finger-shaped bruises marching across her skin. "It's not what you think."

Elaine scooted to the edge of the couch and tucked a strand of Beth's hair behind her ear. The tenderness of this touch loosened something in Beth, and tears sprang to her eyes.

"Don doesn't want to fuck me anymore."

Natalie stiffened.

"I know, I know. *Ladies* aren't supposed to use that kind of language, but it's true. Don and I fuck. Like rabbits. We don't make love. We're wild and rough and loud. Sex is a huge part of our marriage, and we're not having any."

She picked up her glass and tossed back the rest of her drink.

"Last night, Don was already asleep by the time I finished getting ready for bed, so I thought I'd wake him up in a really nice way. I started touching him, and he got hard. I thought everything was okay, even when he grabbed me by the arms and pinned me down, because he's done that before. But before, it was playful. Sexy. Last night, he just held me there. I couldn't move and there was nothing playful about it. I screamed at him until he let me go."

Elaine stared at Beth's arm. "Maybe it was an accident. Maybe he didn't realize he was hurting you."

"It wasn't an accident. He said, 'For fuck's sake, I'm trying to sleep. Don't touch me again!'"

Beth pushed back her sleeves and held out both her arms. A school of purple bruises swam over her skin.

Natalie picked up Beth's clipboard and pressed it into her hands. "We'll make sure Mrs. Smith is too busy to bother Don anymore. Won't we, Elaine?"

Elaine knocked her glass against Natalie's and whispered, "Fuck yeah."

10

Mrs. Smith

Mrs. Smith sat in her hot tub, thinking about the letter the woman in white had pushed through her mail slot two days ago.

The woman who lived in the house with too many windows had passed through Mrs. Smith's electronic gate with the cool dignity of a priestess. After slipping around the gate behind the yard crew, her sandals click, click, clicking on the driveway, she'd marched up the flagstone path and across the porch to the front door.

She didn't knock. Instead, she removed her sunglasses, tucked them in the oversized pocket of her blouse, and pushed a collection of gold bracelets higher on her wrist.

While the woman was adjusting her jewelry, Mrs. Smith had studied her face. She could easily see through the closed window shade, and she examined her neighbor with the emotional detachment of a leopard watching a beetle scuttle over its paw.

The woman's eyes were a bright blue, like a lagoon awash in sunlight. When she glanced up to face the door again, Mrs. Smith saw determination mixed with fear in those eyes.

She'd seen this look on the woman's face before. If fact, she'd seen the full range of the woman's expressions because she'd been watching her for years.

She watched all the humans within her line of sight. Not because she was intrigued—gelatinous sea snails were more interesting—but because she distrusted them.

After all, what did these humans do other than consume? They were entirely focused on the acquisition of *things*. They were like the rats infesting Mrs. Smith's basement. Except the rats were smarter. They knew to be silent when she slithered down the wheelchair ramp from the first floor. The rodents recognized her power. The woman in white did not. If she knew what Mrs. Smith truly was, she'd cower inside her block of a house and never leave again.

Having fixed her bracelets, the woman had knocked on the door with her weak fist. Then she waited several seconds and knocked again. And again.

It had been a while since a neighbor had been this dogged. For the most part, they left Mrs. Smith alone. They were not like the humans of the previous century. Or the ones before them. And so on.

Those humans had been wiser. They'd sensed her otherness. They'd known she was a threat. They'd come in the night with iron chains. With a noose. With fire.

More than once, they'd destroyed her nest. They'd driven her back into the water, forcing her to seek shelter on another shore.

She was never vanquished. Only inconvenienced.

She always found a new place to hide. Back then, there were dark caves where only the sea was brave enough to venture. She would stay hidden, and she would hunt. She would punish the humans by devouring their man-children. And eventually, she would be reborn.

The man-children restored her power. After gorging on four or five Pure Ones, she could transform into a human so beguilingly beautiful that no one could resist her thrall. Her human form dazzled. When she chose a female form, she was fair-skinned and raven-haired. Her eyes were the blue of a shifting sea. Her body was supple. She moved like a river flowing into the ocean. She had a tiny waist and creamy-white breasts that swelled over her corset like cresting waves. Her voice was low and sultry. Her full lips whispered promises she would never keep.

In this form, she walked among the humans, trading gold coins for the perfect shelter. Solid walls close to the water's edge surrounded by stone or metal fences and an army of trees. A dark lair made of timber and brick.

Money was no object. She could buy whatever she wanted with the treasure she'd reaped from the seafloor. She had piles of coins, gold bars, jewels, and trinkets. She spent a fortune on safety. On privacy.

When she had to conduct business, it was necessary to slip into a man's form and become Josiah Smith. In the past, women did not own estates. They did not captain ships or buy tracts of land on coasts of a dozen different countries.

Women stayed in their homes, tending to the hearth and their young. They fed and nurtured the children who would guarantee Mrs. Smith's next rebirth. In this century, the women were still primarily breeders, but their children spent most of the day away from the home. In their absence, the women shopped or gardened or made themselves pretty. Mrs. Smith saw little point to their existence.

One of these insipid creatures had knocked on her door.

She'd dared to disturb the Mother of Eels.

The woman in white had knocked again and again. Then she'd yelled, "Hello! Can you hear me?"

Mrs. Smith had wanted to whip open the door and grab the woman's fist. She'd wanted to crush her hand like a shell, grinding the bones to powder as blood and tissue dribbled onto the floorboards. She'd wanted to clamp her jaws down on the woman's head, silencing her kitten mewl of a voice for good.

But memories of women from the past had kept her rooted in place.

Women whispered. They whispered to one another. They whispered to their men. With enough oxygen, a woman's whisper could light a torch. It could build a scaffold.

As Mrs. Smith stood as still as stone on the other side of her front door, she'd heard a subtle whoosh of air followed by a gentle thud as a letter landed on the foyer floor.

Mrs. Smith had stared down at it in disgust.

Humans loved their paper. Newspapers told them what to think. Leaflets and catalogs told them what to buy. Bills shoved into the mailbox demanded they pay for what they already owned. They used reams of paper for their fictional stories or to create records of their short, meaningless lives.

Such an ephemeral thing, paper. So easy to destroy.

Mrs. Smith had speared the letter with her hooked nail and unfolded it.

The woman's name swam across the top of the page. The thin, slanting letters looked like blades of seagrass.

Elaine K. Bernstein

Mrs. Smith's black eyes swept across the first three lines. They were full of inane platitudes and held no interest.

In the second paragraph, Elaine K. Bernstein got to her point.

She had a request. No, two requests. She wanted to cut back the oriental bittersweet infringing on the yacht club property.

She also wanted permission to set off fireworks at midnight as part of her son's bar mitzvah celebrations. She then wasted two paragraphs explaining the significance of the occasion.

Mrs. Smith needed no schooling when it came to these ceremonies. At one time, every culture had a ritual recognizing the passage from childhood to manhood. Long ago, when the humans were less numerous, she received a number of these man-children as offerings. Now, she had to hunt for the nine she required.

The thought of their sweet flesh made Mrs. Smith's hunger swell. That hunger would grow and grow until the ninth man-child was in her belly. The closer she got to the harvest moon, the more her cravings would rule her.

This season was the most dangerous phase of her life cycle. It was the time when her hunger was in control. Her desires overpowered her logic. She became a desperate animal—an underwater cyclone of scales, teeth, and claws.

She had arrangements to make before the frenzy took hold. Preparations for her next life cycle must be completed. There were treasures to bury. Properties to purchase. She'd used this nest for too many years. She would not go unnoticed for much longer. This letter from Elaine K. Bernstein was a warning.

Mrs. Smith had been invisible until now. She'd been the one watching *them*. Now, their gazes were turning toward her.

The whispering had begun.

Realizing she would have to reply to Elaine K. Bernstein, Mrs. Smith dragged herself out of the hot tub and half crawled, half slithered to her writing desk. She loaded a fresh sheet of paper into her typewriter, dripping beads of water onto the keys.

She could remain out of the water for longer periods now, thanks to the two Pure Ones she'd eaten. It took several hours for her skin to dry out and itch for the sea's salty caress, and her human form was less frail. She could walk to the boathouse without dragging one foot. More flesh stuck to her bones. The bald patches on her head were now covered with hair.

Power was returning to her age-worn cells, and she was greedy for more.

The Mother of Eels was ready to feed again. She was ready for the ecstasy of flesh, for that blaze of vitality.

Unfortunately, she could not hunt in the same place this time. The humans would be more careful there after the news of the three lost souls circulated.

News.

Mrs. Smith reached for the yacht club newsletter. She flipped through photos of seafood buffets and smiling men brandishing trophies until she came to a list of junior regattas. Cold Harbor's regatta was always the last race of the season, but the shores of Long Island were peppered with yacht clubs. Hundreds of man-children would sail out of their protected coves into deeper waters.

On summer Saturdays, crews of man-children would zigzag their tiny vessels from buoy to buoy. There'd be dozens of fragile boats with shell-thin hulls and tantalizing cargo.

If one boat strayed off course or was swallowed by a patch of fog, she could capsize the flimsy vessel and drag its passengers down into the deep. It would help if rain hampered the visibility, but she couldn't count on the elements to obey her whims.

There had been a time when she could hunt without caution, but those days were gone. If the humans caught her killing their offspring, she would become the hunted one. They'd use their gadgets and machines to track her. Their guns and bombs to destroy her. They could bring their fire to the water now, so she had to move with caution.

Studying the race locations, she pictured the terrain below the surface of each bay. The junior regattas would begin next weekend with a race west of Cold Harbor, in the waters near Port Jefferson. It was a place of ferries, barges, and sports cruiser boats. Men would be racing larger sailboats there, too.

With all that activity, a capsized boat could go unnoticed for a few minutes.

A few minutes was all Mrs. Smith would need to devour a Pure One.

Mrs. Smith knew these boats were manned by two children. The skipper would be older, between fourteen and eighteen. Too old for her needs. It was the first mates she wanted. These children could be as young as ten and as old as thirteen. She could draw a single craft away from the fleet of young sailors. Make it look like the wind's work. A daylight hunt was risky. She would need the camouflage of many eels.

Some of her children would die—their bodies mauled by propellers and tangled in anchor chains—but they would not turn away from their deaths. They knew her survival was paramount. Without her, they would all perish. They'd be netted by the thousands. Their bodies would be used for food or for medicine. The humans would consume them until they were only a memory. A creature existing only in books.

Despite her warnings, too many of her children were caught by human traps. The humans' underwater cages and mesh tunnels littered the seabed. The poison from their engines and factories stole oxygen from the water. Their litter slid into her children's bellies or wrapped itself around their necks.

Long ago, she'd hunted with eels the size of school buses. A swarm of these magnificent animals could kill a whale in seconds.

But when the oceans changed, her first children could not adapt quickly enough. They never learned to breathe the air above the water, and so they perished. The humans grew more cunning. They made weapons and built ships. They took to the seas with harpoons and nets, and the largest descendants of the giant eels vanished, too.

Still, the Mother of Eels endured. She would endure for another hundred years as long as the old ways were honored. The old ways bound her, but they also gave her power.

Setting the newsletter aside, Mrs. Smith recalled what Elaine K. Bernstein had written in her letter.

I respect your privacy, but this event is very important to my family. I hope you understand and are willing to make exceptions for such an important occasion. If there's anything I can do for you in return, like run errands or prepare meals, I'd be happy to return the favor. After all, that's what neighbors are for. We're here to help one another.

The letter had filled Mrs. Smith with rage. The woman wanted to set off fireworks from the end of the yacht club dock. The woman wanted to cut Mrs. Smith's precious vines. To erect a party tent. To play loud music. This soft, weak, useless human was making demands.

Despite her fury, Mrs. Smith knew she had to appease the woman in white.

Elaine K. Bernstein was not a solitary entity. Humans were social animals. They were group hunters. Once they selected a common enemy, they would focus all their energy on that creature's destruction. As of this moment, they had no idea she was their enemy, and she needed to keep it that way.

It had been many years since Mrs. Smith walked the length and breadth of her property, because her human legs were too weak. She cared little about community standards but understood that she would have to pay attention to them now. The neighbors' eyes were upon her.

She would fulfill Elaine K. Bernstein's requests.

For a price.

She would make several very specific requests. On the outset, these requests would appear to serve the woman's purpose. They'd come across as considerate. Even helpful. But in the end, they would benefit Mrs. Smith. They would give her everything she wanted. And cost Elaine K. Bernstein everything she held dear.

With her claws hanging over the typewriter keys, Mrs. Smith's mind drifted to another time.

A time when fireworks meant setting fire to bamboo stems. The minor explosions stayed firmly on the ground. They did not illuminate the whole sky or fill the air with thunderous claps. They didn't drop debris into the ocean. Fish did not feed on bits of charcoal, paper, or plastic because humans wanted to create their own stars.

Swimming through her memories, she remembered when a man had gifted her with fireworks.

She'd just begun a new life cycle, which meant she could easily adopt a human form, and she'd chosen to masquerade as the beautiful and mysterious widow of Captain Josiah Smith.

Suitors and sycophants came out of the woodwork, showering her with costly gifts. One of these suitors, the man who'd presented her with fireworks, had also brought her chests of treasure from the East. Her servants had carried them to her boudoir and thrown back the lids to reveal embroidered silks, jade ornaments, ivory carvings, foo dog figurines, porcelain vases, and exotic plants for her conservatory.

The man was generous by nature, and he gave cuttings of these plants to several acquaintances. Before long, pots of oriental bittersweet were thriving in the protective glass rooms of a dozen Gold Coast mansions.

Two brothers who owned a nursery in Flushing were

enchanted by the new plant and became the first to propagate *Celastrus articulates.* However, they weren't the first to plant oriental bittersweet in the ground. That honor belonged to a female gardener hired by Mrs. Josiah Smith.

Mrs. Smith's servant buried the seeds in the loamy soil right before the spring rains. Shunned by her fellow humans for having a child out of wedlock, the woman whispered to each seed as she dropped it into its dark hole, willing it to cover the land, the houses, the electric lights. Willing it to choke and strangle whatever it touched.

The plants thrived. They drank in the sunshine and nutrient-rich rain. They climbed over the arbor. Surged over the stone walls. Became a green wave cresting over the garden gate.

In late summer, their fruit turned yellow and split. The red berries looked like beads of blood. Sparrows and starlings plucked the berries off the vine and carried the seeds in their bellies.

The birds flew to neighboring yards. They flew to other counties. Other states. Along the way, they deposited their droppings. The seeds burrowed into the earth. The rain found the seeds in their wombs of soil and compelled them to wake.

The oriental bittersweet grew and spread. Grew and spread. It became an infestation. An invader. An enemy.

Though Mrs. Smith did not feel love, she did feel tenderness toward certain living things. The oriental bittersweet pleased her. She admired its tenacity and its invasive power. The humans had taken so much land for themselves. Perhaps her dogged vine could take some of it back.

Mrs. Smith reached an impossibly long arm to the window overlooking the garden and raised the shade. A century ago, servants had filled the garden with things the humans found attractive. There'd been roses and boxwood bushes, benches and sculptures, gravel paths and a reflecting pool.

Now the benches and sculptures had disappeared under layers upon layers of bittersweet vines. Riding over the backs of thorn bushes, the vines fanned out in all directions, their tendrils tirelessly reaching, reaching.

Let them cut you, thought Mrs. Smith. *You will only grow stronger. You will come at them from below. From the deep. From the dark. As will I.*

Then an idea came to her, and her mouth curled in a serpentine smile.

Using a single hooked claw, she began to type.

11
Una

That Sunday, Una and Kristofer were the greeters for the early worship service at the Cold Harbor United Methodist Church.

For most of the year, this service was primarily attended by the oldest church members. They'd shuffle in, eager to get a seat in one of the stiff-backed pews near the front, as if proximity to the shining altar cross could erase their sins as their Day of Judgment grew closer and closer.

On summer Sundays, the grannies and grandpas at the early service were joined by the sailing families. They showed up at the last minute, damp-haired and harried, hoping to cross piety off their list before hustling home to change clothes and then jump back in the car and speed to one of the many North Shore yacht clubs.

For now, the church building was still dozing. The organ was silent. The wooden pews weren't groaning. The bells had yet to toll the hour.

Una grabbed a handful of programs from the wooden table in the entranceway and took her place outside the chapel doors. It wasn't even nine in the morning and already the air was sticky with humidity.

There was no sign of the sun. Clouds drooped from a gray sky, and mist crept over the grass, as diaphanous as a bridal veil. The world felt hushed and heavy.

"You're pretty as a picture," Kristofer said as he took up his position across the sidewalk from his wife.

Una crinkled her right eye in the briefest of winks as the first worshippers headed their way.

Having been a member for years, Una was able to welcome most people by name followed by a "nice to see you" or "I'm happy you're here."

The older women asked after Gunnar or shared a tidbit or two about their own children or grandchildren. Their husbands talked to Kristofer about last night's game, grumbling over the ump's call in the sixth inning.

When the sailing families arrived, the parents took the proffered program and ushered their children into the church without pausing to socialize.

Occasionally, a woman would hold Una's hand a little too tightly while whispering, "I'm *still* waiting for an opening in your schedule."

Extricating herself from the woman's press-on-nails grip, Una would say, "I'm still booked, but you're first on the list."

"There's always that one person," Kristofer said after the entrants had trailed off. "Dale Berger asked me if I look through people's magazines before I put them in the mailbox. Fred Carter wanted to know if I'd been chased by any dogs this week. Then he barked at me as he walked away."

"I heard him. He sounded like a seal."

When it was almost time for the bells to ring, Una saw the Scott family spill out of their station wagon. Justin grabbed Jill's hand and tugged her toward the church. J.J. followed behind, his hands plunged deep in his pants pockets. Natalie smoothed her dress and threaded her arm through Jimmy's. He seemed pleasantly surprised by the gesture.

"Una!" Justin ran down the path and flung his arms around Una's hips.

"Hello, little bee," she said, kissing his plump cheek.

"Why am I a bee?"

Jill tugged on her baby brother's shirt. "Because your shirt is yellow with stripes."

"Then what's Jilly?" Justin asked Una.

Una made a show of studying Jill from head to toe. Jill wore a floral sundress and white sandals. Her hair was parted in the middle and pulled back into ribbon barrettes. The ribbons were blue and white and nearly the same length as Jill's hair.

"Jill's a fairy queen," said Una.

Beaming, Jill took a program and tried to pull Justin away from Una. "Come on. We're gonna be late for Sunday school."

"But I want to stay with Una," Justin whined.

"I wish I could go to Sunday school," Una said. "You're making pinwheels today. And Mrs. Drew baked chocolate chip cookies for snack. With *extra* chips."

That was all Justin needed to hear. He sprinted inside the church.

J.J. smiled shyly as he shook Una's hand, glowing when she remarked that he had a strong grip. A man's grip.

"I bet it helps you when you race today," she added.

J.J. glanced at the trees in the churchyard. "There's hardly any wind."

"You could always pray for wind," Jimmy said as he moved to shake Kristofer's outstretched hand.

Natalie hung back until the rest of her family had disappeared inside. After making sure no one was around, she leaned close to Una and whispered, "You'll never believe this, but Elaine got a letter from Mrs. Smith."

At the sound of Mrs. Smith's name, the air turned leaden. It pressed down on Una's shoulders and sat heavily on the crown of her head.

"A letter?"

Natalie watched Kristofer hand a program to the manager of the local bank. She waited for him to enter the church before saying, "Elaine wrote her first."

As she spoke about vines and fireworks, Una glanced up at the sky. The clouds reminded her of Amma's sheep. Their long fleece was dark gray or jet black, but Amma's favorite, a ram with double curled horns, was dual coated. His fleece was a dirty white and gray. His eyes were black as flint. He was the biggest ram in her herd, and the most aggressive. He'd charge any human who came near, and when a neighbor's ram strayed onto Amma's land, her ram had headbutted the creature to death.

The neighbor had called him Púki, which meant demon.

Amma embraced the name, boasting of her ram's spiteful nature, until he killed a young ewe in her own herd.

"He cannot help his nature," Una's amma had said. "But he is a danger to the others and must be destroyed."

Though Una was elsewhere when Púki was butchered, she sat at the table on the summer solstice as his meat was served for the Feast of the Midnight Sun. It bobbed in a soup of potatoes, carrots, turnips, and herbs. The meat felt slimy on Una's tongue. When she bit down, her mouth was flooded by a sour, rancid flavor, and she spit the half-masticated piece back into her bowl.

Púki's head had been prepared especially for Pappi. *Svið* was one of his favorite dishes, and he grinned with glee when

Amma placed it in front of him. After his brains had been scraped out, Púki's head had been cut in half and boiled for an hour.

Without his horns and black eyes, he looked sad and diminished.

Una turned away when her father stuck his fork behind Púki's cheek and scooped out a hunk of flesh. After one bite, he told Amma that the meat was rotten and gave it to the dogs.

They sniffed and pawed at it but refused to eat it. By the time the sun set and rose again, a legion of black flies had found Púki's discarded head. It was a long time before Una could eat lamb again.

Now the sky above the Cold Harbor United Methodist Church was the color of Púki's fleece, and the buzz of Natalie's voice in Una's ear sounded like a mass of black flies.

"What did the letter say?" she asked Natalie.

Natalie's eyes were feverishly bright. "She agreed to Elaine's requests on two conditions. The first is that she wants to hire Charles, J.J., and Jill to work in her yard. She offered a *very* generous wage."

"No," Una whispered.

Misinterpreting Una's objection as surprise, Natalie barreled on. "I couldn't believe it, either, but I'm thrilled."

Una wanted to dig her nails into Natalie's shoulders. "The children—they're going to work for her?"

"Yes, but don't say anything to them. We need to get through this regatta first."

A woman in a green paisley print dress hurried up the sidewalk. She took a program from Kristofer and then put a hand on Natalie's arm. "Hey! Long time no see. Are you going in?"

"In a minute," Natalie said. "I need to finish up with Una. Let's catch up after the service, okay?"

The woman looked down her nose at Una and then entered the church.

"I need to tell you the second condition. It's even more unbelievable than the first one." Natalie sounded breathless—overexcited—like a child who'd eaten too much sugar. "She wants an invitation to Charles's bar mitzvah!"

Una stared at Natalie in shock.

"That was my reaction, too! I had to pick my jaw up off the floor." Natalie glanced at her watch and began to edge toward the entrance. "I guess we're finally going to see the mysterious Mrs. Smith in the flesh."

Suddenly, the church bells began to peal.

Una tried to open herself up to the melody. "How Great Thou Art" was one of her favorite hymns, but the music failed to reach her. Her head felt thick. Like the cross on the steeple had pierced the clouds and they had fallen around her, cocooning her in a gray miasma.

But then, Kristofer was taking her by hand and leading her into the sanctuary. "You're white as the snow on *Snæfellsjökull.* What did she say?"

"It was nothing," Una said as she slid into the pew reserved for greeters and ushers.

How can she send the children to that house? she thought as the minister asked the congregation to rise for the processional hymn. *Doesn't she feel the presence there?*

As the service progressed, Una stood up or sat down along with everyone else. She closed her eyes when she was supposed to be praying and sang along with the hymns, but none of the messages sank in. It was as if a fog had invaded her mind.

Focusing on the program, she saw that there was to be a baptism today. A baby boy would be received into the church fold and the entire congregation would promise to serve as his guardians.

As the parents walked up the center aisle—the mother in a white dress with padded shoulders and the father in a smoke-gray suit—the baby turned his head and looked right at Una.

His eyes were almost the same blue as her own. They were just a fraction darker, as if a fleck of black had been mixed in with the blue.

The baby's eyes looked exactly like Svana's eyes.

When the family reached the altar, the baby began to cry. He wriggled in his mother's arms, and she tried to soothe him while straightening his christening gown. He pedaled his legs in protest, kicking her in the chest until one of his white socks came loose and fluttered to the crimson carpet.

Una stared at the sock. It looked like a giant's tooth. One of Goliath's, perhaps, knocked out by David's stone.

Una imagined the *thwap* of David's slingshot as his stones rocketed through the air, catching the giant in the nose, the eye, the cheek. She could almost hear the crunch of bone and the sonic boom of the giant's body as it crashed to the ground.

He probably hadn't died right away. He'd probably lain there in the dust, his mouth open in anguish, his broken teeth floating over his tongue until a stream of blood deposited them on the ground by his shattered face.

In the front of the sanctuary, the baby wailed. He was in the minister's arms now, enduring the shock of water on his forehead. Congregants tittered in amusement as the water fanned out over his skull, darkening his hair and soaking the collar of his gown.

"Robert Phillip Peterson," intoned the minister. "I baptize you in the name of the Father, and of the Son, and of the Holy Spirit."

When the rites were completed and the boy was returned to his mother, red-faced and squalling, the organist struck up the opening chords of "All Things Bright and Beautiful."

As the family returned to the back of the sanctuary with as much speed and dignity as possible, Una looked at the words in her hymnal.

"All things bright and beautiful,
all creatures great and small,
All things wise and wonderful:
The Lord God made them all."

As the second stanza began, Una's gaze strayed to the stained-glass window to her right. It was a portrait of a robed man with a shepherd's crook. The Good Shepherd, surrounded by his sheep, had stopped under the shelter of a tree to pray. The shepherd's hands were clasped in front of his chest. His chin was lifted to the heavens, and his eyes were fixed on a point somewhere above the tree branches. Behind his head was a disc of light. Una thought it was meant to be a halo, but to her, it looked like a setting sun. Below the disc was a body of water made of graduating blues.

The shepherd wore dull colors, so it was the golden disc and the striations of blue that captivated the viewer. The lightest blue was closest to the shore. The deep, dark blue was right below the sun. The wavy pieces of glass gave the impression of a current, and the longer Una stared at the swath of midnight blue, the more she wondered if something was in the water, watching the shepherd. Waiting to take him unawares.

Next to her, Kristofer sang the chorus in his rich baritone.

"All things wise and wonderful:
The Lord God made them all."

Why, Lord? Una thought as she turned the page of her hymnal. The music notes bobbed across the creamy paper like black jellyfish. *Why did you make monsters?*

After Svana was lost to the ocean, Una's mother found comfort in scripture. Una preferred Amma's stories. In her worlds, Svana's bones weren't stuck in the sand, down in a cold, lightless place. She was with the fairies, dancing on rainbows and making flower crowns.

Una's gaze shifted to the window showing a crucified Jesus. His face was mournful. A crown of thorns dug into his flesh.

Mrs. Smith's yard is full of thorns.

Una had to do something to keep the children away from that house. The woman in the photograph, the woman with the black eyes, had left her mark on that place. It was cursed. It was full of shadows. And the woman inside was one of those shadows.

Una had never seen this woman, but she'd felt her dark presence for years. Now, after all this time, Mrs. Smith was interacting with the people around her. She wanted to hire the Scott children. She wanted to attend Charles's party.

Monsters could wear human faces, Una knew. She needed to look at Mrs. Smith. She needed to see her eyes. She had to do this for the children.

She turned back to the window of the Good Shepherd, and this time, when she took a long, hard look at the sheep, she saw that their eyes were black with fear. Their shepherd wasn't paying attention, and they were in danger.

Whatever was in the water was coming for them, and by the time the shepherd realized what was happening, it would be too late to save them all.

12

Jill

Jill didn't want to go to the regatta.

Ever since she and her friends had snuck into a showing of *Jaws* last summer, her fear of being on a sailboat had intensified.

The open water made her anxious, but she felt relatively safe on a motorboat. There was comfort in its speed, in the violence of the sharp propeller blade. She liked to sit in the stern and watch the chaotic wake. As long as the propeller sliced through the water and the boat kept moving forward, Jill believed she'd be okay.

But she never felt safe in a sailboat.

Sailboats relied on the fickle wind. Small crafts abandoned by the wind could be stranded far from land. Even when the wind was cooperating, and a boat's sails were bloated with air, the danger of capsizing was always there.

Jill's father loved to skirt that line.

He sailed his boat, a thirty-six-foot Hunter named *Nike*, like he was being chased by the devil. On summer weekends, the man in the business suit shucked off his fatigue and became a man of salt spray and speed. He could read the wind like a Shakespearean soothsayer, shouting at his crew to "trim the mainsail!" or "prepare to gybe!"

His eyes would sparkle with impish glee as he steered the boat upwind.

"Hold on, Jilly!" he'd cry as the starboard side began to lean. When the balloon-like spinnaker hovered inches from the water's surface, taunting the ocean, Jill would cling to the lifeline.

Once, she'd seen the hem of the spinnaker dip into the water. Then, a puddle formed in the middle of the blue-and-yellow sail as the water tried to suck the sail into its mouth. The boat listed so severely that Jill could reach over the side and put her whole hand in the water.

Not that she ever would. Long before she'd made the mistake of leaving the theater playing *The Fox and the Hound* and creeping into the one showing *Jaws*, she'd feared the creatures that could swim under the hull of a boat without anyone knowing they were there. Her fear had turned into an obsession.

Back in March, she'd done a report for science class on the sharks of Long Island. She'd checked out a dozen books on ocean predators from the public library and spent night after night absorbing facts about apex predators. She studied drawings comparing the sizes of the sharks' bodies to human bodies. She learned about their acute sense of smell, how a shark's tail rocketed them through the water, and how they hunted. Sharks could detect the vibrations or electrical impulses of prey, but what stuck with Jill the most was their ability to detect blood.

"From a quarter of a mile away," she'd told her friends on the bus. "One drop in an Olympic-sized pool. Just *one* drop."

There were so many sharks in the waters surrounding Long Island. Sand sharks and sand tiger sharks. The smooth dogfish shark. Blue, dusky, and basking sharks. Hammerheads and makos. The unpredictable bull shark. And finally, the great white. The *Jaws* shark.

She knew the shark in the movie was a machine—that it wasn't real—but it didn't matter. There were very big, very real great whites in the waters around Long Island.

Two years ago, a man had caught a fifteen-footer. It was the same size as Una's car. The Blue Jay boats Jill and the other kids sailed were thirteen feet.

No oxygen tanks or flare guns on board, either, she thought. *Just a stupid wooden paddle.*

As if the sharks weren't bad enough, there were other scary things in the water. Eels. Killer whales. The Portuguese man o' war, which everyone called a jellyfish when it was really a colony of zooids working together as one organism.

A man o' war had washed up on their beach once. J.J. had poked at its kaleidoscopic balloon with a stick, trying to pop it, while Jill hung back, her eyes locked on the dark violet tentacles. The corpse proved her theory. There were dangerous creatures all around them, swimming unseen in the dark water.

That was why she hated being on her dad's boat, but junior sailing regattas were even worse. For one thing, her father was a skilled sailor. No matter how close he seemed to come to losing control, he always adjusted the sails and righted the boat just in time.

"See?" he'd yell, directing his comment to his wife and daughter. Jill's mom didn't like the lean any more than Jill did.

"This isn't fun!" she'd shout. "It's scary! This is exactly why I won't let Justin come."

"J.J. likes going fast, don't you, son?"

"Yeah!" Jill's traitorous brother would answer.

But Jill saw his white-knuckled grip on the lifeline and how he sprang into action to loosen or trim a sail, always trying to stay one step ahead of disaster.

At the end of last summer, Jill's mom had announced that her boating days were over.

"I'm going back to work, so I won't have time for sailing next year," she informed the family while serving them chicken Parm and broccoli.

Jill wished she could get a job, too. She'd much rather babysit or be a mother's helper than be on a boat, but there were hordes of high school girls looking for work over the summer, which left Jill another twelve weeks of swimming and sailing.

The swim meets were okay, but the regattas were pure hell.

After church, Jill's mom went straight into the kitchen to pack bologna and cheese sandwiches, carrot sticks, and apples into two brown bags. Jill and J.J. changed into shorts and T-shirts and hurried into the kitchen to grab their bags.

"Could I come with you instead?" Jill asked her mom. "I could help with the open house."

Her mom was wiping off the counter with a sponge, but she paused to consider the request. "Thanks, honey, but I've got it all under control."

Jill watched her mom swipe breadcrumbs off the counter into the bowl of her hand. She dumped the crumbs in the trash can and unwrapped a bouquet of yellow roses. She started to hum as she stripped the leaves of the roses and clipped the stems. The light spilling through the window fell softly on her face, erasing tiny lines and sprinkling gold into her brown eyes.

"You look pretty, Mom," Jill said.

Her compliment wasn't another attempt to avoid her fate. She said it because it was true. When her mother was happy, she was beautiful.

Leaving the roses in the sink, she crossed the room and

hugged Jill. "What a sweet thing to say. I know sailing isn't your favorite, but it'll be over before you know it."

Resigned, Jill stepped out onto the back deck and looked at the harbor. The sky was a snarl of pewter-gray clouds. The water was flat and calm.

Jill wished she could stay in the kitchen. She wanted to be near roses that looked like tiny suns and bask in the sound of her mother's wordless song. Instead, she slid the door shut and walked to the yacht club.

When she reached the parking lot, she joined Heather and some other friends. Then the instructors began calling out the captain and crew pairings.

Jill glanced around, hoping against hope that she'd get one of the nicer high school girls as her skipper.

J.J. had been paired with the captain of the swim team, and Heather got Marianne, one of the best junior sailors on the North Shore.

They'll probably win, Jill thought sourly.

Her instructor flipped the sheet attached to his clipboard over and said, "And for our final boat, the skipper is Allison Burr. First mate is Jill Scott."

Jill's stomach dropped. Allison was painfully shy. She barely spoke in class and had absolutely no confidence out of the water. Everyone knew she was a terrible skipper.

"Have fun coming in last," J.J. whispered in Jill's ear as he passed by.

Fury made Jill's arm jerk like a pinball flipper. Her fist caught J.J. right in the stomach.

"Oof," he grunted, his grin betraying how ineffective the blow had been. He turned away to grab life jackets for himself and his captain, and as Jill followed him with her eyes, she saw Aaron detach himself from a group of boys and walk over to her. "Tough luck," he said. "I sailed with Allison last summer. She's doesn't know how to catch the wind. You'll have to tell her what to do."

"I guess," Jill said.

She'd had hundreds of pretend conversations with Aaron, and in every one of those, she was clever and entertaining. In these fantasies, he hung on her every word. But now, when she had the chance to dazzle him, her mind went totally blank. She was dying to touch one of the brown curls that fell into his eyes or do something to make him smile. He had the most beautiful smile. *Everything* about him was beautiful. The arch of his brows, his wide shoulders, his sea-green eyes, and his long, tapered fingers.

A Greek god, Jill thought, drinking in the sight of him.

"There isn't much wind, and my dad says there's fog near the shoreline," he continued. "It's gonna be wicked-slow sailing."

"If slow and steady wins the race, then Allison's got this in the bag."

Aaron laughed. "We should just give her the trophy now. See you out there."

All of a sudden, Jill didn't care if she came in last. She didn't care that she had to give up a Sunday afternoon doing something she hated.

She'd made Aaron laugh. After he'd deliberately come over to talk to her. Not to J.J. or one of his friends, but to *her.*

Heather rushed over and grabbed Jill's arm. "Oh, my gawd! What was that about?"

"He was wishing me luck."

Heather put a hand to her heart. "What if he, like, *likes* you?"

Though this was Jill's secret hope, she didn't dare give voice to it. "He was just trying to make me feel better because I got stuck with Allison."

"Because he likes you!" Heather covered her mouth as if she couldn't contain her excitement. "Oh. My. God. You've had a crush on him for, like, *forever.*"

Jill was about to shush Heather when their instructor raised an air horn and issued two short blasts. "Before you get in the launch, make sure you have your life jackets. No life jacket, no race."

You could get out of the race, niggled a small voice in Jill's head. *Just get on the launch without a life vest. After everyone gets dropped off, the launch would bring you back. You could go home, have the house all to yourself. You could listen to records. Read. Eat anything you want.*

While Jill was lost in the vision of putting on her *Xanadu* record and sprawling on the living room couch with a Strawberry Shortcake ice cream bar, Allison appeared by her side.

"Ready?" she asked in her hushed library voice.

In her Bar Harbor T-shirt, black Ray-Bans, and scuffed-up docksiders, Allison almost looked cool. But the smear of white cream on her nose ruined the look. Jill imagined someone pushing Allison's face into a bowl of sunscreen the way a Dairy Queen worker would dunk a soft-serve cone in a vat of vanilla dip.

It's not even sunny, Jill thought with disdain.

She saw Aaron heading down to the dock. He was taller than the other thirteen-year-old boys and a few of the high schoolers, too. If Jill got a seat next to him in the launch, they could talk some more. If not, she wanted to sit where she could see him. She wanted to watch the wind blow his hair off his forehead and ripple his T-shirt.

"Yeah. Let's go," she replied.

Jill didn't get a seat near Aaron. She was stuck sitting with Allison and one of Allison's friends instead. Both girls ignored her as the launch motored through the harbor.

Jill watched Mrs. Smith's house, then the empty lot, then her own house slide by. Next, they passed a cluster of moored sailboats and finally, the jetty of rocks that stuck out into the water like a wart-ridden finger.

The rocks were the boundary between the harbor and the bay. Beyond the bay was the Sound. The bay was much deeper than the harbor, and the currents rushing in from the Sound made the water choppy and unpredictable.

Jill glanced at the wake behind the launch. The bubbling white trail led back to the dock. To safety. Like the breadcrumbs in *Hansel and Gretel*, the path home would soon disappear, leaving the kids to face the wind, the tides, and all the creatures they couldn't see.

A yacht club employee had towed their Blue Jays to the middle of the bay. The sailboats were tied to each other and to a lead line securing them to a motorboat. The launch pilot cut the engine and shouted for the kids to exit over the port side.

"Sailors in the lead boat go first. Go in order so the sailors in the boat closest to the launch leave last."

Having done this before, the kids scrambled over the side into the first Blue Jay. Holding on to the mast for balance, they picked their way to their assigned boat.

Jill looked for their boat number and was relieved to see that it was close to the launch. She and Allison climbed over the side and half crawled to their boat. Heather and her skipper exited last, and then the launch slowly pulled away.

Their first task was to separate from the other boats, raise the mainsail and the jib, and head to the starting line. They'd wait there until the sailors from the competing yacht clubs were also ready to begin.

The Cold Harbor sailing instructors had reviewed the racecourse with the skippers, but Jill wished she'd seen the chalkboard drawing, too. She was relieved they were in the second heat and could follow the boats in the first heat.

Suddenly, several air horn blasts cut through the kids' chit-chat like a guillotine blade.

Jill thought Allison said, "Here we go," but she couldn't be sure.

She watched the boats in the first heat maneuver to the starting line. J.J.'s, Aaron's, and Heather's boats were all in the same heat.

Jill wished she was with them. Too many skippers in her heat were losers. Allison was timid and indecisive and had never even placed in the top ten. Then there was Charles Bernstein's skipper, Tony Pulcino. Tony sailed like he was driving a bumper car. He always got too close to other boats, angling for a collision. And Kim Lahey's skipper, Leslie Feldman, never wanted to stay on course. She thought she knew better than the instructors and was always getting lost.

Four short horn blasts sounded. This was the warning for the sailors in the first heat to prepare to cross the starting line. Twenty seconds later, a long blast meant their race was underway. It was also a signal for the second heat to sail toward the starting line.

When Allison steered their boat toward the two buoys without much difficulty, Jill felt a glimmer of hope.

She knew it was illogical to be scared. Teachers and parents from all three yacht clubs patrolled the water around the racecourse in power boats. They kept their distance so as not to create too much wake for the sailors but stayed close enough to rescue anyone in serious trouble.

Still, the fog hovering around the shoreline was thicker than it was in the harbor, and without the sun to burn it off or a brisk wind to break it apart, fat bands of diaphanous gray seemed to be oozing toward the sailors.

The four short horn blasts sounded again, followed by the long blast. The bow of Jill's boat kissed the stern of a boat from another yacht club and the skipper threw them a glare. When Allison steered into their boat a second time, the boy shoved them off with his paddle. "Back off, bitch!"

Allison turned crab-red and muttered, "Sorry."

Ten minutes later, Jill was ready to shout at her, too. Most of the boats had pulled ahead while they were still floundering in the rear.

"Where's the first buoy?" Jill asked. When she couldn't hear Allison's reply, she lost her patience. "Talk louder! I don't know when we're tacking because I can't hear you."

"Tack!" Allison yelled.

The boom swung from port to starboard and Jill switched seats while trimming the jib. They picked up a little speed, but not much.

Jill scanned the horizon, searching for the course buoy. At this point, it didn't really matter if she knew its exact location because all they had to do was trail the other boats. At least they weren't dead last. That honor belonged to Charles and his skipper. Their boat was close behind a boat from the Huntington Yacht Club, and Jill wondered if Tony was deliberately antagonizing the rival team.

She could see Charles's red head bobbing around as he responded to Tony's orders.

He must be miserable, Jill thought. She knew Tony would call him Upchuck. Then he'd ask who Charles's favorite character was from *Gilligan's Island*, which would lead to jokes about Ginger. Tony would ask the same question about *Scooby-Doo* and *The Flintstones*. No matter what Charles said, he'd be Ginger or Daphne or Wilma for the rest of the race.

Though Jill felt sorry for Charles, she had her own problems.

It seemed to take forever to tack around the first buoy and zigzag toward the second, which was floating closer to the opposite shore. By the time they approached, webbed fingers of fog had crept farther out from the shore. Soon, the buoy would be engulfed.

Most of the instructors were waiting near the finish line or motoring in wide circles at the edge of the fog to be sure that none of the junior sailors went too far off course and ended up stuck on a sandbar.

There were piles of jagged rocks near the shore as well. They'd tear through a Blue Jay's hull like it was made of crepe paper, leaving the sailors no choice but to wait for help or swim parallel to the shore until they cleared the rocks. Only then could they make for the safety of the beach.

"Coming about!" Allison shouted.

They rounded the second buoy and Jill gave her skipper a thumbs-up. Two more buoys and they would cross the finish line and be done.

As their mainsail swelled with wind, the bow knifed through the waves. Jill's ponytail streamed out behind her head like a comet, and for a few heartbeats she felt her anxiety loosen.

Almost there. We're almost there.

Glancing over her shoulder, she saw that Charles's boat and the Huntington Yacht Club team had dropped even farther behind.

Their boats didn't look right. They were so close that their sails seemed to overlap. Jill couldn't tell exactly what had happened—they were too far away—but in her gut, she knew that Tony had rammed the other boat and now both boats were stuck. They were a floating tangle of lines and sails and masts.

"Earth to Jill!" Allison cried. "We're tacking!"

Jill snapped to attention seconds before the boom whipped across the centerline. As she shifted her body to the other side of the boat, she saw a dark mass in the water. It was approaching their boat from the east. From under the fog.

She'd seen shadows created by schools of fish, but as this mass grew closer, she knew it wasn't made of fish.

It was too dense. Too dark. It was like a sea within a sea. It undulated and roiled like boiling water. But it wasn't water. It was a *thing*.

Jill was immobilized by fear.

Shark.

It can't be. The shape is wrong.

It was like an interstellar cloud—black and irregular. But as it slid under their boat, she closed her eyes, gripped the nearest cleat, and braced for impact.

Nothing happened.

Their boat kept its steady pace north. She heard the water slapping at its sides and the whoosh of wind filling the sails.

She opened her eyes and looked down.

The mass was already to the aft of their boat. Watching it recede, Jill expelled a lungful of air.

She was about to turn away when she saw its speed suddenly increase. It was headed directly for the last two boats, which were still locked together.

The next course buoy was coming up, so Jill had to face forward and prepare to come about. But out of the blue, Allison lost hold of the tiller. Their boat turned directly into the wind. The sails shuddered and their momentum stalled.

Allison grabbed the tiller and pulled it toward her, steering the boat the wrong way. As the sagging mainsail blocked Jill's vision, she listened for Allison's command.

Allison didn't give one.

Jill gave the boom a shove and bellowed, "Turn toward the shore!"

With the sail out of her face, Jill could see Allison. Her skipper was wide-eyed with panic. Her sunglasses were gone and the sunscreen on her nose was now smeared across her left cheek. It looked like warpaint made of Elmer's glue.

"I don't want to get caught in the fog," she whined.

Jill was scared, too, but they had no choice. "It's just until we catch the wind again."

Allison mouthed something. *Oh* or *okay*, maybe. Jill wasn't sure. All she knew was that they needed to keep moving. They needed to put more distance between themselves and the black mass in the water.

Glancing at the stretch of water behind them, Jill searched for the two boats.

She saw only one, lying on its side, its sails floating impotently in the water. It looked like a broken bird or the wreckage of a small plane.

The other boat was gone.

It wasn't behind the capsized boat. It wasn't speeding away in another direction. It was just gone.

Suddenly, a sound hurtled toward Jill from across the divide—a high, animalistic shriek that raised gooseflesh on Jill's arms and stole the breath from her lungs. It went on and on, sweeping over the two girls in the boat as they sat in frozen terror.

Jill wanted to cover her ears. She wanted to stop the sound from getting in—from proving to her that nightmares were real.

The noise wasn't coming from an animal.

It was coming from a kid.

One of the boys in the capsized boat was screaming.

13
Mrs. Smith

Mrs. Smith used a tentacle to push the boy's severed arm down her throat.

The boy was a Pure One.

As she chewed his flesh, her mouth filled with his salt-laced blood and the neurons in her brain exploded, filling her vision with a searing light. She was blinded by ecstasy.

The euphoria hurtling through her cells was so powerful that she was temporarily stupefied. She drifted in the water, belly up, her eyes rolling back in their sockets. Her jaw hung open, revealing the strips of skin and strands of hair caught in her teeth.

Like a shark, she'd entered a state of tonic immobility. Her muscles relaxed. Her breathing slowed. Lost in pleasure, she had no awareness of her surroundings.

Her children writhed in agitation. They swam over her and under her, trying to conceal her from above and below. The eels knew she was completely helpless—susceptible to propeller blades or fishing nets. Vulnerable to discovery.

The Mother of Eels had already taken a huge risk by capsizing the boat. She'd arced her lower arms through the water, sending them crashing into the centerboard just as the little craft was tacking. Struck from the side with incredible force, the centerboard caused the boat to careen violently to one side, the mast toppling like a felled tree.

The sails landed in the water with a helpless slap. The young humans shouted in surprise. Seconds later, she saw a pair of legs frog-kicking. She saw sunlight bounce off a watch face. She paused for the briefest moment, watching the laces of an untied shoe dance in the current. The wriggling strings looked like glass eels.

Then, she struck.

She wrapped a tentacle around the man-child's ankle, pulling him under the surface with a vicious tug. She ripped off the life jacket with her teeth as the human screamed. The sound was muted by the water as a frenzy of bubbles poured out of his mouth. Mrs. Smith witnessed his final exhalation with mild amusement before biting into his torso.

Enveloped by clouds of blood, she waited to be electrified by his flesh. But this man-child was not a Pure One. He was sweet and delicious—a vast improvement over shark or whale meat—but she feasted on him quickly, eager to capture the second human and drag him to the bottom.

The other boy, the one climbing onto the centerboard, had to be a Pure One. She couldn't have taken this risk for nothing. She'd read the yacht club's newsletter. She'd researched the rules. She knew the skippers were too old to be Pure Ones but that the crew members were the perfect age.

Mrs. Smith crushed the first boy's bones between her jaws. A nimbus of flesh and clothing fragments floated around her head. The eels darted in and out of the murk, swallowing every tiny morsel.

Maddened by a frenzy to feed, they inadvertently bit their own brothers and sisters. Lacerations appeared on their black skin. More blood oozed into the water. The eels wriggled and twisted in excitement, their lust for meat equal to the Mother's.

Eager to taste the second human, Mrs. Smith didn't bother consuming every bit of the first boy's body. Leaving several digits and a whole ear to her children, she swam toward the surface.

She saw the boy—the Pure One—long before he saw her.

He clung to the centerboard with both arms, his legs hanging limply in the water. As she approached from below, he tried to pull himself onto the hull of the capsized boat, but his life jacket kept getting caught on the edge of the centerboard. Finally, he dropped back into the water and unfastened the life jacket. He kicked and flailed, fighting to free himself of the cumbersome garment.

Now you'll taste better, thought Mrs. Smith.

Watching him struggle with the life jacket, Mrs. Smith recalled the days when her sacrifices would walk into the ocean without a stitch of clothing on their backs. Even in the dead of winter, with clumps of ice bobbing in the water, the Pure Ones would enter her realm as naked as a clam without a shell.

Too often, they would die before she could eat them. Their pink skin would turn blue. Their lungs would fill with water. They'd slip into oblivion without experiencing the searing pain of her teeth.

Sacrificial man-children were convenient, but Mrs. Smith preferred a fresh and lively catch. This boy, for example, with his frantic splashing and kicking, was vibrating with fear. His heart hammered like a finch in a cage. The neurons in his brain were firing at the highest speeds.

Terror would make his flesh taste even sweeter, so Mrs. Smith decided to let the boy see her.

She slowed her ascent, allowing her tentacles to unfurl like a flower opening to the sun. She stretched her mouth into a toothy grin and hovered a few feet under the boat's hull. At this depth, the sunlight still penetrated the water. It put diamonds in Mrs. Smith's black eyes. It made her teeth gleam like pearls.

Having lifted himself halfway out of the water, the boy stared across the centerboard and looked down.

He looked down and saw her.

At first, he seemed confused by Mrs. Smith's humanoid face. But then he took in her hungry stare and open maw. He saw her massive, squid-like body spreading like an inkblot under the boat. He saw tentacles and claws. He saw the squirming eels.

He was arrested by the sight of her. She had to be an illusion. A nightmare.

Whatever she was, the boy knew that he was staring down at Death.

The boy didn't move. He didn't make a sound. He clung to the centerboard like a barnacle. All Mrs. Smith had to do was pluck him off.

She didn't want to give him the chance to call for help, so she gave the boat a violent shove. The boy slid into the water like a coin. A shiny treasure minted just for Mrs. Smith.

She wrapped him like a mummy in her tentacles and dived to the bottom. Resting on a jumble of rocks and broken shells, she severed the man-child's left leg first, rejoicing in the jolt of energy that filled her mouth.

It was like swallowing lightning.

After that first bite, she couldn't control her desire. She bit and chewed, bit and chewed. She ate until there was nothing left. When she was done, she succumbed to the rapture.

The eels watched as she floated, belly up, inches above the

sandy bottom. She'd succumbed to tonic immobility, which meant the two young humans in the other boat were safe.

Mrs. Smith was senseless. The eels, simple as they were, recognized the danger in this.

The rocky shore offered no refuge for the Mother. She was too big to slide between the boulders and wait for nightfall. She would have to stay close to the bottom, seeking protection in the deeper waters, until it was safe to return to the boathouse.

Mrs. Smith didn't hear the boy with the red hair scream. She didn't know that a severed finger had popped to the surface of the water like a cork. She was still in a trance, unaware that her children were battling over that finger, torquing and splashing in an effort to get a nibble before one of their larger brethren could swallow the morsel whole.

The red-haired boy screamed again. And again. And again.

The eels couldn't hear well, but the noise vibrated through the water and pulsed inside their heads. In an instant, they became nervous and unorganized, swimming in figure eights and winding their bodies around one another like licorice twists.

They returned to the Mother and tried to rouse her. They nudged her with their noses. Caressed her with their slimy skin. They nipped her with their little teeth and slapped her with their tails.

By the time she responded, it was too late to capsize the other boat.

The humans heard the boy's cry. They're coming to rescue him.

The purr of distant engines grew louder as the V-shaped bows of motorboats cut through the water.

Mrs. Smith knew that the boats would converge above her, and the humans would begin searching for the missing boys. Soon they would blast their air horns and fire flares into the sky. They might even enter the water.

When they found nothing, they would become frightened. That fear would soon turn to anger.

Eventually, there will be a vengeful mob. There will be torches.

It was what happened whenever her dwelling place was discovered. The humans would band together, their courage growing with their numbers, and take up arms against the monster. Grim-faced and determined, they'd come for her, the orbs of fire on the ends of their sticks punching holes in the night.

As soon as the flames of her home rose into the sky, they would find their voices. They'd curse her to their god, debase her with the vilest language their thick tongues could produce. They'd howl like animals as the fire chewed through wood and blackened walls of stone.

Mrs. Smith had been caught unawares only once. The humans had almost killed her. All these years later, she could still taste the ash in the back of the throat and smell the acrid odor of her charred scales.

The pain had been like nothing she'd ever known. Even after she'd crawled into the water and the salt began to cleanse her wounds, the burning sensation had continued.

It had taken her a long time to heal. For many moon cycles, her new scales were softer than the shell of a molting crab and her tentacles were no longer tipped with hooked claws but impotent black stubs.

Back then, Mrs. Smith had longed to return to the village where she'd been assaulted. She wanted to sink every fishing boat and tear the men apart, limb by limb, until the water turned red with blood. She wanted to hear the women wail, to know that their children would go hungry. She wanted to see their babies shrivel in their cradles. She wanted crude wooden crosses to bloom in their fallow fields.

Despite her rage, she did not return to her ruined home. She could not risk being wounded again. Until she ate her fill of Pure Ones and began a new life cycle, a harpoon could pierce her tender scales and puncture her heart. Without her claws, she couldn't free herself from their fishing nets. She couldn't fight back if they dragged her onto the beach and stabbed her with spears or pointed sticks. Worse still, they might douse her in whale oil and set her ablaze.

For the first time in her existence, the humans had gotten the upper hand. Mrs. Smith had been forced to swim away until she was strong enough to face them again. She'd hidden under ice, hunting seals and whale calves. In the cold, dark waters, she'd found solace. She went into semi-hibernation, drifting among the ghost-white creatures of the Arctic deep.

She didn't know how long this lasted. She ate and swam, ate and swam, until her pursuit of a killer whale brought her close to the surface. Close to the wooden hull of a boat. A boat with nets and a heavy metal anchor.

At the sight of those nets, her anger flamed.

She was herself again. She was scales and claws, teeth and hunger.

The time had now come to seek out humans again. Not only would she feed on them, but she would mate with one of them, too.

Mrs. Smith could rejuvenate her aging body by consuming Pure Ones. She could also wake her dormant reproductive system by mating with several human males. Their competing sperm would stimulate an atavistic need in her to perpetuate her species. She shared more genetic material with her prey than she cared to admit, but it was these commonalities that allowed her to mimic their appearance for periods of time.

Like certain starfish species, Mrs. Smith was an asexual

animal. Her kind procreated through binary fission and reproduction. Unlike the starfish, which sacrificed one of several arms to create a new being, Mrs. Smith had to tear herself in two. While her offspring would survive the ordeal, there was a chance she wouldn't.

She'd come close to reproducing once before, but her own self-preservation had kept her from completing the act.

Now she had no choice. The humans were multiplying at an alarming rate. She had to bear an offspring. And she had to survive the process. If she succeeded, there would be two creatures to collapse oil rigs and sink tankers. Two beasts to puncture the hulls of submarines and trawlers. Together, they would pull thousands of humans down into the dark. The sharks would feed until their bellies were bloated. Until the ocean floor was littered with teeth and bones.

Mrs. Smith was repulsed by the idea of sex with a human, but she would do it. Once they'd given her what she needed, she'd swim to an underwater cave along the Maine coast and undergo the agony of binary fission.

She'd chosen this cave after her long period of hiding and healing.

Abandoning the ice floes and frigid water of the Arctic, she'd traveled south in search of fishing coves. She'd been stunned by the number of boats populating the harbors and inlets. There were nets and traps everywhere. The shores were dotted with buildings. Humans crawled over the land like ants. They'd built machines. They'd tamed the wilderness with steel and guns and fire. While she'd been in a stupor, they'd claimed dominion over the world.

The Mother of Eels had been relegated to the shadows.

However, the shadows in the bay adjacent to Cold Harbor were not deep or dark enough to conceal her for long. She had just devoured two humans, and their absence would not go unnoticed. Mrs. Smith needed to escape. To do so, she had to rely on her children.

The eels swarmed, swimming above her as she traveled east past Huntington Bay. She headed toward the shores of a vast nature preserve where the water was studded with sharp rocks. Boats kept a wide birth of the area, which made it the perfect place for Mrs. Smith to digest her food without being discovered.

The flesh of the Pure One burned in her belly like a star. She wanted more. Many, many more.

But for now, one was all she needed.

Soon, she could transform into a human woman.

She would join humans at their dinners and cocktail parties. She would eat their sugary foods and sip their bitter drinks and smile while they talked about their dull jobs and pathetic dreams. She would listen with genuine pleasure when they spoke about their children, imagining how she would savor the flesh of their Johns and Janes with the same relish they exhibited when masticating a chunk of raw, bloody steak.

Elaine K. Bernstein had already told her where and when these children would gather in a large, delicious group. All Mrs. Smith had to do was secure an invitation, and she would have all the Pure Ones she needed.

She would arrive at the party as a beautiful human woman, but she would leave in her true form. She would shed her human skin and swim away as the Mother of Eels.

And her belly would be full.

14

Natalie

Natalie was in the McCreedys' kitchen, stripping leaves off the stems of yellow roses when the doorbell rang.

She stuck the roses in a cut glass vase and yelled, "Coming!" in a cartoonishly chipper voice.

She'd prepared for today by standing in front of the mirror and smiling as she said things like "Thanks for coming" and "It *is* the best school district in the area" and "It's *so* close to the beach."

She knew she looked the part of a successful Realtor. She'd bought a white skirt suit for the open house, which she paired with a silky black sleeveless top and the gold necklace Jimmy had bought her in Mexico. She'd folded her Gold Coast scarf into a flower shape and pinned it to her breast pocket, right above her nametag. A kiss of pink blush and Revlon's Million Dollar Red lipstick made her look pretty and confident.

She practiced her professional smile as she opened the door. Beth stood on the welcome mat, holding a cookie sheet covered in plastic wrap. The cookie sheet was resting on top of a Tupperware container filled with balls of dough.

"You look amazing!"

Natalie was unable to return the compliment. Beth looked like she'd spent the night partying. She wore a Barbie-pink dress with a stain on the right breast. Her greasy hair was gathered into a messy ponytail and her pancake makeup failed to conceal the puffy skin under her eyes. Her lip liner was three shades darker than her lipstick, her nail polish was chipped, and she smelled faintly of sweat.

"Thanks for bringing the cookies," Natalie said. "Come on in."

Beth followed her into the kitchen and gazed around. "I love seeing the inside of other people's houses, especially the kitchen. It's my favorite room in the house. This one is . . . well . . . you can tell that many meals were cooked here." She put the cookie sheet on the counter and opened the oven. "You cleaned this, right?"

Natalie nodded. "You should've seen this place before I cleaned. It was nasty. I really wish they'd replaced their carpet. It's hard to disguise the smell of old dog."

"Don't worry about that. In about twelve minutes, the whole house will smell like heaven."

"I hope so." Natalie put the Tupperware in the fridge for later. "If the brokers respond well to your cookies, I can bake them again at the next open house. And if people ask where they came from, I can give them your business card. Who knows? Maybe we can launch your career, too."

Natalie expected more enthusiasm from Beth over the idea of getting her home baking business off the ground, but her friend just mumbled, "That'd be great."

"How's Don?"

"He was still asleep when I left for church. I tried to wake him up, but he told me . . ." Tears sprang to her eyes. "He told me to fuck off. I don't understand what's happening to him."

Natalie was shocked. Don had a dirty mouth. He cursed

like a marine and told crude jokes. But in all the years Natalie had known him, Don had never been rude to Beth. He spoke to her in a soft voice and never forgot his manners. He opened her car door, pulled out her chair, and generally treated her like she walked on water. Natalie had always been jealous of how openly affectionate Don was with Beth.

How many cocktail parties or backyard cookouts had the women worked as a unit to set the tables or arrange the food while the men gathered around the stereo or the grill, drinking and smoking? How many times had she seen Don search for Beth with his eyes? He always knew exactly where she was—always sent a smile across the room or gave her a saucy wink when she passed by carrying a stack of dirty dishes or martini glasses.

Whenever Beth moved within arm's reach, Don would grab her ass and call her *foxy lady* or *hot stuff* or *baby doll.* He never wiped off the lipstick tattoos she left on his cheeks, and he loved to sneak up behind her and squeeze her tiny waist. She'd squeal every time. He'd laugh and lean in to cover her neck in kisses.

Natalie, who'd seen them replay this routine a hundred times, couldn't imagine Jimmy nuzzling her neck or tickling her in front of their friends. Sure, he'd put his arm around her or give her a peck on the cheek. And sometimes, if they'd had a few drinks, they'd kiss during a slow dance, but Jimmy didn't search for Natalie in a crowded room. They both tended to seek out friends who could entertain them with jokes or juicy gossip. They wanted to flirt a little and remember who they were before they got married, moved to the suburbs, and had three kids.

But Don and Beth didn't have kids. They only had each other. They were two planets orbiting each other, so it was jarring to hear that Don had forgotten how much Beth meant to him.

Because of Mrs. Smith.

Natalie stiffened her spine and raised her chin. Her open house was about to start. She had to keep her mind in the game.

"It's going to work out, honey," she told Beth in the syrupy sweet voice she used to placate Justin when he wanted to stay up late or have an extra dessert. "Once Mrs. Smith realizes that she has to fall in line or the whole neighborhood will be against her, Don will snap out of it. Whatever power she has over him will be broken. In the meantime, you need to keep it together. Go home, take a shower, and start baking. You and I are going to go door-to-door tomorrow with treats for the neighbors. We'll give everyone a few of your cookies and a menu. Make a list of your items and the prices and take it to the copy shop. Tell them to print it on the prettiest paper they've got. We're going to be success stories. *Both* of us."

Hope sparked in Beth's eyes, and Natalie congratulated herself on her problem-solving abilities. She ushered her friend outside and promised to call her later.

The cookies were barely out of the oven when the doorbell rang.

Here we go, Natalie thought.

"Something smells great!" boomed a man's voice from the hall.

Natalie yanked off Mrs. McCreedy's stained oven mitts seconds before a barrel-chested man in a pin-striped blazer strutted into the kitchen. He put his hands on his hips and surveyed the room. Then he shook his head, as if what he saw was best forgotten, and thrust a hand toward Natalie.

"Mack Bowers, Merrill Lynch."

Natalie shook his unpleasantly moist hand. "I was about to put these cookies on a plate. They just came out of the oven, but once they've had a minute to cool—"

"Don't mind if I do," he interrupted, grabbing one right off the hot tray. "Jesus!" he barked, his fingers spasming as the cookie scalded his palm. He dropped the cookie on the floor and rushed to the sink.

Even though she'd done nothing wrong, Natalie apologized and scooped up the ruined cookie with one of the fancy floral napkins she'd bought at the party store.

She plated two cookies and waited for Mack to dry his hands on the artfully folded tea towel. Natalie looked from the crinkled towel to the water droplets on the faucet and backsplash and pursed her lips to prevent them from turning down in a frown. Mack Bowers had been in the house for less than two minutes and he was already making a mess.

"Want to give me the grand tour?" he asked, breaking a cookie in half and shoveling it into his mouth.

Natalie smiled. "It would be my pleasure."

As Mack moved through the rooms, he issued a series of dismissive grunts. Viewing the house through his eyes, Natalie realized all her cleaning and decluttering had been in vain. She saw only outdated paint colors, old carpet, and cracks in the bathroom tile.

Mack ate his second cookie in the living room. As he turned around, he created a circle of crumbs on the carpet. Natalie's fingers itched for a vacuum. She'd love to suck up the crumbs and then press the metal nozzle to Mack's mouth. It would be hard for him to look smug with a vacuum hose hanging off his face.

"The place has potential," he said. "If someone was willing to fix it up, it could be real nice. Let's see the yard."

Natalie opened the patio door and followed Mack outside. He was about to speak when the doorbell rang again.

"Excuse me," she said.

She retraced her steps to the living room, where an elegant middle-aged woman stood next to a cabinet stuffed with

Hummel figurines. The woman was very slim with a cumulus cloud of blond hair. She opened an engraved business card case and withdrew a card. "Joan Andrews. I'm from Daniel Gale."

Natalie noticed the initials on the gold case. She noticed the way Joan held her card like it was a cigarette. Her nails were long, rounded, and red. She carried herself with a confidence that bordered on hauteur.

"Natalie Scott. Thank you for coming."

Joan fingered the eyeball-sized pearls around her neck and glanced around the room. "The home of an older couple, I assume?"

"Yes. Would you like—"

"I'll just do a quick wander." Joan spun on her heel. "I can see what I need to see in five minutes."

As Joan glided away, Mack came in from the patio. "Spacious yard," he said "Plenty of room for a work shed or a swing set. You've got that going for you, at least."

Someone knocked on the door three times and another agent entered the house. Stepping in front of Natalie, Mack pumped the newcomer's hand. "Steve! How the hell are you? Oh, hey! I didn't see your little guy behind you. You showing Junior the tricks of the trade?"

Natalie was surprised to see a toddler peeking out from behind Steve's leg. She'd never heard of an agent bringing a child to a broker's open house.

How unprofessional, she thought.

Steve, whose face was the shape and color of a chicken pot pie, gave Natalie a sheepish grin. "I'm dying to see the house, but this guy needs to use the bathroom real bad. Where's the closest john?"

Natalie pointed down the hall toward the bedrooms and watched in horror as Steve scooped his son into his arms and hurried in that direction. The pair made it halfway to the bathroom before the little boy started to wail.

"I'm gonna take another look at the kitchen," Mack said. "Maybe grab a cookie or two for the road."

While Mack piled cookies onto a clean napkin, Natalie recited the key selling points of the house.

She had time to mention the school district and proximity to the beach before Mack cut her off. "My current buyers are looking for something more modern, but I'll keep this in mind for future clients. Nice to meet you, Nat. I'll show myself out."

Natalie swiped the crumbs off the counter and refolded the tea towel. When she turned around, Joan was standing in the doorway, her finger pressed to the tip of her nose.

"Do they have dogs? There's an *odor* in the master bedroom."

"They do, but—"

"You might want to rent a carpet cleaning machine. If *I* can smell it, potential buyers can, too." She waved a hand at the cookies. "This is a nice touch. Did *you* bake them?"

"My friend did. She can make anything. Cakes, cookies, pastries—you name it. These are her Polish cinnamon cookies. Please, help yourself."

Joan shrank back. "I *never* eat sweets."

A wail echoed from down the hall. Joan murmured, "Oh, my," and made a quick exit.

Natalie used the lull in action to pick up the cookie crumbs in the living room. She'd just deposited them in the trash when she heard a toilet flush. This was followed by a rush of running water, which seemed to go on for a very long time.

Finally, Steve exited the bathroom, carrying his son in his arms. The little boy's shorts were gone, and his face was streaked with tears and snot. He met Natalie's eyes and then buried his head in his father's chest.

Natalie glanced from the boy's naked bottom to Steve's red face. "Is everything okay?"

"I wanted to take a quick look at this place on the way to a birthday party for this guy's best buddy, but I'm gonna have to come back another time. My boy has a funny tummy, and I need to take him home. Sorry, um . . ."

"Natalie. Natalie Scott."

"Nice touches here and there," Steve said, bolting through the front door. "Love the flowerpots and the cinnamon air freshener. Bye now."

Natalie tried to focus on the compliments, but dread propelled her down the hall. She was ten feet from the bathroom when she was assaulted by the smell of shit.

"*Nononono*," she moaned.

At first glance, the bathroom seemed okay. But as her gaze sharpened, she noticed brown streaks on the hand towel. Smears on the faucet.

"No."

Natalie clamped her hand over her mouth and approached the toilet. Steeling herself, she used the tip of her pinkie finger to raise the lid.

The toilet was stuffed with a mass of water-saturated paper. It pulsated at the bottom of the bowl like a nebula, barely visible under the swirls of fecal flotsam. The seat and lid were shit-speckled.

Retching, Natalie raced back to the kitchen. She drank water straight from the tap and wiped her mouth on the tea towel. Sucking in deep breaths of cinnamon-laced air, she looked out the window and watched the yellow balloons tied to the For Sale sign straining against their tethers. As her nausea abated, her anger swelled.

"Bastard."

She hurried out to her car for her bucket of cleaning supplies. If another agent showed up now, she'd never live it down. Word would get back to Sid that the McCreedys' house had smelled like cookies and diarrhea. Her career as a Gold Coast agent would be over before it began.

"Asshole!" she growled as she yanked on her latex gloves.

Natalie had cleaned up plenty of shit in her lifetime. Dog shit. Cat shit. Diaper blowouts. Toilet training mishaps. It was bad enough to clean up after her own kids. Cleaning up another child's shit was a different level of nasty.

She cleaned the smears on the sink and toilet handle first. There was nothing she could do about the towel, so she shoved it into the bottom of her bucket and started searching for a plunger.

She didn't need to flush the toilet to know that it was clogged. Dipshit Steve had used half a roll of toilet paper wiping his baby boy's ass.

Finding no plunger under the sink, Natalie frantically dug through the cabinet in the master bath and then flung open the door to the linen closet. There, crammed between a stack of old paint cans and a dust-coated box of maxi pads, was the plunger.

With the plunger in hand, Natalie stared down at the toilet bowl in dismay. If she tried to unclog it now, brown water would cascade over the side and onto the floor.

She wished Steve was in the room with her right now. She'd like to use his face as a plunger.

"Asshole."

Sweat gathered in Natalie's armpits and dampened the hair at her temples. She dropped to her knees and, holding her breath, reached into the water to grab a fistful of paper. She dumped the dripping mass into her bucket and went in for another handful.

The transfer was messy. Droplets of brown water dotted the seat. Toilet paper fragments floated in the bowl like loose fish scales.

With the biggest obstacles gone, the water level dropped. Natalie prayed she could simply flush the rest.

It didn't work.

Instead, the paper and poop remnants spiraled, rising higher and higher in the bowl.

"Please no. Please stop. *Stopstopstopstop.*"

To her immense relief, the muck stayed within the confines of the bowl.

And then, the doorbell rang.

Natalie let out the high-pitched squeak of a mouse squeezed between a cat's jaws and shoved the plunger and bucket in the cabinet under the sink. She slammed the toilet lid down and jogged to the front door.

When Natalie found the neighbors from across the street, Samir and Sarah Gupta, standing on the stoop, the smile she pasted on looked slightly maniacal.

Samir waved around the foyer. "How goes the open house?"

"I'm having a bit of a problem in the bathroom, and I need to take care of it before another agent shows up."

Sarah glanced over her shoulder as if a line of agents was forming behind her. "Want us to keep watch for you?"

"Please." She ushered the Guptas into the kitchen and told them to help themselves to cookies.

Back in the bathroom, she waited another two minutes for the water level to fall before giving the plunger a try. When the clog finally gave way, she squeezed her eyes shut in relief. Disaster had been averted.

Helping herself to the McCreedys' bleach, Natalie poured some into the bowl, the sink, and the bathtub. By the time she was done, the bathroom smelled like a hospital ward. Like disinfectant and decay.

She returned the bleach to the laundry room and carried the bucket of rank water and toilet paper to the farthest corner of the backyard. She tossed the contents into the vines and undergrowth on the other side of the fence.

"Eat shit, Mrs. Smith."

As Natalie breathed in the fresh air, she congratulated herself for keeping cool during a crisis. It was over now, and she was back in control. All she needed to do was run a comb through her hair and freshen up her lipstick, and she'd be ready to welcome the next agent.

Only there weren't any.

The Guptas hung around for fifteen minutes, but once their curiosity was sated, they took the rest of the cookies and left.

Natalie turned on the oven, arranged the rest of the cookie dough on the baking sheet, and waited.

The cookies turned golden brown, the ugly brass clock on the living room mantel ticked, and Natalie waited.

The oven timer rang, she took the cookies out of the oven, let them cool, and plated them.

Fifteen minutes later, she began to pace around the house.

No one else came.

The open house was over.

With the bitter taste of disappointment on her tongue, Natalie dumped the cookies into the Tupperware and turned off all the lights.

The last thing she needed to do before leaving was lock the patio door, but as her fingers closed around the dead bolt, she glanced across the yard to Mrs. Smith's woods and froze.

"Impossible," she whispered.

Natalie opened the door, crossed the brick patio, and

stepped onto the grass. She stood there, staring directly in front of her, as ants pole-vaulted off the grass blades onto her feet. They marched over her bare skin and slipped down into her shoes. Their tiny bodies tickled the soles of her feet and the sensitive flesh of her ankles.

Then they started to bite her.

She stomped her feet without looking down. She couldn't stop staring at the fence line. At the vines Jill had cut.

She'd beat them back, revealing the weary wood of the fence. Natalie had seen the result of her daughter's efforts. She'd seen the tangle of vine cuttings Jill had shoved into garbage bags. She'd filled four giant bags. So, what Natalie was seeing now made no sense.

The fence was no longer visible.

The vines had regrown, even thicker than before. They were a lush, green waterfall. A tsunami of leaves and berries spilling into the McCreedys' yard.

As Natalie gawked, a tendril near her shoe uncurled. She watched it wriggle like an inchworm, shuddering forward.

This thing from Mrs. Smith's woods was alive, and it was reaching for her.

Natalie turned and ran.

15

Una

Una surveyed the array of breakfast foods on the Bernsteins' kitchen island. There was a bowl of Froot Loops, a square of Entenmann's crumb cake, raisin toast slathered in cream cheese, a strawberry Pop-Tart, and a fan of cantaloupe slices. A hunk of cheese sat on the counter next to a frying pan of untouched scrambled eggs. The eggs had a rubbery sheen, and the cheese was dry and wrinkled, like an old woman's skin.

In between a box from Dunkin' Donuts and a mixing bowl with an oily coating of beaten eggs were cartons of orange juice and milk. In the corner, a wooden fruit bowl was stuffed with bananas, peaches, and plums.

Una would never get used to the abundance of fruit in the houses she cleaned, let alone the bounty available in every grocery store.

Shopping for fruit was a sensual experience for Una. She would push her shopping cart next to the ziggurats of apples, oranges, or lemons and just stand there, admiring the gumball-bright colors.

She'd lean over the berries, which were heaped into green pulp baskets like caskets of jewels and inhale their sweet perfume before running her palm over the smooth curve of a watermelon.

It was impossible to choose between sun-kissed apricots, succulent peaches, and fat-bottomed pears. The plump grapes that exploded in the mouth with bacchanal pleasure, or grapefruits whose pink flesh yielded when penetrated by the tip of a spoon.

Una was sad to see that the fruit in the Bernsteins' bowl was rotting. The banana was sagging and tiny flies danced over the surface of the brown-spotted skin.

"Una?"

Elaine stood in the doorway, cradling a coffee mug. She wore a white tracksuit with blocks of blue, pink, and purple. Her face was swollen from lack of sleep and her hair looked like the fluff Una emptied from the vacuum bag.

"Why are you here?" Elaine whispered.

Una pictured the Ziggy wall calendar hanging in her kitchen, a Christmas present from Gunnar. The Bernsteins' name was clearly written in today's square. Elaine hadn't swapped with Beth or Natalie. She hadn't called to cancel. If she had, Una would've updated her calendar.

Confused, she said, "You don't want me to clean?"

Elaine moved closer. "Don't you know what happened?"

Una shook her head.

Elaine drew in a fortifying breath and released it again, very slowly. "Two boys went missing yesterday. During the regatta. Their boat . . . capsized. And they just—they disappeared."

Una pictured two boys sinking. Both of them wore Svana's face. Both of them reached out to her as they were dragged down, away from the light.

Tears leaked from Elaine's eyes. "Charles was there. The boat the boys were in was tangled up with his boat. Then a wave separated them and carried the other boys' boat into the fog. That's probably why they capsized—the waves and the wind. Charles saw something—I *know* he did. It must have been horrible because he, well, he refuses to talk."

"How terrible."

Elaine gestured at the dirty kitchen. "He won't eat, either. He's curled up in his bed facing the wall. He used to do that when he was little, after a bad dream."

Una felt time folding in on itself. She was two people at once. She was a schoolgirl in Iceland who'd just lost her sister. She also was a cleaning woman on Long Island listening to a mother talk about her son. Fear wove her past and present together. It felt like a rope around her neck. She couldn't find her breath.

Two boys in the water. Two boys gone. Charles saw something that scared the words out of him.

"The boat," croaked Una. "Was it damaged?"

Elaine plunged her hands into her hair. The mug in her right hand tilted. Coffee dribbled down her tracksuit. "Not a scratch. The boys didn't capsize near the rocks or run into a buoy or another boat. It doesn't make any sense. Their parents—God—their parents must be in hell."

She dropped the mug in the sink and sobbed into her hands.

Una guided Elaine to the sofa and urged her to sit down.

"I'll make you some tea," she said, hurrying back into the kitchen before Elaine could see how her hands trembled.

She put the kettle in the sink and tugged off the lid. As she started to fill it, she saw her face reflected in the water.

Then she saw her sister's face, just below the surface of that dark sea. She saw the black oval of her mouth and the white marbles of her eyes. She saw her hands, two pale starfish, reaching for the surface.

Save me, Svana's hands had screamed.

That was the last thing Una remembered from that day.

She'd woken, many hours later, to find Amma sitting on the edge of her bed, singing to her. A candle burned in the corner of the room, its weak light throwing shadows on the walls.

The shadows looked like tentacles.

"Sleep," Amma had whispered when the song was done. The word was an incantation. It pulled Una into its embrace, and she'd slept for two more days.

Rest would do Charles only so much good. He needed to tell someone what he'd seen. Otherwise, the memory would haunt his dreams for the rest of his days.

Una put a steaming mug of tea on the side table next to Elaine. "Could I check on Charles?"

Thrown off-balance by the question, Elaine fidgeted with the tea bag, slowly raising it in and out of the scalding water like an inquisitor seeking a confession.

"That's sweet of you to offer, but our rabbi's coming over after lunch. I'm sure he'll know what to do." Elaine glanced down at her coffee-stained tracksuit. "I think I'll take a bath. If Charles comes out or asks for anything, please knock on my door."

"I will."

It took Una an hour to package the breakfast items in baggies and Tupperware, throw out the spoiled food, scrub the frying pan, and clean the rest of the kitchen from top to bottom.

She turned to the laundry room next, where she found a small heap of clothes on the floor. The striped T-shirt, socks, and shorts were damp and had a tangy, briny scent. They smelled of the ocean. And fear.

Two boys. Gone.

Una pictured a small boat flung onto its side, its young sailors ejected into the water. Had the boys cried out? Had they struggled and splashed? Or had they been struck so hard by a swinging boom that they'd slid into the water with the slippery silence of a seal?

What did Charles see?

Una pushed the clothes into the washing machine and wiped the salt grit on her apron. She passed her hands over her apron again and again, her gaze locked on the orange-and-yellow Tide box.

You are here to clean. That is all.

She needed to focus on detergent and bleach, lemon-scented sprays, and abrasive powders. Fine rags and feathery dusters. She had to block all thoughts of Svana and try not to think about the missing boys.

She poured the Tide into the machine and started it, comforted by the thought of the blue-white granules obliterating the salt spray and sweat from Charles's clothes. Then she put his boat shoes on the rack in the garage and mopped the floor with hot water and vinegar.

She was dusting the living room when the doorbell rang.

The sound boomed through the quiet house but didn't rouse Elaine. Una quickly opened the door to stop the visitor from ringing the bell again.

Natalie stood on the stoop, looking tired and rumpled.

"I came to see how Charles was doing," she said.

"I haven't seen him. He's resting in his room."

"And Elaine?"

"Also in her room."

Elaine must've heard the bell after all because she suddenly appeared in the hall. Her hair was combed, and she'd swapped her tracksuit for a white blouse and dolphin-gray slacks.

"There you are," Natalie said softly. She opened her arms to her friend, and Elaine stepped into the embrace with a sigh.

Una returned to the living room and resumed her work. She tried not to listen to the two women, but certain phrases drifted out of the kitchen. She heard "nightmare" and "no one knows" and "can't explain" and "Jimmy took off work" and "what can we do?"

After a flurry of whispers, the women seemed to forget about Una's presence and spoke at a normal volume.

Natalie said, "Sailing class is canceled next week."

"I don't think Charles will be going back."

"Has he said anything?"

"No."

"Jill won't talk about it, either. When I got home after the open house, which was a total disaster, I found her on the sofa with her head on Jimmy's lap. He was stroking her hair and drinking whiskey. As soon as I saw them, I knew something was wrong."

Cupboards were opened and closed. The refrigerator sighed. A spoon clinked against porcelain. Then the women carried their coffee into the dining room.

"He had a glass waiting for me on the table," Natalie continued. "We never drink whiskey neat. It scared me. Seeing Jill in his lap like that scared me, too."

"I wonder if Jill saw what Charles saw." Elaine paused for a heartbeat before adding, "Do you think they feel guilty? Like they know something that could get someone in trouble? An older kid maybe? Or an instructor?"

After a short silence, Natalie said, "I don't know. Jill gets this look on her face when she feels guilty, and I didn't see that. She just retreated inside herself. The only thing she said was that she was worried about Charles."

"Really?" Elaine's voice lifted.

"Jimmy got her into bed and was getting ready to turn out her light when she said, 'I hope Charles is okay.'"

Elaine made a strangled sound, and Una pushed the vacuum into the master bedroom and closed the door behind her.

She didn't want to hear any more.

But as she sprayed the bathroom mirrors with Windex, scrubbed the toilet, and picked up Elaine's damp towel, she pictured Charles and Jill in their beds, their bodies curled like nautilus shells, and wished she could wipe away their memories of the regatta.

Two boys.

Lost.

She dusted and vacuumed the bedroom, straightened the wrinkled comforter, and kept her face averted from the window.

All she had to do was raise the shade to see Mrs. Smith's house.

Eel's Nest.

She'd be there, Una knew. Behind those gray walls, watching.

Una had to keep J.J. and Jill away from that house, but how could she explain the danger to Natalie when she didn't understand it herself? She couldn't tell Natalie how the woman in the library book, the one with Mrs. Smith's face, had moved. She couldn't tell her how Mrs. Stapleton had buttoned her lip when Una asked about her father's research.

But Mrs. Smith was changing. After years of avoiding people, she'd bought a car from Don. She'd replied to Elaine's letter. She'd hired the Scott children to do yard work.

Is she going to come out?

The thought turned Una's mouth dry. The dust she'd dislodged from the nightstands stuck in her throat, so she went to the kitchen for a glass of water.

Passing by the dining room, she heard Natalie say, "I'm not going into the office today. I'm working on my mailbox bed and trimming the bushes out front. What's Benjamin doing?"

"He went to work." Elaine sounded embarrassed. "I wanted

him to stay home, but he said he had meetings he couldn't miss. Our rabbi will be here after lunch. I hope he can get through to Charles."

"If you want, I can send Jill over later. The ice cream truck comes this afternoon, just late enough to spoil the kids' dinner. I'll have Jill get something for Charles and bring it to him. What does he like?"

"The cookie sandwich with the vanilla ice cream and the chocolate chips. Thank you, Natalie."

"I'd better get back. Justin's watching *The Smurfs* even though Gargamel scares him."

"He scares me, too," Elaine admitted. "I think it's because he only has that single tooth. It's like a can opener."

Hearing the smiles in the women's voices, Una imagined them clasping hands, just for a moment, before Natalie walked out of the house.

Una finished her water and placed the glass in the dishwasher. Elaine came forward, holding a check in her hand.

"Thanks for taming the chaos in here. I thought I could make everything better if I could find the perfect breakfast for Charles. Silly, I know, but I didn't know what else to do. Anyway, we'll see you next week."

In her car, Una glanced at the check. Elaine had paid her the full amount even though Una had only cleaned half of the house. And because Natalie wasn't going to the office, Una didn't need to watch Justin, which meant she was free for the rest of the day.

Instead of going home, she drove down the Scotts' driveway and parked in the nook near the basketball hoop.

Lady and Tramp announced her arrival. Natalie opened the door but didn't have the chance to speak because Justin skirted around her and wrapped his arms around Una's legs.

"Una!" he cried in delight.

She kissed his plump cheek and looked at Natalie. "I'm going to the library, and I thought Justin might like to come with me."

"Are you sure?"

Putting a hand on Justin's golden head, Una said, "I wouldn't mind the company. This seems like a good day for a quiet place like the library."

"You heard what happened?"

Una gave Justin a little push. "Go get your shoes. We'll stop at the hobby shop after we get our books."

Justin let out a whoop of joy and raced away.

"I heard two boys are missing," whispered Una.

Natalie joined her on the stoop. "There's no sign of the boys, except for one life jacket. The current near those rocks is pretty strong, but . . ." She trailed off.

"Jimmy is looking for them?"

Natalie nodded. "Lots of people are. Harbor patrol, sailors from three yacht clubs, and parents from all over."

Una looked over Natalie's shoulder to the windows facing the harbor. The water was draped in sun-sparkles. The light was too bright. It burned tiny globes into Una's eyes. She looked away just as Justin reappeared, carrying his sneakers and a quarter. "I want a candy necklace," he said, offering the coin to Una.

Natalie retrieved her purse from the coat closet. A movement caught her eye, and she froze in the middle of opening her wallet.

Jill stood in the hall, gripping the stair rail with one hand. She was dressed in jean shorts and a green Izod shirt that was too small on her. Her hair was a nest of tangles.

"Can I come, too?" she asked in a near whisper.

"If it's okay with your mom," Una said.

Natalie pointed at the bathroom. "Brush your hair first."

Una helped Justin with his sneakers and settled him into the back seat. Jill came outside a few minutes later, her hair fastened in a low ponytail.

Normally, she was a talkative child, but she didn't say a word on the drive to Greenlawn. Justin filled the silence by humming the theme song to *The Smurfs* over and over again.

"Can we go to the hobby shop first?" he asked while Una searched for a parking spot at the library.

"Yes, but you can't eat your candy necklace until you're back in the car."

"Okay."

On the sidewalk, Justin took Una's hand and skipped all the way to the hobby store. He stopped in front of the display window and pointed at a group of typewriters. "Jilly wants that for her birthday. She wants the blue one, so she can write real stories. Mom says it's too expensive, but Jilly's going to buy it with her own money."

Una admired the display, but she was really looking at Jill's reflection in the glass. "I bet your sister will be a famous writer one day. All of her books will be in the library."

Jill's vacant gaze skimmed over the sky-blue typewriter. Una could tell that it couldn't hold the girl's interest today. Not when she was so numb inside.

The bell over the door tinkled merrily as Justin entered the shop and made a beeline for the candy display.

"Can you pick out something for J.J.?" Una asked him.

"This." Justin handed her a package of Chuckles.

Jill pointed at a package of wax-shaped bottles filled with colorful liquid. "Nik-L-Nips are his favorite."

Una swapped the candy. "What about you?"

Jill selected a piece of plastic shaped like a bullet. "Candy lipstick. You get two for a quarter."

She chose two pink lipsticks and then wandered to the back to look at a shelf of horse figurines in boxes. Justin sidled up next to her and touched the box featuring a young boy riding a black horse. "What does that say?"

"It's the Black Stallion and Alec, the boy who was on the deserted island with him."

Justin shrank back. "I don't like that movie."

"I know, but I do. There's a fire and their ship sinks. But they save each other. Otherwise, they would've drowned."

A shadow darkened Jill's face and she moved away from the horses to the activity book section. Instead of following her, Justin crossed the store to gawk at a display of car model kits.

When he sat down on the floor to study a silver Camaro kit, Una approached Jill. She put an arm around the girl and squeezed. "I don't know what happened yesterday, but you're strong and brave. You're going to be okay."

Keeping her eyes on a spinner rack of Invisible Ink books, Jill whispered, "Charles was behind us. His boat, I mean. He was behind us, and he was screaming."

"His mother thinks something scared him."

Jill slowly turned the spinner. The plastic-wrapped books winked as they glided past. "I was in the car with him on the way home. He stared out the window and whispered to himself the whole time. Our instructor was talking to her boyfriend, so she didn't hear him, but I did." She swallowed hard. "He kept saying what he saw in the water. He said there were eels. And something else . . ."

She shook her head, unable to finish.

"You'll feel better if it isn't stuck inside you."

Jill gripped the rack until her knuckles turned white. "He saw a finger, floating in the water."

Una's tongue felt like a piece of leather. She knew she could tell Jill not to worry. She could say that Charles was mistaken. That his eyes had tricked him. It was foggy and the water was choppy, so he'd seen something that wasn't there.

But Una couldn't lie to this shaken girl.

Not when she believed Charles Bernstein.

He saw eels.

He saw a finger.

"Do you believe him?" Una asked Jill.

Jill nodded.

"So do I."

Jill leaned against Una, her body heavy with gratitude, as Justin returned the model car box to the shelf.

Ambling over, he tugged Una's hand and said, "Can we go now?"

"Yes, darling."

At the library, Jill disappeared into the stacks and Justin got comfy in a chair in the children's area. Una waited until he was absorbed by a Busytown book and then hurried over to the checkout desk. She asked Mrs. Stapleton if they could speak in private.

The librarian gave her a quizzical look and finished stamping a card. Then she gestured for Una to follow her to her office.

"Have you heard about the missing boys?" Una asked with uncharacteristic bluntness.

Wavelets traversed Mrs. Stapleton's brow. "It's terrible, isn't it? Their families must be worried sick."

"Has this happened before? Children going missing from boats? From the water?" Something flickered in Mrs. Stapleton's eyes. A quicksilver minnow of fear. Una saw it and pressed harder. "Did your father mention something similar in his research?"

The librarian stiffened. "Hardly. He mostly wrote about landmarks."

"Please. I'm worried about the children I take care of. I want to keep them safe. If your father wrote about strange things—things that couldn't be explained—I need to know."

The librarian shook her head. "He didn't—"

Una cut her off. "My grandmother used to tell me stories about things that seemed impossible. When I got older, my friends said that none of the stories were true. But I knew things my friends didn't know. Maybe your father did, too."

Mrs. Stapleton darted a glance at Justin, who was moving his finger over the book page. Una knew he was searching for Busytown's little mouse.

The phone at the circulation desk rang.

"I need to get that." The librarian moved toward the door. "Come back Saturday. I'll have something for you then."

Una returned to Justin and his Richard Scarry book. Busytown was a world of smiles and friendly waves. It was filled with citizens who loved their jobs and lived in homes with glowing windows and families seated around dinner tables.

It was not a world of missing boys or floating fingers.

There were no eels in Busytown.

There were no monsters.

16

Jill

The yacht club was still closed on Tuesday.

Sailing classes had been canceled for the week, and swim practice wouldn't resume until Wednesday at the earliest.

The missing boys had not been found, and with every passing hour, the chances of their recovery shrank.

"It's horrible," Jill's mom whispered into the phone on her nightstand. She'd left her bedroom door cracked, and Jill tiptoed close enough to overhear the one-sided conversation. "They found pieces of orange fabric on the beach this morning. From a life jacket. No, there was nothing else. I don't understand it, either."

Jill pressed her cheek against the wall and remembered how Charles's boat had been so close to the one that had capsized with no warning.

"Tony Pulcino was Charles's skipper, and he didn't see anything strange," her mom went on. "He said as soon as the other boat separated from theirs, it fell behind and got pushed into the fog. I guess they caught the wind and got turned around." A pause. "Well, if what Charles said is true, they must've got hit by a propeller. I *know*. It's awful."

Charles told his mom about the finger, thought Jill.

"She's doing okay," her mother said, still speaking in a hushed tone. "Una called to ask about her, too. She wanted to know if she could take the kids to the movies, but I told her I had plans for J.J. and Jill. She went on and on about how Jill is super allergic to poison ivy and about the wasps she's seen flying around the lot next door. It was bizarre." After another pause, she said, "No, I'm doing cold calls from home today. Stop over after you see Elaine if you want."

Her mother hung up, and Jill slipped into the bathroom.

In the mirror, she saw a girl with a sleep-swollen face and mussed hair. She took her brush out of the top drawer and began working through the tangles. The stiff bristles crunched as they passed over a mass of knotted hair at the nape of her neck. She had to use her fingers to pull some of the strands apart. Jill's scalp prickled with pain, but she kept going.

When she finished, her hair was smooth, and her eyes were glassy with unshed tears. She blinked them away and filled her cup with water. She drank the water in three gulps and felt a little better. After wiping her mouth on the hand towel, she stared at her reflection, wondering if she looked like someone who knew two dead boys. Boys whose bodies might have been mangled by propellor blades. Or sharks.

Jill imagined being interviewed by a reporter. She thought of how she'd describe the fog and the shrillness of Charles's scream. She'd explain how it had given her goose bumps. How she'd been so scared.

The reporter would hang on her every word. All her friends would see her on TV. They'd tell her how good she looked. They'd admire her big hoop earrings and her full-bodied hair. They'd tell her she looked a little like Michelle Pfeiffer. The next time she ran into Aaron, he'd say, "I saw you on TV," and smile at her in a way that meant he liked her back. Then he'd take her hand, pull her behind the snack bar, and kiss her.

"Breakfast!" her mom called from the kitchen.

Jill shoved her brush into the drawer and exited the bathroom just as Justin zipped past her down the hall, Lady right on his heels.

To Jill's surprise, there were mini cinnamon rolls on her plate along with a small mound of scrambled eggs.

"I thought you could use a treat today," her mother said, pouring orange juice into Jill's empty glass.

"Thanks, Mom."

Jill made a show of eating her eggs first. She tried not to wolf them down, even though she really wanted to bite into a cinnamon roll while it was still warm. The moment her mother left the room to call for J.J., she grabbed one of the pastries and shoved the whole thing into her mouth. As the sugary, buttery sweetness coated her tongue and sank into the grooves between her teeth, her entire body tingled with pleasure.

Her mother returned to the kitchen and busied herself at the sink. A few minutes later, J.J. shuffled in.

"Why can't I sleep in for once?" he complained. "We have the day off."

"From the yacht club, but not from other things."

Jill wanted to tell J.J. that Una had offered to take them to the movies, but if she said a word, her mother would know that she'd been eavesdropping.

Why did Una mention poison ivy? And wasps?

Jill picked up the second cinnamon roll. She wanted to eat it slowly, nibble by nibble, until only the central spiral was left. When that was gone, she wanted to lick her icing-flecked fingers, one by one. But she was afraid of drawing her mother's attention, of being reminded for the umpteenth time to eat like a lady, so she took a demure bite and watched her brother's face darken with indignation.

"All of my friends are sleeping in—probably Jill's, too. What do we have to do today? Wait! Are we going to look for the kids from Huntington?"

"Other people are doing that. Anyway, when something like this happens, it's best to stay busy."

J.J. groaned. "Lemme guess. Chores."

"Yard work. *Paid* yard work."

At this, J.J. became more alert. Jill knew he was thinking about the boom box he wanted to buy. "Here?"

"No, at Mrs. Smith's. She's offered to pay you and Jill ten dollars an hour."

J.J. and Jill exchanged stupefied glances. Ten dollars an hour was a fortune. But working for Mrs. Smith? The idea was insane. Other than the small lawn in front, her yard was an untamable, frightening place. Her house was scary. And she was a mystery—a ghostly presence creeping around behind gray walls.

"Did you talk to her?" Jill asked when she got her breath back.

"She put a note in our mailbox. She wants you to start in the back garden. Pull weeds, cut vines, and clear the path. The door to the garden will be unlocked. You'll need gloves, garbage bags, clippers, and a rake. I'll ring the bell when it's time for lunch."

J.J. waved a forkful of eggs in the air. "What garden? It's all pricker bushes and poison ivy. We'd be better off with a flamethrower."

"Start with the vines on the fence. You'll figure out what to do after that."

Jill pictured the skinny windows on Mrs. Smith's second floor. "Will she be watching us?"

Her mother scowled. "I'm sure she has better things to do with her time. Just focus on your work, and before you know it, you'll have earned thirty dollars. If she likes what she sees, she might hire you again."

As much as Jill wanted the money for her typewriter fund, she didn't want to go to Mrs. Smith's. She didn't want to step foot on *her* property.

How could her mother make them do this after what happened at the regatta? Charles's mom would never force him to work for their crazy neighbor. He was probably still in his pajamas, watching *Star Wars* or one of the other hundreds of movies he owned.

If he wanted a typewriter, he'd get it. He wouldn't have to do a thing. No chores. No babysitting. No yard work.

J.J. finished his breakfast and pushed away from the table. "Fine. Let's get this crap over with."

"*After* you put your dishes in the dishwasher. And, Jill." Her mother tapped her own head. "Put your hair in a ponytail so it doesn't hang in your face."

Jill and J.J. didn't speak as they collected their tools and trudged up the driveway. Jill was scared. She could sense the house watching them. Did her brother feel it, too? How the window on the top floor was like an eye, gazing down at them?

The electric gate across Mrs. Smith's driveway had been drawn back, leaving a gap just big enough for the garbage can. Jill knew the door to the garden couldn't be on the side of the house facing the Bernsteins' or she would've noticed it before. That meant it was on the side bordering the woods.

"This way," she said, leading her brother past the front porch and over the lawn.

"There's a door under all this shit?" J.J. dropped his tools and stared at the mass of vines covering the length of the fence.

"Let's just cut until we see it."

Muttering under this breath, J.J. picked up his clippers and began severing vines. It wasn't long before he said, "Found it!"

The door was made of wood so dark that it was almost black. The metalwork was rusted. Vines had wormed furrows into its surface. The pitted handle had a serpentine shape. Above the handle was a keyhole.

"Maybe it'll be locked. Then we can go home."

Jill didn't share her brother's wish. If the door was locked, her mother would make them ask Mrs. Smith for the key.

She stepped forward, placed her gloved hands flat against the wood, and pushed. The door moved inward by an inch at most.

"The vines are in the way," J.J. said. "Lemme try."

He rammed the door with his shoulder until the wood groaned and the vines shuddered. The door moved a few more inches and then stuck fast.

Jill peered into the opening. She saw tall grass in the foreground and vine-covered bushes in the background. She told J.J. to keep hacking away at the vines while she attempted to slice through the clumps of grass behind the door.

It took them twenty minutes to create an opening wide enough to accommodate their bodies. After hesitating a long moment, they slipped into a wilderness that bore no resemblance to a garden.

"Holy shit," J.J. muttered.

Spread out before them was a riot of weeds, prickly shrubs, and more vines. It seemed as impenetrable as a fairy-tale briar patch. Every bush was festooned in thorns or draped in poison ivy.

Seeing no evidence of garden beds or ornamental plants, Jill said, "Should we make a clearing around the door?"

"I guess."

Jill yanked out handfuls of crabgrass and pigweed while J.J. attacked the winter creeper. He wasn't allergic to poison ivy, so he volunteered to tackle those vines as well, leaving Jill free to exhume what appeared to be a brick pathway from beneath a heavy blanket of moss.

As more and more bricks emerged, Jill forgot about Mrs. Smith and the ocular windows of her house. Sweat pearled on her forehead and trickled down the back of her neck. A nimbus of gnats hovered around her head. The air filled with the threatening buzz of wasps, but Jill was too absorbed in her work to notice.

When her trash bag was full, she waved her brother over. "Look at this brick."

He wiped his face with the bottom of his Lake Tahoe T-shirt and crouched down next to her. Brushing bits of orange dirt away from the shape stamped in the center of the brick, he said, "Looks like an anchor."

"I wonder if she ever owned a boat."

J.J. shrugged and returned to the task of rescuing a row of bushes from the greedy vines. The bushes were barely alive. They were spindly and colorless. Their fragility reminded Jill of the prisoners of war in the movies J.J. liked.

Jill tied off her second garbage bag and dragged it to the curb. She had no idea how long they'd been working. And even though she was hot and thirsty, she had no desire to go home. The brick path had curved to the right at first but was now curving back to the left. She wanted to follow the wave of bricks to the center—to the heart of the ruined garden.

She and J.J. didn't talk much. Occasionally, he'd pause to show her a bit of detritus caught in a nest of the vines or speared by a thorn. There was a bleached comic strip, a torn Thurman Munson baseball card, and a scrap of pink ribbon.

"It'd be cool if we found some money. Or old jewelry." He slowly ripped the baseball card until Munson's head separated from his body. "I should bring my metal detector up here."

Jill shot a wary glance at Mrs. Smith's house. There was no window on the ground floor, but there were two on the floor above. Mrs. Smith could be looking down at them right now. Watching.

"Better not," she whispered.

She'd almost filled another bag with moss and weeds when her trowel revealed a line of bricks moving in another direction. It seemed she'd finally reached an intersection. The path continued meandering to the east but also split off, heading north and south as well. There was a round stone in the middle of the place where the paths crossed.

Jill wondered if she'd uncovered a rose compass, but then she saw grooves carved into the center stone. Strange symbols ran around its perimeter.

"J.J.!" she hissed. "You have to see this!"

Her brother was dragging a massive hairball of vines toward the garden door. He was red-faced and sweaty. His arms were mottled with dirt and small lacerations. Glowering at her, he warned, "This better be good."

Jill knew that voice. Her brother was angry. He wanted to hit or kick or swat at something.

She didn't want that something to be her.

"Look. It's a face."

J.J. lumbered over and put his hands on his hips, fully prepared to disparage his sister. But the sneer forming on his lips evaporated when he looked down at the image. "What the hell?"

Jill pointed to the path leading from the door to the side of the face, then to the start of another path jutting out from higher on the face. "I think it's a sun. The paths are, like, the sun's rays."

Grabbing her trowel, J.J. scraped along the edge of the

stone until a series of diamond shapes began to emerge. They looked like snake scales.

"Maybe it's Medusa," Jill said.

"Jesus Christ. You're *obsessed* with her. Just because you did that book report at the end of the year doesn't mean everyone is into Greek myth. I mean, duh. Don't be such a dolt. No normal person would have a Medusa head in their garden."

Mrs. Smith isn't normal.

"Use your brain for two seconds," J.J. sneered. "The bricks have anchors. The face has scales. The house is on the water. It's a fucking mermaid."

He walked back to the mass of vines and dragged them out of the garden.

As Jill scraped more dirt and moss from the circular stone, scales continued to emerge around the edges.

She pulled a tapestry of small stubborn roots away from the bowed lips and wide, flat nose. The eyes were narrow ovals under a heavy brow. The woman wasn't pretty like the mermaids Jill had seen in books. Her unsmiling mouth and lowered brow made her look angry.

Determined to prove J.J. wrong, Jill started probing the ground for more bricks. If more wavy paths grew out of the stone head, this woman had to be Medusa.

Jill worked as if in a fever dream, sliding her trowel under thatches of moss, tugging grass, and yanking out dandelions. She filled another garbage bag. Then another.

The drone of wasps became more persistent. More gnats gathered. The hostile buzz of a horsefly sounded in Jill's ears. She idly swatted the insect away.

Suddenly, a shadow moved though the grass a few feet in front of her right hand. It shot forward quickly, the grass blades shivering in its wake.

The thing could be a field mouse or a chipmunk, Jill told herself. But it hadn't scurried like a rodent. It had slithered. Like a snake.

Jill froze.

She hadn't seen a snake since last summer, when she and her father were working in the vegetable garden. A little green snake, no bigger than the ruler in Jill's pencil case, had poked its head out from under the leaves of a cucumber vine.

"Careful," her dad had said. "We don't want to hurt him. He's good for the garden because he eats bugs."

The thing in Mrs. Smith's grass was much bigger than the green snake. And darker. Jill stared at the spot where the grass had moved, searching for a shape. A shadow.

Behind her, J.J. let out a groan of frustration. Jill turned to see him wrestling with a vine as thick as his forearm.

She turned back to the grass in time to catch another movement. An S-shaped wave formed in the grass, traveling away from her. She caught flashes of dark brown or black, and then all was still again.

Jill didn't resume her work. She stared at the stone face and remembered a Sunday school lesson from when she was Justin's age. She didn't recall everything, only that their class had been learning about Adam and Eve. The teacher had shown them a painting of the Garden of Eden, and Jill's eyes had gone right to the snake coiled around a tree trunk. It had a shovel-shaped head and a forked tongue. The tongue, which was black as tar, caressed the swollen curve of a bloodred fruit.

The horsefly buzz grew louder, and Jill snapped to attention. She didn't want to be bitten by a fly, a wasp, or anything else. She didn't want to startle another snake. There could be a copperhead in this wild garden. Maybe even a rattlesnake.

"They hunt at night in the summer, and I've never seen

one," her father had told her the day she'd seen the green snake. She'd asked him what other snakes lived on Long Island, and if any were poisonous.

They hunt at night.

His words drifted in her head, merging with the angry thrum of the horsefly. The wasps were getting closer. Mud daubers and yellowjackets swooped lower and lower. A mosquito landed on her arm and bit her before she had the chance to flatten it with her hand. Flicking its body into the dirt, she grimaced at the thin streak of blood on her skin and the huge red welt already rising. It itched so badly that she had to take off her glove and scratch it. She scratched and scratched until it no longer itched but burned.

"What time is it?" she asked her brother. She'd had enough of Mrs. Smith's garden for one day.

"Almost noon."

"Why isn't Mom ringing the bell?"

"Because she loves it that we're up here, sweating our asses off and dying of thirst."

Jill was about to put her glove back on when she saw a wink of iridescent green from an object wedged in between two bricks. She leaned over for a better look. Whatever it was had serrated edges, like a bread knife, and a pointy end.

She pinched the object between her fingers and pulled it from the dirt. She didn't know why she bothered. It was probably just a piece of a mussel shell. She'd cut the bottoms of her feet on the stupid shells more times than she could count, but she'd never seen one glow green before. Nor had she seen one that had broken into a perfect diamond like this one.

Using her shirt to wipe off the rest of the dirt, she held it up to the light. The black shell flashed green and silver. Jill was mesmerized by its beauty.

Glancing to her left, she stared at the woman trapped in the stone. Then she looked from the diamond-shaped scales around the edge of the woman's face to the shell cupped in her palm.

Suddenly, the clamor of a ringing bell sailed through the air. The sound startled Jill and she reflexively balled her hand into a fist. The serrated edges of the shell pierced her skin.

Yelping in pain, she dropped the thing on the ground.

"What are you doing?" J.J. yelled. "Stop spacing out and let's go!"

Jill didn't respond. She just sat there, staring at her palm.

Tiny beads of blood appeared where her Head and Fate lines intersected. Then the beads swelled and merged, forming new lines. Those lines became a shape. A diamond, just like ones on the stone woman's face.

It's not a shell.

Jill picked up the black scale. After tucking it in her pocket, she gathered her tools and followed her brother out of the garden.

At home, she washed her hands in the bathroom, horrified and fascinated by the bloody shape in the center of her palm.

The wound looked just like an eye.

17
Mrs. Smith

Magazines were spread across Mrs. Smith's bathroom floor. Every cover featured the headshot of a beautiful woman. There were movie stars and models. Royal princesses and pageant queens. Mrs. Smith leaned over the lip of a hot tub, assessing their faces with a critical gaze.

The female humans had changed a great deal in a hundred years.

The last time Mrs. Smith had worn a woman's shape, her dark hair had been swept high onto the back of her head, leaving a few tantalizing ringlets to frame her face. Her body had been a perfect hourglass with high, soft breasts and curvy hips. Her skin had been pale as milk. Her round, luminous eyes had a doll-like quality. Her pouty lips were as red as a fairy-tale apple.

Back then, women were laced into their garments. Mrs. Smith's corsets enhanced her tiny waist. The low-cut necklines of her gowns showed off her lush breasts. Layers of crinoline under her full skirts made her look like she was gliding instead of walking. The bustles on the backs of her gowns accentuated the swaying of her hips.

Like other wealthy women of the late 1800s, Mrs. Smith's dresses were made of the finest materials. She owned gowns of every color. They were custom-made out of silk, taffeta, and velvet and embellished with lace or exquisite embroidery. She favored items in dark purple, a color reserved for the upper classes.

In addition to her gowns, gloves, shawls, and hats, she had a box stuffed with jewelry. Emerald and diamond necklaces. Jet chokers. Jade bracelets. Pearl earrings. A ruby brooch. Opal pendants. Tortoiseshell and diamond hair combs. She had several tiaras. She needed a separate chest for all of her gold jewelry, and no one ever saw her wear the same piece twice.

Fresh orchids were delivered to her house on a regular basis, and she always pinned the deep purple flowers to her dress or had them woven into her hair before she went out. The flower's shape and color reminded her of an ochre sea star.

Back then, securing a wardrobe had been easy. Dressmakers, milliners, jewelers, shoemakers, perfumers, chemists, and florists came to her. She had servants to dress her, apply her makeup, and style her hair. She paid three times the going rate and deliberately sought out individuals who were mute, deaf, or so desperate for money that she knew she could rely on their discretion.

She did not require their services for long. Even at the height of her powers, she abhorred having to maintain a human form. But it could take many months to stimulate her reproductive cycle and put her finances in order. As impatient as she always was to return to the water, she had to make provisions for her future. During this time, she purchased coastal properties, invested in gold, and sold precious relics harvested from the ocean floor to rich private collectors.

Mrs. Smith never wanted for funds. Her coin collection alone was worth millions. For centuries, she'd pilfered shipwrecks for treasures, accumulating an extraordinary horde of riches. She could open a lockbox hidden in any number of sea caves and pluck out a Persian daric, a Spanish doubloon, or a gold aureus from Rome. By selling a few coins, she gained enough capital to ornament herself, hire servants, and invest in the future.

A century ago, she purchased land along Long Island's North Shore, properties on the Connecticut and Massachusetts coasts, and a private island in Maine. Her assets were managed by the Bank of New York. Her current financial advisor believed her to be the granddaughter of the Mrs. Smith who'd once done business with his grandfather.

On Monday, she'd instructed her advisor to transfer twenty thousand dollars to her checking account. After ending the call, she'd unlocked her wall safe and counted her cash.

Confident that she had enough to purchase a basic wardrobe, she'd begun studying beauty and fashion magazines as well as clothing catalogs. She'd torn pages from Neiman Marcus, Saks Fifth Avenue, and Lord & Taylor catalogs.

These stores were familiar to Mrs. Smith. Having flipped through such publications for years, she'd grown accustomed to the idea that clothing was no longer tailored to the individual but bought "off the rack." However, she didn't want items made to fit any body. She wanted pieces designed just for her—clothing that would help her outshine all other women.

And yet, time was of the essence. The yacht club cocktail party would take place in ten days. During this event, she would select her mates. After that, there was the man-child's bar mitzvah, and the awakening of Mrs. Smith's full power. In between these two significant occasions, she needed to meet with her banker and lawyers. She needed to make provisions for her offspring.

Even if it meant her own death, Mrs. Smith had decided to

reproduce. She would devour as many Pure Ones as she could. Then, when she was freshly reborn and brimming with power and vitality, she'd swim to the underwater cave on her island in Maine and tear herself in two.

However, she couldn't go outside in her human form without the correct attire. The chests of clothes that had languished in her house since the 1880s hadn't aged well. The dresses were moth-eaten. The chemises and slips were yellow with age.

She'd have to build a wardrobe from scratch, but first, she needed to decide what her human form should look like. The ideal body shape of a female in 1982 was taller, slimmer, and more athletic than the women of the Gilded Age. Brows were bushy and dark. Lashes were thick and curled. Lips were full. Cheekbones were high. Teeth were big, square, and white as ship sails.

The women on Mrs. Smith's bathroom floor, smiling out from the covers of *Vogue*, *Harper's Bazaar*, and *Cosmopolitan*, looked healthy and confident. Their gazes were both knowing and playful. They were beautiful and ambitious. They were more powerful than the women who'd come before.

Mrs. Smith could easily adapt their more desirable physical features, but she also had to dress, move, and speak in such a way that every human in her sphere would feel compelled to please her. Especially the men. Men like Don Pulaski.

Mrs. Smith had seen Don's blonde mate come and go from the Bernstein and Scott houses. She was short and busty with a cloud of honey-colored hair. In contrast, Mrs. Smith would make herself taller. Her limbs would be long and toned. Her dark hair would fall in soft waves down her back.

With the power of the Pure Ones' blood coursing through her veins, she could transform into any of the women she saw on the magazine covers. She could be Linda Evangelista, Jerry Hall, Carol Alt, Christie Brinkley, Cindy Crawford, Isabella

Rossellini, or Princess Diana. But as her gaze swept across face after face, the one she kept coming back to belonged to a blue-eyed brunette named Brooke Shields.

Mrs. Smith decided to make herself look like a slightly more mature version of this young woman. She would choose a different eye color, too. In the waterways of the world, blue eyes were found only on an inconsequential Australian fish—a weak sliver of a creature that spent its short life feeding on mosquito larvae.

According to *Vogue*, beauty required an arsenal of cosmetics. To resemble Brooke Shields, Mrs. Smith would have to create a smoky eye. This was achieved with powdered eyeshadow, mascara, and heavy black gel liner on the upper and lower lids. This bold look, reminiscent of the kohl used by Egyptian queens, was one of drama and glamour.

Other makeup trends included bright pink, metallic, or red lips. Sometimes, the lips were heavily lined. Blush was applied generously to the cheeks to create lift and brightness. Nail color often matched the lips. Mrs. Smith studied the popular pinks—which ranged from fuchsia to plum to bubblegum—but didn't like any of them. The shades reminded her of seahorses or sea anemones.

She surveyed the bold palettes from Revlon, L'Oréal, Max Factor, Estée Lauder, and Elizabeth Arden. She dismissed the products made by CoverGirl and Maybelline because they were too pedestrian. Too affordable. Everything she bought must be of the highest quality. She had to light up a room like a firefly squid in a black ocean, to sparkle like a gossamer worm.

This was why she studied the current fashion trends so carefully. In her realm, creatures didn't see in color. The deeper they swam, the darker it became.

In the water, it was best to be as black as a starless night. The women in the magazines wore electrifying shades of pink, orange, red, and yellow. Their clothes had bright patterns, like those of a flame angelfish or the mandarin dragonet. They resembled a coral reef habitat, these women in their wide-shouldered blouses with irregular stripes. They looked like clownfish and guppies, purple firefish and royal grammas.

Mrs. Smith remembered the tropics well, though she hadn't swum in warm waters for centuries. She preferred the solitude and safety of the Arctic. In this black and frigid world, light was more magical than color. And the only visible light produced by creatures in the deepest, most secret ocean trenches was blue. A blinding, electric blue. That would be her color of power for this cycle.

Now that she'd made this decision, all she had to do was find the right dress for the yacht club cocktail party. She flipped through more magazines, which were already dimpled from moisture, and examined designs by men like Karl Lagerfeld, Yves Saint Laurent, and Giorgio Armani. She tore out photo after photo of outfits designed by Perry Ellis and Oscar de la Renta, balling them up and tossing them to the side.

Nothing seemed timeless. Nothing seduced her senses. The dresses were neither fluid in movement nor flawless in construction.

The only designer who came close to her ideal was Dior. He'd made a satin dress in royal blue with beaded velvet floral appliqués. The beads curled up one side of the gown, from just above the ankle to just below the left breast. The serpentine tendrils reminded Mrs. Smith of the oriental bittersweet vines growing wild in her woods.

It'll have to do.

Mrs. Smith found an article detailing the body measurements of the world's top models and decided these bodies were too thin. She wanted to resemble a violin, not a flute.

Throughout the centuries, the human male had changed little. His attention was easily captured by long, lustrous hair, plump lips, the swell of high breasts, and the undulating sway of full hips.

After stacking a pile of photos on one corner of the hot tub, Mrs. Smith willed her vocal cords to adapt to a human voice and then poked at the illuminated number keys on her phone.

"Lord & Taylor, this is Mindy, how may I help you?"

"Hello," Mrs. Smith croaked. Recalling the clarity and softness of a female voice the humans seemed to find appealing, she began to talk in a perfect semblance to Julie Andrews. "I would like to speak with the individual in charge of personal shopping."

"That would be Muriel O'Connell. Please hold while I get her on the line."

Mrs. Smith shifted, causing water to sluice over the edge of the hot tub and soak the magazine pages she'd set aside. The ink began to bleed, seeping into the tub water like fluids leaking from a pestilent corpse.

Irritated, Mrs. Smith flicked them off the ledge with the barbed tip of a tentacle.

"Hello, this is Muriel O'Connell. How may I be of service?"

"My name is Mrs. Smith. I am recently recovered from a long illness, rendering my previous wardrobe obsolete. I require an immediate replacement. Time is of the essence, and money is of no consequence. Do you possess a writing implement?"

After a brief pause, Muriel said, "I have a pen."

"Then I'll begin with my measurements."

She rattled off the numbers and explained that she preferred pieces designed by Christian Dior. "Of paramount importance is a cocktail dress. I have a particular item in mind. A size four would be suitable as long as it can be tailored to my measurements."

"Certainly."

Mrs. Smith was pleased. This Muriel person was as pliable as seaweed. All servants were the same. The slightest whiff of a generous gratuity and they'd grovel like the weakest puppy of the litter.

Mrs. Smith had learned to be generous with her servants. Hers had always been an unusual house. Wherever she lived, there were locked rooms containing oversized bathtubs filled with salt water and at least one indoor pool. Many areas were off-limits to staff. Anyone caught breaking her rules would live to regret it.

Disobedient servants were dealt with swiftly and severely. Mrs. Smith would spread word of their untrustworthy nature among the gentry, ensuring they'd never find employment with the upper classes again. If the recalcitrant servant had children, she'd kill one if not all of them. That was all it took for the rest of her staff to fall into line.

As Muriel struggled to keep up, Mrs. Smith listed her needs. She wanted cocktail dresses, frilly sundresses, leisure wear, delicate lingerie, string bikinis, wide-brimmed hats, sunglasses, stilettos, Capezios, oversized earrings, colorful necklaces, chunky bracelets, wide belts, and handbags. She wanted makeup, hair products, and multiple fragrances.

"I need everything delivered to my house. I have a condition that prevents me from driving."

"Oh." Muriel's voice deflated. "In that case, we would have to ship everything to your home. I'm afraid we don't deliver."

"I'd compensate the driver two hundred dollars for the inconvenience."

"Oh?" Muriel repeated with renewed enthusiasm.

Mrs. Smith recited her address and phone number and then informed Muriel that she would write a check for the total amount.

Muriel said, "It'll take a few days to get everything together."

Irritated, Mrs. Smith gripped the phone headset so hard that it began to crack. "I need the everyday items tomorrow. If you can expedite the process, I'd be most grateful."

Perhaps Muriel heard the hard edge of Mrs. Smith's tone and, fearing she might lose her biggest sale of the year, haltingly explained that the tailoring department couldn't even begin altering the items until they'd been paid for.

Mrs. Smith imagined curling her tentacles around Muriel's body and squeezing until the woman's ribs snapped. She hated entering the human world. She hated their rules and customs. Their ever-changing manner of speech. They rarely spoke plainly or truthfully. They flattered, lied, obfuscated, and deflected. They were a selfish, grasping species, and the sooner she could create another of her kind, the sooner she and her offspring could destroy more humans and the structures and vessels dumping poison into the oceans.

"Very well," she grumbled. "If you can provide me with a figure, I will write a check and have it delivered into your hands today."

Again, Muriel faltered. "I do apologize, Mrs. Smith, but when dealing with such large amounts, we usually wait for the check to clear before starting on the tailoring. It'll take two days. Three at most."

Anger swept through Mrs. Smith's body, electrifying her newly empowered cells. She could morph into a human form right now, call a taxicab, and travel to the department store. She could hunt down this Muriel woman and punish her for putting obstacles in her path.

She could drag her into a storage or fitting room and crush her skull between her hands. Even in her human form, Mrs. Smith was formidable. She would take great pleasure in killing this insipid creature. She would bite her flesh while the woman was still alive. She would paint the walls with her blood.

For a moment, she was overcome with a desire to feed, but as Muriel's simpering voice wormed into her ear, she calmed herself. "In that case, I shall pay in cash. I presume there is no waiting period for cash."

"There isn't, but—"

"Tell me, Muriel. Did I make a mistake? Should I have called Saks instead of Lord & Taylor? Because I'm beginning to believe I might be better served there."

"No, no!" Muriel cried. "And a check is fine. *Absolutely* fine. We'll do whatever it takes to get your order processed and tailored as soon as possible. We appreciate your business and value you as a customer."

Seeing no need to reply, Mrs. Smith ended the call and sank deeper into the water. The time to change had come.

She wasn't slipping into a temporary skin the way she did each night before walking down to the boathouse. That form, featureless as a store mannequin, lasted a few minutes only. This time, she would do a full change. One that would last for weeks. One that caused her a world of pain to perform.

She wrapped her tentacles around her body, creating a cocoon. Her limbs drew in, tighter and tighter, until every inch of her body was underwater.

Then, she released her power.

The water in the hot tub began to bubble. As Mrs. Smith writhed and twisted, water sloshed over the side of the tub. Her cartilage fractured and reformed. Her spine shortened and her lower tentacles fused together. Her arm tentacles split at the ends into hands. The hands split into fingers.

Loose scales and claws roiled in the water. Bits of black fluke stuck to the sides of the tub. The water went from pink to red to vermillion. Chunks of tissue bobbed to the surface.

Finally, the violent movements in the water stopped.

Much later, when Mrs. Smith reached for the phone, she punched in numbers with her human fingers.

When a man answered, Mrs. Smith's lovely mouth curved into a grin. "Hello, Don," she purred. "I've been thinking about you."

18
Natalie

The Thursday following the regatta, Natalie fed the kids and the dogs, cleaned up the kitchen, and went into her room to get ready for work.

The TV in the basement was so loud that she could hear the frenetic music of a Looney Tunes cartoon right through the floor, but she decided to cut the older kids some slack.

Sailing classes wouldn't start again until next Monday. However, after receiving a call from the yacht club yesterday, she'd learned that the kids of working parents could attend a free arts and crafts class after today's swim team practice.

That means your kids. You're *now a working parent.*

Even though J.J. and Jill made it clear that they had no interest in making God's eyes out of yarn, the thought that they qualified for a special class made Natalie's chest expand with pride. That is, until a competing thought wriggled to the forefront of her mind.

You'll be lucky to last the summer. Sid gave you an impossible property because he wants you to fail. And after that disastrous open house? You will.

"No," she said out loud, her lips narrowing as she picked

at a speck of hardened toothpaste in the sink. "I just need to find the right buyer."

In the bathroom, she teased and sprayed her hair until she looked like Michelle Marsh, an evening news anchor. Not only did she and Michelle share an alma mater, but Natalie liked the other woman's voice and how she styled her hair. She often copied her makeup and was inspired by the bold colors of her blazers.

Natalie was just about to apply her lipstick when someone knocked on her bedroom door.

"Come in!"

Jill appeared in the bathroom doorway. She was still in her nightgown even though she should have been getting ready for swim practice.

"Why aren't you in your suit?"

Jill cradled her right hand as if it might fall off without support. Natalie had seen a Band-Aid on her daughter's palm after she'd worked at Mrs. Smith's, but she hadn't asked Jill what happened. Her kids always had minor cuts and bruises, insect bites, and splinters. They were a natural part of any good childhood. Her children were given the freedom to learn things for themselves. To solve their own problems and deal with their own challenges. Because of that, they'd be ready for the real world. If Jill cut her hand, she knew how to clean it and bandage it. Natalie was raising independent, capable children.

Children like Charles, coddled until they were practically adults, wouldn't be able to handle themselves in a fast-paced, competitive world. After the regatta, Elaine and Benjamin should've encouraged their son to go out, to be around other kids. Instead, Elaine would probably put him under glass until his bar mitzvah.

Natalie's sympathy for the boy was waning with every

passing day. Had he really seen something horrible or was he just using the tragedy to avoid sailing class?

Elaine's decision to let him stay home, watching movies and playing video games while she plied him with his favorite foods, was a horrible idea.

"She's raising a mouse instead of a man," Jimmy had said last night. "J.J. and Charles are eleven months apart, but you'd think it was five years."

This morning, over breakfast, Natalie had taken a long look at her eldest son. He seemed even taller than he had at the end of the school year. Sunlight and chlorine had turned his hair platinum, and his torso was tanned and muscular. He'd been upset by the disappearance of the two boys, but he was starting to come around. He ate heartily and chugged two glasses of orange juice. Then he belched near Jill's ear, hoping to elicit a response.

He didn't get one.

Jill didn't even move. She wore the vacant look of a lobotomy patient as she pushed cold scrambled eggs around her plate.

Nothing a little fresh air, exercise, and time with her peers can't cure. She needs to learn how to push through.

Jill and J.J. had spent the last two days clearing debris from Mrs. Smith's garden. There were so many trash bags at the curb that Natalie wondered if any plants were left behind that tall, rusted iron fence. Not that she cared. Her kids were doing the neighborhood a favor by attacking the chaos that was Mrs. Smith's backyard, and they were being paid handsomely for their efforts.

They never saw Mrs. Smith, but at some point during the night, she'd placed two envelopes of cash in the Scotts' mailbox. Natalie hadn't asked her kids how much they'd earned, but she had a feeling it was more than Mrs. Smith originally promised.

The kids were scheduled to work for another three hours that afternoon, and Natalie hoped Jill wasn't going to try to worm her way out of her commitment.

"Why are you holding your hand like that?" she asked her daughter.

"I cut it at Mrs. Smith's. There was this—I don't know—thorn? Scale? It was sharp. I washed my hand when I got home, but it really hurts."

Natalie beckoned for Jill to join her at the sink. "Lemme see."

Of all her children, Jill had the highest pain tolerance. Considering she was also the most accident-prone, that was a good thing. To hear her say that a cut on her palm really hurt was out of character.

Jill peeled off the Band-Aid. Then she moved her hand closer to Natalie's and slowly uncurled her fingers.

The smell hit Natalie like a slap in the face.

Her daughter's hand smelled like their bait bucket. Briny and rotten.

Recoiling, she gestured for Jill to toss the Band-Aid in the trash can under the sink. Then she studied her daughter's wound.

The skin in the center of her palm was puckered. The red-purple lines surrounding a dark purple circle looked like an almond. Or an eye.

Natalie gently pressed on the skin. "Looks infected."

Jill let out a hiss and snatched her hand away.

The reaction took Natalie by surprise. "Did you use iodine? You didn't, did you? I can tell."

"Just soap."

Natalie shrugged. "There you go. You know you have to clean cuts with iodine."

"But it stings!"

"That's why you blow on it. Soap isn't enough. You'll have to soak your hand in a bowl for a few minutes and then use the iodine. Show Una. She'll know what to do."

Natalie turned back to the mirror and applied her lipstick. Next, she dabbed perfume on her wrists and behind her ears. She could sense Jill watching her. Her daughter had more to say.

Annoyed by the weighty silence, Natalie said, "What is it? I need to go."

"Should I go to swim practice after I soak my hand?"

Natalie's eyes moved over Jill's body. "Of course you should. It won't make your hand worse. If anything, it'll help."

"What about Mrs. Smith's?"

Natalie's patience ran out. She shook her hairbrush at her daughter. "You have a commitment. In this family, if we say we're going to do something, we do it."

For once, Jill didn't talk back.

Natalie descended the spiral staircase, her heels clack clacking with every step. In the TV room, she kissed Justin's cherubic cheek and shooed Lady off the sofa.

"Don't be late for practice!" she yelled at J.J. through his closed door. She heard him singing "Fernando" and smiled to herself. J.J. had gotten hooked on ABBA last summer and played their *Greatest Hits* all the time.

Natalie remembered when music had been a huge part of her life. Back when she was single, living in a shoebox of an apartment in the Village, she'd been surrounded by music. And so much more. There'd been art and restaurants and such interesting people.

She and her girlfriends spent their weekends in smoky clubs. She'd heard the Doors, the Byrds, Cream, the Yardbirds, and the Band. She'd rubbed shoulders with Andy Warhol and had drinks with Franz Kline and Roy Lichtenstein. A dozen photographers had asked her to model for them. Other artists wanted her to be their muse. But Natalie's ambitions had nothing to do with art. She was going to be a successful scientist.

She'd been on the right path, too. She'd graduated with a double-major in bio and chem and was hired as a lab assistant for a drug company in Brooklyn. She was the only woman working with a group of scientists studying genetic change and protein expression. Her job was to run experiments to help isolate and analyze DNA, RNA, and proteins. She was fascinated by the work and never tired of staring at bacteria through her microscope. One day, she hoped to be known as the woman who helped eradicate E. coli.

Back then, she still dreamed big.

But after her kind, encouraging boss had a fatal heart attack on the golf course, everything changed. His replacement, the son of the company's CEO, didn't see Natalie as an integral member of the team. He saw her as a conquest.

Ken Hoffman.

"Nope," Natalie muttered as she slid into the driver's seat of the station wagon. "I'm not letting you in. Not today."

It had been years since the man had invaded her thoughts. She'd pushed that asshole's smug face into the far recesses of her mind. This was how she protected herself from the memory of what he'd done. How he'd ruined her career and made her a pariah in the scientific community. No one would hire her after the disaster. No one would have believed her if she'd told what really happened the night of the fire.

Ken Hoffman had threatened to punish her if she didn't give him what he wanted. When she refused, he'd made good on his threat. He'd destroyed one of his own labs and blamed her for the loss of expensive equipment and valuable research.

All because she'd fought him when he tried to rape her.

He'd made a pass at her before, but she'd made it clear she wasn't interested.

"Playing hard to get, eh? That's fine with me, babe. I like a challenge."

He got tired of chasing her very quickly, and one afternoon, after the staff meeting was over, he told her that he needed to speak with her in private. And then he shoved her face against the conference table.

She'd bucked and writhed as he held her head down with one hand and pushed her skirt up with the other. He forced his body between her legs, pinning her with his weight.

She shouted for him to stop. Tried to twist her head so she could bite his hand. He'd just sniggered and tugged at her blouse, ripping off all the delicate pearl buttons at once. His meaty fingers had yanked at her bra, then grabbed one of her breasts. He squeezed her soft flesh with such force that she'd whimpered in pain.

"You know you want it," he'd growled, flecking her ear with spittle. "I've seen how you shake your tight ass and your perfect titties under that lab coat. I've seen you smile at me. No more playing around, baby. I've got what you want right here."

She'd elbowed him as hard as she could, right in his paunch. Then she'd reared back, clocking his face with the top of her head. She freed her legs and ran out of the building, leaving him with a bloody nose and a deflating erection.

Her hands were shaking so badly that it had taken her three tries to unlock her car. When she finally got in and started the engine, she'd kept expecting to see Ken Hoffman in her rear-view mirror. As she drove away and the lab receded behind her, she hadn't known if she could ever go back.

Ken Hoffman had made the choice for her. After all, she'd dared refuse a man who always got what he wanted.

Get a grip. You're not that naive girl from Wisconsin anymore, Natalie told herself as she backed out of the garage.

She needed to be sharp today. She was meeting with new clients this morning, a young couple looking to relocate from Queens. They had two young children and wanted a house with a yard in a good school district. The husband was a doctor, but they were on a tight budget as he had taken out two loans to pay for college and medical school.

It had been a stroke of good luck that Natalie had answered the office phone when Dr. Sherif called earlier in the week.

She should've transferred the call to Rick. His was the next name on the sales board, but he'd already gone under contract on two houses and would be closing on a third before the end of the month.

The spaces next to Natalie's name were still blank, so she took down Dr. Sherif's information and promised to dedicate herself toward finding him the perfect home. He seemed pleased by her enthusiasm and asked for a meeting to review current listings in their price range.

She already knew that there were only two houses available in the good school district, and one of them was very close to the train tracks. The McCreedy house was in a lovely, family-friendly neighborhood. Natalie just had to convince Dr. and Mrs. Sherif that it was the house for them.

Just yesterday, Gina had bragged that her cape would be under contract by the end of the week, so Natalie saw no reason to include it in the listings she planned to show the Sherifs. Instead, she compiled homes for sale at much higher prices than the McCreedy house in an effort to make her listing more attractive.

Her meeting with the Sherifs was scheduled for ten o'clock, so Natalie had plenty of time to swing by the bakery to pick up some Lebanese cookies. She didn't know where Dr. Sherif was originally from, but she knew an Arabic accent when she heard one. When she'd lived in the Village, there were several Turkish families on her floor and the men sounded just like Dr. Sherif.

Even if he's not impressed by the cookies, his wife will be, she thought as she drove slowly up the driveway. Tramp was outside and had a terrible habit of chasing their cars to the street.

At the top of her driveway, she paused, distracted by a slash of red to her left.

Glancing at Mrs. Smith's house, Natalie saw a sports car parked in front of Mrs. Smith's door. Not on the curb outside the electric gate, but right in front of the house.

Natalie recognized the car. It was Don's garnet-red Aston Martin.

"What the hell?"

She hit the brakes and stared at Don's empty car. He wasn't in the car or on the front porch, so where was he?

He's *inside*. With *her*.

She waited a few minutes to see if he'd come out. When he didn't, she wondered if she should knock on Elaine's door and tell her about Don, but she couldn't risk being late. She had important things to do today.

The bakery. The meeting with the Sherifs. Selling the McCreedy house.

Natalie hit the gas and drove up the winding road. When it flattened out near the top, she pulled into Beth's driveway. She shoved the column shifter into Park, left the engine running, and raced to the front door.

She pounded on the thick wood. "Beth! Are you there? It's Natalie!"

She knew it took Beth forever to get ready in the mornings

and wouldn't be surprised if her friend was still in the shower or lingering at her vanity while she painted her nails or nursed a cup of coffee.

"Beth!" Natalie jabbed the doorbell three times in succession. If that didn't convey urgency, she didn't know what would.

Finally, the door cracked. Natalie caught a glimpse of Beth's swollen, tear-streaked face and immediately reached out for her friend.

"What's wrong?"

"It's Don." Beth's voice was hollow. Her eyes were red-rimmed. "We had an appointment at nine. At St. Mary's, a Catholic orphanage. We were going to meet with one of the sisters so she could take us on a tour and introduce us to some of the children. Don doesn't want to adopt, I know he doesn't, but he said he'd go. For me. He said he'd go."

"So, what happened?"

Beth leaned her head against the door frame. "The phone rang an hour ago. I was still in bed, but Don picked it up in the kitchen. He talked to someone for a minute or two and then he took a shower and got dressed. I thought he was getting ready for our appointment, so I got up, too. I was happy, you know? I was so excited to see the kids, but I could tell Don wasn't. He looked mad."

Nothing new there, Natalie thought.

"And?" she prompted.

Beth seemed to shrink. "He said that my only job was to give him a baby, and I'd failed. He said he wasn't going to raise another man's bastard kid—that he'd be better off finding a new wife. Then he left."

"Oh, honey. No wonder you're upset." Natalie rubbed Beth's arm. "Did you see which way he went?"

"What do you mean? He has work. He— Wait. Do you know where he is?"

"I saw his car as I was leaving my house. It's parked across the street."

Color leeched from Beth's face and Natalie hurried to slip an arm around her in case she fainted.

"He's with *her*?"

Natalie hated hurting her friend, but she couldn't lie.

"His car is there. That's all I know. Maybe he's dropping off paperwork for the Porsche or something."

Beth stared at her like she was an idiot. "You didn't see him in the driveway, did you? They weren't out there, chatting about the car. She doesn't come out. That means he's *inside* her house. Isn't he?"

It was impossible to believe. No one in the neighborhood had laid eyes on Mrs. Smith, let alone stepped foot in her home. And yet, where else could he be?

"I *told* you. She has some kind of hold on him," Beth murmured. "She has . . . power."

It was a strange thing to say, but no stranger than the idea of Mrs. Smith wanting something from Don. Loud, brash, uncouth Don. It was beyond comprehension.

Beth's next-door neighbor tooted his horn in greeting as he drove by. As Natalie gave him a perfunctory wave, she noticed the time. She needed to go, but Beth looked so gutted that she didn't see how she could leave her on her own.

"You'll work this out," she said. "All couples go through rough patches. Don loves you."

Her words carried no conviction, and Beth didn't bother responding.

You have a client meeting, said the devil on Natalie's shoulder.

You can't leave her like this, said her better angel.

Yes, you can. You need to sell the McCreedy house.

She's your friend.

Your name isn't on the sales board. Sid said the market dies in August, and August isn't far away. Get on the board, or your career will die, too.

An image of her Electrolux, sitting in the laundry closet like a leashed dog waiting to be walked, flashed in Natalie's mind.

"I'm really sorry, Beth, but I have to go. As soon as Don comes back, he'll tell you why he was at Mrs. Smith's. I'm sure it was just about the car. I'll call you later, okay?"

Natalie tried to give her friend a quick hug, but Beth retreated into the shadows of her foyer. She stood straight as an arrow, her arms pinned to her side. Her eyes were two pinpricks shining out of the gloom. She looked hollowed out. She looked like a ghost.

Staring at her friend, all the tiny hairs on the back of Natalie's neck stood on end. "Is there anything I can do?"

Beth shook her head once and then slammed the door in Natalie's face.

19
Una

Una spread blackberry jam on Kristofer's toast and transferred three sausages from the frying pan to his plate.

Her husband appeared in the kitchen as if magicked there by the scent of coffee and grease. He gave her a kiss on the cheek. "You're up early, love."

Una pointed at the rain-freckled window. "The thunder woke me."

Kristofer poured coffee into his favorite Cornell mug and held out the carafe. "Would you like some?"

"I'm having tea this morning. This gray day reminds me of home."

If Kristofer found it strange that she still referred to Iceland as home after all this time, he didn't show it. "It's a good day for reading, eh?"

Una sat down at their little table. "Reading and baking. I think I'll make enough *Rúgbrauð* for us and the Scotts."

Her husband's eyes creased at the corners as he imagined slathering butter over a slice of his wife's hearty rye bread. *Rúgbrauð* was a staple in Iceland, and though there was plenty of rye bread available in New York, none of them tasted quite right. They lacked the density and mild sweetness of Una's bread.

"I'll stop by the library while I'm in Greenlawn," Una said. "Do you have books to return?"

"I haven't finished any yet. Too much baseball watching."

Thunder rumbled low in the sky and Una glanced out the window. "No one will be sailing today. They'll all be safe at home."

Kristofer studied his wife over the rim of his coffee cup. "How are the children?"

"J.J. seems fine, but I'm worried about Jill. She's been very quiet. I told you about that cut on her hand? Well, it's not healing right."

"I'm sure her parents will keep an eye on it this weekend. If it gets worse, they can take her to the doctor." Kristofer licked a spot of jam from his finger. "Speaking of things getting worse, the tap in the bathroom is dripping again. I'll fix it today."

The hardware store was next to Kristofer's favorite pizza place, and he often looked for an excuse to pop into the former so he could patronize the latter. Una smiled. "So, you're having two slices of pepperoni for lunch. I should go to the library early because you'll need the car."

"You know me too well. Want anything from the market while I'm out?"

"Some cod? I thought we'd have baked fish with our bread tonight."

Kristofer removed a little notepad from his pocket and turned to a fresh page. "Any fruit? You haven't had a nectarine yet this summer."

Una laughed. "You know *me* so well. Pick whatever looks good. A little sunshine on a rainy day."

After breakfast, Una folded the laundry she'd started in between her first and second cups of tea. When all the clothes were put away, she glanced at the clock. The library would be opening in fifteen minutes, and Una planned to be there the moment Mrs. Stapleton unlocked the door.

She packed her library books in her tote bag and zipped up her raincoat. After tying the strings of her rain bonnet under her chin, she rooted around in the hall closet for her umbrella, then shouted good-bye to Kristofer.

The wipers of her VW Bug swished furiously as she drove from Cold Harbor to Greenlawn. She pulled into the library lot, parked the car, and hurried to the front door. Though the library had been open for only three minutes, Una was not the first patron inside. That honor belonged to a twelve-year-old girl in a dripping yellow slicker, wet jeans, and soggy sneakers.

"Jill!" Una cried. "You're soaked."

Jill passed a hand over her damp forehead. "I rode my bike here."

That's almost three miles, thought Una. *Why would she make such a trip in the rain?*

Mrs. Stapleton came out from behind the circulation desk carrying a towel. She handed it to Jill. "It's not pretty, but it's clean."

"Thanks, Mrs. Stapleton. Sorry about the carpet."

Una looked down and saw shoe prints dampening the smoke-gray carpet.

"That'll dry in no time. The carpet can handle anything except for gum, and I haven't caught you with a piece of Bazooka since you were Justin's age." Mrs. Stapleton cocked her head. "Are kids still chewing Bazooka? Or am I hopelessly out of touch?"

"I like Bubble Yum, but J.J. likes Bazooka because of the comic."

Mrs. Stapleton grinned. "Me, too. Now, is there something I can help you find or are you just browsing?"

Jill fidgeted with the zipper pull on her jacket. "I'm looking for books on Medusa."

The librarian's gaze slid over to the wooden card catalog drawers. "I think you've already read most of our Greek mythology books."

"What about monsters like her? From other places besides Greece."

The librarian nodded enthusiastically. "Sure, sure. You can check out myths from other cultures first and then see what we've got in the fables and folklore section. So, you'll start in 291 and end up in 398.2."

"Okay."

Jill was about to move off when Mrs. Stapleton grabbed her arm. "Why don't you leave your jacket with me? I'll hang it on the coatrack, and by the time you're ready to head home, it'll be nice and dry."

Shucking off her jacket, Jill flashed Una a small, apologetic smile before hustling away.

"That child and her creatures. Gorgons. Sharks. Dragons. I remember when she was obsessed with unicorns." A wistful expression came over Mrs. Stapleton's features. Then, she sighed and beckoned for Una to follow her to her office. "I hope you didn't ride a bike because I've got a whole box of stuff for you, which you're welcome to take home. All I ask is that you're gentle with my father's papers. They were very important to him."

"I'll be very careful. Thank you for trusting me with his things."

In her office, Mrs. Stapleton pointed at a cardboard box marked DAD'S RESEARCH—COLD HARBOR and said, "I don't know what you're looking for, and I don't think anything in here will explain what happened to those boys, but if there's the slightest chance it can help, then it's worth the effort. Now, if you'll excuse me, I need to get back on the floor. I'm by myself until noon and I have a pile of returns to process."

Picking up the box, Una trailed after the librarian. When they reached the circulation desk, Una said, "May I leave this here for a minute? I want to see if I can give Jill a ride home."

"Please do. She and the books will both be drenched if she goes back out in this deluge."

Una walked past bookshelves, peering down the 200s–300s aisle without seeing Jill. She found her in the 500s, sitting cross-legged on the floor, books spread out all around her. It looked almost ritualistic, the way the books formed a circle around the girl, especially considering most of the illustrations featured snakes or dragon-like lizards.

"There you are," Una said. "Are you still hunting for Medusa?"

Jill refused to meet her gaze. "No. Something else."

"Another monster that's part snake?"

Jill kept her eyes glued to the book in front of her, which had a double-page illustration of a horned viper. Just looking at it made Una's skin crawl. There were no snakes in Iceland, and Una had yet to encounter one in her garden. Hoping to keep it that way, she'd planted extra garlic, onions, and marigolds around the perimeter and routinely sprayed vinegar on the ground to deter them from slithering into her yard.

As far as Una knew, Jill wasn't afraid of snakes. However, her red cheeks were pink with embarrassment, and she was on the verge of tears. Una knelt down and laid a hand on Jill's shoulder.

"What it is, sweetheart?"

Jill's fist hovered over a book page filled with photographs of reptile scales. The patterns were characterized as tubercular, imbricate, or overlapping. Under these headings were more categories like rhomboid, polygonal, juxtaposed, or granular.

"I was looking for a match for this." Jill opened her fist to reveal a diamond-shaped object. "This is what cut me. I think it's a scale. Like this one."

She pointed at an illustration under a caption reading MUCRONATE SCALES. Una glanced between the scale and the illustration. According to the book, a mucro was a sharp point. The scale from Mrs. Smith's garden had sharp points at both ends.

"But it's also shaped like this one." Jill tapped a photo labeled GANOID SCALES. "Diamond-shaped. Some reptiles have these, but this book says they're also on a fish called a gar. It's a really old fish. It has teeth and it eats other fish."

Jill picked up another book and showed Una a photo of a gar's mouth. Its jaw was loaded with dozens of needlelike teeth.

"Oh, my," Una whispered. "That mouth looks like two saws coming together."

"Gar eggs are poisonous. To humans, anyway." Jill picked up the scale and held it out to Una. "This is too thick to be a fish or snake scale. It's more like a crocodile's, but the shape is wrong."

Una gingerly poked one of the sharp ends into the soft flesh of her finger. "Imagine a whole body covered with these."

Jill didn't answer. She frowned at the stack of mythology and folklore books. She wouldn't be able to fit them all in her bike basket, which meant she had to skim through several of them before she left.

Una regretted that she hadn't been able to convince Natalie to keep the kids away from Mrs. Smith's yard. She'd used the only reasons she could think of—poison ivy and wasps—and her attempt had failed. If only she'd taken the kids to the movies, Jill wouldn't have gotten hurt.

"How's your hand today?" she asked.

"It still hurts, but the soaking helped."

They fell quiet, listening to raindrops pummel the roof. At one point, Jill seemed on the verge of speaking, but then her gaze fell on the strange scale, and she bit back whatever she was going to say.

Una heard murmuring from other patrons and knew she couldn't leave the box at the circulation desk much longer. She also couldn't leave Jill. The girl had ridden her bike in the rain in search of answers. The scale had cut Jill's skin like a scalpel and Una didn't think the wound was healing properly. She understood why Jill was trying to identify it.

The scale came from Eel's Nest.

Una thought of the black-and-white photo she'd seen the last time she'd been in the library. Even now, she felt the darkness of that woman's stare.

Had Jill seen something, too? Something outside the realm of belief?

Turning the scale this way and that, Una said, "You said the gar is a very old fish. Maybe this also came from a very old animal. Like a fossil. Was there anything else in the garden that seemed old?"

Jill met Una's curious gaze. "There's a stone face with a bunch of wavy brick paths coming out of it. I thought it was a sun at first. Or maybe Medusa. J.J. thinks it's a mermaid—that the paths are her hair—but she's got a mean face. She could be a siren, I guess. In some books, they look like mermaids. They sing to sailors until they jump overboard and drown."

"So, it's a mean face surrounded by wavy rays?"

Jill's brow furrowed. "Actually, there weren't any paths coming off the top of her face, like, where hair should be. They were here." She mimed waves originating from her cheeks. "And here." She repeated the gesture under her chin.

"Like an octopus?"

Jill's eyes went wide. "Yes! Totally! It's like the shape in the stained-glass window, except with a woman's face." She leaned closer to Una. "Does Iceland have a story about a sea monster with a woman's face?"

It was Svana's face Una thought of now. Svana disappearing into that dark, roiling sea.

In Una's memories, there had only been Svana's face and those black holes for eyes staring out from just below her.

But last night, she'd dreamed of the thing in the water. She'd seen details that had caused her to bolt awake, drowning in sweat. She'd seen a creature with ropy arms and spear-point teeth.

Rippling shadows in the water had surrounded Svana's body. Were they eels? Or . . .

"Tentacles," she whispered.

Jill waited for her to elaborate, but at that moment, Mrs. Stapleton appeared at the end of the stacks, a patron in tow.

"We're finishing up here," Una told the librarian. To Jill, she said, "Give me the books you want to check out and put the rest back. I'm driving you home."

Jill did as she was told. A few minutes later, she and Una ran out to her little yellow car.

"What about my bike?" asked Jill.

"One of your parents will have to pick it up. You can't ride home in this weather. With library books and only one good hand? It would be a disaster."

Jill's face fell. "Mom's showing a house. I can ask Dad, but he'll be mad that I went out."

Una wiped a stray raindrop off Jill's cheek. "I need to stop at Rudy's Market on the way home. I'm going to make bread today, but I don't think I have enough flour. Why don't you come in with me, and we'll see if he has any sprinkle cookies left? I think cookies taste better on rainy days, don't you?"

Ten minutes later, Jill followed Una into the little shop and held the shopping basket while Una filled it with eggs, flour, and two cookies. Then they stood outside under the awning and ate their cookies, marveling over how the sprinkles turned their rain-damp fingertips green, yellow, and blue.

Back in the car, they stuck out their tongues and laughed at the streaks of color covering the pink flesh.

Jill seemed more relaxed now than she'd been at the library, but as soon as Una turned onto her street and slowly traversed the descending curves, she went quiet again.

"Would you do me a favor?" Una asked.

"Sure."

"Will you soak your hand as soon as you get home?"

Jill glanced at her bandaged palm. "Okay."

"But show it to your dad first. Tell him it's why I wouldn't let you ride your bike."

Jill picked at a curled corner of the Band-Aid. "He doesn't know I went to the library. He thinks I went to Heather's."

Una sighed. Everyone kept secrets. Told white lies. It was part of being human, but she wished Jill could be more honest with her parents. Her fear of disapproval had her constantly saying things she later regretted.

"Why? Don't you think he'd understand why you went to the library today?"

Jill shook her head.

"I'm not sure I do, either. You want to know more about the face you found in the garden, right? And the scale, too. But why today? Why not wait until the storm passed?"

By this point, they'd reached the cul-de-sac. Instead of going down Jill's driveway, Una pulled over next to the Bernsteins' mailbox.

Jill's gaze was immediately snared by Mrs. Smith's house.

She raised her eyes to the roof and stared, even though there was nothing to see. Both the widow's walk and attic windows were shrouded in mist.

"Is it the regatta?" Una whispered.

Jill's eyes drifted to the Bernsteins' house. "I don't think it was a propeller. I think it was . . . something else."

"Because of what Charles saw?"

"Because he saw a finger," Jill said. "And eels. I know he wasn't lying because I saw them, too."

Una's blood ran cold. "You did?"

"Not during the regatta." Jill looked down at her injured hand. "Last night, when I was watching TV, my hand got really hot. It felt like it was burning. Mom told me to let the dogs in. They were down by the water, barking like crazy. I called them, but they wouldn't listen, so I went down to the beach. My hand was on fire, so I stuck it in the water. That's when I saw them."

"Tell me."

Hugging herself, Jill murmured, "Eels. Hundreds of them. Only, they weren't actually there. They were, like, in my head. But it wasn't a dream because I was awake."

"What were they doing?"

"Swimming under a boat. A Blue Jay. Like the ones we use in sailing class. There were *so* many of them. It was gross. Then someone fell off the boat. They were wearing white sneakers and white shorts and a life jacket. Then there was a big cloud of bubbles. Then . . . the water was full of blood."

Tears rolled down her cheeks. Una grabbed tissues from her purse and wiped them away.

Jill's eyes pleaded with Una. "I'm not lying, I swear! I saw the eels swimming through the blood. They were excited—like sharks get in a feeding frenzy. Then I yanked my hand out of the water, and everything went back to normal."

Una smoothed Jill's hair. "Amma had visions from time to time. She said it was like dreaming while she was awake. Some people thought she was just telling stories, but I believed her. I believe you, too."

"I think I saw one of the missing boys. I think . . ." Jill pointed at the library books strewn across the back seat. "If it wasn't a propeller, or a shark, then it was something *else*."

A catalog of sea monsters surfaced in Una's memory. These creatures appeared again and again in Amma's fireside tales. Some came from Norse mythology. Others were part of their island's folklore. All were very old.

Una guessed Jill's mind was filled with monsters, too.

Serpent. Leviathan. Kraken. Sea witch.

What were the curved paths radiating out of the stone face in Mrs. Smith's garden? Were they tentacles? The eels from Jill's vision?

Eel's Nest.

Una cast an anxious glance at the looming gray mass of a house.

"I want to tell you something." Una took Jill's hand. "The box I got from Mrs. Stapleton is about Cold Harbor's history. I borrowed it so I could learn more about that house and the people who lived there."

"You did?"

Una nodded. "We can share what we learn, you and me. We can be a team. Okay?"

Jill's face flooded with relief. "Okay."

Una drove down the Scotts' driveway and let Jill off by the garage door.

Before Jill got out, she leaned over and kissed Una's cheek. "Thank you."

Una waited until Jill scurried inside before turning around and motoring up the driveway. When she reached the top, her car paused as if holding its breath, and Una caught a shadow out of the corner of her eye.

Slowly, reluctantly, she turned her head to the left and saw a woman standing in Mrs. Smith's driveway, her hands curled around the bars of the motorized gate.

She wore a silky blue robe, which the rain had plastered to her skin. Long dark hair framed a phantom-white face. Her feet were bare. Her mouth was a slash of red. Her eyes were deep black marbles. They studied Una with cold malevolence.

Una heard a low moan of terror and realized it was rising out of her own throat.

It was the woman from John Stapleton's book about Cold Harbor. She had the same face. The same soulless eyes.

Una wanted to strip off her own skin, to burn it—anything to stop the prickling, probing invasion of the woman's black gaze.

Instead, she stamped down on the accelerator. Her car shot forward, breaking the spell.

She drove as fast as she dared on the winding road, too petrified to look in the rearview mirror.

She tried to tell herself that she must be mistaken. That the rain was playing tricks on her.

But it was no use. She knew what she'd seen. Her worst suspicions had just been confirmed.

Mrs. Smith was done hiding.

20
Jill

For the rest of that rainy Saturday, Jill searched for monsters in her books. If she found something that could explain what happened to the missing boys, she was supposed to call Una and tell her all about it. Knowing Una was on her side made Jill less afraid.

She started off looking for creatures from Greek mythology that were capable of biting through bone. The Kraken was an obvious choice. It was a behemoth with tentacles and a mouth filled with teeth the size of short swords. It could easily swallow a human whole.

Did Charles see eels? Jill wondered, her fingertips tracing the black-and-white drawing of what looked like a giant octopus. *Or tentacles?*

Turning the page, she examined the illustration of the Scylla, a six-headed sea monster with a dragon-shaped head that reminded Jill of Gidorah from the Godzilla movies. Scylla terrorized a channel of water somewhere in the Mediterranean, guarding one side of the channel while another monster named Charybdis, who was basically a whirlpool, guarded the other.

"You don't bite," Jill said to the drawing of Charybdis.

She added Scylla's name to the list she was compiling in her Hello Kitty notebook and continued reading.

There were dozens of sea nymphs and minor ocean goddesses. None had sharp teeth.

The illustrations of sirens varied. In one book, they were beautiful naked women from the waist up. The water hid their serpent tails. In the second book, which was fifty years older than the first, sirens were birds with women's faces.

The second book had a much longer description of the sirens, including how they'd been created by Demeter and how all three had killed themselves after a man named Odysseus had managed to escape their deadly song.

Jill didn't add sirens to her list. No bird had bitten off the finger Charles had seen floating in the water next to his boat.

Charles said it didn't look like it had been cut by a blade. It had bits hanging out. Like it had been chewed.

After reading about the sea goddess Derceto in the newer book, Jill dismissed her because she was essentially a mermaid. But in the older book, she was not only described as a great whale, but as the Greek version of a Syrian goddess named Atargatis. This goddess was older and more powerful than the Greek Derceto. Atargatis ruled over all the fish. However, fish weren't the only creatures sacred to her. Snakes were as well.

Picturing the stone face in Mrs. Smith's garden, Jill added Atargatis to her list. She also added *Ceto*, a general term for sea monsters. There were different descriptions of these creatures sprinkled throughout the book, but most resembled giant sea serpents.

After reviewing her list, Jill noticed something.

"They're all women. Scylla. Sirens. Atargatis. Ceto."

She still had a hundred pages to go in the older Greek mythology book and hoped that her dad and brothers would leave her alone so she could finish it. It was slow going. The typeface was small and there weren't many illustrations. It was harder to find descriptions of monsters without reading about the heroes who killed them.

She skimmed over the familiar stories of Perseus and Heracles, Theseus and Jason, and the section on wars and temples. Suddenly, all that was left was a glossary on gods and goddesses and the minor deities and creatures under their dominion.

Jill flipped to the page listing Poseidon's underlings. Many of his creatures were familiar to her now, from mermaids to hippocampi, but she was only interested in the ones with teeth. Creatures who had teeth and bodies with snakelike appendages or tentacles.

She was just about to close the book when a line caught her eye.

Lamia. Female demon. Sea monster. Mother of Scylla. p. 114.

Jill turned back to the chapter on the Children of Zeus. This was an abbreviated history of all the women he'd slept with, what form he'd taken to seduce them, what children the union had produced, and what Hera had done to punish the mortal women and their offspring.

The paragraph about Lamia was short. Jill's eyes flew over the words.

> Zeus became enamored with Lamia, a queen of Libya who'd descended from the Titans. When Hera learned that Lamia had given birth to twins, she was enraged. Taking the form of a lioness, she crept up to Lamia's children as they played in the gardens and slew them. Lamia had spent the day swimming in the sea, but when she returned to the gardens and came upon the bodies of her children, her grief knew no bounds. She vowed to spend the rest of her life punishing

the Greeks. Under the cover of darkness, she used her magic to lure their children into the water. Then she carried them beneath the waves and devoured them.

Suddenly, the cut in the middle of Jill's palm blazed in pain and she pressed her fingertips against the layers of gauze her father had used to cover the wound.

She could feel the heat of her skin through the gauze. It was like touching a light bulb.

Blood began to seep into the clean white gauze, forming a familiar shape. A red eye stared out at her from the center of her palm.

The pain lessened to a dull throb, but Jill felt clammy and nauseated. The words in her notebook blurred. The letters seemed to melt together, to slither across the page like dozens of little worms.

"Stop," she muttered through gritted teeth.

She picked up her pen and pressed it down hard on the paper to steady her trembling hand. Her words came out slanted and spidery.

Lamia. Demon. Sea monster. Eats children. Hunts at night. Mother of Scylla.

Jill's pen snapped in half, spewing black ink across the paper.

She rushed to the bathroom for paper towels, blotted up the ink, then sank back against her bed.

Demon. Sea monster. Eats children.

Jill had to tell Una about Lamia. She had to tell her how her hand had started hurting the moment she'd seen the creature's name. The phone in the kitchen had a long cord, so she could stand out on the deck and close the door behind her. No one would hear what she said to Una.

However, her dad was in the kitchen, talking on the phone. Covering the mouthpiece, he whispered to Jill, "Charles is coming over. He has something for you."

For once, Jill wasn't repelled by the idea of seeing Charles. If she couldn't talk to Una, she could show Charles what she'd found.

She opened the front door before he had the chance to knock.

He thrust a bakery box at her. "Mom got you butter cookies."

"Oh. Thanks." Jill took the box and waved him inside. "Can I show you something?"

Startled by the invitation, all Charles could do was nod.

Jill left the box of cookies on the hall table and beckoned for Charles to follow her to her room. She sat on the floor and patted the carpet the same way she would if she wanted Lady or Tramp to lie down.

"I went to the library today," she began. "Una drove me home, and we started talking. I told her about the . . . you know." She held out her index finger. "She totally believes you and she doesn't think we're crazy for thinking there was something out there. Something . . . in the water."

She saw Charles retreat into himself. He drew his knees into his chest and stared at the books scattered across the carpet.

Jill pulled a jewelry box from under her bed and twisted the tiny key in the lock. The lid popped open, and she pointed at the scale nestled in one of the satin-lined compartments.

"Look at this." She waited for his pale blue eyes to land on the scale. "I found it in *her* garden. *This* is what it did to me."

She unfurled her fingers and showed him her bandaged palm.

He immediately recoiled.

"I'm not contagious," Jill snapped.

Hearing her change of tone, Charles nodded contritely. His eyes were fixed on the scale. "Can I see it?"

Jill plucked the scale out of the box and dropped it into Charles's open hand. He poked it, pinched it, and tested the sharpness of its tip.

"What's it from?"

Jill shook her head. "Dunno. I haven't found an exact match. The closest was a scale for a fish called a gar. It has teeth and eats other fish." She waved at the books. "I've been looking for stories about sea creatures. Not sharks, but other things. Things with teeth."

Charles pulled one of the books closer to him. He stared at the illustration of Scylla for a long moment, his gaze tracing the serpentine lines of her tail.

"I made a list of ones with body parts that might look like eels. And . . ." She trailed off, unsure of what to say next.

Charles gave her an expectant look, and she gestured for him to pass her the book in front of him. She turned to an illustration of Medusa. "My mom is making J.J. and me do yard work for Mrs. Smith. Mrs. Smith wrote a note, telling us to start in the backyard. I've never seen what's back there before, but I guess there used to be a garden. There's a bunch of brick paths that come together in a circle. The circle is actually a woman's face. She looks really pissed off, and there are scales carved around the edge of her face."

Charles held out the scale from Jill's jewelry box. "Like this?"

"Yeah. They're the same shape without the little teeth around the sides. I guess that would be kind of hard to carve."

"So, do you think she's, like, a monster? Like, something from one of these books?"

Jill knew he understood that she wasn't referring to the stone face. Neither of them wanted to say Mrs. Smith's name.

"This face in her garden is weird. Her house is weird. *You* know. You see it every day, same as me. Those skinny windows on the bottom. That creepy octopus in the attic windows. The way the air feels colder when you get close to the place. All the wasps and flies and pricker bushes and poison ivy. Those vines that have spread from her house all through the woods. And it always feels like someone inside is watching."

"That happens to you, too?"

Jill nodded. "We're not the only ones, either. I think Una feels it, too. Something's wrong with that house. Because of *her*."

Charles gazed down at the illustration of Medusa and her two sisters. "Maybe she *is* a witch. Maybe she, like, controls something in the water."

Jill waited a moment to see if he was being serious, but she could tell by his deep frown and frightened eyes that he was.

"Maybe. I've mostly read about Greek myths, but I also found this woman called Lamia. She was, like, a combo of witch, demon, and sea monster. And she ate kids."

Charles muttered something in a language Jill didn't understand.

"Is that Hebrew?" she asked.

"Yiddish. It's something my bubbe used to say to ward off evil spirits. It means, 'In the balcony there are three cracks. Go there, Evil Eye, and hide yourself.'"

Charles's cheeks were scarlet with embarrassment, but Jill wished she knew a charm to protect her from demons.

"Is this the grandma who comes over all the time?"

"No, it's the one who died when I was ten. She was really cool. She was in the circus when she was young. She always told the best stories. She was kind of my best friend." He swallowed hard and tried to distract himself by looking around Jill's room. Then he pointed at the book in Jill's hand. "Does that have a picture of Lamia?"

Jill sighed. "No. There are photos of Greek vases showing almost all of the other monsters. The vases are super old. Like this amphora of Scylla? It's from 450 BC. If Lamia is Scylla's mother, then she's even older. I need to look up monsters in other myths. Like from China and Norway. Because if other people wrote about a monster like Lamia . . ."

"Then she might be real," Charles whispered. "What are we gonna do?"

"Tell Una. She—"

A crash came from Justin's room followed by a squawk of dismay. Something thumped against the wall behind Jill's bookcase and Justin let out a wail. Jill heard J.J. trying to placate their baby brother.

"Stop crying!" J.J. barked. "I'll fix it. *Look!* I'm fixing it!"

"What's going on in there?" their dad bellowed from down the hall.

"Nothing! One of Justin's LEGO towers collapsed, but I'm fixing it!" J.J. shouted back.

I bet you knocked it over with Mr. Potato Head. Or your foot, thought Jill.

She heard unintelligible murmuring from J.J. and a few sniffles from Justin. As soon as the house grew quiet again, the carousel music box with the creepy horse began to spin. The twang of an off-key note echoed in the air. After two or three seconds, another dissonant note played. Then another. Every pluck of the metal comb inside the belly of the music box caused Jill's hand to vibrate with pain.

Charles got to his feet and stood in front of the shelf of music boxes. Glancing down at Jill, he said, "Is it hurting you?"

Jill whispered, "Yeah."

Charles grabbed the carousel horse and held it by the base so that it couldn't turn anymore. "I have to go to temple now. Do you want me to take this?"

Jill nodded gratefully. "Throw it in the trash at your house. Don't let anyone see. If my mom asks, I'll tell her I broke it."

She walked Charles to the front door and followed him out onto the stoop. Together, they stared at the mist-veiled shadow that was Mrs. Smith's house.

Charles said, "Do you have to go back there?"

Jill didn't bother to disguise her misery. "Tomorrow. After church."

"Can't you just tell your mom that you don't want to do it?"

"She isn't like your mom," Jill said with a conflicting mix of jealousy and pride. She wished her mom was soft and sweet like Mrs. Bernstein, but she was also proud of how smart her mom was. How strong. If Mrs. Bernstein was Aphrodite, then her mom was Athena. And Jill would rather be the daughter of a warrior. Especially if there was a monster in the water.

Witch. Demon. Beast. Child killer.

Jill said goodbye to Charles and returned to her room. Feeling a little better now that the music box was gone, she reached for a book called *Mythical Beasts of the World*. She ignored the beautiful illustrations of unicorns and griffins, searching only for creatures with a woman's face.

She'd gotten through half of the book before her dad asked her to help make bologna and cheese sandwiches for lunch. Suddenly hungry, she yelled, "Be right there!"

After she ate her sandwich and a bowl of fruit cocktail, Justin asked her to play with him. She wanted to get back to her room, but he looked at her with his puppy dog eyes and she couldn't say no.

They played Candy Land, which Justin won, followed by two rounds of Chutes and Ladders. Justin landed on the cookie jar space and had to go all the way down the long slide, but he didn't pout, even when it was clear the action meant he'd most certainly lose. He just shrugged and waited for Jill to take her turn.

"Charles brought us a box of cookies," she said after packing up the game. "Want to ask Dad if you can have some while you watch a show?"

"Yeah!" Justin trotted down the hall.

Back in her room, Jill continued looking though *Mythical Beasts of the World*. She was reading a description of an Inuit sea monster called the Qalupalik when her dad knocked on her door.

"Phone's for you, Jilly Bean."

"Okay."

Her dad surveyed the array of library books. "Working on your summer reading for school?"

"It's research. For a story."

As she passed him in the doorway, he gave her a one-armed hug. "My little Hemingway. Maybe you'll work in the city one day. Your brothers and I will be on Wall Street, and you'll be a reporter for *The Times* or *The Post*. We could have lunch. I'd take you to all my favorite places."

Jill didn't want to be a reporter, but she loved the idea of meeting her dad for lunch. Even more, she loved that he saw her as being smart enough to land a job with a major newspaper.

She paused for a second to lean against her father's warm chest. He kissed the top of her head and then gave her a gentle push. "Phone's off the hook in the kitchen."

Jill picked up the handset and said, "Hello?"

She fully expected to hear Heather's voice and was startled when Charles said, "Jill? Hey. It's, uh, Charles. I—I wanted to tell you something."

"Okay."

"I had to stay after the service today to talk to the rabbi. He wanted to make sure I was ready to come back to Hebrew school after, you know, after the regatta." Jill heard the rustle of paper in the background. "We were in his office, and I asked him if there were other creatures in the Torah like the Leviathan. The Torah's basically the Old Testament of the Bible and the Leviathan is a sea monster."

Jill stared out at the harbor, her eyes searching for shadows between the moored boats. "Okay."

"The Talmud, which is all these Jewish laws and other stuff, mentions a bunch of monsters and demons. So, I asked Rabbi Greenberg if one was named Lamia, and he gave me a funny look. Then he went to his shelf and pulled out this really old, old book. It was brown with big, yellowy pages. There was no title on the cover or anything. He read to himself for a bit and then told me that Lamia *is* in the Old Testament. Not in our Torah, but in a Bible like you'd use."

"No way."

"Yeah. The lines are from the Book of Isaiah. I wrote them down. They say, 'And demons and monsters shall meet, and the hairy ones shall cry out one to another, there hath the lamia lain down, and found rest for herself.'"

Demons. Monsters. Lamia.

"So, she meets with other demons and then rests? I don't get it."

"That's just one version. In another version, she doesn't have a name. She's just called the Night Monster. In other versions, she's Lilith. My rabbi said Lilith is older than Judaism. She was around before the Bible. Some translations call her the Night Demon. Guess what horrible thing she did?"

Jill was scribbling notes as fast as she could, but now she stopped. She felt clammy again. She didn't want to hear what Charles was about to say, but she knew she had to. "What?"

"She devoured children."

Jill's gaze shifted to the shallow water directly behind her house. "This can't be real. It just can't. It's totally crazy. If there was a demon swimming around, eating kids, people would know. I mean, where could she hide?"

"I asked the rabbi what Lamia looked like, and he said he didn't know. He said there are demons called *shaydim*. They're shapeshifters. The only way you can tell they're not human is if they take off their shoes. The *shaydim* will never take off their shoes because they have chicken feet."

Charles let out a nervous giggle, but Jill glanced from the gray, rain-needled harbor to the bloodstained bandage on her hand. "Maybe the shapeshifters who lived on land had chicken feet," she said. "And the demons from the water—the night monsters—had something else that showed what they really were."

"Like what?"

Jill closed her hand and rested it over her heart. "Scales."

21

Mrs. Smith

Mrs. Smith ushered the housecleaners into the foyer. She gave the team of women in starched aprons and sturdy shoes the once-over. They looked strong and hungry, which meant they'd be good workers.

"All the rooms on this floor require attention, but I'd like you to start in the bedroom," she said. "When that's clean, the items in my car need to be arranged in the wardrobe. New furniture is being delivered at noon, and I'd like the rooms prepared ahead of its arrival. There'll be a hundred-dollar bonus for each of you if you can complete your work to my satisfaction by the end of the morning."

The cleaners gave her a bovine stare until finally, a woman with streaks of white in her black hair stepped forward and said, "We'll do our best."

Mrs. Smith left them to their work and entered the kitchen. The dust-coated room was noticeably antiquated. The room had no appliances. No built-in cabinets. An antique icebox stood on one wall, flanked by a cast-iron stove and a crockery cupboard. A swaybacked butcher block on legs and a large porcelain sink occupied the opposite wall. An oak table sat in the center of the room. The Yellow Pages was splayed open on its scarred surface next to a letter bearing the town seal.

The letter, signed by some pencil pusher named Cliff, directed her to expunge certain plant species from her property. The missive threatened steep fines or possible legal action if she failed to comply within thirty days.

She balled up the thin sheet of paper and tossed it on the floor. Soon, she would be gone, and men like Cliff would have far bigger concerns than plants.

Turning her attention back to the phone book, Mrs. Smith ran a pointy nail down the list of hair salons. An ad for Premier Salon caught her eye because it used the words *exclusive* and *elegant*, which was code for *pretentious* and *expensive.*

She dialed the number.

When a chipper young woman answered the phone, Mrs. Smith asked to speak with the owner.

"He's with a client right now. May I take a message?"

"It's a personal matter, and it's rather urgent."

After a brief hesitation, the young woman said, "Please hold."

Thirty seconds later, a brusque male voice came on the line. "This is Peter Jacques. Who's calling?"

"A future client willing to pay ten times your going rate. I am making my debut in society after a very long hiatus, and I require a true master to style my hair and apply my makeup. I also require discretion."

Having read dozens of magazines a week for years, Mrs. Smith knew that humans were enamored with fame. If this self-important coiffeur was like the rest of the herd, he'd trip over himself for the chance to assist a celebrity.

Peter Jacques lowered his voice to a conspiratorial murmur. "May I have Madame's name?"

Mrs. Smith thought of all the names she'd been called over

the millennia. There'd been a hundred, in an equal number of tongues.

"You may call me Mrs. Smith."

By the end of the call, the man was eating out of her hand. He agreed to come to her house next Saturday to prep her for the yacht club cocktail party. He would style her hair while his assistants took care of her nails and makeup.

Until then, only the cleaners, the deliverymen, and Don Pulaski would be permitted inside her home. Don's access would be limited to the furnished areas on the ground floor, but Mrs. Smith knew he wouldn't wander too far from her bedroom. If all went well, the room would be as seductive and beguiling as her human body.

To accomplish her vision, she'd ordered a California king poster bed with a canopy. The thick pilasters had a serpentine shape. Silk curtains hung from the canopy. The headboard was gently curved, like a woman's back.

In addition to the grandiose bed, she purchased a changing screen with a cherry blossom design and a red velvet chaise. *Cosmopolitan* had taught her that men liked to watch themselves having sex, so she'd had a floor mirror with an ornate frame positioned across from the bed. To enhance the hedonistic atmosphere, she'd purchased a series of nudes to hang above a French-style vanity. Her final touch was to scatter soft rugs over the floor and scent the air with Chanel perfume.

Mrs. Smith wanted to lure men into this room and use them until they had nothing left to give. It would likely take several men to trigger her reproductive system, especially if her encounters mimicked the fast, frenzied coupling she'd had with Don.

This hairy, blustering dimwit of a human had been easy to persuade. He'd come running when she called, entering the garage where her new Porsche sat like a black beetle in the dark.

When Mrs. Smith turned on the light and revealed herself, he'd been rendered utterly speechless. But he didn't need to talk. She could sense lust in his slack jaw and glowing eyes.

With no suitable clothes to wear, she'd had to make do with a white cotton shift. Its scooped neck and lace trim looked demure, but the material was so thin that it was nearly transparent.

Moments before Don's arrival, Mrs. Smith had held her head under the kitchen tap until her hair was wet. She'd then twisted the excess water from her hair and let it fall onto her shoulders, where it saturated the front of her shift, revealing the hard caps of her nipples.

She'd extended her hand to Don and softly whispered his name. He'd moved toward her like a man in a dream.

"I just got out of the shower, so I'm not dressed for a driving lesson." Slipping past him, she'd run her fingers over the sloped hood of the car. "Perhaps you could show me a few of my car's interior features."

She'd lowered herself into the passenger seat and waited until he stood next to the open door. Then she'd said, "How far back can this go?"

Don's glance had roved the length of her body. He drank in her long, sculpted limbs and the graceful curve of her neck. He stared at her lush, round breasts with their eager nipples, and let out a low, animalistic groan.

"You're the expert," she'd said. "Show me how this works."

Don had watched her caress the leather under her right thigh. Finally, he found his voice and stammered, "I, uh, I don't think . . ."

But even as his lips tried to form words of protest, his legs had propelled him forward.

"Show me," she'd whispered, shattering what remained of his resistance.

He'd lunged at her, thrusting his tongue into her mouth. His fingers clamped onto her breasts, squeezing and pinching. He twisted her nipples until she gasped. He bit the tender skin of her neck, oblivious as to whether her cries stemmed from pleasure or pain.

He sucked on her neck while his hand probed under her shift. She'd parted her thighs, inviting him to touch the dark, wet place between her legs.

"Show me," she'd whispered.

Groaning, he fumbled with his belt, undid his zipper, and freed his erection.

Pulling her by the arm, he'd yanked her out of the car and took her place in the seat. Then he guided her on top of him, angling his hips so he could penetrate her.

"That's it, baby. Take it. Take it all."

As Mrs. Smith moved up and down, he pulled at her nipples with his front teeth and kneaded the flesh of her backside.

They'd barely gotten into a rhythm before Don had cried, "Ready, baby? Ready? Here it comes!"

Then he'd shuddered, grunted like a rooting pig, and gone limp.

As his erection deflated, Mrs. Smith had felt the liquid warmth of his seed trickle onto her thigh and soak into the fabric of her shift.

"This is only my first lesson. I hope we have many more," she'd said as she exited the car. "Before you go, would you do something for me?"

Still caught in a postcoital haze, Don had nodded.

Mrs. Smith had opened the glove box and removed the instructions for collecting her items from Lord & Taylor as well as an envelope stuffed with cash. To her utter annoyance, that cow of a saleswoman had telephoned to say that they were unable to deliver her items until tomorrow. After expressing her displeasure in glacial tones, Mrs. Smith informed her that a member of her staff would collect them by the end of the day.

Handing Don the envelope, she said, "Stop by the men's department and pick out a suit while you're there. Wear it to the yacht club cocktail party next week. I'll be there."

This had startled Don out of his stupor. "You will?"

"There's no need for concern," she'd soothed. "I don't have designs on you. All I want is more lessons, and I know how to be discreet. Think of me as a satisfied customer. *Very* satisfied."

Mrs. Smith had met men like Don before. His type couldn't imagine a woman being left unfulfilled. As long as he'd felt pleasure, he assumed his partner had as well.

The closest equivalent Mrs. Smith had to a human orgasm was the act of devouring a Pure One. And the heights of that gratification were beyond anything such an inferior species could understand.

"Take my car to collect my clothes," she told Don. He blinked at her stupidly, as if struggling to understand her directive. "That way, you can just leave everything in the Porsche and hurry home afterward with your new suit. No one will be the wiser. When you're ready to give me my next lesson, just knock on this door."

She'd slipped into the house before he could reply. She was tired of looking at him and disappointed by his performance.

She required a more explosive coupling. Three minutes of panting wouldn't suffice. She and her human mate needed to rut like animals. They had to scratch and claw, wrestle and snarl. The human male needed to dominate her. To pin her down and hold her wrists and take her again and again until he was too spent to move.

She would find other men to bed. As many as she could coerce at once, or within a handful of hours. Such a variety would create competition on a cellular level, lighting up her reproductive system like fireworks.

After Don left, Mrs. Smith had shucked off her shift and stepped into her hot tub. The water didn't refresh this body like it did her true form, but it was still her element. She'd picked up a random magazine and began flipping through it.

It was last month's issue of *New York Homes and Gardens*, which Mrs. Smith had yet to peruse. When she came across the title "Do You Live on the Most Beautiful Street in New York?" she'd read the contest rules and smirked.

What did humans know of beauty?

The natural world was spilling over with beauty, which they ignored, corrupted, or bastardized. Humans and their hothouse roses and orchids. Their hybridized corn and wheat. Their grafted trees and artificial turf. Their cemeteries strewn with plastic flowers.

Pushing aside the frayed curtain, Mrs. Smith had glanced out at her backyard. It had been many years since she'd last seen the stone face in the center of the garden. Once, she'd taken great pleasure in knowing that her likeness had been surrounded by toxic plants.

A century ago, her poison garden had been lovingly tended by one of the villagers—a woman who'd been ostracized for having an illegitimate child. Her family had driven her out of their home, tossing a single suitcase and globs of spit in her wake.

The woman had poured all of her anger and bitterness into the poison garden. The foxglove, wolfbane, and lupine she planted were as tall as the fence. She grew thick mounds of jimsonweed, stinging nettle, and water hemlock. She mixed and manipulated the soil, encouraging colonies of deadly mushrooms. She nourished plants with thorns, plants that oozed sap, and plants with toxic berries. She sang to the poison ivy, the creeping spurge, and the wart weed.

She planted oriental bittersweet along the property line, watching with delight as it grew and spread, grew and spread.

She lured bees to the garden by singing to them. She watched them pollinate the plants and attract birds. After the birds gorged on berries, they'd shit in the villager's fields, sowing poison into the rich, fertile soil.

The village woman was long dead. But the remnants of her legacy were now being unearthed by the neighbor's children.

Mrs. Smith liked to watch them work.

She had been watching them since they were infants in their mother's arms, just as she'd been watching the red-haired boy next door.

Thinking of the redhead made her smile. After all, his party would grant her access to dozens of Pure Ones. In a fortnight, she would consume the boy's friends, including the Scott child.

Round and ripe, the girl would pop like a grape in Mrs. Smith's mouth.

Until then, she and her brother would clear the paths and pull weeds. In doing so, there was a chance they'd dig up artifacts from Mrs. Smith's hunts.

They might find teeth. Metal fillings. Watches. Rings. Things that Mrs. Smith had regurgitated. Things that were hard to digest.

These items would intrigue the children. And possibly frighten them. The girl might run to her mother and beg to be released from her commitment. But Mrs. Smith didn't think the mother would oblige. Like all humans, the woman was swayed by the promise of cash.

Mrs. Smith had seen the children working in their own garden. She'd heard their mother and father speak to them about saving their allowance. She'd seen the woman's face when she'd retrieved a pile of bills from the mailbox. The pinched look she wore when she thought of money. Mrs. Smith knew that she could sway such a human by offering to pay her children a generous fee in exchange for a little labor.

When the work was done, she would add a gratuity along with a short missive praising the children's diligence. After this, the Scott woman would no longer view Mrs. Smith as the strange creature who hid from the world, but as a misunderstood benefactor. Hoping her children would be hired for another task, she would try to quell any whispers about her neighbor. Mrs. Smith would gain an ally. And for such a paltry sum.

However, if the girl told the silver-haired woman who drove the yellow car, that might be cause for concern. The mobs who came after Mrs. Smith had always formed because one human—usually a woman—was too observant.

For years, the silver-haired woman had avoided looking in Mrs. Smith's direction, but today, they had locked eyes. Mrs. Smith had seen fear and surprise in the woman's glacial-blue gaze. But there'd been something else, too.

The woman had recognized Mrs. Smith.

This wouldn't do at all.

I will have to kill her. If I don't, she will be the flame that lights the first torch.

22

Natalie

Natalie was in a good mood when she walked in the house at quarter to five. The dogs met her at the door, their tails wagging wildly, and she gave them some cursory pats as she kicked off her shoes. She dropped her purse on the hall table and went downstairs in search of her oldest child.

J.J. was parked in front of the TV, mashing buttons on his Atari controller as multicolored lightning streaks blazed across the screen.

"Did you feed the dogs?"

J.J. kept his eyes on the game. "Not yet."

"It's almost five."

"I'll do it as soon as I finish this level."

Natalie noticed a crumb-dusted plate and an empty cup on the coffee table. They were probably J.J.'s lunch plates, which he hadn't bothered to clean up because she hadn't been home to nag him.

It was always like this when Jimmy was in charge of the kids. He fed them, refereed their fights, and occasionally made them do a chore, but that was the extent of his interaction.

They'd watch TV in the basement for hours on end while he watched sports in the living room.

He was there now, stretched out on the sofa with a beer in his hand.

"How was your day?" she asked him.

"All quiet on the Western Front. How'd it go with the Arabs?"

Natalie sank into a chair and kicked off her shoes. "They're *very* interested in the McCreedy house."

Jimmy arched his brows. "They are?"

"Yep. It fits their budget, and they love the neighborhood. Sure, it needs a little TLC, but—"

"TLC?" Jimmy scoffed, his attention returning to the baseball game. "In the form of a nuclear bomb?"

Natalie felt her good mood slipping away. "Can you make me a drink while I change?"

Jimmy sprang off the sofa and took her in his arms. "Don't go changing." Then, in his best Billy Joel voice, he started singing the opening lines of "Just the Way You Are."

She rewarded him with a kiss for making her laugh. "If you keep singing, the dogs will howl."

Jimmy sang louder.

Heading down the hall, Natalie poked her head into Jill's room. She saw a pile of library books on the bureau and a plastic bag stuffed with used paper towels.

She moved deeper into the room and took a closer look inside the bag. The paper towels were stained black.

If she got ink on the carpet, I'm going to kill her.

Natalie hadn't sighed all day, but she sighed now. When Jimmy came home from work, the house was always in order. Why couldn't she come home to that, too?

Satisfied that the carpet hadn't been stained, she went into Justin's room. She'd been hoping for a hug, but Justin wasn't there. In her room, she walked to the window overlooking the backyard and saw Jill and Justin sitting on the seawall, playing with Justin's army men and what appeared to be the shells of two horseshoe crabs.

When Justin's laughter floated up to the window, Natalie smiled. She was happy to see her kids playing outside.

Watching them, she felt an unexpected rush of gratitude for her daughter. Jill had always been a good sister to Justin. She played games with him and read him stories. She comforted him when he was upset and protected him when J.J. was in one of his tempestuous moods.

Natalie put on a Yankees T-shirt and a pair of white shorts. Then she hung up her work clothes and joined Jimmy on the sofa.

"Cheers," he said, saluting her with his martini glass. "Here's hoping the Arabs buy the McCreedy house."

"I'll drink to that."

A roar of applause came from the TV. Jimmy leaned forward and shouted at the umpire. Natalie sipped her drink and felt her body loosen a little. She was just starting to unwind when J.J. appeared in the doorway, followed by the dogs.

"What's for dinner?"

Jimmy was too engrossed in the game to respond, so Natalie said, "Pizza."

J.J. ruffled Tramp's fur. "Did you hear that, boy? Pizza! But not for you. You get grody Alpo."

Natalie nudged Jimmy. "When will this be over?"

"Fifteen minutes, give or take."

"Can you pick up the pizza in fifteen minutes? I'll call Sal's after I finish my drink."

Jimmy frowned. "I'd rather have a real meal. We had sandwiches for lunch."

"Are you going to make the real meal?"

Jimmy looked at her like she had two heads. *"Me?"*

Natalie gave him a blank stare. "You could grill. Do we have any ground meat?"

Sweeping his arm in a wide arc, Jimmy said, "It's not like I had time to go to the store. I washed the car, mowed the lawn, and watched the kids."

"Then I guess we're having pizza."

The crack of a bat colliding with a ball reverberated from the television and Jimmy whipped his head around to see what he'd missed. He put his feet on the coffee table and jiggled his right foot, a telltale sign that he was annoyed.

Natalie made herself another drink and carried it to the kitchen to call Sal's. A few minutes later, she heard Jimmy collect his keys from the bowl on the console table.

"By the way," he said on his way out, "you might want to look at Jill's hand."

The door slammed, prompting a chorus of barks from the dogs.

"Lady! Tramp! Want a treat?"

The dogs raced into the kitchen. Natalie opened the cookie jar she kept in the laundry room and pulled out two rawhide chews. The dogs trotted off to eat their treats on the living room rug while Natalie headed to the back deck, where she called out a hello to Justin and Jill.

"Mommy!" Justin shouted. He ran across the lawn, scrambled up the stairs, and threw himself into Natalie's arms.

"How's my baby?" she asked, sweeping his golden hair off his brow and planting a kiss on his warm skin.

"Jilly and I were playing."

"I saw you. Dad's getting pizza. Want to go in and wash your hands?"

Justin slid off her lap and leaned over the deck railing. "Jill!

We're having pizza!" He let out a whoop and disappeared into the house.

Natalie expected Jill to jog up the stairs in excitement, but her ascent was surprisingly slow. She looked pale and wore a hangdog expression.

"Let's see that hand." Natalie thumped the empty chair beside her.

Jill sat down and rested her bandaged hand on the table. Tears beaded her lashes.

Natalie gently turned Jill's hand over, revealing a dark brown stain in the center of the gauze. "It started bleeding again?"

Jill nodded.

A fetid smell came from the wound, which was more alarming than the bleeding. "Come into the kitchen."

With her daughter's hand hovering over the sink basin, Natalie sliced through the gauze. It was obviously stuck to the dried blood, so she turned on the faucet and told Jill to hold her hand under the stream of warm water.

After waiting a minute, Natalie removed the gauze. She tried to be careful but the scab over the wound came off anyway.

Bright red blood pooled in the center of Jill's palm, mixing with bubbles of pus. The smell of rot intensified, stimulating Natalie's gag reflex. She had to turn away and breathe through her mouth until the sensation passed.

Get a grip. Your daughter needs you.

Natalie looked at the wound again. It was still oozing, and the skin around the wound was inflamed. In some areas it was cherry red. In others, it was the color of a dried prune.

"Does it hurt all the time or only when you touch it?"

"Sometimes it's sore. Other times it gets really hot. Like it's burning."

Goddamn it, Jimmy. You think you're a hero for mowing the lawn and making a few sandwiches. You should've taken your daughter to the doctor, but the game was on, so you left it for me to deal with. Like always.

Later, when Jimmy strolled into the kitchen carrying two pizza boxes, Natalie shot him a poisonous glance.

"Jill's hand is infected." Her tone dripped with accusation. "I tried to drain it, but I think there's something in the wound. She should've gone to the doctor today. Now she'll have to wait until Monday."

Unfazed by her anger, Jimmy's eyes lit with interest. He dropped the pizza in the middle of the table, called the boys, and joined Jill and Natalie at the sink.

Before Jimmy took a job on Wall Street, he'd entertained the idea of going to medical school. He handled the kids' injuries calmly and enjoyed bandaging wounds, removing splinters, and popping Justin's shoulder back in the socket whenever it was dislocated, which seemed to happen on a regular basis.

After washing his hands, Jimmy began poking Jill's palm. "Does this hurt? How about here? Sorry. And here?"

Natalie grabbed his arm. "Stop it, Jimmy! Can't you see how tender it is?"

"It needs to be debrided. She might need antibiotics, too."

Jill couldn't take it anymore. She snatched her hand back and closed her fist.

"Sorry, Jilly Bean." Jimmy hugged Jill to him. To Natalie, he said, "Saline soak tonight."

"She's *been* soaking it. I told you yesterday that I didn't think it was healing properly."

Releasing Jill, Jimmy grabbed a beer from the fridge. "Maybe it'll clear up if she does a soak tonight and a bunch of times tomorrow."

It didn't clear up, and when Monday morning came, Natalie had to call the office to tell Sid that she had to miss the team meeting.

"Don't you have a babysitter?" Sid demanded. "It's a team meeting, Nat. Are you on the team?"

"Yes, but—"

"Do I need to remind you that your position with Gold Coast is not secure? You have ninety days to make a sale, little lady. It's the middle of July. Summer's half gone. If your job is interfering with your home life, maybe this isn't the place for you."

It's a fucking team meeting, not the Geneva Conventions, she thought. Aloud, she said, "I'll be on the board by the end of August. That's a promise."

"I really hope so, Nat. I'd hate to lose you, but if I'm going to have women on my team, they have to be go-getters. Look at Gina. *She's* on the board. *She's* on time for the morning meeting. *She* wants this."

Picturing Gina's tight blouses and flirty smile sparked Natalie's ire. Of course Gina was at the meeting. She didn't have to take care of anyone but herself. She didn't have kids. Or dogs. Or a husband that left her in the lurch. She could spend an hour in front of the mirror, curling her hair and putting on slut-red lipstick. She could swing by Dunkin' Donuts and get a Boston cream for Sid. She was probably serving it to him right now while he stared at her tits.

Everyone knows I'm a go-getter, Natalie thought.

She picked up the phone cord and imagined winding it around Sid's thick neck until his face turned purple and his tongue hung out of his mouth like a fat, slimy slug.

Instead, she apologized. But her words were met by dead air. Sid had hung up on her.

Natalie slammed the earpiece into the cradle. "Asshole."

Dr. Young went to the same church as the Scotts and made room in his busy schedule to accommodate Jill. After numbing Jill's hand, he gave the wound a thorough cleaning. While he worked, Jill told him how the injury had occurred.

"An animal scale?" His Einstein brows twitched with amusement.

"I think so."

Dr. Young reached for a pair of tweezers and dug around in the raw flesh of Jill's palm. Unable to watch, Natalie grabbed an issue of *Good Housekeeping* and flipped to a random page.

"Got you." Dr. Young brought the tweezers closer to his face. "This tiny splinter was keeping you from healing right. Sometimes, the body breaks them down or pushes them out through the skin, but this guy wanted to stick around. Now that it's out, we'll use butterfly bandages to help close the cut. Is she up-to-date on her tetanus shot, Mom?"

"Yes."

Dr. Young grunted in approval as he applied the butterfly bandages. "Do you have the scale with you, young lady?"

Jill's good hand disappeared into her shorts pocket. Natalie couldn't see what she gave to the doctor, but he slid on a pair of magnifying glasses and studied it with interest.

"I think you're right. It's a scale. I don't know where it came from, but it's a nasty-looking bugger, isn't it?" He turned to Natalie. "I'll write a script for antibiotics. Just to be on the safe side. We can't have this mermaid missing any swim meets."

Because she didn't have time to drive Jill home, Natalie had arranged to meet Una at the library. She would've preferred to have Una come to the office, but she had to load Jill's bike into her station wagon.

Jimmy could've picked it up on Saturday but had chosen not to. Natalie wasn't surprised. Everything always came down to her. He only helped with the kids if she left him a specific list. If something unexpected happened—like their daughter riding her bike to the library in the rain or having an infected hand—he either didn't notice or didn't care.

"Do I have to go to sailing class?" Jill asked before getting out of the car.

Natalie pictured her daughter pulling or releasing ropes with one hand. "No. You can help Una with dinner instead."

Jill smiled for the first time that day. "Thanks, Mom."

Having taken care of one problem, Natalie waved at Una and drove away.

As soon as she was alone, she practiced what she'd say when she called Dr. Sherif at noon. She was gesticulating to an imaginary Dr. Sherif when a red car with a thunderous engine pulled up next to her at a red light. It looked and sounded like Don's car, but when Natalie glanced to her left, she saw a brunette in the passenger seat.

She was about to turn away when she noticed the white fuzzy dice dangling from the rearview mirror. Don had received the same pair last December at the neighborhood's white elephant party.

As Natalie leaned forward to get a better look at the driver, she saw a large, masculine hand slither down the front of the brunette's low-cut blouse. As the hand fondled the woman's breast, she closed her eyes and arched her back in pleasure.

Though Natalie was still unable to see the man's face, she couldn't stop staring at the brunette. Her beauty was otherworldly. Her every movement was sensual. As Natalie watched, she grabbed the man's hand and started sucking his index finger.

The light turned green, but Natalie didn't move. She was mesmerized by the man's gold pinkie ring.

Behind her, someone honked, and the sound jerked Natalie out of her trance.

She gave a wave of contrition to the driver she was holding up and then darted a final glance to her left. She saw Don Pulaski grab a fistful of the brunette's hair as he guided her head toward his crotch.

Natalie hit the gas, and the station wagon lurched forward. Behind her, Don's car remained stationary.

And as it receded in Natalie's rearview mirror, the fuzzy dice looked like the eyes of some cartoon character, laughing at her as she sped away.

23
Una

Una stood on the threshold of the Bernsteins' dining room, wondering what she could clean.

The room was a complete mess. Sample menus, music playlists, and color swatches were strewn over one end of the table. The other end was covered in color printouts.

Una's gaze swept over images of china patterns, balloon arches, floral centerpieces, and buffet items. She made it a point never to look at people's personal papers but was unable to avoid the photos of champagne fountains, ice sculptures, macaron towers, and platters of chilled caviar.

When she saw the cost of some of these items, she gasped. Then she clapped her hand over her mouth.

You are here to clean, not to judge.

But what to clean?

Boxes of Atari game systems and Sports Walkmans were stacked on top of the sideboard next to a bowl filled with little blue Tiffany boxes. The painting that once hung above the sideboard had been replaced by a bulletin board showing a seating chart for Charles's party.

The top shelf of the china cabinet had been emptied to make room for RSVP cards and invoices.

Dirty coffee mugs littered every surface. Una counted twelve in all.

"It's chaos, I know," Elaine said, stealing up behind Una. "The party's in two weeks and I still have *so* much to do."

The doorbell rang and Elaine frowned. "Oh, brother. I was just about to get to work."

She marched to the front door and Una heard her exclaim, "Beth! Oh, my goodness! I feel like I haven't seen you in ages. I was just about to have a cup of coffee. Care to join me?"

"I came to drop off this raspberry-walnut rugelach I made for Charles, but I also wanted to see a friendly face."

Elaine hesitated a beat too long before replying, "That's so nice of you. Come in."

Trailing Elaine into the kitchen, Beth spotted Una in the hall. "Morning, Una."

Una was shocked by Beth's appearance. She looked hollow, as if she hadn't eaten for days. Her cheeks were gaunt and the thin skin under her eyes was puffy and discolored.

The poor girl isn't eating or sleeping.

She smiled warmly at Beth. "Good morning."

Una vacuumed the dining room and waited until Elaine and Beth had relocated to the living room before carrying the dirty coffee cups to the kitchen.

As she loaded them into the dishwasher, she heard Beth say, "The thing is, he's been super sweet to me for the past few days. He's been complimenting my cooking and telling me I look beautiful. He took me out to dinner and held my hand under the table, just like he did when we started dating."

"You see! It's just a rough patch. All couples have them. As a matter of fact, Ben and I are in one right now. He thinks my plans for Charles's party are spiraling out of control. He won't let me spend another dime." Elaine let out a dry laugh. "I pretended I'd scale back to keep the peace, but I have money of my own, and I'll empty my bank account if it means giving Charles what he wants."

"Don and I aren't in a rough patch." Beth's voice sounded brittle, as if she might break down if she kept talking. "He feels like a stranger. He'll hug me or kiss me on the cheek like I was his mom or kid sister. He told me he wanted to take a break from baby making—that we should just focus on the two of us right now. He wasn't even looking at me when he said it. He was gazing out the window. It's like he's not all there."

Una ran the water in the sink even though there were no dishes to clean. She didn't want to hear such intimate details about the women's marriages. Her brain was already overloaded from having spent the last few days poring over the papers and notebooks belonging to Mrs. Stapleton's father.

Jonathan Stapleton's research on Cold Harbor dated back to the 1700s when the Matinecock Indians sold the land to a group of white settlers in exchange for a cartload of household goods.

His notes on the settlement's early history were reflected in his book, which Una had already read. After reading his notes, however, she finally came across a reference to Eel's Nest. In 1878, Captain Josiah Smith purchased fifty acres of land from the village of Cold Harbor. According to property records, Smith planned to build a house on a twenty-acre parcel. He also gifted thirty acres along the waterfront to be designated as a nature preserve.

Other than property records and tax payments, my search on Capt. Smith came up empty, Jonathan wrote. *As he kept only a gardener and housekeeper on retainer, I suspect Eel's Nest was not his primary residence. With no information on his place of origin, the name of his ship, or records of his voyages, he might as well be a ghost.*

Jonathan didn't run across Smith's name again until an 1882 article in *The Long-Islander* highlighted two Suffolk County homes built by Gilded Age architect Stanley Morris. One of those houses was Eel's Nest.

Jonathan had a copy of the original article, which included the grainy photo of Mrs. Smith that Una had seen at the library.

She didn't want to risk looking into the woman's black eyes again, so she immediately covered it with a Post-it note and didn't breathe easy until Mrs. Smith's smudged profile was hidden under the square of yellow paper.

In the article, Eel's Nest was described as the summer residence of Mrs. M. Smith, widow of Capt. J. Smith. The writer focused on the unusual architectural details of the Victorian home, including the layout of its garden and its large boathouse. When asked why the octopus in the stained-glass windows had been crafted with nine limbs instead of eight, Mr. Morris stated that the design had been his client's idea.

"The creature is meant to remind us that we cannot know all of the ocean's secrets," said Morris.

The circumstances of Captain Smith's passing weren't mentioned in the article, and there wasn't a single biographical detail about Mrs. Smith other than her title as benefactress of the Young Oystermen Society. Jonathan's notes indicated that the organization was founded as a means of expanding the oyster industry by creating paid apprenticeships for children between the ages of ten and fourteen.

There were two more articles tucked inside Jonathan's notebook. The first of these was a short and mournful paragraph from July 1882 listing the names of the nine boys who were "swept away by a sudden storm" near Port Washington, a town twenty-seven miles west of Cold Harbor.

The boys were enrolled in the oyster apprenticeship program, Jonathan noted in the margin. *I've found nothing to explain why they were together or why no other boats went missing in the storm.*

Finally, there was a single paragraph in the August edition

about the tragic death of Mrs. M. Smith in a fire that destroyed the boathouse at her Eel's Nest property. The cause of the fire was cited as a lightning strike.

Jonathan's notes revealed his frustration.

How were the remains identified as belonging to Mrs. Smith? What is her Christian name? Why no obituary? Estate bequeathed to a cousin residing outside the country. Property records for Eel's Nest show M. Smith as owner from 1878–present day. Was the estate put in a trust? Billy Phelps says mail to Eel's Nest has been addressed to Mrs. M. Smith for as long as he's worked at the post office. Current boathouse erected in 1968. Why not earlier? Attempts to contact new owner thwarted. No one picks up the phone or answers the door, but I feel a presence inside the house. Interviews with neighbors unhelpful. No one has seen or conversed with the resident. I'm determined to solve this mystery.

But Jonathan Stapleton hadn't solved it. He'd finished his book and died shortly after its publication.

Una filled a bucket with warm water and vinegar and began to mop the floor in the dining room. She started in one corner and mopped backward until she reached the next corner. As her mop made circular patterns on the wood floor, she thought about the patterns in Jonathan Stapleton's research.

The octopus in the window of Mrs. Smith's house had nine limbs.

Nine boys had been lost in a storm.

For the past hundred years, the name on tax and property records and on every piece of mail delivered to the sinister gray house had remained the same: M. Smith. No one had seen or spoken to the current M. Smith until recently.

What does the M *stand for?*

Girls' names floated through Una's mind. Mary, Maria, Margaret, Molly, Morgan, Mae, Matilda, Mildred.

She shook her head in dismissal. The woman who lived

in that house—that creature with the bottomless eyes—was no Mildred.

A crash came from the living room followed by a cry from Beth. "Oh, no! Your rug!"

Una guessed that Beth had dropped a mug. It had shattered, spilling coffee on the white shag rug. She was already moving to the pantry to grab some clean rags when Elaine shouted, "Una! Help!"

"Coming!"

Una dumped her bucket of mop water down the drain and refilled the bucket with a mix of vinegar, dish soap, and warm water. She hurried into the living room to find Beth kneeling on the floor, collecting pieces of broken crockery.

"Let me do it. You might cut yourself," she told Beth.

As she blotted the spill, she noticed that Elaine's face was in her hands and her shoulders were shaking. Without a word to Una or Beth, she got up and fled to her bedroom.

Una looked at Beth. "I can get the stain out. She'll never know it happened."

Beth pressed her fingertips to her temple. "It's not the spill. She's upset because I asked her if Charles really wanted this party. He's such a shy kid, you know? I just wondered if she'd asked him if it was okay to plan all these over-the-top things. They just don't sound like him at all."

Una wasn't about to get in the middle of an argument between two clients, so she kept quiet and continued blotting the rug.

"I shouldn't have said it," Beth went on. "I know how important this party is to her."

Una made a sympathetic noise. In truth, she agreed with Beth. This party was right up Elaine's alley. Charles would probably prefer a quiet celebration at home. Instead, he would have to stand under a spotlight, surrounded by hundreds of people.

Having soaked up the excess coffee, Una began to dab the rug with a rag soaked in the dish soap, vinegar, water mixture. She heard tiny granules of porcelain crunching under her palm, which made her think of the cut on Jill's hand.

Beth got up to toss the pieces she'd collected into the can under the kitchen sink. Leaning against the doorway, she said, "Una? I'm going to go. If you see Charles, can you tell him I made his favorite rugelach?"

"Of course. I know he'll love it."

Fifteen minutes later, Una walked into Charles's room, the vacuum trailing behind her. She was surprised to see the boy lying on his bed. His eyes were closed, and a pair of yellow headphones flattened his curly orange hair. His fingers tapped out a rhythm on his chest.

Una knocked on his open door. He slitted his eyes and then bolted upright in surprise. "Hi! Sorry. I didn't know you were here."

Una grinned. "I didn't know you were here, either."

Charles reddened. "I'm supposed to be studying—like, memorizing stuff for my bar mitzvah."

"My son always listens to music when he studies. He says it helps things soak into his brain."

Charles nodded. "Same here."

They smiled at each other, enjoying this small moment of kinship.

"Mrs. Pulaski made you a treat."

"Cookies?" he asked hopefully.

"Rugelach."

His face fell. "I like her Polish cookies the best. The ones with the jam."

"I like them, too."

"My mom says she wants to start her own business. She totally should. She's the best baker on Long Island."

Una sprayed Endust onto a rag, while surreptitiously studying Charles.

Despite what he'd seen at the regatta, he looked well. And even though she couldn't linger, chatting about music and cookies, she wanted the boy to know that she was in his corner. She wanted to tell him that she'd also seen something horrible when she was close to his age. She'd survived it, and he would, too.

Before she could raise the subject, Charles crossed the room and put a hand on the stack of books on his desk. "Me and Jill have been trying to figure out what I saw. She told me how you drove her home from the library—and that you knew why she took out so many mythology books. She said that . . . we could tell you things. Even if they sounded crazy."

Very softly, Una said, "Yes, you can."

Charles opened one of the books and took out a piece of paper from between the pages. It was filled with letters written in black ink. The language was unfamiliar to Una, but she thought the letters were beautiful. "Is this what you're studying?" she asked.

"It's Hebrew, but it's not what I'm supposed to be memorizing." He traced the letters with his fingers, coming to a pause on what Una assumed was a particular word. "This line is about a demon called Lamia. It was written a really long time ago."

He paused for so long that Una didn't think he'd continue. She noticed that his hands had begun to tremble.

"It's okay" she said. "You can trust me."

Shoving his hands under his armpits, he curled inward, like a pill bug. "I don't think we're safe. Me, Jill, J.J., Justin—none of us are safe."

"Because you think Lamia's real?"

Charles pointed at his window and whispered, "Yeah. And I think she's in that house."

Not anymore, thought Una, her skin prickling with fear. *She's come out.*

24

Jill

Jill was caught between a rock and a hard place.

Her mother had just told her that she could spend her Saturday morning cheering on her teammates in their swim meet against the Dolphins or working for Mrs. Smith.

"Her yard men prepped the beds on either side of her driveway yesterday. They even dug the holes for the flowers, but the flowers weren't delivered until after the guys left. All you have to do is put the flowers in the holes, cover them with dirt, and toss the pots in the trash." Jill's mother waved a piece of bacon in the air as she spoke. Lady and Tramp tracked the glistening piece of meat with hopeful eyes. "She offered to pay you *twenty* dollars an hour because she feels bad about your hand."

Jill watched her mom split the bacon in half and give a piece to each dog. They chewed once and swallowed, then whined for more. Looking down at the crispy bacon strip on her plate, Jill's stomach roiled.

"How does Mrs. Smith know about my hand?"

Her mother shrugged. "She probably saw the bandage. She might not come outside, but her house has windows. Anyway, she called this morning to ask if you and J.J. were free. I told her that J.J. had to go to the swim meet, but you could skip it if you'd rather earn some money. Or if you think you can swim well with your hand, then you can swim. It's up to you."

Jill hadn't made it past the second sentence. "She *called* you? Like, on the phone?"

"Yes, and she was perfectly pleasant. She even apologized for being such a standoffish neighbor. She has a rare skin condition, which made her very shy, but after trying new medicine, she's completely cured. She said she doesn't want to waste another minute hiding in her house, and wants to get to know her neighbors. She's actually going to the yacht club cocktail party tonight. I'll *finally* get to see what she looks like."

Jill's head was spinning.

Mrs. Smith had called her mom.

Mrs. Smith was coming out of her house.

"Another few hours of work, and you'll be able to buy that typewriter." Jill's mom gave her a conspiratorial smile. "We're both working to get the things we want. Isn't that great?"

The pleasure of her mother's approval was intoxicating, and suddenly, Jill was smiling, too. "What time does she want me to start?"

"Whenever you want. You're supposed to keep track of your hours. If you'd like to do extra work after you finish the flowers, she said to weed the small beds in the back garden. Do you know what she means?"

The spaces between the brick paths, Jill thought. *The ones around the woman's face.*

"Charles isn't swimming in today's meet, either. I have no idea why, but when I told Mrs. Bernstein about Mrs. Smith's phone call, she said Charles might come over and hang out with you." Her mother pulled a face. "Get him to help you. That boy needs to get his hands dirty."

Before Jill left, her mom wrapped her hand in a clean Ace

bandage and gave her a new pair of gardening gloves. "We want this to heal before the bar mitzvah. If I sell the McCreedy house, you and I will both get new dresses for the party. How does that sound?"

"Good," said Jill. For once, she wanted a new dress. She wanted the prettiest dress she could find.

Ever since she heard that Aaron was going to the party, she'd been fantasizing about making him fall for her. She pictured herself stepping onto the dance floor when suddenly, a spotlight would snap on, illuminating her white dress and the white ribbons in her hair. There she'd stand, glowing like Olivia Newton-John in *Xanadu*. All the kids would fall silent, dazzled by her beauty.

In her fantasy, Aaron would surge forward, determined to reach her before anyone else could. While the other kids watched, he'd take her hand and lead her away from the dance floor to a private place where they could still hear the music.

In this secluded nook, Aaron would smile at Jill. He'd tuck a strand of hair behind her ear and whisper, "I've liked you forever."

Then he'd lean over, almost in slow motion, and kiss her. His lips would be soft as velvet. He would taste like sugar.

"Jill!" her mother barked. "Did you hear what I just said?"

Jill shook her head.

"I told you to have peanut butter and jelly and a pear or baby carrots for lunch. *No sweets.*"

Twenty minutes later, Jill was sitting on the curb in front of Mrs. Smith's house, planting impatiens. The holes were so close together that no dirt would be visible when she was done, only a sea of pink, white, purple, and red petals.

Jill had finished the first bed and was starting on the second when Charles and his mother exited their house, heading in her direction.

Mrs. Bernstein paused at her mailbox and waved at Jill. "You're doing a *lovely* job." She shielded her eyes against the sun. "Do you need a drink? It's awfully hot out today."

"I have water." Jill pointed at the orange thermos near her feet.

"Well, Charles will be happy to get you some lemonade if you change your mind. You just say the word. Did your mom tell you when to water the flowers?"

Charles looked like he'd rather be beamed aboard the Starship *Enterprise* than spend another second standing close to Jill while his mother prattled on about the best time of day to water impatiens.

Finally, Mrs. Bernstein seemed to remember the mail. As she reached out to open the mailbox, a sleek convertible came roaring around the last bend in the road and screeched to a stop in front of Mrs. Smith's driveway. Mrs. Pulaski jumped out of the car. She wore big sunglasses, a cherry-red dress, and lipstick that matched her outfit. Jill thought she looked like a movie star.

Mrs. Pulaski grabbed a plate of cookies from the passenger seat and came over to admire the flower beds. "This looks so nice! I heard that Mrs. Smith wants to meet her neighbors, so I brought her some of my Christmas in July cookies."

Charles peered at the silver plate with interest. "Are they Polish?"

"Yes, but they're *not* for either of you." Her voice was unusually stern. "Even if she offers you one, don't take it. I added an ingredient that isn't for kids. If you get sick, I'll get in trouble with your parents, so promise me you won't have a single bite. If you promise, I'll bake a batch just for you. Do we have deal?"

Jill and Charles exchanged confused looks but readily agreed.

Mrs. Bernstein glided over, her arms held out to Mrs. Pulaski. "Aren't you gorgeous! What's the occasion?"

"Well, after Natalie told me she saw Don in a car with a strange brunette, I thought I'd introduce myself to the woman who's fucking my husband."

Mrs. Bernstein put a hand to her heart. "Beth! Not in front of the kids!"

Mrs. Pulaski glanced at Jill and Charles before moving closer to Mrs. Bernstein.

"Oh, of course. *You'd* never swear in front of your kid. Not Elaine Bernstein, the perfect mom." Her voice rose in anger. "But I don't have kids, remember? I might *never* have them! I might always be poor little childless Beth. The only woman in the room who can't talk about swim team or PTA meetings or sleepovers. Who doesn't have a labor story or a breastfeeding story or a first-day-of-kindergarten story. All Beth has is her marriage. And now that's turned to shit! Because of *that woman*!"

Mrs. Bernstein reached out to stop Mrs. Pulaski. "Please don't do this. Charles's party is in two weeks. She could revoke her permission. She could—"

"Jesus Christ, Elaine! All you care about is this fucking party. No matter how many checks you write, there *are* some things you can't buy. Like happiness or love or friends for your son!"

Mrs. Bernstein looked like she'd been slapped, but Mrs. Pulaski didn't seem to care. She clenched her jaw, stormed up to Mrs. Smith's gate, and slipped through the opening. Then she marched up to the front door and rang the bell.

Jill held her breath. Was she about to see Mrs. Smith for the first time? Would she answer the door? And if she did, what would happen? Mrs. Pulaski was an unpinned grenade.

What was she going to do? Shout at Mrs. Smith? Throw the cookies at her?

The tension was almost unbearable, but Jill couldn't look away. She knelt in the dirt, unmoving, her gaze fixed on the front porch.

When nothing happened, Mrs. Pulaski knocked on the door. Again, she waited. She knocked again, harder this time.

And just when Jill thought Mrs. Pulaski was ready to give up, the door cracked open.

From her vantage point, Jill could see only Mrs. Pulaski. She heard the murmur of women's voices but couldn't make out any of the words. Mrs. Pulaski didn't raise her voice. If anything, she sounded friendly.

And then, an arm snaked out through the opening. It seemed very long and pale to Jill. A hand closed around the cookie plate and instantly withdrew back into the gloom. The door closed with an audible thud. Mrs. Pulaski marched back to her car. Without looking at Jill or Charles, she gunned the engine and drove away.

As soon as the convertible disappeared around the bend, Mrs. Bernstein hurried into her house.

Jill picked up an impatiens and eased it out of the pot. Keeping her eyes on the soil, she whispered, "Did you see anything?"

Charles took the plant from her and put it in the ground. "No."

They didn't speak again until the flower beds were done. The work hadn't taken very long, which left Jill with a decision to make.

She wanted to earn more money, but she didn't want to be in the backyard alone. Everyone knew Charles was a wimp, and Jill wasn't looking to him for protection, but if he stayed, there'd be another pair of eyes to watch Mrs. Smith's house and another pair of ears to listen for suspicious sounds.

"Want to see the back garden?" she asked Charles. "That's where the face is."

Too curious to turn her down, Charles grabbed the box of black trash bags and followed Jill through the garden door. When he saw the stone face, he paled.

"She's gotta be a monster."

Worried that he'd bolt, Jill put a hand on his back. His T-shirt was soaked in sweat. "We don't have to stay long, but we might find another clue. You know, something to help us figure out *exactly* what she is. All we have to do is weed between the paths. Do you have gloves?"

Charles produced a pair from his back pocket. Focusing on the ground seemed to steady him. "How can you tell the difference between the weeds and the plants?"

"Just pull out all the grass. And the dandelions. I'll do the rest."

Jill was soon lost in a rhythm of grabbing weeds by the base, yanking them from the dirt, and tossing their bodies into the trash bag. She sat cross-legged on the bricks and tackled the weeds on the left while Charles focused on the bed to the right. They worked in silence until Jill pulled out a dandelion and felt something heavy dangling from its roots.

"Charles! Look at this."

Charles detached the piece of rusty metal from the roots. "It's a belt buckle. Kind of a weird thing to find here."

Their eyes met and Jill knew they were both thinking the same thing.

The tooth with the braces. A belt buckle. Things that might be found in a grave, not a garden.

Charles put the buckle next to the thermos and went back

to work. A half hour later, after they'd both finished weeding their areas and had started on a new area, Charles made a discovery of his own.

"Hey," he hissed, shooting an anxious glance at the house. "I found something."

Jill tried to ignore the prickly sensation on the back of her neck. Mrs. Smith was watching them; she was sure of it. But from which window?

Charles scuttled over to Jill and opened his hand. A coin sat in the middle of his palm. "I rubbed off most of the dirt. It's from 1870!"

Jill picked up the silver-colored coin and stared at the woman's profile and the date. Its reverse side showed three straight lines that looked like the columns on a Greek temple.

"Do you think it's worth anything?" she asked Charles.

"Maybe. But what if she finds out we took it?"

Jill pinched the coin between her thumb and index finger and slipped it inside her sock. "We need to show everything we find to Una."

Charles opened his mouth to argue when a shadow fell across the path. They both pivoted to find a tall, dark-haired woman in a sky-blue halter dress standing over them.

"Good morning, children. I've been watching you work with such diligence. You must have built up quite an appetite by now and Mrs. Pulaski brought me these lovely cookies." She held out the silver plate piled with cookies. "As tempting as they look, I've never taken to sugary foods. Would you care for one?"

Unable to meet the woman's dark, bottomless eyes, Jill studied the hands holding the platter.

Milky-white skin stretched over bony fingers. Her long, pointy nails were the yellow of old paper. They were the hands of a fairy-tale witch disguised as a princess.

Jill lowered her eyes to the ground and said, "No, thank you."

"What about you, young man?"

Charles lurched to his feet. "No, I c-can't. I'm s-sorry. I have to go home now."

Jill's chest tightened. Charles was going to leave her alone with this terrifying creature?

She turned to him, wordlessly begging him to stay, but he scurried away in that quick, awkward gait that made him look like a rodent being chased by a feral cat.

Jill had to swallow twice before finding her voice again. "I need to go, too."

"I owe you remuneration. How many hours did you work?"

Jill grabbed the trash bags and her tools. She still didn't meet the woman's eyes. "Two."

"I'll put an envelope in your mailbox. After the carrier comes, of course. Perhaps he would like these confections. He looks like a man who indulges in sweets all too often."

Jill mumbled a goodbye and hurried off. The trash bags made it impossible to run, but she could feel the slithery caress of the woman's gaze on her back.

She cursed Charles for abandoning her. He was supposed to be her ally. He was supposed to help her figure out a way to defend themselves against something neither of them understood. But he was too much of a wimp. She could only rely on Una.

As soon as she was safely inside her house, Jill turned on the kitchen sink and drank deeply from the tap. Then she washed her hands, her arms, and her face, scrubbing hard to get rid of all traces of dirt from Mrs. Smith's garden.

But no amount of soap could erase the snake-tongue feeling of looking into that creature's soulless black eyes. Mrs. Smith had assessed her in the same way her mother inspected a piece of meat at the butcher counter.

"She's gotta be a monster," Charles had said.

He'd been talking about the stone woman, but Mrs. Smith had the same eyes. Arrogant, angry, and old. Too old to belong with such a smooth, sculpted face.

Jill turned off the water. Her hands were shaking so badly that she gave up trying to dry them with the dish towel. Instead, she called the dogs. When they trotted to her side, she sank down on the floor and buried her face and hands in their soft fur.

She didn't care how much money she was offered. She didn't care what her mom said. She was never going back to that house.

25

Mrs. Smith

Mrs. Smith studied herself in the mirror with satisfaction. She looked like an older, sultrier version of the Brooke Shields girl.

Most of the men at the cocktail party would want her, but she was only interested in the most virile specimens. Tonight, she would have sex with several partners, hoping that a little sperm competition would fire up her anatomy.

She found her first partner while crossing the parking lot.

"Hot damn!" cried the valet as she passed by.

She paused to look him over. He was young, barrel-chested, and hairy. She spun in a slow circle. "Do you like what you see?"

He clutched his chest and said, "Lady, you must be a parking ticket because you have *fine* written all over you."

Mrs. Smith gestured at the valet booth. "Is there enough room in there for two?"

"If we stand real close."

She brushed her fingertips over the crotch of his black polyester pants. "How close?"

Within minutes, she was straddling the hairy young man. As she rode him, she closed her eyes and imagined tearing him apart with her teeth. When he came, he twisted her nipple like it was a radio dial. She waited until he'd released his seed before leaning forward and biting his ear hard enough to draw blood.

He shoved her off his lap. "Ow! What the fuck, lady?"

Mrs. Smith licked her lips. The man's blood stirred her hunger, but she was not here to feed. It was time to find another partner.

"Crazy bitch!" the valet shouted as she walked away.

She strode through the front door and approached the banquet room, wishing she could tune out the raised voices and peals of laughter.

She was over an hour late, which meant her neighbors were probably on their second or third cocktails. Here in their private club, with its leather chairs and trophy cases, their defenses would be lowered. All Mrs. Smith had to do was pick a man and get him to meet her in an empty room. As long as that man kept his mouth shut, she could continue luring partners to the same space for the rest of the evening.

She was walking down the hall behind a tall, broad-shouldered man when he suddenly ducked into the coatroom. Taking note of his thick legs and big hands, she followed him.

The man had his back to her. As she closed and locked the door, he continued rifling through a cardboard box. Grunting in frustration, he tossed the box on the floor and began digging through another box.

"Goddammit," he muttered.

Mrs. Smith said, "Lose something?"

The man cried out in surprise and swung around. He opened his mouth to berate her for sneaking up on him, but his jaw went slack.

"I've been watching you," she said, pointing a red nail at his chest.

His gaze probed every inch of her body. His eyes shone with lust. His face clouded in confusion. "Do I, uh, coach your kid? Mrs. . . . ?"

"Smith."

He was taken aback. "Is Kirsten your daughter?"

Mrs. Smith walked her fingertips down her neck to her collarbone. "As much as I *love* children, I don't have any of my own."

"But you've been watching me?" The man shoved his left hand in his pocket in a lame attempt to hide his wedding band. "I'm Coach Patrick."

"Patrick." His name was a reverent whisper on her lips. "Could you help me? I lost an earring. A round, lush pearl. I could go down on my hands and knees to look for it—" she slowly ran her hands over her dress, lingering on the fabric covering her breasts "—but this is so tight. It might tear right down the middle."

The man's eyes widened. The tip of his tongue probed the corner of his mouth. A pulse danced on his neck.

"There's no need to speak." She pressed the tip of a nail against his lips. "I followed you in here because I want you." She withdrew her hand and put the same nail in her mouth, biting down on it as she stared at him, her dark eyes daring him to make a move.

"I—I can't," he stammered.

Mrs. Smith tucked a finger under the shoulder strap of her dress and eased it over and down. She pushed the strap lower and lower until the swell of her right breast was exposed. She leaned back until her nipples strained against the blue silk. Even in the dim light, the man could see how they begged for his touch.

An animalistic groan rose from his throat.

He tugged at the top of Mrs. Smith's dress, freeing her

perfect breasts. His mouth was suddenly everywhere. He licked and bit her. He sucked on her. Drooled on her.

When she couldn't stand his fruitless pawing anymore, Mrs. Smith shoved him away and told him to take off his pants. While he unbuckled and unzipped, she bent over the table.

Glancing at him over her shoulder, she commanded, "Don't be gentle. I want you to take me. Prove to me that you're in charge."

This seemed to release something primal in the man—an atavistic, biological need to dominate.

Digging his fingers into her hips, he thrust himself inside of her. He rammed into her slowly at first. Then he picked up speed. The table struck the wall with a forceful *bam, bam, bam*, but he didn't stop. When he climaxed, he grabbed a fistful of her hair and pulled so hard that a clump of black strands came away in his hand.

He dropped the hair in revulsion and backed away from her.

While Mrs. Smith stood and began to adjust her dress, he growled, "This never happened. You got me? This *never* happened."

Mrs. Smith retrieved a comb and a compact from her purse. Studying her reflection, she said, "It's already forgotten."

After he fled the room, she worked the tangles from her hair and reapplied her lipstick. After using powder to conceal the bite marks on her neck and décolletage, she spritzed herself with perfume and stepped out of the coatroom just as Natalie Scott exited the ladies' room across the hall.

Mrs. Smith contorted her mouth into the semblance of a smile. "Hello, neighbor."

Natalie let out a soft gasp. "Oh, my goodness! Are you Mrs. Smith?"

Mrs. Smith disliked shaking hands, so she performed a small bow instead. "One and the same."

"It's lovely to finally meet you," the Natalie woman gushed. "I know I'm staring, but I can't help it. You're *stunning.* I can't believe you ever had a skin condition."

"How very kind."

Natalie made a visible effort to stop gawking. "Did you just come in? If so, I can introduce you to everyone."

"Perhaps not everyone. I am unaccustomed to crowds. My immediate neighbors will be enough for this evening."

Natalie blushed. "Of course. I almost forgot that you've . . . kept to yourself for a long time. The Bernsteins are at the bar. Let's start with them."

As she entered the room, Mrs. Smith saw heads turning her way. Men and women openly ogled her. And then the whispering began.

"Who is *that*?"

"Is she a model?"

"A movie star?"

"She *has* to be someone famous."

"Look. Natalie is introducing her to the Bernsteins."

"Figures. They've got more money than the rest of us put together."

Mrs. Smith felt every eye on her as she ordered a Manhattan from the bartender.

"Do you have a bourbon preference?" he asked.

Mrs. Smith gave him a reproachful look. "I prefer rye."

Benjamin nodded in approval. "Rye is what they used back in the day. Did you know that the cocktail you just ordered was invented at the Manhattan Club in the 1870s at a party hosted by Jennie Churchill, Winston Churchill's mother?"

Mrs. Smith shook her head. "Impossible. At the time of

the party, which was thrown to honor presidential candidate Samuel Tilden, Jennie Churchill was in England, preparing to give birth to her famous son."

"How do you know that?" asked Elaine.

"Having spent a good part of my life indoors has made me a voracious reader." She smiled warmly at Elaine. "How is your son's *d'var Torah* coming along?"

Elaine lit up with delight. "You're familiar with the bar mitzvah ceremony?"

Mrs. Smith dipped her chin. "I am. Such a sacred rite of passage should be celebrated on a large scale. I'm looking forward to wishing your son *mazel tov* in person."

"Just two weeks to go," crooned Elaine.

Mrs. Smith took a delicate sip of her cocktail. Then she speared the cherry with the tip of the stirrer and held it between her plump lips. The Scotts and Bernsteins were hypnotized by the sight of her mouth closing around the bright red cherry.

"How many guests will be in attendance?" she asked after swallowing the cherry whole.

"Over three hundred," boasted Elaine. "We invited the whole synagogue, people from Benjamin's company, Charles's school, and everyone on our street. We're a tight-knit group on Tidewater Terrace, and we're happy to welcome you into the fold."

Natalie held up her glass. "I can't raise a toast to you as Mrs. Smith. What's your first name?"

"Mare."

"Like the horse?" asked Jimmy. His face was alcohol-flushed, and he wore a lopsided grin. Natalie shot him a dirty look.

"As in Latin for 'the sea,'" corrected Mrs. Smith.

The two couples raised their glasses to Mrs. Smith.

Elaine put her empty glass on the bar and was about to speak again when her attention was suddenly diverted. Her smile slipped and she turned to Natalie and whispered, "Don and Beth just walked in."

"Uh-oh." Natalie grabbed her husband by the arm. "Quick. Buy Don a drink and take him to the lounge."

"Why?"

"Please, Jimmy. Just do it."

While Jimmy ordered a whiskey neat, Benjamin gave his wife a puzzled look. "What's going on?"

"*Tsuris.* Natalie and I will handle it." Elaine put a hand to her heart. "Excuse us, Mare."

The women hurried away, leaving Mrs. Smith alone with Benjamin Bernstein. Unlike most men, he was unaffected by her beauty.

He is used to beauty, she thought. *His wife is like a ghost jellyfish, ethereal and elegant, but lacking in substance. He yearns for something else.*

"What kind of trouble?" she asked.

Benjamin gazed at her with renewed interest. "You know Yiddish?"

"I have a gift for languages and an aversion to crowds." Mrs. Smith glanced around the room. "Is there a quiet corner where we might sit?"

"Certainly. Let me show you."

Benjamin led her away to a sitting area overlooking the harbor. Though Mrs. Smith had no interest in seducing this man, she did want to extract information from him. After disarming him with questions about his business, she turned the topic back to his son's bar mitzvah.

"Are you looking forward to the party?"

"Am I looking forward to being crammed on a luxury power yacht with three hundred people?" He snorted. "No. But if it makes my son happy, that's all that matters."

Mrs. Smith pumped him for details for another ten minutes. When she was satisfied, she bid him a good night and left the party.

As soon as she reached the beach, she took off her heels and left them on the seawall. The sand was soft beneath her feet, but she longed for the cool caress of water. Wading in up to her ankles, she headed for her boathouse.

She scanned the quiet harbor. Her children were out there, swimming under docks and boat hulls. She would rejoin them soon enough.

"Hey!" a man shouted from behind her. *"HEY!"*

Mrs. Smith didn't turn around. Recognizing Don Pulaski's heavy breathing, she smiled to herself. She'd known he would follow.

Human men were all the same. When she wanted them, they were as pliable as warm wax. But when she was done with them, they turned combative. Their lust morphed into a different breed of desire. A simmering, heated rage.

This is why she wasn't surprised when Don's hand closed around her arm and he yanked her out of the water. He smelled of booze, sweat, and cigars. His tie hung loose. There was a red stain on his white shirt. Fury danced in his eyes.

Grabbing her other arm, he shook her like she was a rabbit in a hound's mouth. "Did you fuck the valet?"

She gazed at him flatly. "Yes."

"Whore," he spat.

She found his anger amusing. "I don't belong to you. I belong only to myself."

"But why *him*?" His fingers burrowed into her arms. "He's a total loser."

"You're all the same to me."

His face clouded with anger. He cupped her jaw and squeezed. "Fucking whore."

Her hand whipped through the air, striking Don's cheek with such force that his head rocked back.

The slap echoed over the surface of the water. In the distance, there was a splash. Then another. And another. Her children were close. They'd sensed her hunger. The possibility of violence.

Mrs. Smith needed to couple with another man tonight. A virile man. If she wanted a better performance than Don Pulaski had delivered thus far, she needed to bring out his baser self.

Don grunted, sounding more pig than man, and slapped her back.

The blow sent her careening to the ground. She fell on a patch of broken shells, which sliced through her silk dress and the skin on her lower back with the precision of a scalpel.

Her mouth curved into a smug grin. And then, Don was on her.

He tore the bottom of her dress and shoved his body between her thighs. His hand searched for a pair of nonexistent panties.

When he hesitated, Mrs. Smith worried that he might walk away, so she punched him in the chest. He caught her hand and pinned it over her head. Eyes blazing, he pushed her dress high up on her belly and penetrated her.

She laughed softly, stoking his ire, and he responded by wrapping his hands around her throat.

By the time he came, Mrs. Smith's crimson face was flecked with spittle. Her back was bleeding. Her arms and neck were a garden of blooming bruises.

She leveled a dangerous look at Don.

"You have served your purpose," she said, lying in the sand with her pelvis tilted toward the night sky. "Do not come near me again. Disobey me, and I will cause you more pain than you've ever known."

Don looked into her black eyes and blanched. Suddenly disorientated, he fumbled with his pants and lurched across the sand.

When he was gone, Mrs. Smith peeled off her ruined dress and walked into the water.

Her children surged forward and wound themselves around her legs and torso. The blood from the cut on her back excited them. They thrashed from side to side. Their mouths opened to drink in the metallic taste in the water. When it finally dissipated, they grew calmer. They swam languidly, weaving in between her legs, stroking her flesh with their flesh.

She ducked under the surface, her hair spreading out like a spiderweb.

Suddenly, a spark ignited in her human womb. Warmth spread over the center of her torso.

Bathed in diaphanous moonlight, the Mother of Eels glowed with power and possibility.

She was ready to create life.

In two weeks, when the same moon was little more than a scythe blade, she would attend the man-child's party. She would eat her fill of Pure Ones, swim to her secret cave, and tear herself in two.

She closed her eyes, reveling in the sensation of eel skin against her naked body.

My children. It's almost time to feast.

26

Natalie

The following Friday, Natalie and Elaine were in the Scotts' living room, talking about Mrs. Smith.

They'd had multiple phone calls since the cocktail party. During these calls, they dissected every detail of her appearance and wondered where she'd bought her dress. They spoke about the ripples her presence had sent through the yacht club community.

"She's got all the wives worried," Natalie had said toward the end of Tuesday's phone call.

"Benjamin didn't say a thing about her looks, but he went on and on about how clever she is," Elaine had responded in a sour tone.

On Wednesday, Natalie called Elaine to complain that she'd overheard Jimmy telling one of his buddies that his neighbor was "foxy as hell."

Ever loyal, Elaine had said, "So are you."

"Not to Jimmy. Not this week. He's been in a pissy mood ever since the cocktail party. I don't know what's gotten into him."

Now, perched on the edge of a chair in Natalie's living room, Elaine said, "Did you hear about the fight in the parking lot? It happened after we left."

Natalie handed Elaine a glass of white wine. "No. Between whom?"

"Rod Kerry and the valet. Apparently, the valet ground the gears of Rod's new Porsche or something like that—you know I'm clueless about cars—and Rod yelled at him. Instead of apologizing, the valet jumped out of the driver's seat and hit Rod in the face."

"No!"

Elaine nodded. "Broke his nose. The valet got fired, of course, but if you ask me, he probably did Rod a favor. His nose was pretty awful before."

The women cackled.

"*I* have a story, too." Natalie took a swig of wine and continued. "I ran into Judy Strauss at the dry cleaner's, and she told me that Coach Patrick was completely soused by the time he left the cocktail party. She said he was nasty to the kids during Monday's practice. She even saw him pull Misty Duncan's ponytail because she was talking while he was giving instructions."

Elaine tutted. "That's a bit much."

Natalie glanced at her watch. "I thought Beth would be here by now. Did you talk to her today?"

"Yes. She said she was coming."

"I've called her a bunch of times this week, but she never picked up or called me back. How did she sound?"

Elaine took a sip of wine, considering. "She sounded okay, actually."

Natalie's brows shot up in surprise. "Really? Do you think they'll work it out? She and Don?"

"I hope so. I mean, what would Beth do if they got divorced?"

This gave Natalie pause. "Start her home baking business?"

"From what home? Without Don's income, she'd be in an apartment over someone's garage."

"That's true." Natalie glanced around her comfortable living room. "What would you do in her shoes?"

Elaine let out a soft laugh. "Benjamin would never cheat on me, but in the unlikely event that he did, I'd keep it to myself. You and I aren't in the same boat as Beth. We're mothers. I wouldn't tear apart my family over an affair, would you?"

"No," Natalie admitted. "If Jimmy and I got divorced, I'd have to do even more than I do now. I probably wouldn't be able to keep Una on, and if I had to quit my job to do nothing but clean and take care of the kids, I'd be crushed."

"Speaking of your job, congratulations on the McCreedy sale." Elaine saluted her with her wineglass. "May it be the first of many."

Natalie felt a rush of affection for her friend. "Thank you. I *am* very pleased. Just between you and me, I was getting worried. In the time it took me to convince the Sherifs to put an offer in writing and to negotiate with the McCreedys, Sid gave Gina another fantastic listing."

"What will you do if he gives you another dud?"

"Oh, I fully expect another challenging property. And since I won't make enough money selling duds, I've come up with a plan." Natalie smiled slyly. "You see, all the agents are supposed to take turns answering the phone, but the guys never do it. Gina will put promising leads right in the guys' laps because that's what we've been told to do, but I'm going to keep them for myself. That's how the Sherifs became my clients and that's how I got the listing for the colonial down the street from our church."

"The Richardsons' house?"

"Yep. They're moving to Port Washington because Phil wants to be closer to the city. Phil wanted to work with a male agent, but I got lucky because he didn't call Gold Coast. Barbara did. When I told her the men didn't have much time to give their property the attention it deserved—not with their busy golf and tennis schedules—she talked Phil into giving the listing to me."

"Do all the men play golf and tennis?"

Natalie flicked her wrist. "I have no idea. Technically, it was Gina's turn to receive a cold call lead, but she doesn't have three kids to send to college and Sid will always throw her a bone. I have to bend the rules to get ahead."

Natalie had done more than bend the rules. She'd crossed a line. She would never tell Elaine, or anyone else, what she'd done after Gina cornered her in the break room for a little "talk between us girls."

"Don't rub Sid the wrong way, or he'll give you the garbage listings forever," Gina had advised. "Try being nicer to him. Compliment him once in a while. And smile more when you're around the guys. I know you're a mom and all, but you're still pretty. You may as well use it while you've still got it, am I right? After all, it works for me. I'm top of the sales board this week. *Again.*"

Gina had done a little shimmy, grabbed her coffee cup, and walked out of the room, leaving Natalie rigid with fury.

That bimbo thinks she's better than me!

Natalie had seethed all day. She kept staring at the sales board, noting the addresses of Gina's listings.

The closing for the cute cape near the school was coming up. The family had already moved out and the house was empty.

After work, Natalie drove down the quiet street. She'd parked a block away from the house and walked toward the Gold Coast sign. Everyone in the office knew that Gina used her birthday as the code for her lockboxes, so Natalie had no trouble gaining entry to the house. Once inside, she'd wriggled the dishwasher out of its cubby and used a serrated knife to make several small, jagged holes in the water hose.

"Mice will chew anything," she'd mumbled as she pushed the dishwasher back in place. Then she'd set the machine to its longer run cycle, started it, and left the house.

Two days later, Sid had erased the address from the sales board.

"Kitchen flooded," he'd told Natalie. "Deal's off. Gina can try again when everything's fixed up."

No, Natalie had thought. *That's going to be* my *listing.*

The doorbell rang, startling Natalie from her reverie and causing a riot of barking from Lady and Tramp, who were downstairs with the kids. She told the dogs to hush up and opened the front door.

She expected Beth to be haggard and disheveled, but her friend looked completely put together in tight jeans, a pink tank top with a ruffled neckline, and wedge sandals. Her nails were done, her hair was recently permed, and she wore a bold, musky fragrance instead of her usual floral scent.

"Here's our Beth, looking lovelier than ever." Natalie gestured at the sofa. "Get comfy while I make you a drink."

Elaine held out a hand. "I'm so glad you came tonight. How are you?"

"I'm good," Beth said, squeezing Elaine's proffered hand. "Don confessed everything to Reverend Koterba. We met with him on Wednesday and the reverend believes what I believe—that that woman put a spell on Don. He said that demons come in many forms and that we should strengthen our marriage so we'll be prepared to fight evil together. And Don agreed to go to the orphanage with me next week. If we can't have children the natural way, we're going to adopt. We also met with someone at the bank, and I'm finally going to start my baking business."

Natalie and Elaine tripped over themselves to congratulate her.

"I have some news as well," Natalie said. "The McCreedy house is under contract."

A shadow passed over Beth's face. "I'm happy for you, but I feel sorry for the new owners. Those vines will grow back. They'll creep over that fence and bring her darkness into their lives. I hate living on the same street as *her*. I hate being here right now—being so close."

Natalie felt hurt by Beth's comments. Her friend had every reason to be mad at Mrs. Smith, but couldn't she see how important the sale was for Natalie? Why was she trying to make her feel guilty for succeeding at her job?

"The McCreedys have lived behind her for years. Nothing happened to them," she pointed out.

Beth rolled her eyes. "That couple is barely alive. What could she possibly take from them?"

Having no idea how to respond to this, Natalie walked over to the bar cart to make herself a second old fashioned.

Elaine pasted on a smile. "Maybe she'll move. Now that she's healed and can go anywhere, there's no reason for her to stay here. This is a family neighborhood. She doesn't fit in."

Beth's eyes narrowed. "Have you seen her since the cocktail party?"

"Only glimpses of her getting in and out of taxis. They show up first thing in the morning and bring her back late in the afternoon. One of the drivers almost hit the new mailman. I thought they might start a fistfight in front of my mailbox."

"We have a new mailman? Since when? What happened to Paul?" asked Beth.

Elaine told Beth how Paul's wife had found him at the bottom of the stairs. "Must've been a heart attack. Paul's wife was out of town, and he was supposed to pick her up at LaGuardia on Sunday. He never showed up, so she had to take a taxi home. When she walked in, she saw him on the floor.

He'd obviously been dead for hours. There was a crushed cookie in his hand, so at least his last meal was a good one."

Beth had gone very pale. "How do you know all this?"

"Una told me. Paul and Kristofer were friends. They were supposed to grab a beer after work on Friday, but Paul said he wasn't feeling well. If only he'd gone to the doctor then."

Natalie thought Una had been unusually taciturn on Monday. Now she understood why.

Why did she tell Elaine about Paul but not me?

"Speaking of Una," continued Elaine. "I have an awkward situation involving her and Charles's party."

Natalie groaned inwardly. *Of course. Every conversation comes back to the party. What will Elaine do when it's over? Start making plans for a high school graduation extravaganza?*

"What's the situation?" she asked with a notable lack of enthusiasm.

Perceiving the slight, the corners of Elaine's mouth dipped down. "Charles wants to invite Una. He actually insisted, though I don't understand why. I mean, she's great, but she won't really know anyone other than the three of us."

"Maybe he's just being polite. I doubt she'll go even if you invite her."

Elaine hurried to contradict Natalie. "I gave her an invitation earlier this week. She said yes on the spot. She's coming by herself, too."

Natalie thought it was sweet of Una to give up her Saturday night to hang out with a bunch of strangers for Charles's sake. Like everyone else, she probably felt sorry for the boy. And Una was nothing if not kind. That's why J.J., Jill, and Justin loved her so much.

Natalie was about to ask Beth what she planned to wear to the party when Beth suddenly doubled over as if she was going to be sick.

Elaine laid a hand on Beth's back. "Honey. Are you okay?"

"Oh, Jesus," Beth whimpered. "Oh, Lord."

She's going to puke all over my sofa, thought Natalie, casting around for an alternative.

Grabbing the ice bucket, she thrust it in between Beth's knees. "Here."

As Beth clutched the bucket, Natalie told her to take deep breaths. When it seemed like the immediate danger had passed, she plucked a starlight mint from the stash in Jimmy's desk, unwrapped it, and dangled it under Beth's nose.

"Peppermint helps with nausea," she said. "I wouldn't have survived my pregnancy with Jill without these mints. It's funny because it's the one candy she doesn't like. Suck on this. By the time it's gone, you'll feel much better."

Taking the candy, Beth said, "Excuse me," and hurried down the hall to the powder room.

"What was that about?" Natalie whispered to Elaine.

"She turned white as snow when I mentioned Paul."

"It's not like she knew him well. Maybe she's just putting on a brave face. This stuff with Don must have her twisted up in knots. Any mention of you-know-who is bound to make her feel bad."

Elaine smoothed the fabric of her cream-colored slacks. "What am I supposed to do about Charles's party? All three of them are coming, and I don't want a scene. All of our friends from the temple will be there. And the rabbi. My parents and sisters. Everyone!"

"You have to uninvite Mrs. Smith," Beth said from the doorway.

Natalie's and Elaine's heads swiveled in unison. Neither of them had heard Beth return from the bathroom.

"Excuse me?" said Elaine.

"You have to uninvite Mrs. Smith," repeated Beth, her gaze

boring into Elaine. "How could you even consider letting her come after what she's done?"

Elaine put a hand on her heart. "I'm sorry about what happened, Beth. You know I am. But she signed off on all of my requests in exchange for an invitation. I can't go back on my word. There's no telling what she might do."

Beth advanced into the room. "Let me get this straight. A fireworks display is more important than my feelings?"

Elaine shifted uncomfortably. "It's more complicated than that."

"I don't think it is," Beth snapped. "I'm asking you to choose between Don and me—people who've been your friends for years—and the witch next door. And you're going to pick the witch? You know what that tells me? That she got to you. To both of you."

"What do you mean?" asked Natalie.

"You think because she planted some flowers or hired your children to work in her back garden that she's being neighborly? Wake up and smell the coffee. She'll be after Jimmy next. Or Benjamin." Beth jabbed her finger against her temple. "Think about it! Why would she finally come outside after all this time and decide to attend a kid's birthday party? Because she's on the hunt for her next married man, that's why. She's looking to come between another couple."

Natalie thought back to the cocktail party. There was no denying Mrs. Smith's powerful presence. She'd silenced the room when she first walked in, but she hadn't stayed long. She'd socialized only with her immediate neighbors and then left without saying goodbye.

"It is a little odd that she'd want to spend an evening with three hundred people when she ditched the cocktail party after forty-five minutes because she's not used to crowds," Natalie mused aloud. "I'm not buying her story about the skin condition, either. She had perfect skin. Perfect hair. And a perfect body. She's younger than all of us, but she seemed much older. It was the way she talked. There is something strange about her."

Beth said, "She's a witch. You're inviting a witch to celebrate your son's bar mitzvah. You know what she did to Don. How she hurt *me*, and you still want her there? Are you serious?"

Elaine folded her hands in prayer. "Please. I won't have anything to do with her after next Saturday. Not a thing! But I gave her my word. Just come to the party and—"

"It's us or her," Beth said flatly. "You have to choose."

Elaine opened and closed her mouth like a fish. Finally, she murmured, "I can't."

"Actually, you just did."

Beth stormed to the front door, opened it, and then whipped around to face her friends. "She's dazzling you. You don't see it, but I do. It's exactly what she did to Don." Her hand closed around the cross pendant hanging at the base of her throat. "That woman is evil, and as long as she's in your lives, we can't be friends. I'll be praying for you and your families, but don't call me until you're done with her."

The door had barely closed behind her when Natalie turned on Elaine. "Beth needs this party. She needs to dress up and feel pretty. She needs to drink champagne and dance with Don. How can you do this to her?"

"My son's happiness comes first. I'll fix things with Beth when it's over." Elaine stood up and carried her wineglass to the bar cart. "I feel a headache coming on. I think I'll go home and lie down. Good night."

Natalie let out a huff of exasperation and carried their dirty glasses into the kitchen. By the time she returned to the living room, Elaine was gone.

Feeling out of sorts, Natalie went out to the back deck and sank into a lounge chair.

She was annoyed with her friends. She'd wanted to celebrate her triumph. After all, she'd done the impossible. She'd sold the McCreedy house. Her friends knew how important this was to her, but they were too wrapped up in themselves to care.

In the rafters, she heard the electric bug zapper fry insect after insect. The sound pacified Natalie. She sank deeper into her chair and tried to absorb the serenity of the quiet harbor and the star-filled sky.

The kids were downstairs watching TV and Jimmy was out with two of his sailing buddies, which meant she had at least another hour to herself. There was nothing she had to do. No one needed anything from her. The kitchen was clean. The dogs had been fed. She could take a long bath, paint her nails, or read a book.

Instead, she made popcorn for herself and the kids. Then she went downstairs and joined them for the end of *Time Bandits*.

When the credits started rolling, Justin climbed onto Natalie's lap. She kissed the top of his head and told him it was bedtime.

To J.J. and Jill, she said, "No more TV. You can read until ten."

After tucking Justin in, Natalie got ready for bed. She turned on the small TV in her room and settled in to watch *Death on the Nile*. During commercials, she flipped through a Spiegel catalog, folding down a page featuring a long denim skirt and another showing a smart-looking red blazer. She made it halfway through the catalog before the dogs appeared next to her bed, whining to be let out.

With a sigh, she threw off the covers and followed the dogs to the front door. On her way back, she poked her head into Jill's room. Her daughter had a book open on her lap and two more stacked near her feet.

"Still reading about monsters?" Natalie asked.

"They're African folktales," Jill said. "Some have monsters. Some don't."

"I was about your age when I got really into mysteries. I'll have to give you one of my old Agatha Christie paperbacks to try."

Closing her book, Jill stared at its cover. Without looking at Natalie, she said, "Would your parents have believed you if you told them something was evil? Like the kid in *Time Bandits* tried to do?"

Natalie glanced around her daughter's room, idly searching for anything that might be out of place, but all was in order. "Probably not. Because I was a big-time reader. Like you. They would've thought I was telling them a story—something from a book or my imagination."

"What if you knew something was evil, like the black rock in *Time Bandits*, but you couldn't get any adults to believe you?"

"I'd do what the boy in the movie did. I'd try to be brave and figure out how to solve the problem myself." Natalie began to close the door. "You'd better hit the hay. If you want a trophy like J.J.'s, you'll have to swim like a shark tomorrow."

"Okay."

Natalie smiled at her daughter. She almost said, "I love you," but "sweet dreams" came out instead.

"You, too," Jill whispered back.

Climbing into bed, Natalie picked up her Spiegel catalog again. As she studied the glossy pages, her thoughts turned to Beth. Could she and Don continue living up the street from Mrs. Smith, or would they feel compelled to move?

Natalie pictured a Gold Coast sign with her name on it in front of their house. A vase full of yellow roses in Beth's kitchen. She saw herself in her gold blazer, opening the door to a crowd of eager buyers.

She drifted off long before Jimmy came home. By the time he slipped into bed, she was dreaming of Gold Coast signs up and down the street. Every sign bore her name. In the kitchens of every house, there were vases with yellow roses.

In her sleep, Natalie wore the ghost of a smile.

27

Una

Una was looking through the clothes in her closet, wondering if the dress she'd worn to a wedding two years ago was fancy enough for Charles's party. Though it was the nicest dress she owned, it wasn't very summery.

It was a silvery blue and shimmered like a fish scale. When she'd tried it on and stood in front of the mirror in the JCPenney fitting room, she'd caught a glimpse of the pretty girl she used to be. She'd also tried on a purple dress, though she wasn't sure why. Perhaps because purple had been Svana's favorite color.

Try as she might, her routines failed to restore a semblance of balance to her world. She couldn't concentrate on simple tasks like gardening or baking brown bread. Pests were chewing craters in her flowers. The last loaf she'd made had burned in the pan.

The shadow at the bottom of Tidewater Terrace was beginning to spread. It had gotten to Don first. Then to Beth. Then to poor Paul Campbell.

Kristofer believed that Paul had a heart attack, but when Una saw the plate with the daisies around the rim that had been recovered from Paul's mail truck, she knew what had really happened.

The plate was one of Beth's. She always used a daisy plate when gifting her baked goods.

But the treats she'd made weren't meant for Paul. Una had seen the hole in Beth's garden when she'd gone outside to shake out a rug. All the foxglove was gone.

Foxglove. *Foxes glofa.* Fairy gloves. Witch's thimbles. Dead man's bells. No matter what name it was called, it was extremely poisonous. Every part of the plant was toxic, especially the leaves.

Una pictured Beth drying the leaves and crushing them into a fine powder. She must've mixed that powder into her pastry dough along with lots of sugar, honey, and jam. Lots of sweetness to disguise a bitter taste. She'd given the finished product to Mrs. Smith.

Did Beth want to make her sick? Or to kill her?

Whatever her intentions, Beth's scheming had cost Paul his life.

Paul, who'd been Kristofer's friend for a decade. How many beers had they shared on a Friday night after work? How many Sunday afternoons had they wiled away fishing? How many winter Saturdays were spent at the bowling alley, hoping to be the best in their league?

Mrs. Smith knew the cookies were poisoned but gave them to Paul anyway. If Una needed proof that the woman was a monster, she had it.

She saw no point in sharing these thoughts with her husband. Paul was dead. Nothing was going to bring him back, and Una had to focus on her plan to protect the children. Not just Charles and the Scott children, but all the children at the party. Any of them could become Mrs. Smith's next victim.

Una hadn't been able to save Svana. But she wouldn't let that *thing* drag another innocent down into the deep.

Early that morning, she'd met Jill and Charles at the neighborhood park, which was little more than a playground with two benches and a picnic table. Sitting at the table, the three of them had shared their fears about Mrs. Smith.

"When I saw her standing outside her house, I knew she was the monster who drowned my sister," Una had begun. "She knows that I recognize her—she might even remember me, too—so I am a threat to her. She will come after me tonight. And you children, too." She glanced at Jill. "Did any of your books say how to defeat her?"

Looking hopeless, Jill had tossed a pebble into the road. "If she's Lamia, she's been around for at least a thousand years. How are we supposed to fight a demon?"

As if expecting this question, Charles said, "We have to get her before she goes in the water. She's in a human form now. If she bleeds, she can be killed."

"I'll bring a sewing needle and prick her with it, just to be sure." Una patted her purse. "I will also bring this."

She pulled out a bundle of cloth and unwound it, revealing a knife with a bone handle. Symbols had been scratched into the blade, and a fish with teeth had been carved into the handle.

Charles had leaned closer to the weapon. "Is that from Iceland?"

"Yes. It belonged to my *afi*. My grandfather. He was a fisherman. He made this knife out of whalebone and steel. My grandmother added these runes. They're for protection." Una rewrapped the knife and placed it back in her purse. "You should have a weapon, too. Both of you. Something sharp. Something you can take out quickly."

Jill and Charles nodded.

"We have to make sure none of the children are ever alone with her," Una continued. "We must watch her at all times. If she goes off alone, we must assume she is hunting.

I will go after her. If I end up in danger, you must warn everyone else."

Charles splayed his hands. "How?"

Jill replied before Una had the chance. "We can tell the DJ there's an emergency. Or grab his mic. Or we could set off the smoke alarms. Cruise ships have smoke alarms, so I bet this boat does, too."

"Good," Una had said. "Or find the captain. Tell him that one of the guests is trying to hurt a child. Do whatever it takes to get people to listen."

Thinking back on this conversation, Una wished she'd had more answers for Jill and Charles. She wished she had a more powerful weapon than an old fishing knife. She wished there was an army to stand between the children and Mrs. Smith. She would give her life to save them, but would that be enough?

"Picking out your party clothes?" Kristofer asked from the doorway.

Una turned to him. "I am. I just hope you'll be okay without me."

He came into the room and put his arms around her. "I'll be fine. After I drop you at the yacht club, I'm going to Wendell's house. We're going to grill burgers and watch the game. Try to enjoy yourself. Drink champagne. Eat cake. Go crazy on the dance floor."

"The only person I want to dance with is you."

Kristofer led Una to the living room. He switched on the radio and held her tight as the Flamingos sang "I Only Have Eyes for You."

Una smiled at her husband. "You promised me a lifetime of rainbows the day you asked me to marry you. I'm glad I believed you. I'm glad I said yes."

"I was the luckiest boy in Iceland," he said, kissing her on the cheek. "Now I'm the luckiest man in America."

Later, after an afternoon of laundry and lawn mowing, Kristofer drove Una to the yacht club, where the valet stopped them and signaled for Kristofer to roll down his window.

"Are you here for the Bernstein event?"

"Just me," said Una.

"The party's on the boat at the end of the dock. You can't miss it."

Kristofer drove on, whistling when the luxury motor yacht came into sight. Spotlights illuminated its modern lines and sleek prow. Guests in tuxedos and sparkling dresses followed the red carpet to the boarding platform. Music blared from the boat's top deck.

"It's the James Bond song," said Kristofer. "I hope I don't lose you to a handsome spy with a British accent."

"I wouldn't worry. You know I don't like martinis."

Kristofer laughed, kissed her, and whispered, "Have a good time, my sweet."

Una looked at the boat, which was shaped like a sharpnose shark, and knew she might never step onto dry land again.

"I love you," she told Kristofer. She kissed him tenderly on the mouth and held his face in her hands for several heartbeats.

"*Ég elska þig líka*. I love you, too," he said as she got out of the car.

She stood in the parking lot and watched him drive away. Then she took a deep breath and stepped onto the dock.

Jill was standing next to the boarding platform, waiting for her.

She looked so grown-up in her white satin dress with a ruffled skirt and sleeves. She'd woven ribbons into the tiny braids framing her face and wore glittery eyeshadow. Her lips were slick with berry-colored gloss. For a moment, Una felt she was looking at a brown-eyed Svana.

"You're beautiful," Una told her.

"You, too," said Jill.

Una glanced up at the boat. "Where's Charles?"

"His mom's making him hand out spy gadgets for the scavenger hunt. I told him I'd get you and bring you back to where he is." She patted her dress. "This has pockets. I've got sharp things in both of them. Charles has stuff, too."

"Good. Remember, Charles will be busy with his guests, so it's up to you and me to watch Mrs. Smith."

Jill's fingers brushed the skirt of her dress. "I know."

Steeling herself for the night to come, Una walked up the boarding platform and under a black-and-gold balloon arch.

A crew member in a starched white shirt and navy slacks helped Una step from the platform to the teak deck.

"Welcome aboard," he said. "The main party is on this deck. You'll find the bar in the front of the boat and the buffet and dance floor in the back. If you're looking for a place to sit, there's seating on deck two. The very top deck is for crew members only. Have a great time!"

Una followed Jill down a narrow corridor to a set of double doors that opened up to a large carpeted space. Buffet tables had been arranged in a U shape, and guests were already filling their plates. Waiters circulated the room, offering champagne to the adults and soda to the kids. The room was noisy and warm, and most of the seating had already been claimed by old men in yarmulkes. The old women had formed a circle around Charles. Their braying laughter and tooth-baring grins reminded Una of a pack of hyenas.

Charles waved at Una, and the old women grudgingly departed to give her access to the guest of honor.

"You did it," she said, giving Charles a hug.

"I thought the ceremony would be the hard part. Let's see if I can survive all this," he joked, waving an arm around to incorporate the guests, the hedonistic display of food, and the James Bond–themed decorations.

"Is *she* here?" asked Jill.

Charles pointed at the ceiling. "She's upstairs, talking to some people from our temple. My mom introduced her to everyone like she was her new best friend. Even my dad thinks she's great. None of the adults will believe us if we tell them she's dangerous."

The champagne Una had just swallowed burned in her throat.

"I was too nervous to eat lunch, so I'm starving. Should we get some food?" Charles asked.

"Sure." Jill pointed at the buffet. "You go first. It's your party."

A blush spread over Charles's cheeks. Standing tall, he said, "You're with me, so you don't have to wait in line."

Una had never seen such a decadent spread. There were baskets of bread, platters of cheese, and small bowls of caviar. There was salmon in dill sauce, roast beef, lemon chicken, baked ziti, roasted potatoes, five different kinds of salad, and an assortment of pickles and olives.

Though most of the guests heaped their plates high, Una wasn't very hungry. Kristofer would want her to sample the sumptuous food, but she had very little appetite. She took a small piece of salmon, a few potatoes, and some asparagus. Jill's plate contained mostly cheese, bread, and pickles while Charles had gone for roast beef and glazed carrots.

"Let's eat outside. It's stuffy in here," Charles said.

Una and Jill followed him to the back deck, where tables were arranged around the perimeter of the dance floor.

As Jill spread butter on a slice of French bread, she glanced around. "After we eat, we should start watching her."

"She probably won't do anything until we leave the dock," said Charles.

Una put her forkful of salmon down. "We're going somewhere?"

"Just around the harbor." Charles looked at Jill. "I heard my mom tell your mom that we're going to stop just past the channel markers. That's when we'll do the cake and fireworks. It was Mrs. Smith's idea, you know. To rent a boat. She told my mom it would be safer to shoot off fireworks over the water. More impressive, too. The party planner almost lost her freaking mind finding a boat big enough for all these people."

It was her idea.

Suddenly, the ship's horn blasted, and a voice boomed out of the wall-mounted speakers.

"Good evening, ladies and gentlemen. I'm Captain John and it's my pleasure to welcome you to Charles's bar mitzvah celebration. It's come to my attention that some Russian spies have learned of the secret cargo we've got on board, so we're going to cast off in hopes of staying one step ahead of them. As soon as we're anchors up, the scavenger hunt will begin. Ask any crew member for a clue sheet and put your spy skills to the test. We expect a smooth cruise around the harbor tonight, but just in case, there are life jackets on every deck and lifeboats on both the stern and port sides. Now, let's cast off before the Russians have a chance to crash this party."

The deck vibrated under Una's feet as the engine thundered to life.

We're going out to sea, she thought in a panic. *Into her territory.*

Guests flocked to the rails to watch the crew detach the boarding platform and untie lines.

Una's mind was spinning. Their plan had been desperate at the start. Now, with the dock sliding away, it was bound to fail.

What could she do? Beg the captain to stop? Find Elaine

and tell her that she was playing into Mrs. Smith's hands? And even if she could still disembark, she wouldn't. She couldn't leave Jill and Charles and J.J. alone to face whatever was coming. And something was definitely coming. Icicles of foreboding formed in Una's chest.

She saw the fear in Jill's eyes and whispered, "It will be okay."

The boat cleared the dock and headed toward the channel. Una stared at the trail of white froth behind it. The path to land. To safety.

The DJ started playing the James Bond theme song.

"Kids!" he shouted into his mic. "See if you've got what it takes to be a secret agent! Get your scavenger hunt sheet from any crew member and don't forget to grab a Polaroid camera. Put any pictures you take in this big bowl to my left. Who knows? One of you might snap a photo of a Russian spy."

"Come on, Charles." Jill motioned for him to get up. "If we team up, we can pretend to play while keeping an eye on *her.*"

The kids rushed toward a crew member, their fear momentarily forgotten. Una saw J.J. waiting in line with a handsome boy with dark hair and broad shoulders. Seeing Jill, the handsome boy smiled and performed a small bow. Jill lit up like a star, but didn't leave Charles's side.

Una gave the kids a head start before ascending the same staircase. The music still permeated to this deck, but it wasn't nearly as loud. Scanning the groups of people, Una saw Benjamin in conversation with a gorgeous woman in a one-shouldered midnight-blue gown.

The woman's gaze landed on Una. Her dark eyes narrowed into hostile slits.

Mrs. Smith.

Suddenly, a group of kids swarmed Benjamin. They shouted excitedly, explaining their need to search under the cushion of his bench. Finding a clue taped to the underside of the cushion, they whooped in triumph and raised their Polaroids to capture the moment.

Camera flashes struck Mrs. Smith like bullets, and she snarled. Seeing her distress, Benjamin took her elbow and steered her to the other side of the boat.

"*Ohmygawd*, look at her! She's *totally* pissed." A girl in a hot pink dress showed her photo to her friend.

Mimicking Mrs. Smith's scowl, the other girl said, "Like, chill out, lady. It's a freaking party."

The first girl threw the photo to the floor and rushed off after the other kids.

A whorl of air blew the photo in front of Una's feet. She picked it up and went rigid with terror.

The woman in the photo had become a beast. Her eyes were two black wells illuminated with firefly sparks of hatred. Her lips were pulled back uncannily far, revealing a mouthful of white teeth. It was the lethal smile of a viper.

Una felt dread coil around her bones. The creature in this photo was not here to dance or make friends. She was here to hurt.

To hunt.

Shoving the photo in her purse, Una decided to take stock of the boat. She needed to locate the exits, the lifeboats, and the smoke detectors. She needed to find the wheelhouse and lay eyes on the radio in case she had to call for help. Finally, she needed another weapon. Something bigger than her hunting knife.

There were grappling hooks and boat hooks secured to the rails of every deck. After cutting partway through the ties of a boat hook with her knife, she ignored the NO ADMITTANCE sign and approached the bridge.

The captain was irritated to see a guest in his command center, but Una smoothed things over by saying that her father, a lifelong fisherman, would've wanted her to introduce herself to the man piloting such a fine vessel. Hearing this, he told her all about the boat. Una pretended to listen while studying the instrument panel. Once she'd located the radio, she craned her head around the wheelhouse. There, hanging on a hook next to the door, was a marine harpoon kit in a plastic carrying case. The slogan on the bag read ALL YOU NEED TO STICK A MONSTER.

"Best seat in the house for fireworks," the captain said.

Una smiled and said, "And they'll be set off from . . . ?"

The captain pointed at the ceiling. "Bow of the sundeck. We'll drop anchor just past the channel buoys and then—boom!—we'll light up the sky. It'll be like a second Fourth of July."

Una thanked the man for his time. Tipping his cap, he said, "You should head back to the main deck. They're serving the cake in fifteen minutes. You'll want a front-row seat when they wheel that baby out."

Una had seen the cake when she'd cut through the kitchen. It was a three-tiered behemoth, decorated to look like a tuxedo, and had *0013* piped along the base in gold icing. The figure of the spy on the top tier wore a yarmulke and carried a scroll instead of a gun.

Fifteen minutes later, just as the captain had predicted, an announcement came over the speakers, asking for the guests to congregate in the buffet area. Una waited until the other guests headed down before following them to the main deck. Once there, she scanned the crowd. She found Jill and Charles, but there was no sign of Mrs. Smith.

Una's heart thudded in her rib cage. All of the children were gathered together, so where was she?

As soon as the lights went out and the cake was wheeled in, Una climbed the stairs back up to deck two.

Other than a few crew members, the deck was deserted.

Una paused next to the port-side lifeboat. The corner of the cover had been untied. Una hadn't noticed this before, but it seemed an odd sight on a ship run by such an exacting captain.

Walking around to the starboard lifeboat, she found its cover untied, too.

She heard a noise directly above her—a faint *clip clip clip.*

Cheers burst from the deck below. As Una imagined the guests parting to make way for the giant cake, something flew past her and struck the water hard.

Una couldn't see what had fallen off the boat. Leaning over the rail, she caught a flash of white in the dark water, then nothing.

She's above me.

Closing her hand around the knife inside her purse, Una whispered, "Be with me, Amma," as she ascended to the sundeck. When she reached the top of the stairs, she saw a woman in a midnight-blue dress pouring gasoline from a red plastic container onto a crate of fireworks.

"Stop!" Una cried. "Stop that!"

Mrs. Smith emptied the can and tossed it over the rail. Then she flicked a lighter. Its small flame danced in the night breeze.

"You're going to die tonight, *Islendingar.*" Mrs. Smith's voice was a low growl. "I have tasted your blue-eyed brothers and sisters before. Now, it is your turn." Her mouth stretched into a terrifying grin. "This fire will send you all into my realm. While I feed on the children *you* love, *my* children will pick your bones clean."

Mrs. Smith knelt and touched the lighter flame to a Roman candle fuse. With a *whoosh*, the fire galloped over the rest of the gas-soaked fireworks.

In that searing flare of light, Una saw that Mrs. Smith's hands were stained with blood.

28
Jill

Jill was waiting in line for a piece of cake when she thought she heard someone scream from the upper deck. It was hard to hear anything over the pulsing music and Heather's raucous laughter. One of J.J.'s friends had been imitating their swim team coach, and all the kids were cracking up. Jill was too worried to join in. She didn't see Una or Mrs. Smith and was afraid to search for them by herself.

She wanted Charles to come with her, but he was surrounded by flushed and happy adults who couldn't stop touching him. He was hugged, kissed, and patted on the back. Grandmas squeezed his cheeks. His mother adjusted his yarmulke.

Jill wondered what it would feel like to be lavished with so much affection. Would she ever do something to earn that kind of praise and attention? She doubted it.

She flashed back to earlier in the week, when her mother had taken her to the mall. Jill had been so excited to try on dresses. Despite her fears about the party, she still held on to her fantasy of enchanting Aaron.

Inside Macy's, the rows and rows of glittering colorful dresses were like wishes waiting to be granted. If Jill chose the right one, her wish might come true.

"That won't look good on you," her mother had said when Jill had run her hand down a purple sequined number. "Your shoulders are two wide to go strapless."

For every dress Jill admired, her mother had found something about Jill's body that wouldn't work. Her waist was too doughy. Her thighs were too thick. Her hips were too curvy.

Finally, her mother had picked out several dresses and told her to go try them on.

The moment she'd felt the white satin dress slide over her tanned skin, Jill had known it was perfect. It hugged her on top and the gauzy, tiered skirt floated around her legs like the bell of a jellyfish.

She didn't need to try on anything else. She'd found her dress.

"Let me see," her mother had commanded.

Jill hadn't wanted to leave the sanctuary of the fitting room. In that space, she was beautiful.

"Come on," her mother had urged. "I have things to try on, too."

Jill had stepped out and done a twirl. That was how confident she'd felt in that dress.

"It's a little short," her mother said. "Try the pink one. It'll cover more of your legs."

Turning to the mirror, Jill had examined her reflection. "I like it."

"Well, I don't think you should wear—"

Something inside Jill snapped. She'd rounded on her mother and screamed, "Just forget it! I don't want to do this anymore! You're mean! You're mean and I hate you!"

She'd gone back into the fitting room, changed into her shorts and T-shirt, and stormed out of the store. Her mother had called after her, but Jill didn't stop until she reached the car. She slid into the back seat and sobbed. Her mother had come out twenty minutes later with a garment bag in her arms. She scolded Jill for causing a scene.

Jill hadn't replied. She hadn't looked at her mother or asked her what she'd bought. She'd stared out the window and willed her mother to start the car and take her home.

She'd barely spoken to her since. Even when her mom presented her with the white satin dress, she'd only mumbled a thank-you. It had taken Una telling her that she was beautiful to restore the feeling she'd had in the Macy's fitting room.

I wish I was Jewish, she thought now as a waiter handed her a sliver of cake with alternating layers of chocolate and vanilla and a cookie shaped like a gun.

Normally, Jill would devour the treats right away, but she was too worried about Una.

Just as she was looking for a place to leave her plate, the music came to a screeching stop.

"*FIRE!*" a woman near the DJ shrieked. She pointed to the upper deck.

Jill hurried across the dance floor to the aft seating area. Looking up, she saw a black cloud shift against the dark sky. She smelled smoke but couldn't see the fire.

A high-pitched squeal burst though the speakers and then the captain began to speak. He told the elderly, parents with young children, and guests who couldn't swim to proceed to the lifeboats in an orderly manner.

"Crew members will hand out life jackets to every guest. Please put them on immediately and listen for further instructions. The most important thing is to remain calm."

The tail end of his sentence was cut off by an explosion.

Jill clapped her hands to her ears as a maelstrom of light and thunder engulfed the top of the boat.

The night blazed with color. Mortar shells of light detonated on the sundeck, assaulting the sky. Rockets shot off in every direction, creating sparkling mushroom clouds in the air or barreling into the water with banshee cries.

The boat was under attack from an unknown enemy. Shrill whistles and cannon fire booms reverberated through its hull. The noise and flashing lights disoriented the guests. The smoke pouring down the deck stairs terrified them.

People were running in every direction, screaming. They shouted names, knocked over tables as they reached for each other, crashed into furniture. The deck was instantly littered with shattered glass and broken plates. Ash began to rain down from the sky.

Jill dropped to her knees and crawled under a café table. She watched people swarm to the rails. Kicking off their shoes, they straddled the rails and disappeared over the side of the boat.

A hand clamped around her arm and yanked her out from under the table. Her dad held her by the shoulders, searching her for injury.

"Are you okay?"

"Yes, but—"

"We need to get in the water and swim to those boats." He pointed to a cluster of boats beyond the ship's bow. "Jump overboard and follow your brother." Misjudging her hesitation for fear, he shifted his hands to either side of her face. "You can do it, Jilly Bean. You're strong. I'm going to get your mom in a life jacket and stick close to her. We're not the swimmers—you guys are. Other kids from the swim team are already in the water. *Go!*"

Her dad pushed her over to where J.J. stood and then darted toward the life jacket locker.

"Come on!" J.J. shouted.

"I can't! Una's up there!" Jill saw kids she knew from swim

team, from school, and from her neighborhood climb over the rail and leap off into space. In between explosions, she heard splash after splash after splash.

J.J. grasped her hand. "She can get in one of the lifeboats! You heard Dad. We have to get off!"

Jill's eyes flooded with tears. "You go! I'm not leaving without her!"

"Goddamn it, Jill!" she heard her brother yell, but she ran in the opposite direction without looking back.

Before she reached the stairs, someone grabbed her arm.

It was Charles. "Where's Mrs. Smith?"

Jill started pulling Charles up the stairs. "I think she's up here. With Una. Get your weapon out."

At the top, Charles said, "You take this side. I'll take the other one. Meet you at the bow."

Jill swerved around a man with a bleeding forehead. "Rose!" the man called. "Rosie, where are you?"

A woman in a gold gown stumbled toward Jill. She made a shooing motion at her. "Go back! The lifeboat's on fire!"

Ignoring her, Jill hurried toward the bow.

Smoke poured from the lifeboat's canvas cover as two crew members tried to douse the flames with fire extinguishers. A third crew member used a long hook to peel off the burning material and flick it into the water.

"We're good! Lower it down!" she heard one of them shout as she raced past.

Heat from the sundeck poured onto her head and shoulders. Every time another firework went off, she hunched her shoulders, expecting sparks to rain down on her.

The door to the interior areas was propped open. Tongues of black smoke escaped from within, probing the air. Jill's eyes and lungs burned.

She coughed and yelled Una's name. Coughed again.

No one was alive in there. The heat and smoke were too intense, but she shouted until it felt like a cheese grater had rubbed the tender flesh inside her throat.

Finally, she lurched toward the bow.

Through the haze of smoke, she saw a figure hunched over the rails. It took Jill a moment to recognize that the woman with the whirlwind of silver hair was Una.

"*UNA!*" Jill croaked. "We need to go!"

Una's hands clutched the rail. Her eyes bulged as she stared into the water. She rocked back and forth, muttering something Jill couldn't hear over the mayhem.

Wrapping her hand around Una's wrist, Jill was about to tug her away from the rail when a pillar of flame rent the sky. It lit up the water around the bow, illuminating the thick shadow moving under the surface.

It wasn't a solid mass like a whale or a big shark. It was almost arrow-shaped with a rounded head, streams of hair, and a nest of rippling arms.

It was the creature in Mrs. Smith's stained-glass window. The creature in her garden. The creature with the woman's face and tentacles for arms. It was the monster.

And it was swimming toward the kids in the water. The kids trying to reach the cluster of moored boats.

"*Hey!*" Jill shouted. "There's something in the water! It's coming your way! Come back! *Hurry!*"

Her smoke-scratched voice was lost in the smack of the lifeboat hitting the water. She tried again, but the noise of the fire chewing through the teak decking drowned her out.

The air was polluted with the smell of gunpowder and melting plastic. When Jill sucked in another breath, the grime singed her throat.

Next to her, Una kept muttering. She said something that

sounded like "swan" over and over as she watched the monster draw close to the group of swimmers.

Suddenly, a head disappeared under the surface.

"No," Una whispered. "No, no, no."

Another head vanished. And another.

The swimmers began to scream. Some put their faces in the water and swam as fast as they could, racing back toward the burning yacht. Others kept moving toward the moored boats.

The fire shifted in the wind, and the spotlight of flame that had lit up the water beyond the bow winked out.

Jill strained to see what was happening in the dark. She heard howls of terror. Brief and terrible shrieks of pain. She heard desperate splashing.

And then, just as one of the swimmers got close to the bow, Jill saw the monster hovering directly beneath her.

She saw a woman's face, distorted by a flattened nose and too-wide eyes. Saw a mouth filled with daggers. A flash of scales.

"Oh, God," she whispered.

Two arms, long and eel-like with hooked claws at each end, wrapped around the swimmer.

"HELP!" the girl keened. "HELP ME!"

Jill reached out a hand in a futile gesture. A sob rolled up her throat and tumbled into the night as Mrs. Smith's arms tightened around the girl and pulled her under the surface.

In the illumination of the hull lights, Jill saw the water cloud. She saw a severed arm float by, a cord of flesh flapping out of the shoulder like a puppy's tongue.

"Jill!"

Jill was lost in a fog of horror. Adrift in fear. She thought she heard her name, but the sound was swallowed by too many other sounds. Even when a hand rattled her shoulder, she didn't move. She couldn't look away from the water.

"Where is she?" she murmured.

Next to her, Una said "swan" again.

Suddenly, Charles shook Jill's shoulder. "What are you guys doing? We have to go down and wait for the lifeboat! They're going to drop people on the beach and come back for us."

Jill pointed down at the arm. It bobbed on the surface for several seconds before it was struck by a serpentine shape. Suddenly, a swarm of eels was biting the arm, tearing and nibbling.

"It's *her,* Charles! It's Mrs. Smith."

"Where? I don't see her!"

"She's killing all the kids! If we go in the water, she'll get us, too!"

Charles shook his head. "This can't be happening. What are we going to do?"

Jill put her hands on Una's cheeks and turned her head away from the water. "Una. We have to get on a lifeboat. *We have to go now!*"

Una's eyes were haunted. She tried to look at the water again, but Jill wouldn't let her. "I must stop her."

Charles tugged on Una's arm. Together, he and Jill finally got her to move.

As soon as they led her away from the bow, Una seemed to come back to herself. Wrenching her wrist out of Jill's grasp, she scooped a rectangular plastic bag off the floor and told the kids to hurry.

Bent over, as if the smoke and falling ash were pressing down on them, they hurried to the lifeboat station. The wind shifted again, and the air around that part of the boat almost cleared.

As they paused to suck in a breath of clean air, Jill scanned the dark horizon, searching for the lifeboat's bow lights.

"Listen," Una said, putting a hand on Jill's and Charles's

shoulders. "When the boat comes back, you two need to get on it. I'm not going with you. I need to wait. For her."

She unzipped the plastic bag and removed a pair of steel poles. One of the poles looked like the tip of a spear. Jill saw the lettering on the bag and realized what Una planned to do. Her eyes flooded with tears.

"No, Una! A harpoon won't work. You'll never get close enough. You have to come with us!" Jill started crying hard. "*Please!* I won't go without you."

"You must," Una said, already heading for the stairs leading to the lower deck.

The guests who hadn't jumped overboard or found a space in the lifeboat were milling around the aft section, sticking close to the rails. Everyone wore a life jacket. Jill didn't see any little kids in the crowd. Most of the kids her age were gone, too.

Unable to find her parents or her brother, Jill felt a fresh stab of fear. Were they in the lifeboat? Were they in the water? Out there, with *her*?

Are they still alive?

The lights of the houses along the shore were a world away. There, behind walls of wood and glass, people were watching TV or reading books. Some were asleep. To them, the darkness was a comfort. It shrouded them in silence, invited them to rest. To Jill and the other partygoers, the dark night with its eyelash of a moon provided cover for the demon in the water.

The stars turned their shining faces away from the burning boat. Smoke blotted out the impotent moon. The air tasted of poison. The wind threw ash like confetti.

"The lifeboat's coming back!" a man shouted.

Jill heard the panicked voice of a woman. "Where are the kids? I can't see the kids!"

People surged to the starboard side, desperate to secure a seat on the lifeboat.

A crew member tried to instill order. "Stop pushing! Form a line! Women and children first!"

Jill looked around for J.J., or Heather, or Aaron, or anyone she knew. Every face was turned toward the shore. Every head was veiled in soot. Jill couldn't tell who was who. She pictured the chewed arm and the heads bobbing in the water like a pod of seals. She pictured the monster pulling them under, one by one, and biting them. Heather, Aaron, Lisa, Christine, Billy, Jason, Kim, Brian, Michael.

Bile surged up Jill's throat, and she rushed over to the rail to vomit. As she heaved, tears escaped from the corners of her eyes. The wind snatched them away before they could fall into the harbor.

When Jill stopped retching and could stand upright again, Una took the towel-wrapped knife out of her purse. She gave the towel to Jill and pressed her grandmother's knife into Charles's hand.

"Mrs. Smith is killing the children. She killed my sister. I must stop her."

The lifeboat glided to the yacht's side. "Rescue boats are on the way!" the crew member shouted up to the guests. "ETA is five minutes! Stay calm!"

"We don't have five minutes!" a man cried. "This thing's gonna blow!"

As if on cue, a bang rocked the boat from bow to stern and a dragon puff of fire erupted from the bridge. People screamed and began leaping into the lifeboat. Some were too far away and ended up in the water. Others fell on top of other passengers. Jill heard bones crack. She heard the smack of skulls.

Overloaded with wriggling, shrieking bodies, the pilot cast off.

Guests wailed as the lifeboat disappeared into the darkness.

Suddenly, the captain was there. He lowered the bandanna he'd tied around his nose and mouth and bellowed, "Everyone in the water *now*! Swim for the shore. The rescue boats will find you!"

The remaining guests began to jump overboard, but Jill couldn't move.

A crew member frantically gestured for the three of them to get off the boat. "There's gas in the bilge! Go! *Go!*"

Charles held out a hand to help Una over the rail. "We have to get off. Even the crew's jumping!"

Refusing to let go of the harpoon, Una stepped off the side of the boat. Charles tucked her knife into his waistband and motioned for Jill to jump.

"Wait!" she cried, spying a boat hook rolling across the deck. She grabbed it and, together, she and Charles leapt off the boat.

The moment the salt water stung her eyes and her dress ballooned around her waist, Jill expected tentacles to wrap around her chest. She tensed, waiting for a hundred barbed wire teeth to tear into her meaty thighs.

She was afraid to swim. Afraid of any movement that might attract Mrs. Smith.

When gargled screams echoed from the darkness off to her left, Jill's body kicked into survival mode. She pivoted her right hip toward the sky and began to do a sidestroke.

"Swim like this," she called quietly to Una. "You won't splash."

Unburdened by a harpoon or boat hook, Charles opted for breaststroke. It wasn't long before he pulled ahead.

The lights on the shore seemed impossibly small. Behind Jill, a curtain of black smoke fell over the yacht.

We'll never make it, she thought, her tears falling into the uncaring water.

Somewhere in front of Charles, a woman squealed in terror. A heartbeat passed and then she cried out again, but the sound was abruptly cut off by a violent splash.

Suddenly, Jill heard engines. A searchlight wandered across the water to her right.

"HERE!" she shouted, pausing to tread water and wave. "We're here!"

A light landed on her face. Held there. Grew closer. It was as bright as the summer sun. It was a beacon of hope.

Please, God, Jill prayed. *Please save us. Please get us out of the water.*

An inflatable dinghy approached with agonizing slowness. Something brushed against Jill's back. She shivered at its touch.

Eels.

She shoved the boat hook toward it, but it was already gone.

The dinghy drew up next to Una. A man said, "Give me your hand!"

Jill didn't wait for an invitation. She swam over and clasped the lifeline.

"I got you," said the man.

Jill tossed her weapon in and let the man pull her into the dinghy. As soon as she regained her balance, she pointed at the black water between their rubber boat and the shore. "My friend is there!"

Before the man could respond, the gas tanks on the yacht exploded.

Jill's back was turned, so she didn't see the blooming fireball, but she felt a blast of heat and the force of the man's hand, pushing down.

She lay flat, holding Una's hand, as the echoes of the explosion roared over the water. Waves pitched the dinghy violently from side to side. Jill clung to Una with one hand and to a lifeline with the other. Fresh ashes stuck to their wet skin and clothes.

The man was the first to sit up. Hearing him stir, Jill and Una did the same. They waited for him to restart the motor, to speed them to safety, but he just sat there, staring into the water.

"What the fuck?"

Jill didn't want to look, but she did.

Mrs. Smith was right under their fragile little boat. She floated inches below the rubber hull, her arms fanning lazily in the current. Her scales gave off an iridescent sheen. Her eyes were half closed. Her tongue protruded from the depths of her cavernous mouth like a piece of seaweed.

She didn't attack. She didn't do anything. She seemed to be in a daze.

"What the fuck?" the man repeated, raising an orange flare gun into the air.

"Nooooo!" Jill shouted, but it was too late.

He fired the gun, sending a red flare high into the sky.

Mrs. Smith's eyes snapped open. Two tentacles shot out of the water and wound around the man's neck.

Una roared and buried her harpoon into a tentacle. Jill picked up her hook and stabbed the same tentacle. They stabbed again and again while the man clawed at the scaly flesh cutting off his oxygen.

Then, there was a sickening crunch and the man's head popped off his neck like a champagne cork. It dropped into the water, a grotesque buoy bobbing in the current.

Mrs. Smith rose out of the water. First came her head, then her serpentine neck, and finally, her calloused torso. She opened her mouth wide, revealing the bits of skin and flesh between her teeth.

"You took my sister," Una said.

A series of low clicking noises resonated from Mrs. Smith's throat. It sounded almost like laughter.

"They will hunt you," Una went on. Her voice was irrationally calm. "Like they hunt whales or sharks. There is no place for you to hide. This is not your world anymore."

Tentacles torpedoed through the water. There was no time to warn Una. No time to do anything but stab at the ones that slipped over the side. One curled around Jill's waist. The second roped around her ankle.

The boat hook made holes in Mrs. Smith's tentacles, but she didn't let go. Jill stretched out her left arm and grabbed the flare gun box. There were two flares left.

"Una! Give me the gun!"

Una tossed the gun to Jill seconds before a third tentacle immobilized her arm. She kept hacking away at the one attached to her leg as Jill loaded the flare gun. As the tentacles tightened and pain coursed through her body, Jill aimed at Mrs. Smith's mouth and fired.

The flare buried itself in Mrs. Smith's right eye. She threw her head back and released a high-pitched keening. Her tentacles went slack and slipped back into the water.

"Hit her again!" Una yelled.

Jill reloaded the gun and fired. This time, the flare struck the water and was instantly extinguished.

The light from the burning yacht bounced off Mrs. Smith's scales as she sank. Blood streamed out of the charred hole in her face, and for a moment, Jill dared to hope she was dead.

And then, she heard claws tearing the dinghy.

More searchlights swept over the water. More boats were approaching.

"HELP!" Jill screamed as the middle of the dinghy began to sag.

Una crooked her finger at Mrs. Smith, daring her to come closer.

"Una, *no!*"

"Give me that hook."

Jill passed it to her as the water lapped their calves.

"Tell my boys that I love them." Una flashed a smile at Jill. "Maybe one day, you'll write about me. Because you can be anything you want, Jill Scott. Anything at all."

And then, Mrs. Smith's head broke the surface. She lunged at Una, her jaw stretching impossibly wide, her teeth flashing white.

Balancing on her knees as the dinghy crumpled under her, Una crossed the harpoon and boat hook over her chest.

When Mrs. Smith bit down, the points of both weapons went straight through the roof of her mouth and into her brain.

Her powerful body went limp, and she fell back into the water, taking Una with her as she sank.

Jill saw Una's silver hair spread out like the spikes of a star. A sequin on her dress gave a final wink.

After that, there was nothing but darkness.

29

Mrs. Smith

As Mrs. Smith sank, her brain was flooded with memories.

The sublime ecstasy of biting into the Pure Ones. The sheer joy of sinking her teeth and claws into their fragile tissue. Their blood filling her mouth. The shock waves of power surging through her body after swallowing the flesh of the ninth Pure One. The long-awaited feeling of satiation.

Her blissful stupor hadn't lasted long. The orb of red light from the man's gun had jolted her awake. The humans on the rubber boat had cut her.

The images in her head faded. All that was left was rage. And the sharp, stabbing pain in her skull.

The pain.

She'd never felt anything like it. Had never been wounded in this way. Not in all her centuries.

The pain swelled like a wave. Hot, searing, clawing.

She wanted to crawl out of her own body like a crab seeking a new shell. She wanted to drift weightlessly in the current. She was tired. So very tired.

She was dying.

Her world was dying.

For a moment, the pain loosened its grip and memories rushed in like a breaking wave. A kaleidoscope of shifting images from a thousand years of life. Long-extinct creatures swimming through unspoiled oceans. The images swirled around and around like a whirlpool until they became shapeless blurs.

As Mrs. Smith sank, and the blackness closed in, a single thought sparked in her brain.

Survive.

The thought was a pinprick of light. Not the glaring light of the sun, but the ethereal blue of the light that existed miles below the surface. The light of the ocean's heart.

The will to endure pushed the darkness back. It burned through Mrs. Smith's newly rejuvenated body, directing her synapses to fire. Her limbs, acting autonomously, pulled out the spikes lodged in her flesh.

The pain was a supernova inside her skull. She was completely blinded by it. Blood streamed out of her mouth.

She kept sinking.

When her back came to rest on the sandy bottom, the eels gathered around her. They grazed her skin with theirs, agitated by her stillness and by the blood ribboning from her mouth. In an effort to rouse her, they nipped her arms, wound themselves through her snakelike hair, and nuzzled her ruined face.

They felt the Mother's life ebbing away.

They also felt the vibrations of many engines above them. They saw lights trying to penetrate the water. They smelled the taint of gasoline.

The eels knew danger was coming, but they didn't flee. They wouldn't leave the Mother, not while she still lived.

These creatures of the dark sensed the spark of light within her chest. The drumbeat of that ancient heart. They would stay with her until the beat grew louder. Or until it fell silent.

Far below the swarm of boats, the eels blanketed Mrs. Smith's body with their bodies. From above, they were indistinguishable from the dark water. They were a shield made of flesh and shadow.

In the shadows, they would wait.

30
Jill

Jill pulled on a sweater and went into the bathroom to brush her hair.

The girl in the mirror looked like any other thirteen-year-old. Except for the eyes. Those belonged to someone much older. Someone who'd seen things.

Of course, no one believed Jill's version of what happened that night in July. The only living person who could've backed her story refused to talk about it.

Jill's parents handled the tragedy by running away. They dropped the dogs at the kennel, packed up their kids, and drove a rented RV to the Great Smoky Mountains.

While divers searched for bodies in Cold Harbor and families the Scotts had known for years planned funerals for their lost loved ones, the Scotts went canoeing and toasted marshmallows. They stayed at the Jellystone campground for a week, hiking and fishing and eating lots of hamburgers and hot dogs.

On the way home, Jill's dad stopped at a pay phone and made a few calls. She overheard him tell her mother that the search and rescue team had found what they could, but a dozen empty caskets would be lowered into the ground the following week.

Jill's parents delayed their return by another three days.

The family visited museums in DC and the Philly Zoo. They stopped in New Jersey to see Lucy the Elephant and spent their last day at Adventureland, riding the Frisbee and the Dragon Wagon roller coaster.

By the time they got home, Una had been laid to rest.

Twelve children and fourteen adults had died the night of Charles's party. Because their bodies were either missing or any recovered parts were, as officials stated, "mutilated by aquatic animals," their deaths were blamed on the fire. Cited as the responsible party, the yacht rental company would later file for bankruptcy.

July turned to August, and Jill's parents whispered when they thought she was out of earshot. They talked about taking her to the psychiatrist Charles was seeing or sending her to live with her grandparents until school started. They talked about how the newspaper coverage made the Bernsteins out as villains for their extravagance, how the Pulaskis had dodged a bullet, and how lucky they were to have survived without a scratch. They exchanged theories about how the fireworks had caught fire and where Mrs. Smith had disappeared to.

"She's not in the house," Jill heard her mother say one night. "You can feel how empty it is. Her damned vines are still growing, though. They've covered the McCreedys' fence again."

"The new owners will have to deal with them," her dad replied. "I have a feeling you're going to be too busy to do other people's yard work."

His prediction was correct.

In September, J.J. was sent to boarding school in Connecticut and the Bernsteins moved to Great Neck. When they hired Jill's mom as their Realtor and she found them a house away from the water, the only thing the Bernsteins asked for was a thirty-day closing. A Gold Coast sign went up in front of their Cold Harbor house in August. It finally sold in November for tens of thousands less than the asking price.

Natalie became the seller's agent of choice for all the families moving out of the area. She had so many listings that she had to share some of them with Gina. She put a vase of yellow roses in every kitchen. She had platters of Mrs. Pulaski's cookies at every open house.

Mrs. Pulaski wouldn't drive to the end of the street anymore, so Jill's mom had to get the cookies from her house. If Jill was in the car, she'd be sent to the door to collect the cookies. Mrs. Pulaski would always invite her in. While she wrapped the platters in tinfoil, she'd give Jill a special treat and talk about the baby she and her husband were adopting.

As more and more houses were put up for sale, Mrs. Pulaski's cookies appeared in their kitchens. Buyers sampled them in Heather's house. In Coach Patrick's house. And in Aaron's house. By Christmas, Jill's mom was the top agent at Gold Coast. She bought herself a gold necklace and enrolled Justin and Jill in private school. They'd start in January.

At seven each morning, a bus would pick them up at the top of the driveway, and it would drop them off at three thirty every afternoon. Jill would be in charge of Justin until one of her parents got home from work.

There would be no more babysitters.

There would be no more counseling sessions with the minister from their church. Jill's mother had decided it was time for Jill to move on.

It was a thirty-minute drive to her new school. The building was a converted mansion and looked nothing like Jill's boxy brown public school. The classes were small, there was a strict dress code, and lunch was served family style, with a teacher at the head of every table.

Most of the kids in Jill's class had known each other since nursery school. On her first day, they stared at her like she was a specimen in a museum. They were fascinated to be so close to someone who'd survived the Bar Mitzvah Tragedy. But they were also unnerved by her.

She didn't talk much. She rarely smiled. When a teacher called on her, her answers were mumbled. When she gazed at her classmates, she seemed to be looking right through them. They had no idea that she saw ghosts at every empty desk.

At home, she struggled with her homework. Every subject was ten times harder than it had been at her previous school. Her papers bled from all the red ink her teachers used when correcting her work. Her grades plummeted.

In early February, Jill had to use another study hall period to seek extra help in math. When she got to the classroom, her teacher was packing her bag.

"Sorry, Jill, but I'm leaving early today." She touched the soft mound of her belly. "We have a doctor's appointment. I know the word problems are giving you trouble, but I see how hard you're working. Why don't you stop by before homeroom tomorrow? We'll tackle those problems then."

Jill nodded and her teacher left the room. From down the hall, someone shouted, "It's snowing!"

Moving to the window, Jill put a hand on the cold glass and stared out at the snowflakes spiraling through the gray sky. The math classroom overlooked the garden. The spindly bushes and brittle grass were already dusted with snow.

"Hello," said a voice from the doorway.

Jill turned to see her English teacher, Mr. Tippy, smiling at her.

"Hi."

Joining her at the window, he peered down at the garden. His smile widened, and Jill noticed that his eyes were the same color as the sky. Tapping lightly on the glass, he said, "This reminds me of a poem by Ralph Waldo Emerson. Have you heard of him?"

Jill shook her head.

"It goes:

'Announced by all the trumpets of the sky,
arrives the snow, and, driving o'er the fields,
seems nowhere to alight: the whited air
Hides hills and woods, the river, and the heaven. . .'"

They stood in comfortable silence for a moment. Then Mr. Tippy said, "I get the feeling you like words more than numbers."

Jill laughed softly. The noise sounded foreign to her own ears. "Yeah."

"Your writing is a bit like this snow. It's a little hesitant. It drifts here and there. But I can tell you have a gift. A special spark. Do you want to do more writing? Outside of class?"

"Like, for extra credit?"

Mr. Tippy shrugged. "Sure. But also because I think you have lots of stories in you. Stories that other people will want to read. Some folks are born storytellers. I have a feeling you're one of them."

Jill's calcified heart cracked a little. A flicker of warmth stirred in her chest.

"What's the last thing you wrote about that wasn't for school?"

The word slipped out before Jill could stop it. "Monsters." She swallowed hard, forcing the memories that threatened to pour out of her throat. "It was a story about monsters. But I didn't keep it, and I don't want to write that kind of stuff anymore."

Still looking out the window, Mr. Tippy stroked the stubble on his chin. "Have you ever written about yourself as a monster?" Seeing that Jill was thrown by the question, he added, "It's easy to paint ourselves as the hero of a story. Who doesn't love a hero? But I think the villains are interesting, too. Why are they so angry? Why do they want to hurt those around them? What's the story behind those emotions? That would be my first challenge for you. Write a poem—a short one—from the monster's point of view."

"I'll try."

Jill didn't return to study hall. She closed the door and pulled a desk up to the window. As she watched the falling snow, she thought about her typewriter—the blue one she'd gotten for her birthday and had never used.

She touched the keys sometimes, when she felt grief roll over her like a boulder. She'd gently push the *U*, then the *N*, then the *A* keys. She'd do this over and over, letting the tears fall.

Her parents said to put the past behind her.

Her minster said to trust in God's plan.

For months, no one said anything that resonated with her.

Until now.

Jill could already see herself feeding a piece of paper, white and unblemished as the snow, into her typewriter.

She could hear the *click click* of the keys as her words marched across the paper like a line of ants.

She would accept Mr. Tippy's challenge.

She would use her writing to grieve the loss of Una. Of her friends. She would use it to keep them alive, too. To memorialize them on paper.

She would write to make it easier to endure the sight of the harbor. And Mrs. Smith's house.

She would write to think about something other than that terrible face that had risen out of the water. The face that haunted Jill's dreams, night after night.

Jill's voice had been silent for months, but she was ready to use it again.

Tomorrow, when the storm hardened the water into stone and the harbor was completely frozen over, when all the boats were hidden under a thick layer of snow, Jill Scott would go to her room, sit down in front of her typewriter, and become a monster.

Acknowledgments

If it takes a village to raise a child, the same can be said for a book.

My friend and agent, Jessica Faust of BookEnds LLC, would be the Wise Woman of my book village. Her hut would have a kettlebell, a dog or two, a Wonder Woman mug, and an endless supply of coffee. Jessica and I have been together for over twenty years, and I hope we're still doing what we love best twenty years from now. I wouldn't be a career writer without this amazing human being, and I'll never stop being grateful.

I totally believe that some things are just meant to be. For example, this book was meant to be in Leah Mol's extremely capable hands. In my book village, she'd be the Magic Woman. The seer and the healer. Not only did she champion this unusual story from the start, but she made it shine as only the best editors, aka book shapers, can. Thank you for taking a chance on Mrs. Smith.

There are many people from the dedicated and talented Hanover Square Press/HarperCollins community I'd like to thank. Art director Tara Scarcello created the cover of my dreams. I literally made a noise on a decibel level only known by dolphins when I first saw it. Copy editor Tracy Wilson polished my draft until it glowed, as did proofreader Vicki So. Thank you to the publicity and marketing teams. Sophie James,

Brianna Wodabek, Megan Beatie, and Kathie Bennett, I am grateful for your hard work.

I also owe a long-overdue thanks to Peter Senftleben for checking over my final drafts for years and for always having something lovely to say about my work.

Writing can be a solitary existence, which is why I often pack up my laptop and drive to my favorite café, Joe Van Gogh in Chapel Hill, NC. I wrote most of this book there, and the combination of music, kindness, and foam hearts in my big-ass lattes were a consistent source of inspiration. For this, I want to express my gratitude to the entire staff: Mckenzie Matherly, Coline Oxton, Drew Wansink, Brianna Underhill, Samuel Williams, Steve Burham, Maddie Morrison, Nicole Tester, and Luke Jordan.

To the booksellers, librarians, Bookstagrammers, and Book-Tokers who've supported me from my first release in 2015 until now, I love you. Your reviews and recommendations make a difference. Your shout-outs, posts, and DMs matter. My book village wouldn't thrive without you.

Finally, I want to thank my family for being such good sports considering how awful I made them look in this book. Luckily, they know it's a work of fiction. They also know that *I* know what an amazing childhood I had. Thank you for all the memories and adventures.

To Tim Harrison, and Sophie. I'd swim with eels for you. That's how much I love you.